THE LONGER
WE DWELL

THE LONGER
WE DWELL

◆ ◆ ◆

A Billie Dixon Novel
Book Two

D. L. Pitchford

Straight on till Morningside Prints

First published in 2018 in the United States
by Straight on till Morningside Prints

Cover Design by Sarah Anderson of No Synonym Book Covers

ISBN   978 0 9987 9457 0

Straight on till Morningside Prints
11923 NE Sumner St., STE 709378
Portland, OR 97220

www.DLPitchford.com

For my Coven:
You are, and always will be,
the best friends I ever could've hoped for.

*Life is thickly sown with thorns,
and I know no other remedy
than to pass quickly through
them. The longer we dwell on our
misfortunes, the greater is their
power to harm us.*

Voltaire

One

"Are you sure you have the right address?" Jimmy asks as we wind through the buildings of University Park, the largest and most sprawling section of upperclassmen housing.

"Positive," I snap.

I never intended to come back to these cookie-cutter buildings—let alone the interior of one—but it's a bit late for that now. I didn't realize Dahlia's directions would lead me here.

Jimmy releases an irritated huff. "Then where is it?"

I pause and examine our surroundings. My gaze lands on the lettering beside the nearest apartment doorway, 4B, and I nod in that direction. "Just over here."

We turn the corner and follow the heavy beat.

Inside the apartment, the living room is nearly vacant—it is only 10:30, and according to Jimmy and Xander, Bradford parties don't really start till eleven. Even still, the bass reverberates off the walls.

Jimmy steers me toward the breakfast bar, where the hosts have set up the liquor and mixers, but I hesitate.

Of course, he chooses the only area with another person.

1

The guy in the kitchen is dressed as a pirate captain, complete with a flowing white shirt, black vest, and an eyepatch. He grins a toothy grin through his ruddy-brown beard—drunk enough to throw himself fully into character—and Jimmy plops down on one of two barstools and requests a drink. He's done this a lot because he pours out Jimmy's rum and Coke with precision, then turns his one eye on me.

"What can I get you?" He flashes me an overpowering smile and grabs a red Solo cup, ready to fill it.

"I'm not having anything, thanks." I glance at Jimmy, who takes a sip of his drink and smiles at the cup appreciatively.

"What?" The bartender gleefully raises an eyebrow. "You're not drinking? Party foul!"

I frown at his over-the-top reaction and step closer to Jimmy.

Even in the dark atmosphere, the setup of this apartment is too familiar. My stomach drops at the memories as I lean against the stool—it looks like the exact same stool—but Jimmy smiles and nods toward the bar.

I glance at the bartender, uncertain. "Half a shot."

"You got it." He fills the plastic cup with Mountain Dew and a small pour of Absolut vodka, and I hold the cup by the rim as he passes it to me.

I stir the liquid with my pinky finger and take a sip. Vodka is disgusting, but I swallow it down.

Beside me, Jimmy examines the room. "You talked to Prudence, right?" I internally roll my eyes before he voices his actual question. "Do you think she and Cynthia will show up?"

"I don't know." The room is already filling with people.

"You don't have to keep me company. You should go have fun."

He turns his worried brown eyes on me. "And leave you here alone?" In the low light, he looks like Robin Hood more than the Hero of Hyrule—part of that has to do with his unmanageable brown hair. I'm just glad I convinced him to leave his recorder at home. "Billie, I'm not going to abandon you."

When I assess the living room again, the number of party-goers has tripled since our arrival. The room isn't full in the least, but it's well on its way. I shudder to think how nerve-wracking this will be when everyone is here and drunk.

Although, the terrible dancing and the couple groping each other on an armchair indicates some people did a little pre-gaming.

"I think I'll manage."

Jimmy's bushy eyebrows draw together under his thick-rimmed glasses, and he lowers his voice. "Are you going to sit here and wait for Xander? He could be at work for another hour if they're busy."

"Seriously, go." The last thing I want to do is work the room with him. "I need time to adjust."

He stands, cup in hand, but the frown on his face says he does not approve. "Fine, but I'll be back soon."

He disappears into the crowd, and I sip my drink while people-watching.

The group on the makeshift dance floor is growing, even if many of them are grinding instead of actually dancing. The Bradford standard-issue coffee table and entertainment center are missing—probably shoved in someone's bedroom to make space. University Park apartments were designed with utility in mind. Not costume parties.

Behind me, the kitchen has its own special alcove and is separated from the living room by a narrow walkway and the peninsula I'm sitting at. The bedrooms and bathrooms, though, are located at the ends of two symmetrical hallways on either side of the apartment entrance, two beds and one bath attached to each.

From one of these hallways stumbles a guy in a white toga. He was too drunk to notice blacklight doesn't reflect off whatever sheet he used. His tighty-whiteys, on the other hand…

He grips the wall, and another guy catches him by the shoulders before he falls. "No, Darius, this toga party isn't going to happen!"

I move on.

Near the front door, Jimmy has found David Wright, our RA from Lincoln Hall last year. They have a vocals class together this semester—apparently, David's voice is "divine," though I haven't heard it yet. David pauses to chat and offers Jimmy a Blue Moon from his six pack.

"We're not all terrible people, you know."

I jump, nearly falling off the stool.

The bartender is on my left—too close for comfort. My amber hands tighten around the cup, knuckles turning white, and I force down the panic. This position is far too familiar.

"Unless you're into terrible people." He quirks a smile, flashing white teeth that glow in the blacklight, but I shift away.

I clench my eyes shut, breathe, and open them again.

4

"I'm Brent." He shoves a pink calloused hand in my direction, inches from my chest, too drunk to notice my discomfort. "You are?"

"Billie Dixon." I offer my hand in return.

His grip is firm, but instead of shaking, he presses his lips to my knuckles in a wet kiss. I jerk away, but he doesn't notice. "This is your first party, right? You a freshman?"

"Sophomore. And yes, mostly. I don't imagine you'd count picking up my drunk friends as attending a party."

His laughter booms in my ears, and he grabs his drink from the counter behind us. "Then you don't know any of these people, do you?"

I shake my head and look around. Jimmy and David are the only ones I recognize.

"Well, I live here, along with Darius, the one who's about to pass out in the hallway in his underwear, and Seymour—he's the guy making out with his girlfriend—and Kai's dancing with all those women." Brent laughs and leans against the counter, his thick arm brushing mine. "He gets away with it because he's in a six-year relationship with a girl in Sweden—at least that's his story."

I force a smile and sip my drink.

"And this—" his face lights up "—this is Dahlia."

Dressed in a skimpy dark violet fairy costume, Dahlia Finnick looks ready to grant more than a few wishes tonight. Her long, honey-brown hair is pulled up into a tight ballerina bun, with a few curled strands framing her peach, heart-shaped face. Her makeup is pristine, her skin lacks blemishes, and her white and purple fairy wings glow. She's perfect.

She stretches up to wrap her thin arms around Brent's

robust torso. "Why aren't you dancing?" Giggling, she clutches his hand and drags him toward the dance floor, but he stays in place.

"Lia." He tugs her, and she stumbles into his side. "Have you met Billie? This is her first party."

She turns her attention to me and slips from his embrace to throw her arms around me. "You came!" My drink splashes on my black pants, but she doesn't notice, even after pulling away to examine my costume. "Who're you dressed as?" She cocks her head to the side, her hands digging into my shoulders.

I finish my drink to prevent further spills and drop the cup on the counter. "Have you seen *Fullmetal Alchemist*?"

Her frown persists, but after a moment it abates. "Why are you covered in blood?"

"Riza Hawkeye. The final battle." I reach for my belt to withdraw the pistol—the closest I could find to her Enfield No. 2 snub nose.

Then, I think better of it.

They're drunk—probably drunk enough to think it's real. Thankfully, the overshirt hides it well.

A smile spreads across her petite face. "It's so unique."

I scoot backward on the stool and take a steadying breath.

It's no surprise, but her tone is a dead giveaway. No other girl here is dressed as an anime character. They're fairies or cats or Catholic schoolgirls or the female lead in the latest superhero flick—whoever they need to be to show as much skin as possible.

Brent chuckles. "It's refreshing to see a girl wear something other than underwear and tights."

I snort, but they don't notice.

Dahlia is already moving on. "Come on, Brent." She grabs him by the hand again and tugs him toward the dance floor. "I need a partner."

He sends me an apologetic smile and allows her to drag him away.

When they're gone, I can breathe again. I hold my hands close to my chest and shut my eyes. I'd prefer not to talk to Dahlia and Brent for long, but that's true for most of my interactions. Being alone in the middle of a party, however, is much worse.

I don't know why Dahlia invited me. I don't do well in crowds, and she should know that. We are suitemates, after all. Even if we rarely spend time together.

"You seem uncomfortable."

I lock on to deep cerulean eyes, and a smile spreads across my lips. "Well, this is kind of new. I don't usually go inside the party."

Xander snorts as he takes the seat beside me. When he peruses my costume, a smirk lights up his tawny face, and he leans closer to tug at the neckline of my black turtleneck. "How in-depth did you go with this, Lieutenant?" His hot breath tickles my neck. "Do you hold the secrets to Flame Alchemy on your back? Can I study them?"

I smack his hand away, laughing. "My gun might be fake, Xander, but I can still hit you."

He releases a low laugh. "And I'm sure I'll deserve it." When he leans back, he continues examining my appearance. "You know, you did a good job putting this together. You even got all the blood."

"Yeah, but it's going to be a bitch to clean."

He scoots closer, and I stiffen under his sharp scrutiny. Is he staring at my tits?

His mouth twists in concentration. "Is that my shirt?"

I toy with the hem of the white overshirt affectionately. The material is stiff but soft. "I might have snuck into your closet. I'll buy you a new one—I'm not sure how well I can get this fake blood out."

Xander pulls back, nodding, and heads for the empty kitchen. His face has a hardened expression, but there's a twitch at the corner of his lips.

Is he upset about the shirt?

"Don't worry about it." His voice is clipped. "You look good in my clothes."

Behind the bar, he yanks open the bottle of vodka and pours several shots into a new cup, then reaches for one of the mixers. "Do you want some?" I nudge my cup closer to him, and he fills it—with decidedly less alcohol than his.

He returns my drink as he sits down again, and we knock our cups together.

"Thanks." When I look over, it's my turn to study him. "You don't have a costume."

Xander's dressed in his work clothes: a black t-shirt tucked into black slacks and black slip-resistant shoes. The shirt has a rearing stallion in the middle of an intricate crest, and the words 'Draft Horse' arch above the design. No part of him glows in the blacklight.

He takes a long drink before answering. "I knew I wouldn't have much time after work, so I decided not to bother." He casts a sidelong glance my way. "Although, now that I see you, I wish I had."

A big smile spreads across my face. "Who would you

have dressed as? Roy Mustang?" When he chuckles, I add, "That makes way too much sense. Egotistical womanizer working his way up the ladder."

Xander leans close and nudges me with his elbow. "Doesn't sound so bad to me. He got to strip Hawkeye naked and study her for hours."

Heat rises to my cheeks.

The way his eyes wander my costume says he wouldn't mind stripping and studying me. I'm not opposed to the idea, but those ideas are better reserved for my dreams. Dreams I wish were lucid.

But Xander moves on like this is a totally normal conversation—although, for us it is. "This place is pretty calm compared to where I just came from."

While he examines the scene around us, I take full advantage of his distraction. Even in his dirty, sweaty work clothes, he is the picture of confidence, completely at ease in his own skin.

"How was work?"

He flashes me a smile, and I avert my eyes. He doesn't need to catch me ogling him. "Work is work," he says, "but I have to say, the old men at the bar could drink all of us under the table."

Before I can say anything, my phone buzzes in my pants pocket, and I lean back to retrieve it.

The text is from Imogene, and I heave a sigh before opening it. *Why haven't you called Mom back yet?* I picture her lips pursed in irritation. *She needs to talk to you about the wedding.*

I turn off the screen and shove the phone back in my pocket, not bothering with a response. Imogene has spent the past two months berating me for not helping enough, but I don't know what I'm supposed to do from halfway across the country. I never wanted to be a bridesmaid in my mother's wedding ceremony anyway.

Xander nudges my arm. "More wedding shit?"

"Mo's texting me two or three times a day with reminders that I'm supposed to participate."

He snorts. "How much can you do from Vermont?"

"Exactly." I lift my hands into the air—a reminder of my forgotten drink. "It's not my wedding. I'm not the one who needs to study ballroom dance or whatever else my mom's doing now. I mean, I understand she wants it to be the perfect night, but she's going to extremes."

"I could teach you."

I pause as he extends a hand. "What?"

"Ballroom dance." His eyes hold me steady. "Or we can just dance."

It takes another short moment to gather myself together. "Right now? It took me months to work up to attending a party, and you're not going to let me hide on the sidelines for the first one?"

His lips curl to form a grin. He finishes his drink, then offers me his hand again. "This is me you're talking to. I don't let you get away with anything."

I take another sip.

On the dance floor, everyone—women, plus a few men on the sidelines—are grinding on each other. That's not a move Xander and I should mimic.

"I can't dance." I also can't look at him. "Definitely not in front of people."

He chuckles. "You're making this harder than it needs

to be, Dixon. Don't get your panties in a twist." He pauses for effect. "Unless you're not wearing any."

I shove him, and he struggles to stay atop the stool. "Whether or not I'm wearing underwear is no business of yours, perv."

He laughs and gives me a playful nudge in return. "You know I'm joking."

"You're very lucky I do know that." But I kick back the rest of my drink and drop my empty cup inside his. "When are you going to stop making those idiotic comments?"

Xander doesn't wait for my acquiescence. He slips his hand into mine and threads our fingers together. "When you actually tell me to stop. Now, come on." He tugs, but I stay put. "You don't have to worry about anything. Just hold on to me; I'll take care of the rest."

He will not be swayed, and I wordlessly rise and follow him to the edge of the dance floor.

Without preamble or hesitation, he pulls me into his arms, and when I lean against his chest, he tucks my head under his chin. We sway.

The music isn't slow, but the steady beat pumps through my veins. I don't recognize the song—not that I know much pop music—but there's a woman rapping and another singing. The words elude me.

Xander holds me by the waist, and his fingers find the thin line of skin where my turtleneck has ridden up. His skin is hot against mine. I press closer.

Like he said, he leads, even as the song transitions to the next. His movements don't change with the music. The beat is a little faster, but his grip is the same. Firm but gentle. Sensual but reassuring.

I pull back slightly to study the room. We're the only couple slow-dancing. Does he realize that?

"See?" He smiles at me. "Not so bad."

I don't know what to say, but a reply stumbles out. "Right. Not so bad." I bury my face in his chest, and he rests his head atop mine again.

"Stay right here, Dixon. I've got you."

And he does.

All I have to do is follow his lead. In his arms, I'm stable and secure, even if I don't know how to stand on my own.

Two

THE AIR OUTSIDE IS COLD, AND THIS OVERSHIRT ISN'T THICK enough to block the chill. But it's refreshing compared to the interior. Now that it's after midnight, the crowd is thick and overwhelming, and the apartment is hot—made more so by being wrapped in Xander's arms for four or five songs. I lost track.

University Park is the largest of the upperclassmen housing options at Bradford. It's a series of two-story buildings with two apartments on each level and four students per apartment, like Brent and his friends. Between the buildings are occasional maintenance sheds and small green spaces with picnic tables and young oak trees. Outside and in, the apartments are exact copies with the same structure, same furniture, same breakfast bar, same barstools.

Last year, I came to this area twice. Zane's apartment was only two buildings over—easily visible from where I now stand.

In the opposite direction, the landscape is equally bland.

A few other party-goers are outside. No one I know. Halloween is one of the biggest parties on campus, but most are on Frat Row. I have no interest in attending one of those.

13

The only reason I'm here is because Dahlia was kind enough to invite me and my friends. We don't talk often, despite sharing an apartment in the Towers, one of the nicer upperclassmen housing options and the tallest building on campus. But that has far more to do with my being a recluse than anything. She has been nothing but nice since we moved in. It felt rude to decline.

Behind me, the door opens and closes. Uneven footsteps approach on the concrete. Another drunk person.

I pull out my phone to check my messages. I never responded to Imogene—not that she's unused to my silence, especially in regards to our mother's upcoming nuptials—but she hasn't pressed the matter. No new texts. Yet.

"Having a good time?"

I jump. My phone almost slips from my fingers.

Brent, a small smile on his flushed face, leans against the wall a couple feet away.

"What?"

"Are you having a good time?" He has the eyepatch shifted upward now. His eyes are deep-set and a reddish brown, the same color as his tousled hair and scruffy beard.

"Uh, yeah." About as good a time as expected.

"Billie, right?"

"Yeah."

He assesses me slowly, the smile almost gone. "You don't get out much, do you?"

I cock an eyebrow. "Why do you say that?"

Brent shrugs. "You've talked to four people since arriving, and I'm the only person you didn't know. You're really uncomfortable."

I pocket my phone.

Maybe he did notice my discomfort from his close proximity—either he assumes that's how I normally behave, which isn't far off the mark, or he doesn't care.

"That guy your boyfriend? The one you danced with?"

"We're friends. I don't date."

Brent laughs, but then his face falls. "Like ever? Are you saving yourself for marriage or something? That's cool."

I snort. "Hardly."

"Then what?"

I take a long drink from my water cup. The question hasn't been a dominant conversation topic in the months since last semester's fiasco. I wish it weren't part of this conversation either. Why does he care anyway? I'm some random girl who came to his party.

"It doesn't matter."

He scoots along the wall. "Well, I don't believe you, but I'll let you keep your secrets." I imagine the smile that follows is supposed to be charming. "It makes you more interesting."

I look away again. What does that have to do with anything? "I'm not that interesting."

Brent leans closer with a wolfish grin, and I shrink back. "You know, I don't believe that for a second."

I push away from the wall and put some space between us. "Well, it's a good thing it doesn't matter what you believe." My hands, clutching the cup, are shaking.

But when I glance over my shoulder, all he does is smile.

I'm overreacting. He's perfectly nice, and I'm overreacting. There's no need to panic just because he's near me. Drunk people have no concept of personal space. Why else would Xander get clingy after a couple shots of whiskey?

"Why didn't you tell me you live with Lia?"

I breathe a sigh of relief at the subject change. "I didn't know who you were. And why would I introduce myself as being her housemate?"

His thunderous laughter echoes between the buildings. "That's a fair point. I can't believe I've never met you. It's almost November, and as you can see, I'm pretty close to her and her brother."

"Brother?"

"You're at a Finnick party and you haven't met one half of the duo?" He joins me on the grass, his hands shoved deep into the pockets of his harem pants. "Darius. I pointed him out while we were at the bar. We got him to his bed, thanks for asking."

I nod.

"You know, Lia said we should adopt you."

I raise an eyebrow. "'Adopt'?" I'm not a stray puppy.

"She thinks you're cute and you could use some friends. Maybe a little feminine guidance. She's selfless, isn't she? You guys must get on well, living together and all."

I push down the anxious laughter in my throat. "Yeah, she's great."

But as kind as she is, we barely know each other.

"How old are you?"

I take a moment to assess him, but he's too drunk to be bothered by my scrutinous stare. "Nineteen. Why?"

"We're all turning twenty-one this year, but most of the bars don't let in minors after ten." He laughs at my skeptical face. "Thinking ahead."

I finish my water and glance toward the door. Now sounds like the perfect time to make my exit, but Brent is oddly observant for a drunk person.

"You want another drink? Let's go make you something." He leads the way toward the door, not waiting for me, and I hesitate before following him inside.

Brent doesn't give me the opportunity to refuse before taking my cup and returning to the bar, and I hesitate in the doorway.

Jimmy and David are still talking on t!he other side of the room. David's six pack is down to two, and Jimmy's bright pink. He's such a lightweight.

On the dance floor, Dahlia and Kai are falling over with laughter. They struggle to keep control while performing "The Time Warp" instructions. I'd rather be curled up on Xander and Jimmy's couch watching the movie.

But where is Xander? He said he was going to chat with Jimmy and David while I took a breather. He's not standing with them.

"Here you go."

Brent is back, and he's filled my cup to the brim with a pink liquid that emits a sickly-sweet aroma. I shouldn't have anything else to drink.

"It's Kinky lemonade."

I bite my lip. "'Kinky'?"

"Grapefruit liqueur." He offers the cup again. "And some Sprite and vodka. You don't strike me as the kind of person who drinks often. Citrus covers vodka well."

"I'm really not."

But he pushes it into my hand, his arm quaking from the motion, and I clasp my fingers around the cup so it doesn't fall.

I glare at the quivering liquid, somehow in my hand despite my desire for it to be anywhere else, and look away. I need an excuse to leave. Maybe Jimmy will see me and wave me over. I haven't talked to him since we parted ways, but he's still immersed in his conversation with David. The six pack is empty now. They're probably talking about bands and music, and Jimmy will be arguing about who does a better version of "Blackbird," even though David doesn't listen to the Beatles.

Maybe I could go to the bathroom, though.

But when my eyes drift toward the nearest darkened hallway, there's Xander. Halfway down the hall, he's leaning against the wall, lips pursed as a girl in a skin-tight white dress, white pumps, angel wings, and a halo stands close to him. She places her hand on his forearm and leans her head back as she laughs.

Who the hell is that? And why is Xander talking to some random drunk, half-naked woman?

I sip the drink and force down the nausea welling up in my chest. The cocktail is sweet and tangy, and the carbonation and vodka leave a bitter aftertaste, but I take another sip and a breath to cool down.

There's no reason to be upset anyway. Xander's single and has never kept it in his pants before. Halloween should be his time to shine. All the girls are drunk and wearing as little clothing as possible. Isn't that a male undergrad's dream?

Although, I'm pretty sure all the women he's slept with have been sober and willing for their rendezvous. I definitely was.

In the hallway, the girl runs her hand up his arm and steps closer—and his response?

He smiles.

I turn to Brent and take a gulp of the pink lemonade. He grins when I down half the drink. The vodka is more apparent with each swallow.

"Nice!" Brent claps me on the shoulder. "We'll make a college student of you yet."

I frown. I've been a college student for over a year, and there hasn't previously been a prerequisite for alcohol use. But before I say anything, my phone starts to vibrate.

I can't hear the ringtone over the music, but when I withdraw the device, the caller ID shows the house phone. The only person who uses that anymore is Mom. Imogene stopped the second she got a cell phone in eighth grade.

Brent stares expectantly, and I offer him a quick apology before heading out the door into the quiet night.

"Mom?"

The line crackles to life as I pace the sidewalk outside the apartment. The lemonade sloshes in my cup. If I hadn't drank so much while inside, it would've sloshed right out of the cup.

"What's going on?"

"Oh, good. You're awake. I was worried you'd be in bed."

I stop pacing. "What are you doing up, Mom? It's almost one. You were supposed to go to bed three hours ago."

She releases an anxious laugh, and the earpiece crackles. "I'm finalizing the guest list so I can mail out these save-the-dates, and I wanted to remind you I'm giving you a plus one."

I heave a sigh. It's one in the morning, and she wants to make sure I know I'm supposed to bring a date. How in the world is that her top priority?

"Mom, I know that. But you need to go to bed. Where's Rob? Isn't he there with you?"

"No." Her voice is tired. "He's in California visiting his nephew. Giovanni and Carmen had their new baby."

"What about Imogene? Where's she?" I drain the cup and set it on the concrete under the eaves.

"She's staying the night at Heather's. I'm trying to talk to you about something important, Billie."

I can't believe Mo left her alone at the house. Mom must be managing her mental health well for Mo to be comfortable doing that.

"Imogene says she's going to bring a date, and it would be nice for you to put yourself out there. So, you're bringing a date."

The words are final—not a question anymore—and I sigh. "Sure, why not."

"Good." Her long sigh is the opposite of my short one—relieved instead of irritated, happy instead of angry. "What about Alexander?"

"Who?"

It takes a second to realize who she's talking about.

"Your friend. Jimmy's roommate."

"Xander," I correct, imploring her to remember this time. When he introduced himself to her by his full name last Christmas, it stuck. "His name is Xander. And what about him?"

Behind me, the apartment door opens and closes with a loud *thump*. I shift to look over my shoulder.

Speak of the devil.

"Well," Mom says over the line, "he's sweet and your

friend, so I'm sure he'd be happy to do it as a favor."

Xander smiles as he approaches. "Hey…" But he zips his mouth shut when he notices the phone.

I turn away again to focus on my mother. "Do what as a favor?"

"Be your date."

"What?"

My alarm doesn't faze her. "I don't know how else you're going to come up with one, Billie. You're both single, right? I don't see what the problem is. He's a good friend, isn't he?"

"Right." Why else would he agree to do it? "Mom, I don't think that's a good idea."

"Then come up with something better. I expect you to have a date."

Xander steps around me and mouths, "You okay?"

I shake my head and turn away again. "Mom, the wedding is six months away. Why are you awake right now, worrying about this? You should be in bed."

She doesn't bother acknowledging that. "Have you gotten your bridesmaid dress? You need to get measured for that. Everything needs to be ready."

"Did you not just hear me? Six months."

Fingers press to my upper arm, and I send a glare over my shoulder. Where's the handsy girl in the angel costume now? Did he get bored with her?

"Six months is not as long as you think it is, Billie," Mom says over the phone, and I shrug Xander off.

"I understand how time works and how to read a calendar. Six months is six months, and you should've agreed to a courthouse wedding like Rob suggested." I heave a sigh. "Planning a wedding is too stressful."

"Thank you for your concern." Her voice is curt. "Speaking of stress, what do you think of Dr. Byrd? He seemed qualified when we spoke over the phone."

My entire body stiffens. If she's pissed off, I might as well be honest.

"I haven't seen him."

The line is silent.

Finally, I turn back to see Xander watching me, brow crinkled, lips in a tight line. He steps closer at the recognition and cocks his head to the side.

I cover the mouthpiece. "Wedding shit. Apparently, she's too stressed to go to bed. What are you doing out here?"

He gives a one-shouldered shrug. "You were gone for a while. I got worried."

My jaw clenches, and on the other side of the line, the phone sputters with movement. "You didn't look worried with a pretty angel wrapping her arms around you in a dark, secluded hallway," I snap, and then, Mom's back on the phone.

"What do you mean, you haven't seen him?"

I stumble away from him so he can't hear.

"Billie, those appointments cost money, and you're scheduled for every Thursday until the end of the school year. Tell me you've had the decency to call and cancel them."

Xander's staring, a hardened look on his face, and I avert my eyes before answering.

"No, Mom, I didn't call them. They'll figure it out."

"I have to pay a fee when you skip the appointment, Billie." She chooses her words carefully. "This is completely disrespectful to me and to Dr. Byrd, and you will go to your next appointment."

"No, I won't." Xander's still watching me, and I cover the mouthpiece again, pulling the phone away. "Why are you still here?"

He reaches for me but doesn't make contact. "Dixon, I don't know what you think you saw, but—"

"I'm a little busy with my mom." I level him with a glare. "Go back inside to your angel. I'm sure she'd love to see your apartment—at least the ceiling. Unless you've already gotten her in bed, which wouldn't surprise me in the least." I don't give him a chance to respond before stalking off in the direction of my apartment.

When I press the phone to my ear again, Mom is talking. "Do you need a female psychologist? No one else was as highly recommended in St. Clare as Dr. Byrd, but if you want a woman, that's a simple fix."

"Mom, it doesn't matter who you make an appointment with, I'm not going."

Behind me, Xander doesn't follow, but he has no qualms yelling after me: "What the hell are you so upset about, Dixon? Last I checked, you weren't invested in who I sleep with."

On the phone, Mom is talking, but I can't focus on her words. I stumble on the uneven sidewalk.

"Thank God I can tell when you're lying your ass off!"

I round the corner and follow the sidewalk along the Lane toward King Street. My heart is racing, and Mom is still talking.

"...and quite frankly, I don't know why you're sabotaging everything like this, Billie. This is an important opportunity, and your sister is worried about you. Do you eat? She says you don't eat."

23

I focus on my boot-covered feet slapping against the pavement and the sound of her voice. "If Mo's worried, that's her problem and not my fault. Besides, she's not here, so neither of you have any idea what's going on in my life."

Unless…

Jimmy and Imogene talk a couple times a week. She's been able to needle her way under his skin since we were kids, and Jimmy cannot deny her once she's made up her mind. She is as ambitious and stubborn as I am.

"I won't go to therapy, Mom, and you can't make me."

My hands are numb from the cold. Or from the alcohol. I have no idea how much vodka Brent put in that last drink. I start to pull away the phone—I'm done with this conversation—but the steadiness of her voice makes me pause.

"Yes, you are."

"No—"

"You will attend your therapy with Dr. Byrd, or you will not come home."

"What?"

That's hardly a terrible sentence. I moved to Vermont to get away in the first place.

"You will not be part of my wedding or my new family, you will not step foot in my house, and you will not see or speak to your sister until you fix this."

I come to an abrupt stop at the corner of the Lane and King Street.

"Fix this." She says it with the utmost certainty that this is—that I am—something that can and will be fixed.

Three

Prudence links her arm through mine when we enter Bradford College's Kelley Center for Fine Arts. Like always, she leads the way to our drawing class, happy and energetic. "Seriously, though, how was the party?"

"It could've gone better." We separate at the stairs, and she takes them two at a time. "I wish you'd come."

She throws a grin over her shoulder, and we reach the top landing. "Cynthia was having a freak-out per usual. I spent the whole night in our living room, helping her study for her exam tomorrow morning, and I'm sure I'll do the same tonight too. The things we do for friends."

"That's why you're such a good friend." I match my pace to hers, and her olive face lights up with a smile. "Jimmy was a little disappointed you two didn't make it, though."

She releases a sharp bark of laughter. "Only a little?"

Jimmy was more than a little disappointed at the end of the night. He drunkenly texted me to ask why Cynthia was a no-show. I didn't bother responding. I was too busy starting my Calc III homework at two in the morning.

The door to the drawing studio is open, and we take our regular drawing horses on the far side of the room. The fluorescent lights are on, but the room is primarily illuminated by the awning windows spanning the south wall. Our model typically takes a seat on the barstool sitting atop the small center stage, and we each have a different perspective from our individual benches. But the model isn't anywhere in sight today, and neither is our instructor.

I drop my bag next to the bench and locate my eighteen-by-twenty-four-inch newspaper pad and supply box in my cubby.

"We're doing lunch today, right?" Prudence asks when I return. She's shed her backpack and jacket beneath her drawing horse and has rolled up the sleeves of her peasant blouse. Her pretty brown hair is pulled up into a high ponytail.

"Will Cynthia make it?"

As often as I see Prudence—quite often due to this class, our Honors Program activities, and living in the same building—Cynthia is rarely in sight. A disappointment for Jimmy any time he "happens" to run into us and say hi. He's so obvious.

Prudence frowns. "She said she'll try, but I think when she said that, she forgot about the exam in the morning, so probably not."

I nod. "Alright."

"*Hey!*"

I shift in my seat—and Prudence turns too—to look at the drawing horse on my other side, now occupied by Dahlia Finnick.

A grin spreads across her heart-shaped face, and when I smile back, she pushes a strand of wavy brown hair behind her ear. "You left the party early, Billie. We didn't get to hang out at three in the morning after everyone else left." She shrugs her bag onto the floor. "That's the best part."

I shake my head and flip open my drawing pad. "I would've stayed longer, but I had some shit with my mom that couldn't wait."

Felix Quigley comes in a moment later to introduce the lesson, and Prudence and Dahlia grab their drawing pads and supplies from the cubby wall.

"Alright, folks!" He marches over to a small corner table and connects his phone to the Bluetooth speaker. "Our model's off for the day, so I need everyone to choose a partner. We're going to take turns drawing portraits. A few five and ten-minute drawings. I want you using the charcoal or Conte crayons for this."

Dahlia plops down in her seat with a grin. "Partners?"

"Uh, sure."

Prudence walks back to her drawing horse, carrying her pad and a pack of Conte crayons. I send her a smile while Dahlia scoots her horse closer.

"You pose."

I shift uncertainly.

"Something comfy, but make it interesting."

I stretch my shoulders while she pulls out a piece of vine charcoal, then flips to a fresh page in her pad, but when her intense gaze lands on me again, my muscles tense. I can't imagine I'm doing anything interesting, but she presses her charcoal to the page all the same.

If she's concentrating, it's impossible to tell. Her arm moves fluidly, her motions are brazen, but she spends most of her time studying me instead of focusing on the paper.

"Brent said he had fun hanging out with you."

The room is filled with idle chatter, but the primary sound is that of Felix's music. Ace of Base's "The Sign" is the first song on today's playlist.

"He did?"

"Of course, silly." Dahlia grins, then glances down at her drawing again. "I can't believe I hadn't introduced you before. We've lived together for two and a half months. How is that possible?"

I want to shrug, but I'm not supposed to move. "I don't know."

"Especially when I've already met your friends."

At this, I shift to get a better look at her. "You have?"

"Oh, are we switching positions?" She is unfazed by my movement. She simply flips to another page and begins a new drawing. "My brother and I have been organizing parties since the day we arrived, and people started paying us after the first semester—mostly the frat boys, mind you, because all the others we did for fun."

Brent did say that she and Darius planned the party.

"And your...friend, Xander—well, he went to every party we put together last year. Always flirting with the girls and dragging Jim behind him." Dahlia pauses to laugh. "He doesn't do that anymore, does he?"

I shake my head but make sure to return to my position. "He got a job off campus when he got back. He even came early and lived in his car for a week while job hunting—" something he hasn't explained in the months since "—and he's been too busy working."

"Where's that?"

"A bar downtown."

She withdraws her charcoal from the page. "Which one?"

"Oh, it's called Draft Horse. It's a restaurant too, and they do a whole big thing for the Kentucky Derby—it's their signature event or something." I bite my lip, uncertain. "I've never been there."

Dahlia cocks an eyebrow.

"I don't go anywhere off campus. It's too…stressful."

She studies me a moment before returning to the drawing. "You're majoring in art, right? I am too—well, Arts Administration. It's great to find someone who likes the same sort of things you do, isn't it?"

I blink a moment, unsure how we got from there to here, but I suppose, like Dahlia, I have to roll with the punches. "Yeah." I don't know which of her questions I'm answering, or maybe it's both, but a big smile spreads across her delicate features.

"I've watched your drawings during class. You're really talented. I can't wait to see what you do with me. And Xander's your boyfriend?"

I nearly fall off the drawing horse. "What?"

Where the hell did that come from?

But Dahlia smiles at me, either unaware of how random and personal her question is or not caring.

"No, he's not."

"But you want him to be, right?" She pauses a second to examine her work before flipping to the next sheet.

"We're friends," I say slowly. "I'm not interested in dating."

She inhales sharply. "He must be pretty disappointed."

"I'm sure he's fine."

This is Xander—he's always fine.

"Besides," I add, "he has plenty of women to choose

29

from here, and he's making his rounds. He's certainly not holding out for me." I force a laugh, then remember I'm not supposed to move. "That's ridiculous. Seriously laughable."

Dahlia chuckles too. "Funny story, actually. Halloween last year, Jim was tipsy—from one beer—and talking about this girl he had a crush on, and Xander started berating him for not having any idea how to woo a woman—which he then proceeded to demonstrate on a randomly chosen victim. But the best part was, as sloppy as his so-called seduction was, she kissed him. Probably helped that he was dressed as Deadpool." She sends me a grin, but I can't return it. "Sorry, it was one of those you-had-to-be-there moments. They only made out for a few minutes."

I vaguely recall the costume—he got so drunk that Jimmy, who had happily dressed as Spiderman, had to drag him back to their dorm room at three in the morning, and I was still awake. David helped us get him in bed. That was the first time Xander got seriously drunk, and I haven't seen him that bad since.

But the costume. It was well assembled and tight enough to not leave much to the imagination. Not that I was looking. If he had worn that Friday night, on the other hand…I might have considered paying attention.

"I'm sure it was funny." My voice is flat. "My turn to draw, right?"

As the period comes to a close, Felix switches off his music and unsyncs the Bluetooth. The room falls silent. "Thanks for a great lesson, folks. Remember, we'll do our critique next class, so make sure you have all your drawings from the last month ready."

I close my sketchpad, and Dahlia and I stow our things in the cubbies.

"You don't have plans for lunch, do you?" she asks as she dons her cross-shoulder purse.

I open my mouth, but in the distance, Prudence is putting away her supplies. "I do actually."

"Can't you reschedule?" Dahlia doesn't pause for a response. "You need to eat lunch with us so I can properly introduce you to everyone."

I open my mouth, hesitant. "Maybe, but—"

Dahlia squeals. Before I can protest, she clasps her hand around mine and tugs me toward the classroom exit, leaving Prudence behind.

◆

In the sea of students, the cafeteria's mass of circular tables are difficult to discern. We swipe our ID cards at the reception desk, and Dahlia leads me inside the hall, her hand clamped around mine. To the right, each buffet has a line of at least a dozen students, waiting for food, and Dahlia inhales sharply at the sight before making a dogleg turn toward her regular table.

I've seen her in the cafeteria a few times, but we've never eaten together. Her table is always full, as it is now.

She marches, but I shuffle behind. "Look who I found," she announces when we arrive.

The group of seven turns to greet us. Most of the faces I recognize from the party or around campus, but a couple are new. Brent, a small smile on his face, scoots away to make room for us.

31

Dahlia pulls up a second chair next to the empty one, nudges me into the new seat, and collapses into the chair between me and Brent.

Brent stretches his arm around her to shake my hand, and I hesitantly place my fingers in his firm grip. "Hey, Billie." He releases me immediately, and I retreat.

"Let me introduce you to everybody," Dahlia says. "This is Darius."

She nods toward the guy across the table. They have the same heart-shaped face, the same wavy honey-brown hair, the same smile. The last time I saw him, he was face-down on the ground in a poorly assembled toga, drunk off his ass.

"My idiot brother," she adds before pointing out each group member in clockwise order. "Emily, Anna, Brian, Heath, Elias, and this here is Kai."

Kai, sitting on my right, sends me a toothy grin, and the group murmurs an array of quiet hellos.

"Everyone, this is Billie." Dahlia positively beams. "She's one of my suitemates and my new favorite friend."

I frown at her words—surely someone here would be upset by her use of the word "favorite"—but everyone smiles, and I say, "Hi," in the quietest of voices. My face contorts into an uncomfortable smile.

Despite her declaration, the group is hardly interested in me. It only takes a minute for them to return to their previous conversations, and I sit, the blood beating through my eardrums, drowning out their voices.

My stomach clenches, and I have nothing to do with my hands. We should've gotten drinks first.

I push away from the table. The chair squeaks against the floor, and there's a lull in conversation as they glance my way. "I'm getting a drink," I whisper to Dahlia. The corners of her mouth lift into a small smile.

On the other side of the cafeteria, clutching a cup of ice water, I roll my shoulders and twist my neck. But I cannot relax.

Somehow, this is worse than the party. At least no one knew or cared about me there. Here, I'm expected to have a conversation with people whose names I've already forgotten.

I refill my cup when it's empty and take another sip before perusing the buffet lines in search of something interesting. None of the food options look appetizing.

When I turn away from the drink station, my eyes land on the familiar bespectacled face of my best friend. For the first time in the last hour, my smile is real.

Jimmy stops next to me with a matching foam to-go box and cup. "Hey. How was your drawing class?"

I shrug. "Same as always. What're you doing here? I thought you were doing a full study session before your test at two."

"Thus the to-go box." He brandishes it toward me. "You're eating with Prudence today, right? I figured I'd stop and say hi while I was here."

I roll my eyes. "You wanted to see Cynthia."

But then, I catch myself and turn toward the mass of tables to find them. Prudence is sitting at a table near the entrance with a couple other girls. True to form, Cynthia isn't present.

"Something wrong?"

I shake my head. "Just something I have to fix later."

Jimmy frowns, and I almost laugh. He looks constipated when he's overthinking things.

"Say it."

He releases a half laugh, half sigh. "I wanted to ask you something."

"What?"

He fills his cup at the drink station, and I follow. "Didn't see you much this weekend. You disappeared in the middle of the party."

"I told you, I got tired." I try to shrug it off, but his tone is too nonchalant. He's not buying it. "And I picked up a couple extra shifts at the library this weekend."

"I thought that might be the case." He slips a lid onto the cup and grabs a straw. "Walk with me while I grab food?"

We head for the buffet lines.

"You know..." He grabs a bun, then lays a burger from the grill on the bottom half. "Things have been kinda weird the last few days."

"Really?" I sip my water to hide my interest. "How so?"

He finishes dressing the burger before glancing back. "Xander's been in a bit of a foul mood lately, and I was wondering if you knew anything about it." He tops the burger with the other half of the bun and moves on to the next section. "I mean, he was totally fine when I saw him at the party, but he's been a bigger ass than normal since then."

"I don't know why you're asking me." I cross my arms over my chest. "It's not weird for Xander to be an ass."

He lets out a short laugh. "Which is why I said 'bigger than normal.'" But his smile drops from his face. "Besides, if Xander's in a bad mood, it's usually because of you."

A scoff escapes my lips. "I'm not responsible for keeping

his temper in check. He's a grown adult, not a child, and he should act like one."

He tries to hold it back—I can see it on his freckled face—but he still releases a loud snort. "Right, because you're so good at keeping yours in check. Don't be a hypocrite, Billie."

I take another drink. I don't want to answer the question. I can only hope I've successfully evaded it.

"So, you have no idea why Xander's pissed off right now?"

No such luck.

I shake my head.

Jimmy sighs. "Right." And he moves on to grab some pasta salad.

I gulp down more of my drink.

"It's funny, though. Xander tells me everything, so if he's upset about work or class or whatever, he vents to me." He returns the serving spoon and closes his box. "You're the only thing he's kept from me."

I don't have the capacity to restrain myself anymore—I scowl. "We might've had a spat before I left the party, but it wasn't really anything. I don't know why he's so upset about it."

For a moment, Jimmy watches me, waiting for me to elaborate.

I say nothing.

"What happened?"

My chest constricts, and I look around the cafeteria in search of anything else to focus on. "It was nothing. I was on the phone with my mom, and he kept bugging me, so I told him to leave me alone. He was being ridiculous."

Jimmy raises a skeptical eyebrow. "I'm sure that's the whole story."

"It is."

"Right, of course." And then, he lifts his box in the air and steps toward the exit. "I should get going, do my last-minute cramming."

"Yeah, I'll see you later."

Jimmy's walk to the cafeteria exit is short, and I watch him leave before heading back to Dahlia and Brent and whoever else is at that table. I guess I have to socialize again.

Dahlia's face breaks into a smile when I sit down. "What took so long?"

Four

MOTIVATIONAL POSTERS, PROCLAIMING I SHOULD BE "proud" of who I am and live each day to the fullest, line the walls of Dr. Byrd's office waiting room. Half a dozen chairs are nestled in between end tables with magazines and faux bouquets.

The receptionist, a large woman with hoop earrings, types my name into the computer, then date of birth and appointment time. "Alright, Wilhelmina, you're all checked in." She glances at the nearby digital clock, then hands me a clipboard with a couple pages. "Bring this back to me when you've filled it out. He'll be done soon. Maybe eight minutes."

The waiting area is bigger than I expected for two therapists. There's only one other patient here.

It only takes a couple minutes to fill out the paperwork—medical information, family history, allergies—and I return the clipboard to reception with plenty of time to spare. I lean back in my chair and pick up the closest magazine. *Log Home Living.* I grimace and drop it on the end table again.

One of the doors to the left of the reception opens, and a woman with long black hair and downcast eyes exits the office. She pauses with the receptionist to check out, and I flip through my phone. Have to kill time somehow.

A couple minutes after she's gone, the receptionist calls out my name. "Dr. Byrd will see you now."

Inside, the office is small and minimally decorated. A calendar, a square analog clock, and a couple paintings hang on the wall, and the only furniture is an oak, L-shaped desk with attached shelf, two uninviting green armchairs, and in the far back, a long table with a small tabletop shelf. Two folding chairs are tucked in a nearby corner.

The soft yellow hue of the walls lends the room a warm and inviting atmosphere. That must be useful for a shrink.

"Good afternoon, Billie. I'm glad you're able to join me."

Behind the desk, Dr. Byrd is a tall thick black man with an angular jaw, sitting on a mesh swivel chair. His hair, black and coarse, is dreaded and pulled back into a ponytail. His rich brown skin stretches as he smiles.

I take a seat in the nearest armchair.

"I'm Andrew Byrd. Feel free to call me Andrew or Andy if you like. If you want to call me Dr. Byrd, that's okay too."

I glare at the floor, but my options are limited. I drop my bag next to the chair and look him in the eye. "Hi. I see you know to call me 'Billie.'"

He nods. "Yes, I talked to your mother this morning."

My jaw clenches.

"She called to talk about your missed appointments. She was concerned, so I'm glad you decided to visit me today." He gives me the opportunity to respond, but I have nothing to say. "She was the one who set up your appointments, right? She must be very worried about you to be so proactive from halfway across the country."

The square clock behind him claims it's been a minute. The second hand inches forward. That can't be right.

"She insisted on providing me with some family medical history since you hadn't filled out the paperwork yet. She has a rather severe bipolar disorder, right? It sounds like it took her a long time to get the help she needed, so I'm glad you're here sooner rather than later."

The ragged edges of my fingernails are down to the quick, but I dig at them. I need something to pick at.

"Your sister and friends are worried about you too."

My head shoots up. "You talked to Mo?"

He meets my gaze without hesitation. "Your sister? No, your mother thought I should know."

I don't want him talking to my mother either, but she insisted I sign the release form.

"You don't have to talk if you don't want to, Billie." His chair squeaks as it rolls back a couple inches, and his umber hands clasp atop the desk. "You don't have to be here if you don't want to, but you came here for a reason. If you choose to stay, I would be happy to sit with you until you're ready to talk."

I doubt I'll ever want this conversation. Why discuss my life with a complete stranger?

Not that I have anyone else to talk to.

Jimmy tries so hard to be supportive, but there's a great deal of confusion and a hint of judgment behind his kind eyes. He has never understood.

Dad and I are only now mending our relationship, and I've already relied on him enough. Our structure isn't sound enough to support all my shortcomings.

As much as I love Imogene, she's two years younger than me and has never filled the role of confidante.

And my mom? Obviously, we have a great, healthy, open relationship.

Then, there's Xander.

I can't imagine my relationship with him being anything but rocky. Our fights are a constant, even when we're friends. It's easier to keep him at arm's length. No matter how much it frustrates him.

Behind the desk, Dr. Byrd watches silently.

The clock behind him now reads ten after.

This is going to take forever.

Maybe after the wedding, Mom won't care anymore. Maybe then, I'll be able to get out of this and have control over my own life again. But that's just a maybe, and until then, she's decided to act like a mother for the first time in nineteen years. The fact that I'm an adult now is meaningless.

I clear my throat and lean forward. "I'm not going to skip any more sessions."

He nods. "Thank you for telling me."

"But you should know I have no intention of talking to you about anything."

He raises an eyebrow.

"I don't want to be here. I don't belong here. There's nothing wrong with me. And I'm perfectly capable of dealing on my own."

"I'm sure you are, Billie."

Good.

"But perhaps—" Dr. Byrd lays a hand atop his notepad "—it would be nice to have a conversation instead of sitting in silence for fifty minutes every week. We could exchange pleasantries at the very least."

My resolve softens. "That could be negotiated."

The silence—an emptiness filled by the deafening thoughts flitting through my head—is worse than any conversation of supposed pleasantries could be.

"Billie, can I ask you a question?"

I nod.

"If you don't want to be here, why will you come back?"

I assumed he was aware of the hold my mother put me in to attend these meetings. Part of me assumed he endorsed the idea. Is this a genuine question? Does he not know? Or is he simply trying to get inside my head?

"Like you said, my mother is worried. She's adamant I see you."

He nods. "And would a conversation be an acceptable way to pass the time, Billie?"

What exactly does a conversation entail? How detailed of an exchange does he expect this to be? Is his offer to "exchange pleasantries" legitimate?

"Small talk." I lean forward. "Nothing deep, no diagnoses, no analyzing my dreams."

"Whatever makes you comfortable, Billie." The words are followed by a small smile. "Would you like a water?" He nods toward the mini-fridge hiding behind his desk. He has a plastic water bottle on his desk, half drank.

When I nod, he retrieves a bottle from the fridge and hands it to me. "What are your plans for the weekend?" His deep voice is cool and relaxed.

I twist open the bottle and take a sip. "What I always do. Studying."

This time it's different, though. After a nauseating lunch with Dahlia the other day, she asked me to join them for a group study session Saturday night. I'm not sure why—it might have been her kind smile or the way she said it like I'd already agreed—but I couldn't say no.

There's a moment of silence as Byrd waits for me to elaborate, but I don't.

"Did you dress up for Halloween? You attend Bradford, right? The college usually has a big Halloween celebration with the frats."

I take another drink, this one long, relishing the cold.

The events of Halloween night aren't the optimal choice for small talk, but there's no way he would know that. The alcohol, the discomfort of sitting on that stupid stool, my stranger danger anxiety, and my mother's ultimatum from her sleep-addled brain—that's the last thing I want to discuss with a shrink. Add to that the awful clenching in my stomach, so tight I felt sick, at the sight of seeing Xander with the girl in the angel costume in the dark hallway.

"I'd rather talk about something else."

Dr. Byrd raises a thick black eyebrow but nods his assent.

◆

Dad's in the kitchen when I arrive, stirring a creamy sauce with a bamboo spoon, but nothing gets past him. He must've heard the front door because he glances over his shoulder the moment I walk into the room.

Hazel eyes assess me behind wire-rimmed glasses, and his umber face is twisted in quiet concern. "I was starting to get worried. Dinner's almost ready." On the counter beside him, steam billows from a plate of sautéed chicken breasts.

I lean against the island. "That's why I left you a message. I was…detained."

He raises an eyebrow but redirects his attention to the skillet. With a pair of tongs, he moves the chicken to the boiling sauce, then turns off the burner.

"What are you making?"

"Chicken and asparagus with an herb cream sauce." He lets the chicken sit for a moment before piling it and the asparagus on two plates. Afterward, he pours a healthy portion of sauce over each entrée. "Let's sit." He carries the plates into the dining room, and I grab the two glasses of ice water from the island.

We take our regular seats across from each other, but the food is too hot to eat. Steam blocks much of my view, and I lean back so it doesn't fog up my glasses.

"How are your classes, Mina?"

I take a sip of water. "We've been doing portraits in Drawing. I'm not very good at them, though."

Dad's thick lips purse together. "What gives you that idea?"

"I have to relearn everything." I poke at the chicken with my fork. "I mean, I like having a teacher—and Felix is a great teacher—but everything I thought I knew is wrong."

"That can't be true."

An exaggeration, perhaps.

"Is that what detained you?" He cuts into an asparagus stalk and chews the thick stem. "Your drawing class?"

I frown.

The therapy isn't technically a secret. I haven't told anyone about it, but it's not a secret. And more than anyone,

Dad deserves my frankness. We cannot have a healthy relationship if I keep things from him.

But I also don't want to weigh it down with my mother's drama. Our foundation isn't that stable yet.

"No, Dad, I had a last-minute appointment this afternoon." I drag the fork around the plate, drawing designs in the sauce. "Mom set up weekly therapy sessions for me."

He lays his fork on the table. "That seems rather forward of her. Did she say why this is so important?"

I shake my head. "I don't know. I don't want to do it, but she was...convincing. And you know, I think Mo will be pleased."

"When did this happen, Mina?"

"She wanted me to start at the beginning of the semester, but it got postponed. I guess I'll be doing this for a while, though."

"It might be good to talk to someone."

Dr. Byrd was perfectly nice during our first meeting, but he's a stranger. I won't suddenly tell him all my feelings.

"Maybe."

Dad picks up his fork and knife again and cuts into his chicken breast. Steam rises from the exposed flesh, and he blows on the piece before popping it in his mouth.

But I can't manage to eat anything. "I don't know how to talk to people."

When he swallows, he lays down his knife and stretches his hand across the table. "If you need to practice, you can talk to me about anything."

A small smile forms on my lips, and I place my hand in his. "Thanks, Dad."

Five

Dahlia bounces as she weaves through University Park, but I struggle to keep pace with her.

"I don't think this is a good idea."

But she doesn't let go of my arm.

She releases a melodic laugh and casts a smile in my direction. "You said you wanted to study, so we're going to study. If you get nervous, I can help, but you're not getting out of this, Billie."

"I don't get nervous."

"You do, but that's okay." She nudges me in the side. "They're not going to bite."

There's something haunting about the smile Dahlia flashes. Her face lights up like a child, innocent but bold, kind but assertive, and with that one look, she renders me acquiescent. I am unable to deny her.

Brent and Darius's apartment looks drastically different without the blacklights and drunk people, and I pause at the threshold as a bout of nausea wells up. The living room is back to its natural state of Bradford cleanliness and order, and that only serves as a reminder that each apartment in University Park looks exactly like the next—and the previous.

Sprawled across the couch, Darius flips through the pages of the textbook on his lap, a Coors Light in his hand. On the loveseat next to him, one of the guys from lunch the other day is curled up in an awkward position, his brown hair falling in his face. A blond girl pours a couple drinks in the adjoining kitchen, her long creamy legs stretching for miles. She must be cold wearing little more than short-shorts and a long-sleeve sweatshirt.

They all greet Dahlia when we enter, but no one more zealously than Brent. He jumps up from one of the barstools and shouts her name with uninhibited enthusiasm. If he weren't too busy poking holes in the aluminum foil wrapped around the top bowl of a hookah, he probably would have bounded across the room.

The front door pushes in one final gust of cold air before slamming behind me.

Dahlia drops her bag near the TV and joins him at the counter, but I don't move. She pulls out a circular piece of charcoal from a foil wrapper and offers it to him. "What flavor is it?"

Darius folds up his legs to make space on the couch, and I cross the room to the open seat beside him.

"Rose and jasmine." Brent reaches across a pile of papers and miscellaneous items to extract a lighter. "And I added a little whiskey to give it that rich heavy flavor."

Dahlia nods in approval. "Nice."

Held aloft by a small pair of metal tongs, the charcoal flickers to life, and Brent tosses the lighter back onto the counter while Dahlia wrangles the hose. She sets the three-foot-tall hookah on the coffee table in front of me, and

Brent follows and lays the now white-hot charcoal on the foil-covered bowl.

Only then does he rest an arm on the couch and turn his crooked smile on me. "Hey, Billie. You having a good weekend?"

"I'm not sure yet."

"Can I get you a drink?" He turns toward the kitchen without waiting for an answer. "Anna, can you make another one of those?"

The blonde flashes a devious smile. "I made six. Lia said she'd bring her."

He returns the smile full force before twisting toward me. "Have you smoked hookah?"

Without waiting for a response, he presses the hose lightly to his lips and sucks with all his might. The charcoal, fading to a soft gray, brightens with the influx of oxygen, and he inhales until potpourri-scented smoke pours from his nostrils with each exhalation. He takes one last puff and exhales through his mouth when he pulls back. Then, he offers the hose to me.

For a moment, I hesitate.

Then, my hand snakes out to grab it, and I press it to my lips and inhale slowly. The mouthpiece is damp with his saliva.

The flavor is mild, smooth, and sweet, but when I breathe more deeply, the back of my throat burns. I yank the hose away and force down a cough.

Leaning against the couch, Brent grins. "It's good, isn't it?"

I hand him back the hose. My throat itches and aches. "Good" isn't the word I'd use.

Anna exits the kitchen, carrying three tumblers with clear, fizzing liquid. She offers one to the quiet brunette on the loveseat first, and he gulps down half the drink. The next one is for Dahlia, who smiles in thanks, and then, one for me.

I hesitate, but her face contorts with irritation, and I take the glass so she'll walk away.

She returns to the kitchen and slides one of the remaining three glasses across the counter. Brent lobs the hookah hose toward Dahlia and rushes to catch the drink before it hits the floor. He sends her a short glare after catching it, then nods to the two she has in her hands. "Who's the extra one for?" Darius already has a drink.

Anna sends him a big grin, downs the first drink, and pulls the second closer for a sip. "What extra?"

Brent's hearty laugh reverberates through the apartment, and Dahlia takes a long drag off the hookah before pushing the hose into his hands.

On the couch, I sip my drink and set it in the shadow of the hookah. Vodka tonic, by the taste of it. I slide off my backpack and rummage through the contents. This is supposed to be a study session.

Brent passes the hose over my head to Darius, who leans forward and sets his beer next to my drink. His textbook folds shut from the movement, and several pages crease.

Darius continues the circle. The brunette shifts his position to reach the hose.

Beside me, Darius studies each of us until his eyes land on Anna, leaning against the kitchen counter. "Where's my drink?"

She grins. "You already have one."

Belligerent, he grabs his beer and chugs the remnants. When he's done, he slams the empty can on the table and wipes his mouth with the back of his hand. "Not true."

I drop the papers as I pull them from my bag, and Brent leans over to help. They crinkle in his big hands.

On the other side of the coffee table, Dahlia settles on the floor, cross-legged, discomfort painted on her face. I offer her a small smile as I organize the papers, and Brent sets the ones he's gathered atop my stack. It takes a minute for her to return the smile, but when she does, it spreads across her tight features like a virus.

I withdraw my phone from my pocket and set it next to my drink.

There's one message when I light up the screen. I grab the phone again. From Xander.

You coming over tonight?

Normally, I'm there right now. It's Saturday night, and unless there are extenuating circumstances, the three of us hang out, order pizza, watch some anime, have a couple beers, and I draw. Xander's so tired from work that all he wants to do is peek over my shoulder and ask to see my latest sketches of him. Then, my standard response: I roll my eyes.

But we haven't managed a face-to-face conversation since Halloween.

I push away my phone and grab my notebook and French textbook.

Across the table, Dahlia powers up her laptop and busies herself with making faces at me. When I don't reciprocate, she asks, "Everything alright?"

I glance at the phone again. "It's not a problem."

49

Beside me, Brent offers me the hookah hose again. "What's not a problem?" His voice booms as he speaks.

For a moment, I stare at the mouthpiece, then I shake my head.

Brent frowns before passing it onward. "What's not a problem?" He's quieter this time, but only just.

I gulp down half my drink, but it doesn't do anything for my nerves. Everyone is watching me. "Nothing." Dahlia catches my attention, but I look down. "It's just—my friend and I got into a bit of a fight the other day."

Dahlia leans forward curiously. "Was it serious?"

"Well, he texted me for the first time in a week."

Brent grabs my almost empty cup and downs his own drink, then returns to the kitchen. "You haven't been talking? That sounds serious." Even though he's only five feet farther away, he yells as he sets the cups in the sink. There's no way they weren't drinking before we arrived.

Dahlia shifts her weight. "Brent's exaggerating because he gets along with everyone." She chuckles, and I have to laugh. "You two fight often?"

Since the day we met. Even now that we're friends, the fighting is normal. But the arguments revolve around him being an ass or inconsiderate or nosy. Not his love life of all things. Because really, who he sleeps with has nothing to do with me.

"Yeah."

Brent comes back and sets an unopened Coors Light in front of me, then takes his seat on the stool. The *pop* when he opens his own beer is sharp and loud.

I focus on the silver can. "I guess I shouldn't complain."

I didn't ask for a beer. I don't need it. I've never cared for the taste either. But I take the can from the table, pop the tab, and take a drink. The bubbly liquid is sweet but dry, and my mouth puckers. It's disgusting.

"Don't be like that." Dahlia waves my words away with a flick of her wrist. "Complain as much as you want. That's what friends are for, Billie. One of the best ways to get to know someone is by listening to them bitch."

But before I can answer, my phone lights up. I snatch the device off the table and stand. "I'll be right back."

Outside in the cold, I let the song play for a minute—blink-182's "Feeling This"—only swiping my thumb across the screen right before the voicemail takes over. "Yeah?"

Static and background noise fill the earpiece. Is he not there?

Then, his voice comes through: "Dixon, this is stupid. Come over."

"Thanks for the offer, but I'm busy."

His exhalation is so loud that I can't hear anything else, and his voice is a low grumble. "Are you still pissed off about Halloween? That was a week ago, and this has gone on long enough. Don't say you're busy just because you're stubborn. Get your ass over here."

My jaw clenches. "Or you could stop being a jerk for two seconds to consider that I might actually have plans. Which I do." My grip on the phone tightens. "I'm not blowing you off, and until this moment, I've been more annoyed than pissed off."

Xander groans. "Well, stop getting pissed off over nothing."

"And you should stop assuming I'm lying when I say I'm

busy. For once, take me at my word."

"Then you should take me at mine when I say nothing was happening with Regan," he snaps.

I frown.

The angel, I assume. I liked it better when she was a nameless, faceless entity. Makes it easier to hate her.

"What you do on your time is your business, Xander. I don't care about who or where you're screwing."

"This is why I assume you're lying when you say you're busy." He releases a long sigh, and his irritation dissipates. "Dixon, you know I don't have a lot of free time with school and work. I'd prefer to spend that time with the people I care about. Come over."

My chest constricts with pleasure at the admission. "Of course I want to spend time with you."

"I know you do."

I freeze.

There's something about his tone, his voice, that says more than the actual words—something that says he knows far more than he'll say aloud. My stomach twists at the strange discomfort his words send through my body, and I clear my throat.

Xander sighs again. "Seriously, come over, Dixon. Jimmy's complaining that you're not here."

I almost smile, but my eyes wander toward Brent and Darius's apartment. "I'm studying with Dahlia and her friends tonight." I take a deep breath. "I had to force myself to come here in the first place, so please don't offer me an excuse to leave. I'm trying to push myself."

He lets out a quiet chuckle. "Rain check? I have tomorrow off."

I pause a moment to consider, then frown. "I can't. I have to take a bus to Burlington for that dress fitting, remember? My mom's counting on me."

"Dixon." His voice is flat, and I picture him rolling his eyes. "I have a car. You don't need to take the bus. Let me drive you. Just the two of us."

A grin spreads across my face. "Really? That would save so much time."

And I'd get to spend the whole day with him. Only him. As much as I love Jimmy, there's a twinge in my stomach at the idea of being alone with Xander, an excitement I can't place or explain.

"Yeah, of course. You know, I'm excited to see you wearing a dress. I doubt pictures could do it justice."

Heat rises to my face at the thick anticipation in his voice. My mind flashes through a dozen scenarios. Most of them involve the two of us locked in a dressing room. The amount of clothing varies.

This second twinge is more familiar and decidedly lower than my stomach, but it only happens when he's close to me—close enough to bring back the memories I've spent many nights trying to erase for my own sanity.

I tug at the drawstring dangling from my blue hoody. My voice is quiet and reserved when I respond: "Well, text me in the morning so we can figure out timing."

Unfortunately, those memories—Xander pinning me to the bed and kissing me thoroughly, his naked body next to the dorm room light switch, his rough fingers massaging me till I come—refuse to disappear.

I'm slowly going insane.

Six

Usually, my bedroom is little more than the Bradford-supplied furniture—a twin bed without a box-spring, a dresser, a chair, and a desk with a small attached shelf, where I keep my textbooks when not in use—plus my shoes and sketchbooks thrown wherever. It's a sort of precarious organization. I don't keep many personal items, so the only decorations I have on display are my poster of the Joker a la *The Killing Joke* having yet another psychotic episode and a glow-in-the-dark Gir Funko Pop sitting atop my shelf.

Right now, on the other hand, the room's veering dangerously close to an outright mess. Clothing, torn from my open closet, piles on half my bed and cascades down to the carpet, and boxes litter the floor.

The other half of the bed is occupied by Dahlia, who reclines on my pillow with a textbook, wearing nothing but a thin camisole and Brent's golden-brown harem pants from Halloween. When he bought them for his costume, the deal was she'd get them afterward. Her areolas are vaguely visible through the pink cami.

The sweater has to be here somewhere, and yet, I've

looked everywhere. Nothing to be found in any of the obvious locations. Or the obscure ones.

Maybe I got rid of it. It wouldn't be weird since I only wore it once—and it's been forever since last winter. But surely I would've remembered throwing it out. Besides, I'd bet my mom expects me to wear it every winter I see her— now that she can form long-term memories.

I heave a sigh and push away another box. Another fruitless attempt.

"Billie, are you looking for anything in particular? Or are you enjoying walking around in your bra?"

I send her a quick glare.

There are two more boxes in the closet, and I poke my head inside the dark alcove to pull them out. The first one, as I suspected, is full of old sketchbooks and last semester's textbooks. Nothing remotely fabricy in there.

I open the next box. "I'm looking for a shirt."

Dahlia cocks an eyebrow. "There's a big pile of shirts right here on your bed."

The second box has my spare set of sheets, but beneath that is a shoebox of miscellaneous items and a few Moleskine journals. The gray cashmere with its lavender ribbon sits on the very bottom.

I smile at the sight of it. "This is a particular shirt."

I yank the sweater over my sports bra. It's not winter yet, but it's cold enough for a hoody, which means it's cold enough for this. And this is the only remotely feminine-looking top I own.

"That's a cute sweater. Are you dressing up for something, Billie?"

"Of course not."

She chuckles. "Then why in the world did you spend the last forty minutes searching for this one sweater? Is it a special sweater?"

I shrug. "My mom gave it to me."

"That makes it special?" She closes her textbook and sits up. "Xander's going to be here soon, right? What time did he say?"

I glance at my alarm clock. It's a few minutes after eleven. He should be here any time.

"And you two are going to spend the whole day together, right?"

Despite myself, a smile spreads across my face. "Yeah, we are."

"Like a date?"

I turn to her sharply. "It's not a date. He's helping me out, and I appreciate that."

Dahlia pushes aside her textbook and rises from the bed. "That explains why you're so nervous." When she stands beside me, she lays a comforting hand on my arm.

"I'm not nervous. Not about him at least. If I'm nervous, it's because of my mom's wedding. She stresses me out. I don't even like wearing dresses."

"Well, even if you're not trying to impress anyone, you look cute."

I turn to her with an arsenal of responses, but she tugs at the lavender ribbon with a secretive grin.

My phone rings on my nightstand in the distance. I cross the room to reach the device but pause at the name.

Xander.

That can't be a good sign.

I sit on the edge of the bed and answer it: "Hey, you

running late?"

He releases a low laugh. "I wish that were the case."

Of course.

"I got called in to work. Tiff's got a short-notice school thing, and Kylie asked if I could cover for her. I'm not sure I'm allowed to say no to the owner's wife unless I have a very good reason."

I nod. "Yeah, I understand."

"You know I wanted to take you, right?" His voice is quiet but intense, imploring me to listen. "We can do it next weekend. It's not a big deal to postpone, is it?"

"No, I guess not." I heave a sigh. "The wedding's months away. It's not a problem."

"And we can hang out tonight. It's an early shift; I'm starting at noon, so I'll be done by seven." His voice, normally energetic and teasing, is oddly calm and quiet, reassuring. "Does that sound alright?"

I am not reassured.

I take a deep breath and muster my most upbeat tone. "Yeah, that sounds great. I'll see you then."

When we hang up, I collapse against the mattress, holding the phone to my chest. Yet again, his job ruins everything.

"He can't come?" Dahlia sits beside me and squeezes my knee. "You okay?"

"Of course I'm okay. Canceled plans aren't a big deal." I look at the phone in my hands. "It's not like it was a date, right?"

"Right." She squeezes again. Even through my jeans, her fingers are cold. "And since it wasn't a date, it's not a problem if I take you instead."

"What?"

But when I sit up, she's already heading for the door. "Let me grab my purse."

◆

I've never been inside Dahlia's black Honda Accord before—I rarely leave campus—but the car is sleek and in good condition. We're on the highway to Burlington in no time.

She fusses with the radio, but every station is on commercial, and she shuts it off with a groan.

For a moment, there's only silence.

"So, what are we going to talk about for the next hour?" All irritation is gone. "There are a lot of options."

She waits, but I'm not sure what to say, until the words tumble out: "This is a nice car. What year is it?"

Dahlia snickers. "It's a 2002. Why don't you have one?"

I turn to her, but she's focused on the road. "One what?"

"A car, silly."

"Oh."

"Do you know how to drive?"

"Yeah, of course." I pull out my phone, but Xander hasn't texted at all. I slip it back into my pocket. "Charlie Powell taught me."

"Powell? Like a relative of Jim's?"

Right. How would she know?

"His dad." I shift in my seat to get comfortable. "He taught us how to drive the summer after our freshman year of high school when we were fifteen."

Well, Jimmy turned fifteen the following August, but

58

close enough.

Dahlia casts a quick glance in my direction. "What about your parents?"

Outside, the Vermont trees blur into one long line of brown limbs. A few conifers are mixed in, but most trees are bare.

Normally, a question this loaded, no matter how harmless-sounding, is enough to render me silent, but there's something about the casual way she says it. With Dahlia, there's no expectations and no pressure. The words flow out of my mouth before I consider refraining.

"That was the summer after my parents' divorce. My dad moved here. I was living with my mom, but she was… unable to teach me."

"'Unable'?" She flips on her blinker and switches lanes. She's not looking at me, but her quiet voice betrays the depth of her curiosity. "What's that supposed to mean?"

"My mom's an alcoholic. The year after their divorce was… She was drunk more often than not, and I wouldn't trust her to teach me anything sober either."

"That's fair."

"Plus, there's the little problem of me hating her."

Dahlia stiffens. "You hate your mom?"

I pull a leg up onto the seat; the cab has plenty of room for my petite body. "'Hate' might be an exaggeration, but it's pretty damn close sometimes."

"What do you think of her fiancé?" Her voice is guarded, uncertain.

Roberto Herrera: I met Rob when I got home for summer vacation, armed only with the knowledge Imogene supplied over spring break. He's a first generation Ecuadorian immigrant who teaches Latin dance classes to white middle-class women, most of whom only signed up because he's young, single, and "exotic"—insert eye roll here. He's quiet and reserved, and the majority of what he speaks is Spanish, which I don't understand.

Unluckily for his dance students, he's not so single anymore. He and my mother announced the engagement the second I opened the front door.

"He's fine. He doesn't say a whole lot—not to me—but he seems nice."

She nods, but there's something about the way her jaw slackens. "You're not happy about the wedding, though."

Every time the question comes up, my response is the same: Of course, I'm happy for her.

But the truth is, I'm not.

It's not like I want her to be unhappy—not exactly—but it's hard to care about her impending nuptials when she never made an effort to care about me or be a part of my life.

Until now.

"No, I'm not happy about it."

With no more than a small smile, Dahlia puts me at ease. I can say anything, even the things I don't want anyone to know. Maybe it's because she has no association with my family or any predispositions. Maybe I don't care if she thinks I'm a terrible person; the assessment's probably accurate.

"I hate it," I say after a beat. "She spent most of my childhood not caring about anyone but herself and how the world was against her, but the second she has something good going on, I'm supposed to be one hundred percent supportive. I'm supposed to pretend the last eighteen, nineteen years didn't happen."

There's a moment of silence before Dahlia speaks, but it's not the unbearable seconds of wondering if she thinks I'm unreasonable or selfish or entitled.

I am oddly calm.

"I moved out of my house when I was sixteen." Dahlia keeps her eyes on the road. "Completely cut ties with my mother. Darius was always her favorite, the baby of the family—ironic considering we're twins—and she was very good at playing favorites. She only noticed me when I did something wrong, and honestly, the more time I spend away from her, from there, the more I realize the things I did wrong were average teenager things." Despite what must be a difficult topic, she has the same small smile on her lips.

"What about Darius? Did he leave with you?"

She shakes her head. "No. I was scared about that at first, thinking that without me there, she'd lash out at him. That wasn't realistic. She worshiped him in a weird way; he was the golden child. She took away his phone so he couldn't talk to me, though." She releases a short laugh. "Not that that stopped him."

"And now he's here."

Dahlia glances at me, and I offer her a supportive smile. "Yeah, we never stopped talking, no matter how hard she tried. I got my GED while living with my dad's cousin, and when it came time for college, Dar and I came here so we could be together. She has no idea I attend Bradford, and we intend to keep it that way."

"Wow."

She chuckles. "It's really not that impressive. We're still recovering and sorting things out, and we're juniors. It's

61

been five years since I left."

I shake my head. "But you were able to leave—that's incredibly brave." Outside, the scenery is the same. "I thought about it a lot, but I didn't know where I'd go. In the end, I spent most of my time at Jimmy's house since he lived next door and tried to pretend everything was okay."

When my words fade away, Dahlia has a serene smile on her face.

"If there's anything I've learned since I walked out—" her quiet voice is barely discernible over the hum of the highway "—it's this: It's okay to not be okay."

◆

Inside, the bridal store is sleek and pristine. Long rows of white dresses in see-through plastic bags line one half of the building. The other side has a wide selection of colorful dresses and several mannequins in spring attire. The dressing rooms, mirrors on the outside of the doors, are in the back, and immediately in front of us is the reception desk.

A woman, wearing all black and a headset, looks up at us with a smile. "How can I help you?"

I step forward. "Hi. I need to get measured for a bridesmaid dress."

The lady nods and presses a button on her headset. "Kourtney, I have a young woman here to get sized. Are you available again?" There's a short muffled response, and she looks up. "Have a seat. She'll be right with you."

Dahlia and I step to the side and wait a moment, and she giggles as I fidget with my sweater. "You're really stressing about this, aren't you?"

I roll my eyes. "She probably chose the worst dress so she looks great by comparison. And it's one of my least favorite colors." I glance around the store with a frown. "And what if they don't have it here?"

Dahlia nudges my arm. "Then you order it online. This is fine, Billie."

I send her an appreciative smile.

A moment later, a twenty-something brunette with deep bronze skin and a brilliant smile approaches. "Hi, I'm Kourtney. You're here for a measurement, right?" She glances between us, not sure if the appointment's for one or both of us, and I step forward.

"Yeah, I need to get sized for a bridesmaid dress." I pull out my phone to access my notes. "I have the product number."

She smiles and directs us to the dressing rooms.

We pause in front of a full-length display of white, cream, and ivory heels, slippers, and flats. To our right, there's an even larger display of veils, tiaras, belts, and other accessories, readily available to add a finished look.

Dahlia sits on a viewing chair while Kourtney pulls out her measuring tape. She tightens the plastic strip around my bust, waist, and hips, but I find Dahlia in the mirror. She pokes out her tongue, then giggles when I roll my eyes in response.

The sales assistant steps away and hangs the tape around her neck. "You said you have the product number? I can check to see if we have it in your size." She jots down the code on her palm and disappears in search of the dress.

"Have you seen it?" Dahlia asks once she's gone.

I shake my head. "A glimpse in a magazine."

When she returns, Kourtney is carrying several short dress bags, which she hangs on a nearby hook. "Alright, we have a few different colors. Do you know which one? Or do you just need to make sure it fits well?"

I shake my head, staring at the options, covered and unseen. "It's some kind of pink."

She pulls forward two of the bags and unzips the first one. "It's called blush. You're between sizes, so I grabbed a two and a four."

The dress is a soft dusty pink with a glitter-coated belt. It's strapless, has a sweetheart neckline, and tulle covers the lacy bodice. The full skirt stops below the knee with layers upon layers of tulle.

Kourtney unlocks the nearest dressing room and hangs it on the hook inside, then ushers me in as well.

When the door latches behind me, I strip off my clothes and slip the dress on. The first one is too tight to zip up, and Kourtney supplies the larger dress. I change again, barely managing to zip it all the way up my back without help.

The material hugs my petite form, tight around the ribs but a little loose at my waist. Thankfully, the skirt covers my knobby knees.

"Are you done yet?" Dahlia calls out. "Come show me."

I take a deep breath, open the door, and step onto the platform. I don't want to look at her, though, so I spin to examine myself in the full-length mirror. "I look awful."

Dahlia laughs. "You're a bridesmaid. It doesn't matter what you look like."

The lighting is better out here, and the pale pink matches my freckled amber skin in tone. I'm going to blend together.

"How awful is it?"

Beside me, Kourtney issues a number of compliments I tune out—all attempts to make commission on the sale.

But Dahlia rises from her chair and approaches. I turn to meet her, and she circles me with a predatory gleam in her eyes. My stomach tenses.

Finally, she stops in front of me and steps close enough to lay her hands on my bare shoulders. "It's not as bad as you think. You look sexy." She pulls back with a casual shrug. "I mean, yeah, the color isn't great, but the cut looks good."

I turn to the mirror again. "Yeah, I'll take it." It's not like I have a choice.

Seven

Jimmy slings his bag onto the table and drops into the seat next to me. "Good, you're here."

"Of course, I'm here." I pick at the food on my plate. "We said 11:30, and it's two minutes after."

"Right." Xander sheds his leather jacket on the back of the chair on my other side. "If you're anything, it's punctual."

Jimmy scowls. "That's not what I meant. We just haven't seen much of you lately."

A quick sweep across the cafeteria reveals Dahlia sitting halfway across the hall with Brent, Darius, and the rest of their gang, chatting and laughing per usual. She's been monopolizing my time more than I intended.

"I know, I should've been over this weekend."

Jimmy scoots his chair closer, and excitement flushes his cheeks. "We can fix that."

I raise an eyebrow.

"Do you have plans next Friday?"

"No."

"This asshole—" he nods in Xander's direction "—finally has a Friday night off, and my request off at the Eyrie was approved, so we're throwing a party."

I raise a hand. "A party? Really? Can't we do something else—anything else?"

"I don't care." Jimmy sweeps my protests away with his hand. "We've barely seen you, and you're coming whether you like it or not."

"Seriously," I try again, but this time, Xander draws my attention.

"Nothing big." His voice is quiet and compelling. "Maybe ten people. An intimate get-together if you will."

For a moment, I'm not sure what to say, but I smile. "I guess that wouldn't be so bad. It's not like you can fit a lot of people in your apartment."

"And we don't want security called either," Jimmy says, though that doesn't seem to bother any of the other Bradford students when they plan their parties.

"Which ten people?"

Jimmy shrugs. "I asked David."

"Our RA David?"

"He's not our RA anymore," Xander reminds me. "We haven't asked anyone else yet. Figured you might want to invite Dahlia since you've been spending so much time with her."

"And—" Jimmy leans against the table "—it would be cool if you invited Prudence."

I scowl. "And Cynthia?"

He tilts backward, but his fingers tap an anxious beat on the tabletop. "If she happened to come too, that'd be fine."

The snort escapes my lips before I can stop it, and he sends me a sharp look that I ignore. "Well, I'll ask."

But uncertain, I look back toward Dahlia's table.

Dahlia and I have spent much of the past couple weeks

together, just the two of us. Even when we're with Brent or Darius or any of the others, she sends me those little conspiratorial smiles, like we have our own secret code, not to be shared with anyone. Combining that with my friendship with Xander and Jimmy feels wrong.

When I look at Jimmy, he's grinning, excited despite his attempts to keep his cool.

After perusing the buffet lines, Jimmy returns with a slice of pizza, pasta, and grilled chicken, humming a song I don't recognize. He takes his seat and begins to eat, but he pauses after a glance my way. "Everything alright?"

I smile, but I'm tired. "Yeah, I'm okay. Dahlia and I were up late last night."

He raises an eyebrow. "How late?"

He has a point. I don't get much sleep, but Dahlia wanted to share a couple bottles of wine in her bedroom, and we fell asleep together around four or five.

"Just late." I shrug and turn away before he can give me one of his judgy looks.

But then, I see him.

Or rather, her.

Twenty feet away, Xander's walking back to the table, a salad bowl and small plate of pasta in his hands. And he's talking to her. The angel from the Halloween party. Whatever he said her name was, I don't remember.

He sets his plate on the table and rummages through his backpack. "I should have them with me. If I don't, I can get them to you later."

The angel pauses next to him, a smile on her rosy face, and she leans closer, tits bulging out of her V-neck. "Oh my gosh, I really appreciate it, Xander." She glances at me and Jimmy, short brown hair falling in her eyes with the swift movement. "I feel like such an idiot. I don't know how I could have misplaced my notes."

But he pulls back, shaking his head. "I don't see it. You can come by the apartment later if you have time—I'll be there from two to five—or I can give it to you in class on Thursday."

I feel sick. She's been to his apartment. Has she been to his bedroom too?

A dazzling smile spreads across her face, and he sends her a short one in return. Then, she leans closer. "You're awesome. I'll try to stop by this afternoon."

His eyes gravitate toward the cleavage barely contained by her shirt.

I'm impressed he didn't notice them sooner.

I push my plate away, and Jimmy nudges my arm with a somber face. "Do you think Dahlia will bring her brother?"

"What?"

"To the party."

Right. He's trying to distract me. My discomfort must be obvious, then. Great.

Our discussion has the desired effect, though.

Xander clears his throat and finally takes his seat. "Uh, Regan, I don't think you've met my friends. Jimmy Powell, Billie Dixon. This is Regan…?"

I almost laugh. He doesn't know her last name.

The smile on her face falls. "Foster. Regan Foster." She sends me and Jimmy a smile each, but I cannot return it. She steps back at the sight of my glare. "Nice to meet you."

"Regan's my Chem lab partner," Xander explains, nonchalant once again.

She hovers at his elbow, not wanting to leave yet, but she keeps sending nervous glances in my direction. "Uh, did someone say something about a party?"

Xander gives a half-shrug. "We're going to have a few people over next weekend. Nothing big."

"Oh, fun." She shifts her weight back and forth, her smile still in place, but she doesn't make any move to leave. She's fishing for an invite.

I spin my cup and study the way the Sprite swirls. "You probably wouldn't think so. No dancing, no slutty costumes, no throwing yourself at men you barely know." This would be better with a little tequila.

"Billie."

Jimmy's voice is a warning, but I roll my eyes. I could've sat with Dahlia today, and it would've been a hell of a lot better than this.

Behind me, Xander says, "You're welcome to come." His voice is apologetic on my behalf. "Just, you know, don't expect anything exciting to happen. It's next Friday."

"That would be awesome." Excitement laces Regan's voice, all memory of my harsh words gone at his kindness. "I'll be there."

When she leaves, the table is momentarily silent. But I'm not convinced she's gone until Jimmy speaks:

"Billie, what the hell was that?"

Across the cafeteria, Dahlia catches sight of me and stretches her arm out to wave. Her gleeful laughter carries halfway across the cafeteria, and I smile before turning back to the guys.

On my left, Xander's face is tense and stern. He doesn't

say a word or look at me.

Jimmy, though, frowns.

"I need to get ready for my next class." I rise from my seat before he can launch into one of his spiels.

Jimmy mutters a goodbye as I leave, but Xander remains silent.

◆

"Good afternoon, Billie."

Dr. Byrd settles down on one of the folding chairs in the back of his office and sends me a smile as I join him. He scoots his chair closer to the table. I do the same.

"I thought we might do something a little different." He pulls a booklet from a narrow cubby hole in the corner. "This is something we typically do with younger clients, so it may seem a bit rudimentary."

When he opens the booklet, I look closer. It's a coloring book. A dinosaur coloring book.

"We only have a few different coloring books, so my options were limited. I thought you might be more inclined to work in the dinosaur book than the Disney princess book."

I snicker. That's a correct assessment.

"I'm not looking for you to make a masterpiece," he adds, pushing the booklet toward me. He grabs a golden-orange box of crayons from the table drawer and slides that over as well. "I just want you to color while we talk."

"Okay."

I flip through the book and settle on a stegosaurus. The crayon box requires more force to open than I anticipated.

71

It's brand-new.

"How has your week been, Billie?"

I press a chartreuse crayon to the faded paper. "It's November, which means finals are a few weeks away. My week is a combination of classes, studying, and working."

"Where do you work? I don't think we've talked about that before."

"The campus library." I outline the edge of the stegosaurus's body before filling the interior as a base color. I can go over sections with a darker forest green or yellow where appropriate.

Dr. Byrd nods. "Do you spend a lot of time there?"

"Only when I'm working."

I've always liked the silent professional atmosphere of the library. Its cool interior is calming, relaxing, and in a way, invigorating.

But that was before.

I never expected to get the job in the first place—a library assistant is a sought-after campus position, and I'm a sophomore—but now that I have it, I wish I'd gotten one of the many other campus jobs I applied for in August. There are a lot of unhappy memories in that library. Memories I don't appreciate reliving while stocking shelves or doing my homework in down time.

"What else do you do with your time, Billie?"

I shrug. "I don't know. Nothing really."

"Well, let me ask it another way. What does a typical day in the life of Billie Dixon look like?"

That's a much easier question to answer, but I shake my head. "You'd be bored if I told you."

My typical day starts around six in the morning. Not

because I'm ready to get up, but because once I wake, I can't fall back asleep. I try to get more homework done or fit in some drawing. Classes don't start till 8:30 or nine, depending on the day of the week, and after classes, I usually have a shift at the library or come here. I have a morning shift on Saturdays but the rest of the weekend off, unless I've traded with someone.

In the evening, I occasionally hang out with Jimmy and Xander, but that has to be planned a few days in advance, especially with Xander's rigorous work schedule. Usually, I join Dahlia for whatever ridiculous plans she's concocted. At least once a week, we do a study session with the others. Very little studying actually occurs.

If I have a couple drinks, I'll fall asleep around midnight, often with Dahlia in her bed. If I have more than a couple, we're up late goofing off. Without any, I'm up until three or four, during which time I do more homework.

On the weekends, I spend one night with my dad, and we eat a couple dinners together throughout the week.

"I'm sure I wouldn't be bored," Dr. Byrd says.

I switch to a deep-violet crayon and add some color to the top of the dinosaur's head and spikes, then down to its claws. "There isn't much to tell. I study, I attend classes, I work, I see my friends, I draw, I visit my dad. My life isn't comprised of much."

"Your dad lives in the area?"

"That's why I attend Bradford. He's a professor, so I get a discount on tuition. I wouldn't be able to attend anywhere out-of-state otherwise." The tip of the violet crayon chips, and I purse my lips at the thick dot of wax on my otherwise perfect drawing. "Well, plus Bradford gave me a really good scholarship for graduating Summa Cum Laude."

Byrd crosses his legs and makes a small note. "You're from Missouri, aren't you? They have some good schools there."

I snort. "I didn't care about that." I check myself, stop drawing, and stare at the paper. "I mean, I care about the quality of the school, and Bradford is a high-quality liberal arts school, but there were other factors involved."

The truth is, I wanted to be as far away from my mother as possible, and that desire far outweighed how much I dreaded seeing my dad again.

Somehow, despite everything that happened freshman year, attending Bradford was the right decision.

Eight

BRENT DOUBLES OVER HIS NOTEBOOK ON THE COUNTER, one hand clenched around his mechanical pencil, the other scratching his wiry beard. "Are you sure you can't help me with this, Billie?"

Like most of the upperclassmen housing, my apartment makes use of a simple open floor plan. The living room and kitchen are separated by nothing more than a breakfast bar—our only dining space instead of a table like in Jimmy and Xander's apartment. While the guys have a two-person apartment, this was built for four—myself, Dahlia, and Lacey and Camila, neither of whom I talk to on a regular basis. This living room not only has a couch, entertainment center, and coffee table, but also two end tables and two small armchairs.

I finish sketching out his form in my drawing pad from my comfortable seat on the couch. "I'm not going to help you study just because I'm good at math. You're not supposed to be here anyway."

Besides, the mere correlation leaves an empty feeling in my stomach.

He huffs but laughs all the same, and Dahlia walks out

of her bedroom with her brother in tow. "Okay, you guys need to leave. This is a girls-only night. I made that clear from the beginning."

Darius laughs and nudges her in the side. "I don't know, it'd be fun to see what you do during a sleepover. Isn't there supposed to be a big feather pillow fight?"

I snort. "Only if this were a fourteen-year-old boy's masturbation fantasy."

Brent laughs as he closes his notebook and stands, pocketing his pencil. "We like to think Darius is older than that mentally, but sometimes, I'm not too sure."

Dahlia pushes her brother toward the door of our apartment, and Brent follows.

When at last the door closes behind them, she twists the deadbolt and joins me on the couch. "That's better, right?"

I offer her a smile, but I'm not sure what an appropriate answer would be.

She stretches closer to take a peek at my drawing pad and silently assesses my sketch of Brent. "That's really nice, Billie." She flashes me a smile. "You don't get to draw the whole time we're here, though. You need to pay attention to me."

I chuckle and close my sketchbook.

"And I need a drink." She pushes up from the couch as quickly as she sat down and heads for the kitchen. "You want one too, right?"

"Of course."

Yesterday, she decided she'd whip up margaritas. Most of the ingredients are on the counter next to the blender. Her forethought is the number one indication of her excitement for tonight.

I follow her into the kitchen. I lean against the counter while she double-checks the ingredients: a bottle of Sauza Tequila Silver, a bottle of triple sec, a can of frozen lemonade, a squeeze bottle of lemon juice, and ice from the ice maker in the freezer. Charlie Powell would be appalled at the cheap products, but he's also not on a college student's budget.

Dahlia estimates her measurements and shoves everything in the blender. The machine whirs to life as she holds down the button that says 'Ice Crush,' and the blades slice through the chunks.

When it's done, she pours the liquid into two plastic, neon-colored margarita glasses from the dollar store and offers me one. No slice of lime or salt on the rim, and over half the blender is full.

I sip the semi-frozen drink and shiver at the alcohol. Her estimates were definitely off.

She laughs when she takes a drink. "It's terrible."

I nod but carry the glass back to the living room. "But it'll do."

"Brent and I were trying to decide what to do next weekend." She settles on the couch beside me. Our hips press against each other, and I shift so we're no longer touching. "Do you want to drive to Burlington? Or do you have to work?"

"I have Saturday morning off. I traded shifts with Margaret, so I'm working Sunday afternoon instead."

Then, I pause.

"Wait. I wouldn't be able to do anything then. Jimmy and Xander are having a little party at their apartment Friday night." That's why I traded shifts.

"A 'little' party?"

"Yeah, a few friends, I guess. They said you could come if you want." I shrug. I do not want to make it a big deal.

"How many people? Are you sure we wouldn't be in the way?"

I down a third of the cocktail. "No, it'd be fine." Another sip. "Honestly, it'd be nice to have someone there to buffer."

Dahlia raises an eyebrow. "Buffer what?"

I clasp both hands around the stem of the blue glass. "I don't do well around big groups, and I'm not looking forward to seeing everyone they invited."

"Oh? Like who?"

An image of Regan in her Halloween costume, her hand pressed to Xander's arm, flashes across my mind, and I frown. "No one in particular. I guess I'm worried it'll turn into this boy-girl thing with everyone flirting and me on the sidelines wishing I could just spend some time with my friends."

When I look up, Dahlia has a tight smile on her face. "Is Xander bringing a date?"

I uncross and recross my legs. "Why would that matter?"

I am absolutely positively not jealous.

Dahlia laughs, and after another drink, I turn back to her.

"She's not his date; she's his lab partner, and she's very pretty and has a crush on him." I shake my head. "Not that it bothers me."

But Dahlia presses her lips into a fine line. "How pretty?"

I swallow down the rest of my drink and grip the cup close. "She's at least five-eight and curvy with the straightest brown hair and fair skin and big tits."

Prettier than me. Isn't that enough?

I head for the kitchen again and pour out another drink, this time filling it all the way to the rim. I replace the lid and take a long drink, clutching it with both hands, so I can return to the living room without spilling.

"Really, though, he can date whoever he wants." I take my seat, and she scoots close enough we're touching. "He always has, and I can't imagine that changing any time soon."

"He's a flirt, sure, but I haven't heard anything about him dating or sleeping with girls this year."

I frown. "Maybe he's being more discreet."

Dahlia shrugs. "Maybe."

But that wouldn't be Xander's style, especially with how detailed Jimmy says his accounts are. He would never hide it; he's always prided himself on being upfront and honest with the women he sleeps with, and that's easy because they're aware of his reputation.

"I don't know." I shift in my seat. "I guess, what it boils down to is, I feel like I'm always going to be the awkward third wheel. Sure, Xander and Jimmy aren't dating anyone now, but one of these days, they will, and I'm going to be alone."

She releases a short laugh and places her hand on my thigh. "You won't be alone. You have me."

"And when you get a boyfriend?"

She shrugs, pulling back. "I'm not really into dating. What I typically do is more private."

I cock an eyebrow. "And that's the other thing: If I were to get a boyfriend, I've only had sex a couple times, and I wasn't, you know, in charge of the situation. I don't know what I'm doing."

"Now, sex I can help you with. Dating, not so much."

I take a long drink. "How are you going to help me with that?"

"Tips." She sends me a playful wink. "With anything, the key is confidence, and you might need to build that bedroom confidence up with practice. My general recommendation is finding a fuck buddy. They're a lot easier to find than you'd think." She quirks a smile. "But seriously, if you have any questions, I'm always here if you want help."

"I wouldn't know what to ask."

She frowns. "What experience do you have?"

"Honestly?" I release a nervous laugh and swallow down the rest of my drink. "I've had sex twice. Neither guy was spectacular, but one of them was definitely better than the other. He cared enough to get me off afterward."

"What about oral?" Her drink is almost gone now too.

I shake my head but instantly regret it. Heat rises up my neck, and my head is fuzzy. "Receiving end once, but that was just foreplay, and I've never…"

"Aah." Dahlia draws out her chuckle longer than necessary. "Too scared to give a blowjob?"

Before I can respond, she rises from her seat to grab her laptop from the counter. She brings it out of hibernation and opens a music player. The tinny sound of S3RL's "Pretty Rave Girl" bursts to life from the small speakers. Our music tastes clash dramatically.

"General rules," she says, louder now, "no teeth, focus more on up and down than actually sucking, and use your hands if you want him to come." She ticks them off on her hand. "And if you have a strong gag reflex, don't bother deep-throating. The last thing you want is to ralph all over his cock during sexy time."

I glance down at the empty cup in my hand.

"Otherwise, it's the lifelong debate of spit or swallow." She finishes her cocktail and collapses on the seat next to me. "And if you need advice for going down on a girl, I've been told my tongue is a thing of beauty."

I frown at the cup, uncertain how to respond, then lean forward to set it on the end table. The plastic bangs against the wood at an unexpectedly loud volume.

"No need to get angry about it." She barely holds back a laugh.

"I'm not angry." I shake my head, but that just increases the fuzziness. I shift my weight, but no position is comfortable. My fingers are numb.

She presses a hand to my shoulder and smiles. "Once you've got the hang of it, going down on someone should be as fun for you as it is for them. Oral's my personal favorite. I feel so powerful making someone come."

I force a laugh. "Okay, I don't know when I'd use any of this information, and telling me when I'm drinking isn't going to put it in my long-term memory."

Dahlia pulls me to her side. "Find someone to practice with. That's the best advice I can give you."

"I don't know who…"

"For what it's worth," she yells over the music, "I'm fairly certain Xander would prefer to spend half an hour in bed with you than slow-dancing, but deciding whether to fuck one of your closest friends is something you should think about first."

I pull away. I'm already flushed from the alcohol, but

heat rises to my face as I process her words. Unfortunately, my cup possesses no Bag of Holding abilities, and I cannot will it to fill itself.

"That's not on the menu," I murmur.

Without a word, Dahlia finishes her drink and gets up to grab more. I don't know what I expected her to say to that.

I pull my phone from my pocket to check the time. It's finally after ten. I didn't realize that much time had passed. I flip through my messages while Dahlia pours herself a drink in the kitchen.

Xander hasn't texted me in five days. It's not like I've been there at his beck and call, but that's a long time. We usually text daily, even if we don't see each other. But that's all him. I rarely initiate the conversations.

When Dahlia returns, she pauses next to the couch and looks down at my empty glass. "You want more?"

There's a little left in the blender, and when I nod, she takes my glass to refill it.

On my phone, I open the conversation and read the last text he sent: *Can't tonight. I don't get off until eleven.* He's always working.

I hesitate a moment, but my fingers press the letters on the keyboard with a slowness that only comes from being drunk. Because at some point it changed from delightfully tipsy to actually drunk. It'll hit me the second I move more than an inch.

I miss you.

My thumb pauses over the 'Send' button for a beat, but then, Dahlia comes back with our drinks. I take mine from her, swallow down a gulp before setting it on the coffee table, and press 'Send.'

Against my better judgment, I pull up the keyboard again. No turning back now.

I wish

But I don't know what else to say. There are too many words, too many thoughts racing around my head, and none of them can properly explain what I feel, what I truly wish.

The cursor blinks, and beside me, Dahlia clears her throat.

I turn off the screen with the message half-written. Whatever it is, it's more than I should say. No sense in making a bigger fool of myself.

He won't text back for a while. He's working till bar close tonight, and that's at two. He won't see it till then. There's nothing to panic about.

I grab my drink again and give Dahlia my undivided attention.

Nine

DAHLIA SCOOTS HER DRAWING HORSE TILL IT ABUTS MINE.
"I think I'm still drunk from last night." She keeps her voice
low, but I don't know how much good it does.

I shove her away with a laugh. "Keep your drunk cooties
away."

Class is almost over, and Felix Quigley weaves through
the drawing horses as part of his final walk-through. He
pauses to glance in our direction.

But Dahlia, laughing, doesn't notice. "Don't be ridiculous. You've already got them."

Before I can say anything, Felix addresses the room:
"Alright, folks, that's it for today. I'll see you again on
Monday. Our final critique is in two weeks. Make sure you
have all your work here."

Everyone starts to clean up, and I close my drawing pad.
We used Conte crayon today, and it doesn't smudge as easily
as charcoal, so no need to spray the drawings with fixative
this second. "It's noon. How are you still drunk?"

Dahlia leans close, giggling. "Because, silly, we were up
till four in the morning. How are you sober? You had as
much as me, maybe more."

Because I forced myself to throw up around the time she passed out. Otherwise, I wouldn't have been able to get out of bed this morning.

"You're joining us for lunch today, right?" Dahlia shouts over her shoulder as she crosses the room to stow her supplies in her cubby hole.

"Of course." I follow her to the wall, where I too store my belongings in my assigned cubby. "I have to grab my phone."

She heads for the exit, knowing I'll catch up. She already has everything in her backpack and purse.

"Billie."

I stop.

Next to my drawing horse, where my phone waits for me, Felix stands with a conservative smile. "I was hoping we could have a quick word."

"Yeah." I join him and pocket my phone, then give him my full attention. "Is everything alright?"

He releases a tiny laugh. "I'm pretty sure I'm the one who's supposed to ask that question, Billie. You're a good student: punctual, observant, attentive, on point during critiques, always working to improve your skills even when you're second-guessing yourself—but that's when you're focused." He pauses, and something twists in my stomach. "And you haven't been very focused lately."

I shake my head. "I'm sorry. I know, I need to try harder. I will."

But Felix isn't done yet. "I know the social aspect of college is seductive, but don't forsake your degree for a few nights of drinking."

"I—I'm not."

"I'll see you on Monday. Perhaps you and Dahlia Finnick will be less disruptive."

Dahlia is waiting outside the door, a scowl contorting her normally genial face. "What the hell took so long?"

I pass without stopping, and she rushes to catch me. "Felix needed to talk about something." My feet don't want to do anything but leave the Kelley Center right now. They'd carry me all the way back to my apartment if I let them.

"Whoa, slow down." She yanks my arm, and I stumble to a stop, facing her. "What was that?"

I tug at my high ponytail. "He thinks we're disruptive and asked if we could focus more."

She rolls her eyes. "Ridiculous. If we were that much of a problem, he'd talk to us both. Why in the world would he single you out? How utterly—"

I stagger as someone bumps into me.

Prudence, a solemn look on her face, she pauses to consider me when I look over. "Sorry."

A bolt of guilt surges through me.

"Prudence…"

But she turns away. "I'll see you later, Billie."

"Wait." I pull from Dahlia's firm grip and rush after her. "I'm sorry!" I match my pace with hers, but she doesn't slow down. "I didn't mean to bail on you or blow you off. It just kind of happened."

Prudence shakes her head. "At least own up to your actions. You don't even talk to me during class anymore."

"I'm sorry."

She comes to an abrupt stop and turns on me. "Did I do something wrong?"

I barely manage to stop before plowing into her. "No, of course not. You've never been anything but nice to me."

"Then why are you ignoring me? We don't have to be friends; you don't owe me anything. But please have the decency to tell me to my face instead of parading around with Dahlia Finnick to get your point across."

I take a breath. "Let me make it up to you."

She purses her lips. "How?"

"Jimmy and Xander are having people over tonight. Will you come? Dahlia's going to be there." I cast a glance over my shoulder, where Dahlia is watching us with crossed arms and a deep furrow in her brow. "You two could get to know each other a little better."

Prudence's grip on her backpack strap tightens. "Can I bring Cynthia?"

I almost laugh. There will never be any complaints about Cynthia Allen in Jimmy's apartment. "Yeah, I'll text you the address."

"That sounds like a decent idea." She even gives me a small smile.

◆

No one answers the door when I arrive. I knock two, three times before twisting the knob and walking in myself.

Jimmy, an anxious frown on his face, pushes a vacuum around the small living room. For once, the apartment looks spotless. To my left, the dining table has a few bottles of alcohol and mixers and fresh glasses, but otherwise, the kitchen is the picture of cleanliness—no dirty dishes, no appliances taking up the whole counter, no textbooks or papers on the table. The living room, to the right, is simply the couch and coffee table, along with a fold-up bowl chair, the only extra seating they have. The numerous cords spilling from the entertainment center cupboard are the only indication the apartment's lived in. Xander has too many gaming systems to fit, per usual.

Based on his sweaty brow and clothes, Jimmy's been cleaning for the past couple hours—probably since the moment he saw my text announcing Prudence and possibly Cynthia would join.

He glances up when I shut the door, and I hover at the entrance.

Jimmy moves to the kitchen as, down the hallway, the bathroom door opens. Xander emerges with a towel wrapped around his waist and heads for his bedroom. He's muscular but lean, and water droplets glisten on his tawny skin. He doesn't look in my direction, but I watch his every movement until he disappears into his bedroom.

I lean against the front door, my mouth suddenly dry. I wasn't expecting him to be naked. Or almost naked. Not an hour before people will arrive.

The vacuum shuts off.

My pulse pounds through my ears. A reminder I haven't been spending much time here. Seeing him like that—from far away too—shouldn't elicit such an intense physical reaction.

"You alright?"

I turn to Jimmy. It takes a moment to bury the fierce desire to follow Xander to his bedroom. "Uh, yeah, great. You done cleaning yet?"

Jimmy winds up the vacuum cord. "Pretty sure Xander's

going to murder me if I keep going. He started complaining over an hour ago."

I release a short laugh and push away from the door. "I would've too."

"Xander ordered a pizza since he got tired of waiting for you. It'll be here any minute."

I settle on the couch and pull out my phone. "Yeah, sorry. Dahlia wanted to pick out my outfit."

Jimmy shoves the vacuum into the hall closet, and I shed my hoody on the back of the couch.

A knock sounds from the front door.

I glance back at Jimmy, but he knocks down the broom while shutting the closet door and grunts in disapproval. Xander's still in his room. Which leaves me.

The delivery guy grins when I open the door and holds the pizza warmer aloft. "Large meat lover's pie and buffalo sauce for the pretty lady?"

I frown. I have no idea what Xander ordered or if he paid online. "Uh, maybe…"

He laughs. "You're not sure?"

"I didn't—"

"What's the total?"

I turn to find Xander coming up beside me, and I step to the side, knocking into the door while he exchanges a twenty-dollar bill for the pizza. His hair's wet and dripping— he's barely run a towel through it—and he's wearing nothing but a pair of blue boxers, plain for once. There's a small tuft of black chest hair at his collarbone.

As the delivery guy walks away, Xander turns to me. "If you stop staring, we can close the door, Dixon."

"Oh." I step back into the apartment.

Unfortunately, having my hair up means I have no way to hide the blush rising to my cheeks.

He shuts the door with a laugh and walks around me to deposit the box and sauce containers on the kitchen table. "Come on." He nods down the hallway. "I have to finish getting dressed."

I hesitate a moment before following. Jimmy's in his room with the door cracked as we pass.

"When did you get here?" Xander asks once we're inside.

I don't see his bedroom often—there isn't much reason for me to be here—but it's hardly changed since he moved in. His furniture is the same as mine and every other student's, and like me, he doesn't have much in the way of decorations. He never has more than he can keep in his car.

"Maybe ten minutes ago."

He pulls open a couple dresser drawers to grab a shirt and jeans. Disappointment weighs down my chest as he tugs them on. This is the opposite of what I want to see.

"Do you know how many people are coming?"

He tucks the blue boxers into his jeans. "More than you want to be here." When his pants are done up, he sits on the edge of the bed and pats the space beside him. "Don't be nervous."

I take the seat next to him, and he assesses me silently.

"That a new shirt?"

I look down at the stretchy violet top. "It's Dahlia's." It hangs off my shoulders and stretches so thin it's see-through. Which is why I'm wearing a black cami underneath. "She said I should look pretty."

He cocks an eyebrow. "You do."

I clear my throat. "Nah…"

90

"I wanted to tell you." He nudges me in the side. "I got promoted."

That certainly explains why his schedule's tighter than at the beginning of the semester.

"To what?"

"Bartending. I've been training for the past few weeks."

I frown. I didn't know he was training. How could I not know this? Also, is that legal? He's not twenty-one for another year. "Congratulations, then."

"It's a pay raise. Definitely a good thing. But it does mean working later since bar close isn't till two."

I pick at the denim pilling on my knees. "You've only had the job for a few months. Isn't that really soon?"

He shrugs. "I don't know, but Kylie—she's the front-of-house manager and Javier's wife—insisted, since I have quote-unquote a knack for public relations and learn quickly." Xander laughs. "Basically, the more you flirt with the patrons, the better they tip you."

My stomach falls.

"Don't worry, Dixon." He places a hand on my shoulder. "You have nothing to worry about. No need to be jealous." When I glance at him, he's smirking.

"Why would I be jealous?"

He doesn't say anything, but his eyes bore into mine.

I shift uncomfortably.

After a moment, he dons his leather jacket and grabs his cigarettes and lighter off the nightstand. I follow him to the small balcony off the living room, and we sit in the two plastic lawn chairs. The flame is bright under the dark sky as he lights up a smoke. The chilly breeze blows the smoke in the opposite direction.

"Lashing out at a girl you've barely met because she was flirting with me certainly makes you seem jealous." He takes a long drag and surveys the darkened parking lot below.

"What?"

"Regan. At lunch last week."

I frown. Not my best moment. "I'm sorry. That was really rude."

He shrugs. "I'm not the person you should apologize to."

But the thought of apologizing to her—even though I was out of line—makes my stomach twist. I don't want to talk to her, let alone apologize.

"I'm not sleeping with her." He's still watching the cars. None of them has moved. "If that's what you're worried about."

"I'm not worried about anything."

"Anxious, then. Does the specific word matter?"

I pull my legs onto the chair and rest my chin on my knees. "Well, why aren't you?" When he scoffs, I elaborate. "It's not like you weren't checking her out."

He takes another drag. "Is that a serious question? Or are you playing devil's advocate?"

I'm not sure how to answer. Mostly because I don't know the answer.

"You know—you have to know—how I feel about you. I don't exactly hide it."

My breath catches. I grip tighter around my legs.

Xander leans forward in his chair, resting his elbow on his knee. "It's not some big joke, and me looking at another girl's tits when she sticks them in my face doesn't change that. I'm not going to sleep with Regan."

He takes one final drag, then snubs the filter in the empty

ashtray and heads inside. The sliding glass door remains open behind him.

I linger for a minute in the cold November air.

Despite my need to keep my feelings in check, there's a weightlessness in my chest that I don't know what to make of, and when I return to the apartment, now spotless, everything looks a little different.

Inside, Jimmy has his hand in the pizza box, but Xander is fiddling with his big gaming laptop on the nearest end table. He points toward the kitchen as I shut the door. "Eat." His jacket has been abandoned on the back of the couch near my own hoody.

Music bursts to life from the speakers, and he follows me into the kitchen.

"Do we have to listen to this?" I search inside the box for the smallest slice and take a bite.

"Yes." He pulls two pieces onto a paper plate. "This is the Eagles. You cannot complain about the Eagles."

I chuckle, and sitting at the table now, Jimmy snorts.

"One of these days, I'm going to have to educate you on music." Xander sends me a quick smile. "There are some songs where you need to crank the volume—this is one of them."

I nudge his arm. "I'll take your word for it."

Ten

DAVID IS THE FIRST GUEST TO ARRIVE. I HAVE MY SECOND drink, a whiskey and ginger ale Xander hesitantly put together.

"Hey, guys. Hey, Billie." He drops a couple plastic sacks on the table by the remaining pizza. "I've got a bottle of vodka and some mixers."

I move to the couch as David unloads everything. Why is vodka every college student's go-to alcohol? They chat as they organize, but I'm impatient for the night to begin—so it can end just as quickly.

By the time Jimmy gets himself a drink—something fruity and sweet from the vermilion color—my glass is sitting on the coffee table, empty. He drops in the seat beside me. "You ready for everyone to get here?" He's changed his clothes since he finished cleaning.

I'm not sure I'm allowed to say how little I care about this party, but he sends me his sweet smile, and I have to return it. "Yeah, this is going to be fun."

His face breaks into a grin. "I'm glad you're here. I'm sorry I ignored you earlier. I just, you know, wanted this place to be nice."

I resist rolling my eyes. "You always obsessively clean when you think there's a chance a girl will talk to you." I fan myself, hot from the whiskey. Dahlia insisted on the violet top because it accentuates my breasts, but two layers is one too many.

Jimmy purses his lips. "You and Xander may be *laissez-faire* about these things, but I'm not good at playing host. It's doesn't always have to do with girls."

I let out a short laugh. "No, you cleaned the whole house because Cynthia is coming." This time, I do roll my eyes. "Might be here."

A deep frown spreads across his face. "Is it so bad for me to want to impress her? What's wrong with that?"

Unable to refrain, I sit up and strip down to the black cami. Dahlia will live. "Please tell me you realize how obsessed you are." I look up, but he turns away. "You've liked her for over a year. You even asked her out. At some point, you have to accept that she's not interested."

"I know that." He focuses on his red drink, his hands clasped around the cup. "But my feelings for her don't go away because she doesn't reciprocate. It's called 'unrequited love' for a reason."

I snort—loudly—and rise from the couch to head to the kitchen. I need a refill. "You're an idiot if you think your feelings for her are love," I shout over my shoulder.

Xander and David are chatting and pouring drinks, and they smile when I join them around the four-person table.

Jimmy follows a few seconds behind me. "Yeah, well, what the hell do you know about love?"

Xander and David fall silent.

"You haven't had the best role models when it comes to

95

healthy relationships. Your parents did everything in their power to avoid being in the same room, and your only relationship was with a senior who thought it'd be fun to convince a prudish freshman to take off her glasses, let down her hair, and flash her tits—and you were too stupid to see he was playing you."

I reach across Xander to grab the whiskey and pour a liberal portion into my cup. "You may have grown up with the perfect loving parents—" I enunciate every word carefully "—but you obsess over any random girl the second she looks at you."

"Cynthia Allen isn't a random girl."

I groan and let the bottle of whiskey slam on the tabletop. "Yes, she is." That was a predictable response from him. Too fucking predictable. "She's a random pretty girl, and you like her because she smiled at you when you met. You barely fucking know her. You only like her because you lived across the hall from her for nine months."

I release the handle and take a long drink—only to realize it's straight whiskey. I swallow it down and reach for the ginger ale to fill the rest of the glass.

"What do you think will happen when she gets here? What sort of magical event do you think will persuade her to date you? Because, seriously, she had nine months and wasn't interested. If she's not interested in nine fucking months, move on."

When I look up again, his jaw is tense. "I'm done talking to you about this." Without another word, he turns away from the table and crosses the living room to the balcony on the other side.

Lips pursed, I twist the cap back on the two-liter of

ginger ale, and on my right, Xander pulls the bottle of whiskey closer. "Fine," I mutter to myself—he's out of range. "I'm done talking to you."

The sliding door slams.

I heave a sigh and move to pick up my drink again, but Xander lays his hand atop the glass. "You need to slow down," he says in a quiet voice.

My eyes find his, then David's.

And I glare. "If you're going to subject me to this ridiculous intimate get-together, if I'm expected to socialize with these people and pretend to have fun, then I get to be drunk." I push him away and carry my drink to the living room, where Xander's music has transitioned to AC/DC.

On the balcony, Jimmy's sitting in the dark, his frou-frou drink balanced on the railing, untouched.

My drink doesn't leave my hand till it's empty again.

A couple other guests arrive, but I don't recognize them. Guys Xander knows. From his business classes, maybe work. I don't know or care.

I rise, hand on the couch top to steady myself as I walk.

Inside the bathroom, I pee and wash my hands, then pause a moment to stare at my reflection. The harder I focus, the more it moves. Was that my third or fourth drink? I haven't kept track.

I lean closer to study my distorted reflection.

Someone pounds on the door.

I jump.

I grip the sides of the sink, heart racing. "Fuck."

When I tear open the door, Brent stands there with a stupid grin on his face. "We've been here for like five minutes." His loud voice makes me cringe. "You doing the three knuckle shuffle in here?"

I cock my head to the side but push past him into the hallway.

Dahlia and Darius are hovering at the transition between the living room and kitchen, and when Dahlia turns, her face breaks into a grin. We meet halfway.

She wraps her arms around me in a tight hug. "Oh my gosh, there you are! Xander said you'd been in there a while. You getting drunk without me?"

I hold on to her when she tilts back. "Only a little bit." I search the living room, landing on the empty cup on the coffee table. "Can you bring me the whiskey?"

Dahlia glances in the kitchen, frowning at the request. "Why can't you get it?"

Because I get the distinct feeling Xander is guarding it.

"It's too crowded."

She shrugs and grabs the bottle while I retrieve my cup from the living room. Xander barely glances at her when she withdraws it from his reach. She fills my cup more than halfway, then her own. "What're you mixing it with? Lemonade?"

"Ginger ale. Cheaper."

She returns the whiskey, grabs the soda, and tops off our glasses. After she returns the ginger ale, we cheers.

Dahlia presses a hand to my bare shoulder and snaps the cami strap. "You took off my shirt."

"It was hot."

"That's why I dressed you in it." She flashes me a smug grin. "You pull off braless well."

I fan my face. The alcohol is definitely getting to me.

"Is she here yet?"

A knock sounds on the door.

She must be talking about Regan. Maybe that's her.

But when Jimmy answers the door, it's Prudence with a scowling Cynthia behind her.

"No, not yet."

In fact, Regan is the only attendee not here yet, unless the guys invited someone else.

Prudence gives Jimmy a one-armed hug before approaching me. Cynthia trails behind her. "Hey!" She pulls me into a hug. "You look cute. Showing a little skin."

I glance down at my chest and shrug. "I guess."

Behind her, Cynthia gives me a short wave, and I try to smile in return.

Dahlia smiles from behind her drink. "Hi, Prue."

Prudence sends her a short smile, then turns back to me. "We're gonna say hi to Xander and get a couple drinks. Catch up with you in a few."

In the distance, Jimmy is standing near the door, staring wistfully as Cynthia follows Prudence into the kitchen and quietly accepts a cup. He finishes his drink—his first—and joins them.

"Oh God, no."

"What?" Dahlia twists around, brow furrowed.

I nod toward Jimmy. "He's going to do something stupid, isn't he?"

And sure enough, he stands next to her and strikes up a conversation with a nervous smile—but that's nothing compared to the discomfort splayed across Cynthia Allen's face. Her responses are short, one or two words, but he is undeterred.

Dahlia watches beside me, sipping at her drink. "Is she

the girl he likes?" She wrinkles her nose. "She's so uptight."

I scoff. "No, she's perfect." I turn toward the living room. "Let's sit."

When everyone joins us in the living room, drinks in their hands, Xander's laptop is blasting Boston. Dahlia and I are squished together, legs entangled, on one corner of the couch, and Brent and Darius sit on the floor nearby. Jimmy takes a seat beside Cynthia, who squeezes closer to Prudence.

Regan still isn't here, but Xander is chatting with the only other women available—he's on Prudence's other side.

Dahlia leans close. "Is she going to show up?" Her lips brush my ear.

"I can't imagine she wouldn't show. She was beyond excited when he invited her."

After clearing his throat to draw everyone's attention, Xander retrieves a deck of cards from the end table and holds it aloft. "Game, anyone?"

But David raises an ebony arm, finger pointed. "I've got a better idea. How about 'I Never'?"

I groan and lean my head against the couch. "Can we not? We're not twelve. Could this get any more cliché?"

"No, I think that's a great idea." Jimmy has a determined look in his eyes. "It's a perfect way to get to know people."

Or show how well you already know someone.

"Okay, fine," I say. "Let's do this."

A knock sounds on the door, and being closer than Jimmy or Xander, I open it.

And there she is.

Fashionably late. Dressed in a short black dress that barely covers her big ass and shows off her ghostly white legs. Yet again, she has an ample amount of cleavage displayed for the world to see.

Regan hovers in the doorway.

I'm blocking her path.

Finally, I step aside and allow her entry, and she sends me an anxious smile as she enters the apartment. I shut the door behind her and take my seat on the couch without so much as a hello. Dahlia scoots close to me the moment I return.

I take another drink. "The game?"

"Come on in, Regan." Xander motions her into the living room. "You're welcome to anything on the kitchen table if you want a drink or something."

She grabs a beer and sits on the floor near David, grimacing as she crosses her legs and adjusts her skirt. "What're we playing?"

Brent takes a long swig of his beer. "'Never Have I Ever.'"

"David gets to go first." Xander returns the deck of cards to the end table. "Since it was his idea."

David leans back on his hands with a chuckle. "Alright, let's start simple. I've never been arrested."

I glance around the room but pause when Xander is the only one to take a drink. The game moves on when no one—not even Jimmy—makes an inquiry, and I'm left wondering.

"You need more to drink?" Dahlia whispers. I finish my drink with the next question and hand her the glass, and she heads to the kitchen to refill our cups. "I'm still listening, I promise!"

When she returns, we're a third of the way through the room.

Jimmy levels me with a glare when it's his turn. "I've

never had sex."

He's had enough to drink to be unabashed about this fact. He's normally embarrassed, and I figured that would increase tenfold with Cynthia present.

I roll my eyes when I take my own drink.

No one else is playing the game as ambitiously as he is. No one else is as into it.

In fact, Cynthia has no intention of playing. She says, "Oh, no, thanks," when everyone waits for her to take her first turn, and after a few short complaints from Brent, we move on.

Even Xander, who would normally be trying to get Jimmy, in particular, drunk, doesn't seem that interested in playing. "I've never been kicked out of class," is his first confession. Oddly tame.

When it's my turn, Jimmy hasn't touched his drink, and I scowl at him. "I've never smoked pot."

A number of other people in the room take a drink, but he glares as he takes his first sip since the start of the game. "That was one time, dammit."

I release a victorious laugh.

"Really?" Dahlia nudges me in the side. "We can fix this."

I've never been interested, but I'm not averse to the idea. I shrug, and she smiles before taking her turn.

By the third round, Xander's friends from his business classes have bowed out, and I need another cocktail.

Dahlia and I stumble to the kitchen table, and she, being the more stable one, pours us each a big drink. "So?"

"So what?" I try to whisper, but I don't know if I'm successful.

"The slutty one that's got her eyes on your man."

I snort into my cup, then spend the next minute coughing to clear my windpipe. "Don't say that." My glass clinks against the oak table as I set it down. "He's not mine."

We both look in Xander's direction, but he's sitting in the far corner with a scowl on his face.

"He's not even enjoying himself." Dahlia scoffs. "What's the point of having a party if you're going to be a grouch the whole time?"

"I don't know."

She turns her full attention to me. "So the bitch was late. She's not sitting anywhere near him, and it's totally her fault. It's perfect."

I shrug and take another drink.

"When are you going to make your move?"

My eyes gravitate toward Xander again. Despite his scowl and the fact that he's moving in and out of focus, he's still attractive—his black hair is slicked to the side and slightly spiked, and he's wearing his favorite shirt and a pair of tight jeans.

"I don't have any moves." But I can't take look away.

Dahlia giggles into her cup. "Oh, come on, Billie. Take him by the collar, drag him to his bedroom, and rock his world. Preferably loud enough she can hear."

I take a sip. "I'm not sure how much world-rocking I could manage." I could barely stay up when we walked to the kitchen. How in the world could I do something in bed without falling off?

"Don't say that." Dahlia uncaps the whiskey again and tops me off. "I don't care how much experience you have, confidence will save your ass. And trust me, he'd love a handful of that ass. No guy is going to slow-dance with a girl for six consecutive songs if he doesn't want to screw her. He didn't dance a single song with Regan."

We both look at her. Regan is curled up on the floor next to David, a big smile on her face as everyone takes their turns. But her smile is for Xander. She won't stop beaming at him.

Dahlia laughs. "God, she's so fucking desperate."

My snicker expands into full-blown laughter. Mostly because it's true. She's practically begging for his attention.

Next to the couch, Brent sends us a stern glare over his shoulder, but he can't hold back his smile. He motions for us to come back.

To reach my seat, I clutch the back of the couch to keep from falling. On the other side of the room, Jimmy is flushed from the alcohol, a determined look on his face. It's his turn again.

"I've never had sex with anyone in this room."

I narrow my eyes. "How can that count? You already said you're a virgin."

But half the group takes a drink, and I'm not allowed to get out of this.

Jimmy points a finger at me. "Take your drink, Billie."

"Fine." I swallow down more of the whiskey—the ginger ale is gone now—and crawl onto the couch with Dahlia.

My head is too fuzzy to pay attention as we move around the room. I have no idea whether I should be drinking or not, but I sip at my glass. Dahlia pokes me in the side when it's my turn.

I send a quick glance toward Prudence and Cynthia, who looks uninterested in this entire affair, then turn back to Jimmy. "I've never masturbated to a photo of someone in this room."

If his face weren't already beet red from the alcohol, it would be now. He glares as he takes his drink. "You know," he says after swallowing, "if we opened that up to include all kinds of images, you flicking your bean to some of your more detailed drawings would definitely count."

Heat rises to my cheeks. "I do not!"

"There's no way you'll get me to believe that."

The insinuation is obvious, and I can't look at Xander. All it would take is one look, and he would see. He would know how much I reminisce about our night together. Especially when I'm alone at night in my bedroom. He probably already knows. Sometimes, often, he understands better than I do.

Because I have no idea what I'm doing.

I still know nothing about him. He's been arrested? How the hell did that happen? And has he seriously not been sleeping with every woman he can this year? Is that possible?

I run a hand through my hair, forgetting that it's up in a tight bun, and the auburn strands strain against my scalp.

"Billie, you okay?"

I glance at Dahlia.

She too is drunk—she has a stupid grin on her face, even while she's concerned. "You sure? You're having trouble focusing."

My eyes flit around the room, seeking out the other speaker. It's David. He's talking, and I take a sip of my drink even though I don't know what he says. Then, it's Jimmy again.

How did we go around so fast?

Jimmy's voice is loud, but I strain to comprehend his words. He won't stop moving. "I've never slept with Xander."

I narrow my eyes—half to glare and half to focus my vision. "Liar."

He doesn't say anything.

"You spent three weeks sharing a bed with him last Christmas. You've definitely slept with him." I shake my head, then close my eyes. My head is spinning.

"Do I need to be more specific, Billie?"

I blink.

He's still staring, his face resolute. "Because I have no problem saying I've never had sex with Xander."

"You ass!" I try to rise from my seat, but Dahlia holds me to her side.

"Take a drink and deal with it!"

I raise my glass to my mouth and take my drink.

To the left, in my blurry peripheral vision, Prudence leans forward. "Oh my God, Billie, when did that happen? How did I not know about this? Was it before or after he dated your roommate?" She pauses. "Does she know?"

Xander, sitting next to her, remains silent despite the barrage of questions, but finally, he stands. "Please don't say that like Val and I were actually in a relationship."

He squeezes between the couch and the coffee table on his way out of the living room, and I lean back as he passes. I don't know how to answer Prue's questions. Beside me, Dahlia and Brent are also talking, but I can't follow what, and I lean forward again, thirsty.

My drink is gone.

Not empty. Missing.

I sit up, searching.

The glass, still half full, sits on the kitchen table, and a quiet Xander fills a pint-sized plastic cup with ice water.

"Hey, bring that back."

But he doesn't respond, simply finishes filling the glass with water and walks back to me, pausing behind the couch. "You've had too much to drink." He forces the cup into my hand.

I glare at it. "I get to decide when I've had too much."

"No, you don't." He's silent for a moment, waiting for me to drink, but I don't move. "You may lose all your math skills when you're drunk, but I can still count. That was number six, and it was straight 80-proof whiskey. You've had too much."

The water quivers under my breath, and despite the music, the room is surreally quiet.

"I'm an adult. I don't need you to take care of me."

"Then act like one."

My grip tightens around the cup, and it compresses under the pressure. "I hate you." Angry tears prick the corners of my eyes, but I blink them away.

"I don't care." Of course, Xander never backs down. "Drink the fucking water."

How in the world is he sober?

He clears his throat, and I almost look up, but for the first time, he's not talking to me when he speaks. "Sorry, everybody, I need you to leave." But the second I lean forward, he grabs my shoulder. "You're not going anywhere, Dixon."

A couple people say goodbye. I don't know who. The voices all blur together.

For once, Xander's skin against my bare shoulder is cool to the touch. That must be the alcohol. Apparently, it takes being trashed to be as hot-skinned as he is.

When the door finally closes, he releases me and steps around the couch, talking to Jimmy. I take a small sip of the water and focus on the sound of his voice.

"What the hell are you doing encouraging her? She does not need that from you. Talk about fucking irresponsible— and completely hypocritical when you got pissed at me for giving her a bottle of fucking wine when I didn't know it was a bad idea. What the hell were you thinking?"

But Jimmy's got to be as drunk as I am. Especially with his low tolerance.

I take a long drink of the water and lean against the side of the couch. It's particularly soft. Or maybe I'm more aware of the texture.

"Go to bed."

To Jimmy again. Who doesn't say a word. If he can form coherent sentences.

"Get some water first."

I close my eyes. Clutch the plastic cup between my hands. Focus on my breathing. Everything tastes like whiskey. I swish a little water around my mouth, trying to rinse out the flavor. It doesn't work.

The music shuts off. The room is silent aside from shuffling feet, the laptop closing.

I raise the cup to my mouth again and take another drink. A few drops spill on my black camisole.

Then, Xander's beside me again. "Dixon, do you need to throw up before I put you to bed?" His voice is softer than before.

I shake my head. "I can't sleep," I mumble into the cup.

"Do you want to change? You don't have to sleep in

jeans, and you're still wearing your shoes." His hands find my feet and pry off the Converse. I stretch my toes at the new freedom.

I squint at him. He's sitting next to me in a bright red t-shirt with a few water spots and Charmander's grinning face. His olive skin is smooth and soft. I am lost in the depth of his eyes.

"Are you going to undress me?" My voice is small, but the desire seeps through my words.

"That would be inappropriate."

I want to touch that skin. Run my fingers through his thick black hair. Kiss him. I want to kiss him.

"Only if I don't want you to." I take another drink. "And I want you to."

The smile on his face is a sad kind of smile.

"Are you really not going to sleep with her? With Regan? Have you slept with anyone this semester?"

He doesn't answer the questions. Simply says, "Dixon, you need to go to bed."

"Then take me to bed."

He raises an eyebrow, his mouth a thin line. "You sleep in my bed. I'll take the couch."

I glare down at the cup and shift to set it on the coffee table. He has to help me. "That's not what I meant." I press a hand to his shoulder, leaning close, and he takes in the full view of my cleavage. "Take me to bed, Xander."

But he shakes his head. "You have no idea what you're asking me to do. When you're sober, I'd be more than happy to oblige. But you're drunk right now, and you need to sleep."

I push closer, pressing my body against his, straddling

him. His hands grip my waist. "I know exactly what I'm asking of you. Being drunk doesn't mean I want you more than normal."

"Maybe not, but it means you're more vocal about your desires."

I cling to him, but he pushes me away. I manage to place a few strategic kisses at the base of his neck before he's out of reach. "I can be plenty vocal if you want."

He doesn't respond to that. He continues as if I haven't said it. "Being drunk does make your inhibitions dramatically lower. You would never come on to me sober."

"You don't know that."

"Yes, I do. Five minutes ago, you hated me, and now you want sex. You're too drunk to talk about this. I'm putting you to bed."

He stands, his arms supporting my body. One hand cups my ass, the other braces my back, and I cling to him. He stands as if I weigh nothing. As if I'm a child.

The bedroom is dark, and he doesn't bother with the light. He lays me on the bed, but I don't want him to go. That doesn't stop him from prying himself from my grip and removing my glasses.

"Do you want your hair down?" His lips are entrancing.

"I want you."

And it's true. There's an ache inside me that throbs and swells at the thought of tearing off his clothes. Unfortunately, I don't have the coordination for that right now. He'd already be naked. And hard. And fucking me.

"Remind yourself of that in the morning, yeah?" His mouth curves into a small smile, rueful, unconvinced, and I move closer, but he retreats before I can press my lips to his. "I'll leave your hair up."

Without another word, he slips from my grasp, and I lay against the pillow, defeated.

He disappears. Quickly returns with the cup of water and sets it on the nightstand. But I turn away from him, curl into the fetal position, and wrap my hands in the twisted top sheet.

Xander squeezes my bare shoulder and places a kiss on my temple. "Go to sleep, Dixon. I'll see you in the morning."

When the door closes behind him, I unzip my jeans and press my fingers beneath my underwear. There's no other way I'll go to sleep tonight.

Eleven

Everything smells like Xander. And vomit. But mostly Xander.

My entire body aches. My head pounds. The pain ebbs and flows with the sound of shuffling in the room.

I push up on my elbows and twist to look around. My glasses sit on the nightstand, and I pull them on to see.

In the middle of the dark room, Xander is pulling on a new shirt. He's dressed in tight black pants and socks, and he pauses midway through pulling on his shirt to look at me. "What're you doing awake, Dixon?" Then, his abs disappear under the black fabric.

He sits down next to me, and I struggle to sit up. I don't want to jostle my head.

"I didn't mean to wake you," he whispers.

"What time is it?"

"Just after six." He grabs the cup from the nightstand and hands it to me. "You're dehydrated. You threw up three times."

The cold liquid pours down my dry, aching throat, and I lean against him for support. "Did I fuck up the party?" I have no memory of waking up during the night to vomit.

He shrugs his other shoulder. "Could've been worse."

Why does he always say that when I get trashed and make a fool of myself?

Xander wraps his arm around me and holds me close. "You need to take better care of yourself, Dixon." His lips press to the top of my head, and I relax in his embrace. He smells sharp and musky, and I am heady from the scent.

Or from the hangover.

The cool sheets slide against my bare legs. When did I take my pants off? Fairly certain I had those on when I went to sleep.

"Where are you going?"

His fingers rub a pattern on my arm. "What?"

"You're dressed for something. Where are you going?"

He pushes a few strands of curly hair behind my ear. "I'm going for a run."

My brow furrows. "But it's cold outside."

"Yeah."

"You hate the cold."

He lets out a noncommittal grunt. "It doesn't feel so bad when you're exercising. Besides, I do this every morning."

I pull back. "Since when?"

Xander's face twists into the first real smile since I started drinking last night. "A few months. I had to replace soccer with something, you know."

"I guess." Another drink of water, and I finish the cup. "I never thought about it."

"Of course not." He takes the cup. "You want more?"

I nod. "I have to pee."

He walks me to the bathroom. It's a lot brighter in the hallway without his blackout curtains, but the bathroom is

113

conveniently dark. The campus-supplied lights are shitty incandescents. They don't hurt very much.

I shut and lock the door while he goes to the kitchen, and when I'm done, he's waiting for me on the other side with a full cup.

I rest against the door frame and drink more. "How long will you be gone?"

He shrugs. "Half an hour. Nothing drastic." He presses a hand to my bare shoulder. He's hot against my skin. "Don't do anything stupid while I'm gone."

"I'm pretty sure I'm going to curl into a ball and die." I lean into his touch.

His lips press to my forehead. "I need you to be alive and well when I get back. I won't stand for anything else."

"I'm not sure I'll be able to manage that."

"Take it as an order, Lieutenant." He leads me to his bedroom, our fingers intertwined. "Let's tuck you in."

I set the cup on the nightstand and lie on the bed so he can pull the sheets over my half-naked body. I want more than anything for him to crawl in here with me and keep me warm.

"You need to sleep more. I'll check on you when I get back." His gaze hovers on me, but he pulls back.

When the door closes behind him, I bury my face in his pillow. More than any other part of the room, this smells like him.

The kitchen is a mess when I get up hours later, but Xander fills the sink with scalding water. Bottles of alcohol are spread across the kitchen table, but all the mixers are missing, probably in the fridge. The trash bin is full, and there are dirty cups and glasses on the counter next to him. Otherwise, the apartment is rather clean. The party didn't last long.

I lean against the entryway as he turns off the faucet. His shoes and shirt have been abandoned near the door, but he's still wearing his black exercise pants. "You're back."

It's a nice view.

He glances over his shoulder before returning to his work.

"Can I help with anything?" He shakes his head, but I step into the kitchen. "Are you sure? I mean, I feel a lot better."

"I'm glad you're feeling better," but his tone isn't very convincing. "You should keep resting, though."

"I'm fine."

"Are you?" He drops a couple glasses in the sink and squirts in a generous amount of soap. "Are you really?"

"I—"

Xander twists around, jaw clenched. "Do you seriously have the nerve to tell me you're fine after that ridiculous display last night? Is that why we never see you? Because you're too busy drinking with Dahlia?" He jabs a wet finger toward the alcohol handles on the table. "That's not fucking fine."

I back up against the counter.

He scrubs furiously at a cup, long past the point when it's clean. "You're irresponsible. And selfish. And you're going to get yourself killed. I was up most of the night so you didn't drown in your own fucking vomit. Do you think Dahlia Finnick or Brent Moulder would do that?"

Why is he mad all over again? Did something happen?

He glances at me again. "Put some fucking clothes on."

115

I swallow down the bile in my throat and stalk from the room.

My jeans are on the floor of his bedroom. I pull them on and check the pockets for my keys, phone, and wallet. My shoes, Dahlia's shirt, and my hoody should be in the living room. I return there to put them on.

Xander stops and comes to see about the noise. "What are you doing?"

"Leaving." I don't look up. "You obviously don't want me here. We can talk when you've calmed down."

He wipes his hands on a towel and comes closer. "No, the point is, I do want you here. That's the entire fucking issue. I want you alive. But you're not taking care of yourself."

"I do just fine, thanks."

"Obviously, you don't. You barely eat. You're never here anymore. How much do you drink in a given week? A drink every night? Two? To help you sleep? You don't get much of that. Are you even passing your classes?"

I grit my teeth and push down the memory of my awkward after-class conversation with Felix yesterday. "My grades are fine. My drinking habits are fine. I'm fucking fine."

"If you were fine, last night wouldn't have happened. You wouldn't have had half a bottle of whiskey and spent the whole night fighting with Jim. You wouldn't have spent ten minutes in the kitchen with Dahlia making fun of a girl who's too shy and too nice to defend herself. You two aren't as discreet as you think you are."

My cheeks flush with shame, but I cannot admit he's right. "You're overreacting. Why the hell are you mad all of a sudden?"

He slams the towel down on the counter. "The second you woke up this morning, you're back to pretending everything's okay, despite the fact that your little alcohol stint last night was, what, to help with nerves? And it could've fucking killed you. Do you have any idea how terrified I was last night? I had to take care of you because you can't fucking take care of yourself."

Xander has never been this angry before.

"Why can't you talk about your problems? And why the hell can you only have a conversation about your feelings for me when you're wasted?"

I step closer to the door. "You don't know what you're talking about." My voice has lost its edge.

"Enlighten me."

"I don't...I don't have feelings for you."

He releases a hollow bark of laughter. "It's hard to be enlightened when you're blatantly lying to me." He gives me a second to respond, but only just. "I haven't slept with Regan. I have no intention of doing so. In fact, I've barely fucked anyone in the past six months, and you'd know that if you paid any attention. But instead, you're off in your tiny little corner of the world being jealous for no fucking reason."

I grip the doorknob. "I'm not jealous. I have no reason to be. That would require me to have feelings for you. Which I don't." I twist the knob, but it doesn't turn, and I have to fiddle with the lock to open it. "We're friends. We're supposed to be friends."

"Then maybe you should act like one," he yells after me, but I'm already out the door.

"So should you."

117

The door slams before he can say anything else, and I bolt down the stairs. My Converse aren't tied, and I stumble as I run, but I refuse to stop.

Twelve

"Come on. Time to wake up."

I pull the sheets tighter around my head. Despite all the water, the hangover is unavoidable. The sheets are yanked away, and I curl up, back to the room, and cover my face with my arms.

"Seriously, Billie."

I peek through the crevice between my arms, but all that's visible is my off-white bedroom wall.

The bed creaks. Gravity pulls me toward the opposite side as Dahlia sits on the edge of my mattress. "I've got something to make you feel better."

Finally, I pull my arms away and twist to look at her.

The room is intensely bright. She turned the light on, and she sits beside me with the biggest grin and something in her hands. "You are absolutely crazy, and I love it."

I tug at the satin fabric covering one ear—I put my hair up in a wrap before heading back to bed—and grab my glasses from the nightstand.

She's clear now. Her honey-brown hair is freshly washed, and half of it's pulled into simple braids tied in the back. And what's she holding? A tall, narrow glass filled with a

119

thick, red-orange liquid and several ice cubes. She brandishes the glass toward me, offering, and I accept it with a hesitant hand.

"Bloody mary," she says as I take a sip.

And it certainly is that. Spicy and tomatoey, a few seeds—and a healthy dose of vodka. I choke it down, thankful it's not followed by the need to throw up.

"Counter-irritant in the morning. I've had one, but you—you need this more than anyone."

For a moment, I stare at the glass. My second drink is decidedly bigger. "Last night was…"

She grins. "It was. That was a lot of fun—until, you know, Xander decided to go all passive aggressive and guilt-trip you. What the hell was that about?"

Even after a couple more hours of sleep, the fight is fresh on my mind, but all I can say is, "I don't know."

"He's so melodramatic. Like, are we not supposed to drink at parties? Wasn't that the point?" She releases a curt laugh. "Regan was pretty unhappy with how the night ended, though, so at least there's that."

I swallow another gulp. "I don't care about Regan."

Dahlia snorts. "That's hardly believable, Billie. I mean, I wouldn't consider screwing him after that complete over-reaction, but let's not pretend you don't have a huge crush on him just because you're insecure."

I finish the drink and slide the glass onto the nightstand. I want to deny it, but what's the point? Dahlia sees right through me, and lying about this would be a complete insult to the friendship we've built.

"Okay, no pretending." I turn to her expectant face. "It's possible I have feelings for him, but if I do, it's a crush, that's all. What do I have to offer anyway? Certainly nothing compared to nice girls like Regan Foster. I'm…not nice."

"Nice is overrated."

I shake my head. "Even if that's true, she's beautiful. Tall and so curvy. Did you see her tits?"

Dahlia snorts. "I'm pretty sure the world saw her tits. And she may be tall and curvy—and nice—but looks aren't everything." She takes a deep breath, and for once, her voice is calm and reserved. "I was diagnosed with anorexia when I was thirteen. Comparing yourself to girls like Regan Foster isn't going to get you anywhere."

I examine her thin frame. She's as tall as her brother, but she must be as skinny as I am. "I'm sorry."

She shakes her head. "Nothing to be sorry about. Now, my mother, on the other hand…"

I frown.

"She refused to put me in therapy, even after the diagnosis, and outright told me she'd rather I starve myself so she didn't waste money on food for me."

"Wow."

But Dahlia doesn't miss a beat, doesn't pause, doesn't even act sad. "What happened after Xander kicked everyone out?"

I struggle to focus on the new conversation topic. "Nothing really. He sent me to bed, that's all."

She scoffs. "'Sent' you? Really?" She grabs my glass off the nightstand and rises from the bed. "Who does he think he is? You can't 'send' someone to bed like they're a kid." In a frustrated huff, she stalks from the room, leaving the door open.

Xander apparently can.

When she returns, she carries two more glasses of the stuff, this time with a few green olives on umbrella toothpicks. She hands one to me and sits down again, lips pursed.

"He wasn't trying to be a dick." I sip the thick cocktail. This one is spicier. "He thinks he's looking out for me." Before she can say anything, I shift, sitting up all the way. "We had a big fight this morning. He says I drink too much."

She snorts. "He does realize there's a saying about pots and kettles, right?" She gulps down half her glass, and when she turns to me again, there's a bloody mary mustache above her top lip. "This is the guy who was trashed every time I met him last year."

It's true. Or so I imagine. I don't think they encountered each other outside of a party setting, and there wasn't a single time Xander attended a party without coming back to Lincoln Hall drunk off his ass. At the beginning of the school year, those were the times his jokes were the cruelest. By May, it was also when his words and his smile were the most affectionate.

"I'm sure he's aware of the hypocrisy."

Through the hallway, a knock echoes, and we pause. Then, Camila emerges from her room to answer the door.

"Whether he's aware or not," Dahlia says, relaxing enough to continue the conversation, "he's making a conscious decision to be an asshole. I know your crush won't disappear overnight, but if he's going to get that upset about a fun night of drinks with your best friend—" she flashes me her most charming smile "—then he's a complete waste of your time. You could do so much better."

My stomach bubbles with unease, but it's not from the

bloody mary. I'm not sure I could do better. Xander's already too good for me.

"Hey, Billie."

We turn to the open door, where Camila is paused on the threshold.

"Yeah?"

"Your friend's here." She nods behind her before heading back to her room, leaving a particularly pale and sick-looking Jimmy in her wake.

"Hi." He steps into the room awkwardly. "I didn't realize you'd be…with company." His eyes move to the drinks in our hands.

Dahlia smiles and motions him closer. "I won't bite. You're cute, but you're a little too innocent for my type."

The furrow in his brow deepens, but he walks farther inside and hovers by my dresser. "I was hoping we could talk about something a little personal."

He's asking for privacy, but he doesn't want to ask her to leave.

I'm not sure I want to hear what he has to say.

"Yeah, go ahead."

"Oh."

For a minute, he doesn't say anything.

While he tries to find the right words, Dahlia scrunches her nose and cheeks together and sticks her tongue out at me. I bury my face in the cocktail to hide the laughter.

"So," he says, drawing our attention again, "I overreacted a bit last night. I'm sorry for the part I played in that fight and for blurting out what I said about you and Xander in front of everyone—or what I've been told I said; I don't remember." He sighs. "But mostly, I'm sorry for what I said about Zane. That was totally out of line."

I stiffen at the words. "It's fine. It wasn't a big deal. Besides, I was pretty rude too."

"And badass," Dahlia murmurs.

"Honestly, Jimmy, I don't know why you're making a big deal out of it now. We were drunk. Totally forgivable." I take a long drink of the bloody mary.

His jaw slackens, and he glances between us. But he persists. "Look, I've come to terms with the fact that nothing's going to happen with Cynthia, and I know I have a tendency to…idealize women, but you're not an expert on relationships either."

I roll my eyes.

Beside me, Dahlia snickers. "That's why you have me." She leans closer, excited, and I turn my full attention to her—anything to avoid this awkward conversation. "You know, I'm kinda glad Xander's out of the picture."

I cock my head to the side. "What?"

"I meant it when I said you could do better, Billie." Then, she flashes me a bright smile and reaches over to smack my arm. "We could set you up with someone…"

The drink in my hands is now watered-down and mostly ice. "I'd prefer not to be set up." The umbrella was long ago abandoned on my nightstand.

Dahlia's face lights up. "Good. I'd rather keep you to myself."

"Xander."

We turn to Jimmy, who has an anxious frown on his face. He's looking at the floor, not me.

I return my attention to my glass. "What about Xander?"

"Why would you consider dating someone else when

you know you have feelings for him? And he has them for you too. That's stupid."

I scoff. "I don't know where everyone gets the idea that I have feelings for Xander."

"Because it's true." He pushes away from the dresser, belligerent. His shoulders are squared and tense, and his eyes narrow.

But before I can respond, Dahlia presses her hand over mine. "Everyone has room for improvement. And finding someone who doesn't throw a fit over a little alcohol would be an improvement."

"He wasn't throwing a fit." Jimmy turns to me, pleading now. "He was upset because he doesn't want you to get hurt."

Dahlia snorts. "Oh, please—"

"Can we stop talking about Xander?" I set my glass down on the nightstand. "Please."

She shrugs. "Of course."

On the other side of the room, Jimmy inches toward the exit. "I'm going to go. I'll talk to you later, Billie."

"Yeah, bye."

He shuts the door behind him, and while my stomach turns with nausea, Dahlia laughs as soon as the apartment door closes. "How ridiculous. It's his roommate—of course he defends—"

"Dahlia, when I said I didn't want to talk about Xander, I meant it."

"Fine, whatever." She eyes my empty glass. "Do you want another bloody mary?"

Thirteen

DAHLIA LINKS HER HAND WITH MINE AND TUGS TOWARD the door. "Lunch, right?"

"Absolutely."

Felix finishes his final round of the class and stops a few feet behind our drawing horses. "Have a good weekend, everybody. We'll meet back here on Tuesday for the final."

Dahlia takes her drawing pad to the cubbies.

The moment she's gone, Felix pauses beside my bench. "Billie, could we talk for a few minutes in my office? I want to discuss your schedule next semester since I'm your adviser now." His voice is quiet. He doesn't want to draw attention to this.

What's going on?

"Yeah, sure."

He's gone by the time Dahlia's back.

She grabs her purse and sits on the edge of her horse, watching while I grab my backpack.

"I've got something I need to do first. Can you wait for me downstairs?"

She purses her lips. "What do you need to do?"

"I want to ask Felix a question. Adviser stuff."

"I can go with you."

"It'll only take a couple minutes." I shrug. "And you know, he can't discuss my classes and stuff with someone else in the room."

She frowns but agrees, and when she leaves, everyone else is gone too.

Felix's office is a small narrow room with a glass-top desk, a couple chairs, and a skinny shelf beside the lone window. The white walls, illuminated by light from outside, brighten the room, and behind the desk, he sits at his Mac computer.

He looks over when I take the seat across from him. He's been waiting. "I'm glad you have time in your schedule. This is important, Billie."

I nod. "Do I need you to okay my classes next semester? I already signed up for all of them."

Felix shakes his head. "I was hoping you'd consider not overloading next semester."

"What do you mean? I did twenty-two credits both semesters last year without a problem."

He levels me with a stern gaze and studies me for a moment. "Billie, your grades last year were near perfection, even with seven classes a semester."

My stomach drops. "Am I failing?"

"No, but I have to admit, I'm concerned." He turns to his Mac and clicks around. When he spins the screen toward me, he has my grade for Drawing I pulled up. "I've talked to your other professors too. Your performance has dropped dramatically in the last month. If there's something going on in your life outside of classes, maybe cutting back your credit hours would help you manage."

On the computer, my grade has fallen from a 98 to an 82 in a little over three weeks.

I shake my head. "I don't want to drop anything. I have to take French so I can go on the study abroad trip over the summer."

"You also have to have the grades to qualify." He twists the screen back and glances over my progress. "If your performance continues in this fashion next semester, you will fail one or more of your classes. You need a 3.5 GPA to qualify for the Paris trip. To graduate with honors, you need a 3.75, and I shouldn't need to remind you that your merit scholarship requires you to have a cumulative GPA of 3.5 or higher at the end of each school year. At your current rate, you'll be lucky to have a 3.0 after next semester."

I'll be "lucky" to have a 3.0? I'm scared to ask what my other professors told him.

Felix offers me a small smile. "Billie, you're signed up for four studio classes next semester. You've taken a minimum of twenty credits each semester, and you are continually taking on an enormous workload."

"I can't drop anything. I'm still trying to catch up."

He shakes his head. "I know you're under a lot of pressure because you switched majors and you're taking core classes a year late. But you have plenty of time to catch up—time you won't have if you lose your Presidential Scholarship. My drawing class is elementary, which is why it's the first required studio class for art majors. Not all studio classes are this easy. Painting, Photography, and Sculpture all have intensive out-of-class requirements, and you're scheduled to take those in addition to the required Fundamentals class."

My hands clench around my backpack straps.

"It's a wonder you haven't worn yourself out entirely, especially when you factor in homework, social activities, a job. I don't imagine you have much time for sleep."

Not sleeping has been the main way I've managed such a rigorous schedule.

Felix offers me a sad smile. "Billie, I don't want you to lose your scholarship. I need you to drop at least one studio class next semester. Just this once, take less than twenty credits."

My stomach swells with nausea, but all I can do is nod.

◆

Dahlia settles into the seat next to me with her typical smile. "Okay, first day of finals week." Her voice bubbles with excitement, but I don't know what she finds so entertaining. I'm still shaken from my conversation with Felix at the end of last week. "What're you doing for your break?"

I poke at my food. Nothing looks appetizing. "I'm staying with my dad for the holidays. He lives here in town."

This will be the first Christmas we get to spend with each other since the divorce. The first Christmas together in four years, and he's thrilled. It's barely December, but the house is decked out in holiday decorations, except the tree. The Douglas fir is up, but he insisted on waiting for break. He wants to hang the ornaments together.

"Cool." Dahlia scoots her chair closer. "Not going to see your mom, then?"

Thankfully, no.

I don't know how well they're taking that. But after a summer with my mom and Rob's constant PDA, I have no desire to go back.

Besides, Jimmy's taking Xander home with him for the holidays again. He got three weeks' leave from work.

We haven't spoken since our argument.

"Definitely not."

Staying here means I have to continue attending my therapy, though, which I'm not particularly keen on.

"What are you guys doing?" I glance between her and Darius, due to the nature of their predicament.

Dahlia shrugs like it's no big deal. "I'm staying on campus. Dar's going home for a couple weeks, not the whole break."

I nod.

She nudges me again, her grin back in place. "We have to hang out since you'll be in town." Then, she glances at everyone else. "Brent, you're staying in town, right?"

He sends me a big grin. "Of course."

But Kai and Anna both report their departure over the break, and I look away, uninterested.

When I finish my water, Dahlia pokes me. "Come on, let's get more to drink."

She leads me toward the soda machine by the hand, weaving in and out of the circular tables.

As we pass, my eyes lock on a table not far from Prudence and Cynthia's normal location—a table where Regan is sitting with a few friends. When we pass, she returns to her conversation without a second glance. I feel sick.

At the soda machine, Dahlia pours herself more Sprite, and I wait till she's done. "You're being quiet." She steps out of the way with her bubbling soda.

I fill my cup with more ice. "Sorry. I guess I'm distracted." When I press the button, water pours into the cup.

"Billie, you can't still be upset about this." Dahlia releases an exasperated sigh, but when I turn to her, she's searching the crowded tables. I follow her gaze, already knowing what—who—she's looking at.

On the far right side of the cafeteria, Jimmy is eating lunch with David, and there's a plate in Xander's usual seat, though he isn't currently there. David sits with them more and more often. I, on the other hand, haven't joined them in the past ten days. I don't imagine Xander wants to see me.

Jimmy sends me a small smile, and I force one in return. We've talked occasionally, but everything has been guarded.

I turn to Dahlia, but ten feet behind her, Xander's in line to grab a quesadilla. The two people in front of him serve themselves and disperse, and he takes a couple slices with the tongs, then turns back toward the table.

He freezes.

This isn't the first time we've had a fight that lasts longer than a week, but it's the first time it's been unbearable. I already spend most of my time with Dahlia, but I didn't anticipate my separation from Xander to be this difficult. I didn't anticipate missing him this much.

Dahlia steps close, her arm brushing mine, and Xander retreats into the distance. I release a breath I didn't know I was holding.

"I say good riddance." At my elbow, Dahlia shrugs. "If he's going to be an asshole, why would you want anything to do with him?"

I frown.

How could I talk to her about this? How can I try to explain my feelings when she's so against him? Apparently, all it takes is one party, and all the good thoughts she had about him are gone. And I'm not sure Dahlia is willing to accept redemption.

She drags me back to our table, where everyone but Brent has left for classes.

He grins when we sit down again. "Thank fucking God. Thank you for not leaving me."

I send one more glance toward Jimmy and Xander's table. His back is to me, stiff and hunched; he's not eating. It takes a lot for Xander to lose his appetite.

How could I be such a fool? Outright hitting on him. Asking him to sleep with me. And if I'd been physically able, I would've been a lot more proactive in my attempts to drag him into bed.

When I turn back, Dahlia and Brent are talking, and I give them my undivided attention.

"Okay," Brent says, "you're coming over tonight, right? This is finals week, so we need to get in some serious studying."

"We'll come over as soon as we can, right, Billie?"

I lean back in my chair, my fingers toying with the condensation on my plastic cup. "Yeah, let's do it."

◆

"Are we going to color again today?"

Byrdie rolls his chair over to the small table. His thick dreads jostle when he shakes his head. "No, but it's something just as simple. You said you like to draw, right?" He pulls out a small sketchbook and a couple pens and pencils. "I thought you might like to draw while we're talking.

Nothing specific. Whatever comes to mind."

I frown, taking one of the pencils, and consider the blank page. I don't know where to begin.

"It's the end of your semester, isn't it?"

"Yeah, I've finished all but one final, and then, a month of winter break." I heave a sigh. "I'm ready for a break."

"Oh? Why's that?"

I shrug and press the pencil to the white paper. "It's been a long semester."

The curved line turns into loops and then lightning, but I'm not really drawing anything. It's stream-of-consciousness for art. I trail my pencil all around the page without lifting it.

But Byrdie doesn't press the matter. He sits and waits for me to expand.

My pencil drags across the paper, covering the open spaces with shimmering gray lines. I stop paying attention to what I'm doing, close my eyes, let the pencil lead the way. And hope this ends soon.

Not the exercise. It's simple and easy. Not even tedious.

No, the session. I want the session to end. The day to end. This fucking semester. This whole fucking year. My mother's wedding and her micro-managing.

And Xander.

I don't know how to resolve anything with Xander, but I know it needs to be done. I can't stand it when he's mad at me.

I stop the pencil and open my eyes. The paper is a mess now. Swooping, curling lines. Jagged lines. Faded lines where I didn't press hard enough. Thick, heavy lines where I almost tore the paper.

133

"It's been a long year. It's been a long few years. I don't..." I hesitate, then force a smile. "I'm sure this isn't worth talking about."

But Byrdie shrugs. "Whether it's worth discussing is up to you."

I shift in the seat and set down the pencil. "The thing is, I'm not okay."

"What do you mean?"

"At least Xander doesn't think I am," I say, quickly recovering. I snatch up the pencil again and continue drawing. "And I don't know if he's a good judge when it comes to something like this, but it's the only perspective I have."

"Xander's your friend?" I nod, and he continues: "No other friends have presented their opinions?"

I shake my head, but it's not entirely true. Dahlia, for one, won't stop singing my praises.

"Do you think you're okay, Billie?"

My grip tightens around the pencil. "I'm okay," I say after a beat, "but maybe things aren't going well. I don't think I'm in a good place, but I'm still okay."

Byrdie shifts in his seat. "Are you happy?" When I frown, he adds, "That may be too personal, and if that's the case, you don't have to answer."

I open my mouth to speak, but I don't know what to say.

"Let's word it better: Are you happy with the direction your life is going? Do you think you'll reach your long-term goals?"

That would require me to have long-term goals. I never got any farther than switching my major from Math to Fine Arts. Since then, I've been struggling to improve in my art classes, and I have failed every step of the way.

"Things aren't going exactly how I'd like. I don't know when the last time I was truly happy was."

Byrdie doesn't say anything.

"I mean, I experience joy and excitement, but…I don't know, can you be miserable while still experiencing joy? Is that possible? Because that would be me."

"Billie," he says, matching his quiet tone to mine, "has anything you've done improved this situation? Has anything made you feel better?"

I pause, uncertain. "I don't know. No?"

His black eyebrows scrunch together for a second, then pull apart. "You might consider this: If nothing you've done has helped, why are you doing the same things over and over, still hoping for better results?"

I set the pencil down on top of my paper. I hadn't considered that.

Fourteen

THE ONLY PART OF MY FATHER'S HOUSE NOT DECORATED FOR the holidays is the tree near his fireplace. He has the same decorations up as last year: glittering lights, green garlands wrapped around the walls, candles and a display of decorative balls on the coffee table.

I don't know why he bothers with the decorations. Dad has never observed any religious practices, but he's happy to celebrate Christmas. There's a second stocking hanging at the mantle, and I am speechless at the sight of it.

Dad carries a box of tree decorations into the living room. He's been ready to decorate the tree since I arrived, but I had to get settled in. He didn't have a tree last year.

"Okay, I don't have much, but I figure a few ribbons and the lights can make up for the few ornaments we have."

I smile. "If worse comes to worse, we can always go pick up some pine cones from the park and pretend they're ornaments. That's what everyone else does."

Dad lets out a soft laugh as he opens the box.

"Or we could buy a box of candy canes." I shrug. "Lights first, right?"

He hands me a neatly wrapped string of white lights.

"Check for damaged bulbs."

I start at the top of the tree and unroll the string as I move downward. It's not long enough to cover the whole tree. "We're going to need one more of these."

"I have three."

The lights reach halfway down before I need to retrieve the second string.

"I'm glad you're here, Mina."

I glance toward the second stocking and smile again. "I'm glad I'm here too, Dad." We finally get to make up for lost time. "I wish I could spend more time here during the semester."

But Dad shakes his head, and I pass the bundle of lights between my hands on the other side of the tree. "Nonsense. You spend many of your nights here, even if we don't get to have dinner."

Not as many as I did at the beginning of the semester. Not since I started spending more time with Dahlia.

"I have been wondering, though." His voice is quiet but tense. "I feel like I've barely seen Jimmy and Xander. They used to come with you for dinner every once in a while."

I pause. "Well, Xander's busy with his job. And Jimmy…"

I've barely seen them myself, so how in the world would my dad see them?

"I've been…trying to make more friends, expand my horizons."

"Jimmy's been your best friend for years." Dad opens a small case of ornaments and examines the contents. "Has something changed?"

I finish hanging the string of lights and approach for the third. When he hands it to me, his brown face is wrinkled with concern.

"No, not as such." I return to the tree. "Everyone says I should try making friends with more girls instead of spending all my time with guys, so I have a girl friend now."

"Why haven't you told me about her before?"

I shrug it off, but there's a very good reason I haven't told him about her. "I don't mean to keep her a secret. Her name's Dahlia. She's one of my housemates." I don't want him to know how much alcohol we consume in our free time.

He's silent while I finish the lights, and when I return to him, standing next to the box, he examines me. "Mina, is everything alright between you and Xander and Jimmy?"

I open my mouth, fully prepared to say the practiced, "Of course it is," but I can't lie to him.

"Xander and I have been fighting a lot." I dig down into the big box, searching for ribbons. "Not that that's weird; we always fight. But this has been different, and I don't know what to do to make it better. I don't know how to fix whatever I fucked up."

"Have you asked him?" He pulls another box out of the way, revealing a couple different rolls of gold and silver ribbon. "There's no shame in asking for help."

I grab two rolls and head back for the tree. "I'm not sure that'd work, what with him being away. Besides, we've barely talked in the past two weeks." I unwind the first ribbon, three inches wide with wire edges, and begin to wrap the tree. "That included finals week, but still."

"You have to wait, I suppose."

I heave a sigh. "I hate waiting."

Dad releases a quiet laugh. "I know, Mina, but if that's

your only option…"

"You're right." The shimmering ribbon leaves glitter all over my hands and the floor as I unravel it. "And fights with Xander tend to seep into my relationship with Jimmy. We still talk, but it isn't often when me and Xander are having one of our little spats." Needles and glitter are all over the floor. "We're going to need to vacuum."

He carries a case of ornaments over, with hooks attached, and hangs them on the section I covered with ribbon.

I turn to him with an inquisitive smile. "Dad, are we exchanging gifts?"

He pauses, arm outstretched toward the tree. "I hadn't considered that." He hangs the dangling snowman ornament on a protruding branch. "I don't expect anything. Having you here is the greatest gift I could receive."

"Dad…"

He turns to me with a small smile, and I pull him into a hug, my hand still clutching the roll of ribbon. He wraps one arm around me and presses his head against mine. I hold him for a moment, then pull away and continue as if it didn't happen, and he reaches into the box for another ornament.

The only evidence of the hug is the glitter on his shoulder and the small smile on his face. I smile too.

"You know," he says a second later, "sometimes, people react poorly because they're concerned."

I frown. "Xander?"

"It's a thought."

An accurate thought, I suppose, even if Xander is overreacting.

But Xander has never been the one to overreact. That

was always Jimmy, overly concerned and worried despite my own autonomy. This was Xander voicing his concerns in his perfectly Xander way—bluntly and without remorse.

If he's upset, though, how seriously am I supposed to take his accusations?

◆

"Oh, thank God!" Dahlia pulls me into a hug the second I push open the apartment door. She drags me into the living room and forces a drink into my hand before I take off my coat. "Brent is driving me crazy, and he doesn't have any roomies to distract me."

The liquid is dark and red in a white plastic cup. Some brand of cab by the taste. Nothing expensive.

"I'm so glad you're here."

Brent is in the kitchen, noticeably red, laughing loudly at nothing. He glances over when I enter the living room and flashes me a crooked grin that stays on his face longer than necessary. He raises his drink to me, laughing again, and takes a long gulp.

"When did you start drinking?" I glance between them and sip at my wine. It's tolerable at best but strong enough to be worth the flavor.

Brent grabs for his phone on the counter next to him, misses the first two times, then barely manages to bring it close enough to read. "Twenty-six minutes ago." His booming voice echoes through the room.

"You need to catch up." Dahlia yanks on my arm—luckily the one not holding the wine—and beams at me over her own drink.

I take another sip, set the cup on the coffee table, and drop my hoody and sneakers by the TV.

Dahlia watches with approval. "Much better. Get comfy because I do not want you going anywhere tonight. It's winter break, and we're going to get trashed and it will be glorious."

I snort into my cup. "Glorious" is hardly the word I'd use to describe us when we're drinking—not that it's word I'd use to describe anything.

She sends me a critical look, her lips pursed, a small crinkle between her sculpted eyebrows. "You don't want to spend the night, Billie?"

At that, all I can do is shrug. "I hadn't considered it."

I shouldn't, though. Dad's gone to bed. If I'm not there in the morning, he'll be concerned. The last thing I want to do is worry him.

"Well, sorry, you don't get a choice." She shrugs, smiling, like it's something that's up to her.

Finally, Brent comes out of the kitchen with his drink and two bottles of wine, one half gone, and the three of us sit on the couch, me awkwardly squeezed between them.

"I'll stay as long as I can," I say, hoping that will appease her.

Brent laughs, and his wine sloshes in the cup as he shifts his body to get a better look at me. "Then you have to stay. You're an adult; your dad doesn't get to give you a curfew anymore."

"Exactly." Dahlia finishes off her drink, then leans forward to grab the open bottle. When her cup is full, the depression on the bottom of the bottle juts out of the wine, and she tops me off to empty it.

"He hasn't given me a curfew. He's content that I'm spending Christmas with him."

Dahlia snorts. "'Content'?"

I frown. "Why is that funny?"

But Brent laughs too, nearly spilling his drink for the third time in as many minutes.

My eyes return to the empty bottle, but then, I stretch to see into the kitchen. There has to be another empty bottle or two because they have to be trashed to find the word "content" funny under any circumstances.

The couch starts to vibrate.

For a moment, I'm the only one to notice, but then, Dahlia shifts and pulls her phone from her back pocket. Her face lights up when she reads the caller ID.

"It's Darius!" She holds the phone to her ear, her enormous grin brightening her ghostly features, and answers the call.

On my right side, Brent leans forward to twist open the next bottle, then eagerly fills up his cup. "You need more yet?" He glances toward my cup, but I shake my head. He clucks his tongue in disapproval. "You need to catch up, Billie."

"I'll get there."

"Then drink up." He presses two fingers to the bottom of my cup to lift it toward my mouth, and I take a small drink, humoring him. "We need you drunk."

I pull the cup away, frowning. "Why's that?"

Brent's grin is smug and insatiable. "For fun, of course."

Something about the way he says this sends a shiver down my spine, and I readjust my position to put more space between us. Much like every other time I've felt discomfort in his presence, he doesn't notice I've moved.

The adjustment puts me close enough to Dahlia that our legs press together. She's too distracted to notice. Her lilting voice is loud and excited—impossible to miss, even if I can tune out her words.

When I look at her, she smiles and shifts her attention toward the wall.

I don't imagine she and Darius get to talk often when he's away from Bradford. He needs to be discreet, but with her that happy, it's worth it.

Fifteen

THE BLACKOUT CURTAINS IN MY BEDROOM MASK MY AVER-
sion to light, but they don't prevent the pounding headache
when I wake up. Thankfully, I forced myself to throw up
when I got back at three in the morning.

I crawl out of bed, barely able to reach the floor without
falling, and clutch the nightstand before attempting to walk.

I don't bother with my glasses, grabbing the liter water
bottle instead and chugging a third of it. There's two gel
ibuprofen pills on the tabletop, and I swallow them with the
water. I'm impressed I had the forethought to get them out.

When I put on my glasses and check the time, it's well
after eleven.

I lean forward, resting my elbows on my bare knees, and
massage my temple. There have been a number of times
in the last two months I wished pain relievers kicked in
immediately. This is one of those times. But there's no time
for wishful thinking.

Getting dressed is a struggle.

The bright screen of my laptop is pain-inducing.

Opening the curtains is worse.

But it's been eight days since the end of finals week, and

grades were posted at eight a.m. today. I don't want to be awake or even alive right now, but I need to know.

It only takes a minute to log in to my account and pull up the page. But like all the Bradford web pages, loading is slow, and I fiddle with my hair, still in a bun, aside from the few strands loosened by sleep.

The page, primarily white with a banner of Bradford blue and gray at the top, finally loads, and I bite my lip as I scroll down to the current semester. My breath hitches.

B- in Drawing. B in Personal Wellness. C+ in my Arts Theory class. B- in Physics. B in Honors lit. B+ in Calc III. Somehow, I managed an A- in French I.

And the GPA is listed right there at the bottom: 2.96 for the semester. 3.51 cumulative.

I close the laptop with a shaky breath and push it away.

The lowest grade I had last year was a B+ in U.S. Politics spring semester, and that would've been nerve-wracking if I hadn't been recovering from an impromptu surgery the weekend before finals. I haven't gotten a C since I was in seventh grade. If I get below a 3.5 next semester, I won't qualify for my merit scholarship.

I grab the water again and take a drink. The nausea from the hangover is waning now, but the headache refuses to budge.

Downstairs, Dad is putting together a couple BLTs on whole wheat and a quinoa and tomato salad for lunch. He offers me a smile when I enter the kitchen, clutching my big water bottle to my chest.

"You must've been out late." He tops each sandwich with the second layer of toast and slices them in half. "Tired?"

I take another drink. The bottle's almost empty now. "Very."

"You might be getting sick." He piles the tossed salad into bowls. He doesn't look up as he speaks, and his voice doesn't betray any emotion. "You're quite pale."

Surely, he knows why I'm pale. Vodka has a distinct smell, and Dahlia has begged me to come over every night of the break. Not that I've followed through every night, but she makes it very hard to say no.

"I don't know. Maybe."

He slides one of the plates to me and rinses the empty salad bowl in the sink. I usually wash the dishes after we eat. "When was the last time you spoke to Jimmy?"

I climb on the nearest stool and grab a fork. "A few days ago."

Jimmy texted me on Monday to let me know he and Xander made it to Springfield without a hitch. For some asinine reason, Xander insisted they drive; apparently, he wanted a road trip. But I haven't heard from either of them since. Today is Saturday.

"What about Imogene?" Dad stuffs a forkful of salad in his mouth.

I shake my head. "We've exchanged a couple texts."

Most of which were sent by her, plus several unanswered phone calls. They were all related to the wedding, and that's the last thing I want to discuss.

Dad smiles and picks up his sandwich, only pausing to add, "Eat something, Mina. That's the best cure for a hangover," in a quiet voice.

I flush but do as I'm told.

He's right, after all. He's been the one here the past week, watching and observing, making sure I eat and drink water every day. Trying to keep me from falling apart.

My pocket vibrates. The phone says 12:22 p.m. when I pull it out, and Dahlia's name lights up the screen.

7 p.m., the text says. *Dinner, piña coladas, and movies. You're staying the night. No discussion.*

◆

When Dahlia hangs up the phone after a thirty-minute conversation, she's grinning like a fool.

As happy as I am for her after every long-distance call with Darius, I wish they could happen when I'm not forced to talk to Brent, especially once he's drunk.

"Sorry about that." She happily accepts the fresh piña colada when Brent returns from the kitchen. "Dar is counting down the days till he gets to come back, and I cannot wait. Day after Christmas."

I've never spoken with Darius for longer than a minute, but they can talk on the phone for ages, and she doesn't dominate the conversation.

I accept the other drink from Brent, and he heads back to grab his own cup from the counter.

Dahlia turns to me once he's gone. "The mother has taken to searching his things when he's away from the house—probably for any sign of us communicating. She thinks he has no idea." Despite everything, she laughs. "Dar erased his browser history so she doesn't see all the porn. Not the best way for her to learn her golden child is gay."

From the kitchen, Brent cackles.

"What about your mom?" Dahlia takes a sip, cocking

an eyebrow.

"Oh…" I hadn't expected the sudden subject change. "I wouldn't know what's going on with my mom. We don't talk."

"But the wedding?"

"Yeah, I know. Less than three months away now." I inhale sharply. I got the invitation in the mail yesterday and quickly dumped it in the trash. What a waste of paper. I'm well aware of her wedding date. "Imogene, my little sister, she keeps calling me to talk about it. Every conversation we have now is about my mom's wedding, and Mo should know by now it's the last thing I want to discuss."

Although, maybe not considering I have six messages in my voicemail, all from her. Unopened.

Brent comes back to the living room, then, and sets his glass on the coffee table. "I've gotta piss."

And we're alone again. I prefer it when it's just me and Dahlia.

I take a sip, but when she doesn't say anything, I shift closer. "Can I ask you something?"

Dahlia doesn't miss a beat. "Of course. Anything."

"What was it like when you left home? Have you talked to your mom since you walked out?"

Oddly, the smile doesn't leave Dahlia's face as I expected. Instead, she laughs. "I haven't stepped foot in that house since my sixteenth birthday, and we haven't spoken either. When I cut her out, it was one hundred percent. No going back."

My fingers trace the top rim of my glass. "You said you stayed with your dad's family?"

"Yeah, his cousin—he was shunned from the family ages

ago, so it was safe. I lived with him and his husband in Oregon until I got my GED, and then, I came out here."

In the bathroom, the toilet flushes, but Brent doesn't come out.

"What about Darius?"

When I look at her, Dahlia cocks an eyebrow. "What do you want to know?"

"How have you stayed so close? How'd you stay in contact after you left? Why does he go back there?"

She laughs again. "The thing about Dar is, he's the responsible, sentimental one. Even though she's awful, she's still his mother. I mean, I get that to an extent, but it's also bullshit—but it's his bullshit. I don't have to deal with her anymore, and I am so thankful for that. But I worry about him every time he goes back. I worry he'll get sucked in again like when we were little, and I worry she'll turn him against me, and I worry he won't come back to me—"

Her voice cracks, and she clears her throat. "But then, I remind myself that no matter how long it's been, we've been together through thick and thin. He's been the one to watch out for me and I for him. No matter how hard she tries to keep us apart, she hasn't been successful. I love him so much."

A thick wave of guilt jolts through me.

I wish I could say the same for myself after Mom's threat to deny me access to my baby sister. That's the entire reason I agreed to see Byrdie. But the truth is, the only one keeping me and Imogene apart is myself. I'm the one avoiding her calls and barely responding to her texts.

"Hey." I look up to find Dahlia smiling. "No wonder I drink so much, right?"

She laughs then, like it's a big joke, and despite how accurate the statement is, I laugh too. Anything else would make the conversation awkward, which is almost impossible when you're talking to Dahlia.

Finally, the bathroom door opens, and half a minute later, Brent stumbles into the living room, grinning his stupid drunk grin.

Dahlia helps him into the armchair and sits on the armrest, her hand on his shoulder, an affectionate smile on her face—and he returns it wholeheartedly.

She glances back. "You seem a little down tonight, Billie. Something wrong?"

I heave a sigh and look away.

Between my mom's wedding, my rocky relationship with Imogene, not talking to Xander, barely talking to Jimmy, the therapy I've been too scared to tell anyone about, and those grades, being here with Dahlia is the only thing in my life that doesn't feel like a nightmare.

I tilt my head to the side. "Oh, you know, everything. The usual."

She rejoins me on the couch and wraps an arm around my shoulders. Brent mopes at her departure but leans his head against the chair, sighing.

"How did you meet Brent?"

Dahlia gives a little shrug. "The three of us lived in the same hallway. First floor, left wing of Coolidge Hall. Brent and Kai shared a room, and Darius and Heath shared a room, and the four of them shared the tiniest little bathroom—have you been in Coolidge?"

I shake my head, but the quality of the Coolidge dorm rooms is well-known. Coolidge was the original dormitory, and it's obvious from the exterior that the whole building needs more than a little work.

"I lived with Anna. We were super close then. She was my first female friend, and we kind of dated for a few months. I'd never been close with anyone aside from Dar until moving out of my mom's house, and I was too scared to leave the house while living in Oregon, so Bradford was a revelation. I will always love this place for that—even though, let's be honest, college is complete shit."

I laugh in solidarity.

"But yeah—" she easily brushes off her moment of sentimentality with a flick of her shoulder "—that first month cemented the whole thing, and we've all been friends since. Obviously, times change, and a lot of us have drifted, but I can't imagine Brent not being part of our little group—and you."

The smile spreads across my face before I can think of something to say. This right here is why I'm so glad I met her.

Sixteen

DAD POURS ME A CUP OF TEA AND SLIDES IT OVER WHEN I join him at the dining room table. The thousand-piece Ravensburger puzzle, only the border and a few four-piece sections within, has been pushed to the side to make room for the tea and newspaper. "Good morning, Mina."

"Morning." The scent of spearmint hangs in the air, and the hot tea is mild and sweet. "Merry Christmas, I guess."

He flips to the giant Christmas crossword puzzle and hands me the page.

Growing up, Christmas was both my favorite time of year and my least favorite holiday. Dad spent every minute working at the university, but winter break meant he didn't teach classes for a whole month. We spent those long hours together.

Unfortunately, this also meant we spent the holiday with my Baptist-raised mother. My dad—and me by extension—could never stomach religion.

The holiday is far more relaxing and comfortable with just the two of us.

"Are you going out again today?" He's only answered half a dozen clues while waiting for me. "To see your friends?"

My head shoots up. "Of course not, Dad. It's Christmas—we should at least pretend to celebrate the holiday, right? We're spending the day together."

Dad chuckles.

"Unless you have other plans…"

"No," he says, "no plans whatsoever. I'm more than happy to spend the day with you. What would you like to do?"

"I have no idea." I shift down to the next clue. "Well, aside from this crossword, right? And we should finish the puzzle…"

A smile spreads across his tight features. "Maybe we could start with breakfast. What do you want to eat? Biscuits and gravy? Pancakes? Omelette?"

On the corner where I left it, my phone starts to vibrate, shaking the whole table. I stretch to grab it and frown at Imogene's smiling face on my caller ID.

It's Christmas. I shouldn't ignore her calls on Christmas.

"Hey, Mo," I say when I answer the phone. "Merry Christmas."

"Merry Christmas, Billie." Her voice is happier-sounding than I expected considering how many of her calls I've let go to voicemail. "Are you having a good morning?"

"Uh, yeah. What about you? How's Mom?"

On the other side of the table, Dad pours himself more tea and sips while reading the paper. He's far more patient than I am.

"We just opened gifts, and we're going to join the Powells for brunch—Thea insisted last night."

Right, the Christmas Eve party. This is the first party of theirs I've missed since we moved to Springfield at age eight.

153

"Did you see Jimmy and Xander?"

A stupid question. Why wouldn't she have seen Jimmy and Xander?

"Yep." She pauses to laugh, but her voice is strained. "I've been hanging out with them when we're not doing stuff for the wedding. You know how mushy Mom and Rob are—it's disgusting."

Nausea wells in my stomach. She's spent more time with Jimmy and Xander in the past two weeks than I have in the last six.

"Right."

"They've gotten their asses handed to them in *Mario Kart*," she continues, "so at least I'm not bored without you here."

"Yeah."

"Speaking of which—" and there's the edge I expected from the start "—I know you're having a great time with Dad and all, but winter break is the only opportunity you have to come help with wedding stuff before the actual wedding. Billie, why aren't you coming home?"

I take a shaky breath. "I am home."

She scoffs. "Your break is a month long and you can't take a short trip here to help out? Mom is freaking out about this wedding, and you're nowhere to be seen."

My hand clenches atop the table. "I don't know why it matters."

"You're a bridesmaid. This is our mother's wedding. She needs you here for emotional support, and you're bailing on her yet again."

Red and gold candles sit in a small circle at the center of the table, a thick red ribbon wrapped around each of their bases.

Across the table, Dad fiddles with the newspaper.

"Okay, fine. I'll come for New Year's or something. Will that satisfy you?"

"Yes." She releases a relieved laugh. "Let me know when your flight is, and we'll come get you."

"Sure. I'm thrilled."

"You better act thrilled." She has no time for my sarcasm. "Mom's determined to take care of everything. Do you know how stressful planning a wedding is? And we're supposed to help—you included."

"Maybe she should've considered the stress before taking on the planning of a big wedding."

The first time we had this argument was over the summer: Mom wanted to have an enormous wedding in the Japanese Gardens, but they don't allow weddings, and even if they did, Mom and Rob wouldn't be able to afford it. But was I allowed to point out the faults in her plan?

Absolutely not.

"At least Rob talked her down from inviting every single person she's met. Is she still taking her meds? She's going to bring on a relapse."

Imogene sighs. "Rob's making sure she is. And this is why you need to come home. Having you here would help."

I take a sip of my tea. "Yeah, okay."

The line is silent for a beat.

"Is Dad there?"

"Of course." I pull the phone away without any parting words and hand it to him. They don't talk as often as they'd like to. Their schedules don't match up.

I retreat into the kitchen for a glass of water. An attempt

155

to wipe the slate clean for my special day with Dad. This is why I've been avoiding conversations with Mo.

Fifteen minutes later, Dad joins me in the kitchen and hands me my phone. The screen is black. They hung up.

He leans against the island beside me.

Should we talk about it?

"I don't know why I need to go back." I close my eyes and breathe deep. "Mo says I should be there for emotional support, but Mom and I have never been close. I don't know why she wanted me to be a bridesmaid in the first place. It's idiotic symbolism that isn't applicable in this situation."

Dad chuckles. "I will admit, I'm disappointed you have to leave early. I was looking forward to spending the whole break with you."

I glance over—his eyes are closed, his forehead's creased—and I thread our fingers together. "Me too, Dad. I'm sorry I can't stay."

"No, it's fine."

We're silent for a moment. I lean on his shoulder.

"Maybe…" His voice is quieter than before. "Maybe it will be good to get away from St. Clare, though."

I lean back, but his eyes are still shut. "What do you mean?"

"You've been quite stressed this year, Mina, and I imagine that's taken its toll. Getting away from the college atmosphere could give you a chance to relax."

Around Mom? Unlikely.

"You could talk to Xander." He squeezes my hand. "I know how much you want to make amends. You could spend time with him and Jimmy and your sister. No classes getting in the way. This could be a good thing. You deserve good things, Mina."

I press closer and bury my face in the crook of his neck.

"In the meantime, let's make breakfast." He wraps his arm around me in a big hug before untangling himself from my grip. "I'll show you how to cook pancakes. You have your own kitchen now that you're not in the dorms. You should at least know how to use it."

Seventeen

"How was your holiday?" Byrdie leans his elbow on the table. "Do you celebrate Christmas? Kwanzaa?"

I drag the rake through the white sand. "We don't celebrate either. Christmas was for my mom growing up, and since this was the first holiday with only my dad, we didn't bother with anything special." I draw a few lines down the long end of the zen garden, then retrace my steps. "I think my dad's family celebrates Kwanzaa, but they live in Cincinnati, and I haven't seen any of them since I was ten."

"Why so long?"

The white sand is soft and fine, and it gives at the slightest touch.

"My grandma insisted we visit them, especially as she got older, and we were never in a place to travel after we moved away. The only time I got to see them after the move to Springfield was when my dad and I went on a trip together."

He nods. "What about your mother's family?"

I huff, and bits of sand fly out of the square container. "Sorry."

But Byrdie chuckles and helps me sweep the sand to the edge of the table and then back into the box. "Why such a strong reaction?"

I have to retrace my lines to cover up my blunder. "Because I've never met my mother's parents. They weren't exactly thrilled when she announced she was pregnant at seventeen. She talks to her sister occasionally, though."

"That must be such a shame not to know your grandparents, Billie."

I shrug. "It's nothing new."

For a few beats, we sit in silence, but I shift uneasily in my chair. The silence always leaves me feeling cold and alone.

"When you spoke with my secretary, you said you won't make next week's meeting, correct? You're going back to Missouri for New Year's?"

"Unfortunately." I twist the tiny rake between my fingers before switching positions. A set of four lines appears as I drag it perpendicular over the ones I already did. "Is this supposed to be relaxing?"

Byrdie laughs. "That's its purpose. If it's not working, we can find something else."

"No, it's fine."

"Why is it unfortunate that you're going to see your mom and sister for New Year's?"

I pause, lips pursed.

There are a number of reasons I don't want to go to Springfield, of course. The tension between myself and literally every other person there for one thing, and all the stupid wedding shit I'll have to deal with during my week-and-a-half visit for another. I'll have to talk to Xander—or avoid him. I don't want to hear Mom and Rob having sex during this visit—that happened far too often over the summer.

And I won't be able to drink.

The rake falls from my fingers into the sand, but I don't move to pick it up. "How do you classify an alcoholic?"

Byrdie takes a moment to respond.

When he does, his deep voice is quiet and curious. "Any diagnosis can be complicated. Many people who depend on alcohol put themselves in dangerous situations or have trouble with their families or friends or school due to their alcohol use. Some have such a dependence that they can't think of anything else or go through withdrawal when they don't have enough. But there are also a number of alcoholics who go about their day without those problems. There are still significant health risks with high alcohol intake, of course. It's a serious disorder." He pauses. "Why do you ask?"

"My mom. In addition to the bipolar, she drank. A lot." I shift in the seat and reach for the rake, but I hesitate. "Is that considered a symptom of her bipolar, or is it a separate diagnosis?"

"There are a lot of factors to determine that, and I'm not her counselor. I couldn't make an overarching claim."

I push the box away. "What about eating disorders? I have a friend who said she's struggled with anorexia since she was young."

Byrdie studies my face with his lips in a tight line. "What do you want to know?"

"Does an eating disorder diagnosis require you to be obsessed with your body? Like thinking you're fat when you're below average weight? Compulsive dieting, things like that?"

In my periphery, Byrdie nods. "Most people who suffer

from eating disorders have a severe dissatisfaction with their physical appearance and an intense fear of gaining weight, even when they're the exact opposite."

"But what if you don't care what you look like? You're not dissatisfied or scared of getting fat, you just don't care—what then?"

"From my experience, if that is the case, what looks like an eating disorder is usually related to something else. Depression often leads people to over or under-eat. Many issues like anxiety can cause you to feel sick to your stomach so you lose your appetite. Or not eating could be a symptom of a serious physical disease like cancer or the treatment of that disease. That doesn't mean there isn't comorbidity, though. It could still be an eating disorder."

I twist to check the clock. Less than ten minutes left now.

"One thing that isn't discussed often is that not eating can be a form of self-harm. A punishment for the person's self-perceived failures."

I turn to him sharply. "You mean like cutting?"

He nods.

My stomach clenches.

"Can I ask you a question, Billie?"

I shrug.

"Your mother has concerns about your mental health, and with her history, that's a serious possibility. Mental illnesses and chronic diseases are often genetic. And your mother isn't the only person concerned. Why do you think people are worried about you?"

The list goes on and on. Especially if Xander is the one spouting off the accusations. No one else is as blunt as him.

"Xander says I don't take care of myself."

Byrdie takes a moment to reply to my limited explanation. "Do you think you take care of yourself?"

I shake my head. "I'm not unhealthy. Everything's fine."

"What do you think makes him so concerned?"

"I'm antisocial. I have trouble talking to people about my feelings—though I doubt you need me to say that." I crack a laugh, and Byrdie smiles. The zen garden has been completely abandoned now.

"For what it's worth, I don't think you have bipolar, but there's something I want to discuss."

"Oh?" I cock an eyebrow.

"A couple weeks ago, you told me you don't know how to be happy anymore, and when I asked if anything you'd done had made a difference, you said no."

I remember the conversation distinctly.

"I was wondering," Byrdie continues, "if you'd be willing to try something. A few simple lifestyle changes to see how you feel."

I clasp my hands together on my lap. "Like what?"

"I have a small handout with more information—" he nods toward his desk "—but the steps are easy to implement. Try to eat more foods heavy in serotonin: high-protein foods, fish, coconut oil. I don't think you exercise often, but that's a good way to blow off some steam and get your endorphins flowing. Plus, exercising outside in the sun means additional vitamin D. Avoid things like caffeine and alcohol. They boost your serotonin temporarily but lower it over time."

I frown at my hands. "What does serotonin have to do with anything?"

But Byrdie is already standing and retrieving the handout

from his desk. "These are a few starting points to consider." He takes a seat again. "If they help, even a little, we can work with them. If not, we can look into something else."

The paper he hands me has a list of ten talking points. And the title? *Natural Treatments for Depression Before You Consider Meds*, written by a fellow psychotherapist.

It's flimsy in my hands and shakes as I read it.

"If you don't want to, we can do something else." His words are quiet. Reassuring. "But I want you to remember this: You've been struggling for a while in silence, trying to sort everything out on your own, and you've been unsuccessful. Perhaps to the point where you've stopped trying. It's put a strain on your relationships because you don't know how to be open with yourself or others. What you need more than anything is to talk about your concerns in a safe environment and find healthy outlets. If you're willing to try, I can guide you. But you have to let me help. I can't do it without you."

◆

Brent fills four glasses halfway with vodka before topping them off with a couple ounces of tonic water each. Grey Goose, this time, in celebration of our last night before my flight to Springfield. They went all out.

He distributes the drinks, but when he offers me one, I signal him to lay it on the coffee table.

They have the TV on, watching a rerun of *Kitchen Nightmares* for God knows what reason, and Dahlia curls up on the couch with me, wearing her typical grin. Darius, who got back to St. Clare two days after Christmas, stretches across the nearby armchair and slurps at his drink. On his phone, he's flipping through the front page of Reddit and sharing every cat and porn GIF he finds entertaining.

"Something wrong, Billie?" Dahlia presses closer and pokes my ribs. "This is your sending off party. At least pretend to be happy."

"Right." I wrap my fingers around the chilly glass and raise it to my lips. The liquid is cold and bubbly, and I force it down.

"I know it sucks." She sets her drink on the table and scoots flush with me so Brent has room to sit on her other side. "But we'll have a huge celebration when everybody gets back. It's so lonely over winter break."

It was hours ago, but I'm still shaken by the therapy session.

"Is going home bugging you that much?" Brent collapses on the cushion. "What's the big deal?"

Apparently, Dahlia hasn't told him anything from our long conversations about my mother and how much I dread seeing her. I'm glad for that.

"Because," Dahlia answers for me, "Xander's going to be there."

When I glance up, Brent's forehead is twisted with confusion. "Why is Xander there?"

Dahlia's giggles shake my ribs. "He went home with Jim, who is also Billie's neighbor. Keep up with the rest of the class, Moulder."

He takes another drink. "Oooh, that makes sense."

She rolls her eyes. Her breath grazes my face.

"Is that stupid party still a problem?" Brent scoffs. "Please don't pay attention to his shit. We think you're awesome."

I break eye contact with Dahlia.

Why?

We see each other regularly, but we never do anything of consequence. Our late-night conversations are fueled by alcohol instead of baring our souls. Dahlia is the only one I've had a serious conversation with.

Dahlia slips her arm around my waist and pulls me to her side, laughing. The liquid in my glass sloshes. Small flecks fall on my jeans, and I rub at them with my free hand.

That party was three and a half weeks ago. In the time since, there have only been a handful of nights I didn't drink with Dahlia before going to bed. Usually only one or two to help me sleep. Sometimes far more than that. The hangover has been perpetual.

I stretch forward place the glass on the faux-oak table, but a disgruntled Dahlia yanks me back into our little nest on the couch. My stomach wells with nausea. Dahlia, drunkenly giggling again, snuggles close as Brent turns up the TV volume. And I stare at the half-full glass on the coffee table.

When in the world did I start turning into my mother?

Eighteen

Sometimes, I forget how small the Springfield airport is. The flight is fast, and I spend the time listening to Linkin Park, but when I arrive, I'm ready to jump on the next plane back to Vermont.

They don't give me the opportunity.

Imogene stands near the exit, her long blond hair recently relaxed, a lavender pea coat hugging her athletic frame. She smiles at the sight of me.

Behind her, my mom stands with a nervous smile on her soft features, and her fiancé, tall, bronze-skinned, and practically half her age, holds an arm around her shoulders.

The whole family came for this ridiculous affair.

I shoulder my backpack carry-on as I approach. I don't need more than that for a week-and-a-half-long trip.

My mother steps away from Rob to wrap an arm around me, and despite my flinch, I allow her to press her cheek to mine. "I'm glad you're here, Billie."

I wait for the hug to end. Eventually, she pulls back with a smile.

Imogene stays behind her, and her smile is reserved. "Hey."

Before I can respond, she nods toward the exit and begins the short trek to the car. In the back, Rob gives me a warm smile, and I follow Imogene.

Mom walks in step with me, Rob following a few feet behind. "We thought we'd stop and grab food on the way home since it's dinnertime. There's a tapas restaurant downtown we haven't tried. How does that sound?"

I shake my head. "I'm fine with anything, really."

"Then we'll go there."

When we reach the parking lot, Imogene is several yards ahead. She doesn't wait for us to catch up. All I can do is follow.

Mom slows down and links her hand with Rob's. "We're going over to Thea and Charlie's for New Year's. That's tomorrow night if you've forgotten."

"Of course I haven't forgotten. I had to know the date to get here."

Oddly, she doesn't respond with a biting remark, but I'm not going to turn back to judge her reaction. She moves on. "And I know you came here to spend time with us and help out with the wedding, but it'll have to wait till Tuesday."

"Because of New Year's?"

"Rob and I are going on a weekend trip after the party tomorrow night."

I wait for them to catch up. "You're leaving on a trip the day after I get back? Where are you going in the middle of the night?"

They come to a stop beside me, and Mom sweeps a strand of long hair behind her ear. "We're doing a little weekend getaway. Thea insisted we not skip the party, so I told her we'd stay till midnight."

I came all this way to help with the wedding, and she's not going to be here for half my visit.

"We made plans for Imogene to stay with the Powells while we're gone, but you two can stay at the house if you like." She casts a frown in Imogene's direction—she's disappeared from view now. "I'm surprised she didn't tell you."

We resume walking and quickly reach the car. Mom pulls out her keys to unlock it, and Imogene, who was tapping her foot impatiently when we arrived, climbs inside the back seat without a word.

"We'll do our wedding errands after Rob and I are back from the trip," Mom says as she opens her door.

I take the seat next to Imogene. "Whatever you want, Mom. It's your wedding."

Up front, Mom climbs in the driver's seat, and Rob sits beside her, his hand clasped over hers as we back out of the parking spot.

◆

The restaurant is a long, narrow strip of an apartment building's ground floor, situated right next to the stairs. It's small, but the owner went all out on decorations. The entire restaurant is decorated in Spanish red and gold, and vintage-style drawings of lions line the walls.

The host seats us in a dark corner, and I poke at the cloth-wrapped silverware.

"This is lovely." My mother glances around the restaurant. I must not be the only one who's never been here before.

The server approaches, a pad and pen in his hands and

a smile on his copper face. "Have you had a chance to look at the wine list?" He nods to the small alcohol and dessert menu in the middle of the table.

Mom glances at the small menu before returning to the dinner menu in her hands. "Water's fine."

"We have a wide selection of reds and a few whites. Most of them are imported from Spain, but we do have the local favorites." The server lists off a few of their best sellers.

"Water." Rob lays his hand over my mother's atop the table. "Four waters." This is the first time he's spoken since my arrival. I'd almost forgotten his thick Ecuadorian accent.

The server is momentarily taken aback by the firmness in his tone, but he quickly recovers. "Right, water, of course. I'll give you a few more minutes to look over the menu."

He disappears, and I read through the food options. Tapas are Spanish appetizers, food meant to be shared. Cheese and meat trays, Spanish meatballs, shrimp in garlic, cheese and chorizo on toasted bread, spicy lamb kabobs, pita and hummus.

The other customers in the restaurant aren't sharing their food, though. They opted to order a personal plate.

"How was your semester, Billie?"

I turn to my mother and close the menu. "Uneventful."

Beside me, Imogene makes a small sound as she peruses the menu. What insight does she think she has on the subject?

"And your classes? Have you gotten your grades back?" Mom smiles encouragingly.

She's still trying to force her way into my life.

"Yeah, over a week ago."

"And?"

I shrug, but my stomach tightens. "Mostly A's and B's."

Imogene folds her menu shut, then opens it again.

The server returns before my mom can ask another question and deposits four glasses of water on the table between us. I grab the nearest one and take a drink. "Are we ready to order? Or would you like a little more time?" he asks.

Mom glances between us. "I think we're ready."

He starts with her, then circles around the table, ending with me. I hand the menu to him, saying, "I'll have some hummus."

"The hummus and pita plate?" He tucks the menu under his arm with the others and jots down my order.

When he's gone again, I pull out my phone to check the time. Airplane mode is still on. I switch it off and wait to see if any messages float in from the ether.

"Did you bring the dress with you, Billie?" Mom asks, breaking my concentration. "It would be easier to keep it here."

I frown. "I didn't think about that." No texts or missed calls.

Beside me, Imogene harrumphs.

"I'll bring it with me on spring break."

Mom nods, failing to suppress the heavy crease in her forehead.

She never got her perfect wedding with Dad, and Rob's never been married. This wedding is going to be a big deal, even if it's a small affair. Rob's parents are flying all the way from Salinas.

"Well, your sister and I got a few things done before Christmas." Mom twirls her water goblet between her fingers, then takes a drink. "We mailed out invitations and ordered the cake. Rob and I picked out our rings."

"What is there left to do?"

She smiles. "I have a dress fitting on Tuesday, which means I need my shoes. We have to decide on bouquets, finalize the menu with the caterers, organize the ceremony and reception. I have to talk to the officiant sometime this week."

I raise an eyebrow. "That's a lot."

Beside me, Imogene scoots out her chair. "You'd know if you answered my calls. I'll be right back." She retreats to the back of the restaurant. The restrooms must be back there.

Across the table, Rob smiles at me, his hand entwined with my mother's. The server returns with the first round of food, including my hummus dish, and four dessert-sized plates. Mom and Rob separate at last and fill their plates as the server returns to the kitchen. We're still waiting on all the foods that need cooked.

I push away from the table. "I, uh, have to pee."

The restrooms are singles, and I stand next to an oval mirror hanging on the opposite wall and wait. When the ladies' room door opens, Imogene pauses at the sight of me. She steps aside so we can trade places, but I don't move.

"What is your problem?"

She assesses me with pursed lips. "I don't know what you're talking about, Billie."

I scoff. "Why are you in such a bad mood? I'm here to be supportive and help with wedding things, and I'm acting happy for her like you told me to. This is me acting happy."

"It's a good thing you're not an actress."

"Why are you so mad at me? This dinner is supposed to be a celebration, and you're glaring at me the whole time."

171

"Do you think I have no idea what's going on with you?" She levels me with a glare—the same look that made Jimmy stutter and blush when we were kids. Probably the same one she used on him the second he and Xander arrived to get him to spill everything.

"You don't know what's going on."

"You're neglecting your classes, you're neglecting your friends, you're not talking to Xander—" she ticks each item off on her fingers "—and Billie, are you drinking?"

I'm almost surprised.

Not really.

Jimmy can't keep a secret to save his life—and it's not like he was sworn to secrecy.

"You can be mad at me all you want, but I'm doing exactly what you asked." I push away from the wall. "Food's here."

At the table, Mom and Rob are picking at their food, waiting for us.

Nineteen

THEA POWELL PUSHES PAST ROB AND YANKS ME INTO HER embrace the instant the door opens. "I didn't know you were coming home." Her long gray hair falls in my face, but I don't mind.

"I wasn't planning to. I'm glad I get to see you, though."

When she retreats, still smiling, she pulls Imogene, my mother, and even Rob into their own hugs and invites us inside. She leads us to the living room, her arm wrapped around my shoulders, and nudges me in the direction of Jimmy and Xander when we arrive.

The Powells' living room, as per every holiday season, is still decked out in twinkling lights, though the other decorations were taken down the day after Christmas, but the centerpiece, their ten-foot tree, remains near the piano. Thick red ribbon twists around the tree, along with clear white lights, but what makes it truly magnificent are the embroidered ornaments Thea made herself. A delicate porcelain angel sits on the very top. They won't take the tree down till after the New Year.

On the opposite side of the room, the guys are sitting on a loveseat, chatting idly and each playing a game on their

DS. They're leaning against opposite armrests so there's an open spot in the middle, just large enough for me.

I hesitate, but Thea nudges me again, and I force my legs to move.

Jimmy smiles when I approach, but Xander makes a point not to look when my shadow falls across his face.

"Hey. Can I sit?"

"Of course." Jimmy scoots over to make room, but my hips graze each of them as I sit. "When did you get back?"

My hands clasp awkwardly on my lap. "Last night. We went out to eat after my flight got in." I try to get more comfortable without jostling the loveseat. "How was your Christmas?"

Jimmy powers down his DS to give me his full attention. "I think my parents have doubled the amount of gifts since they don't see me all the time anymore."

I force a laugh.

Xander stiffens.

"You going to help your mom with the wedding stuff since you're here?" Jimmy asks.

I scoot closer to him. The space between me and Xander is too narrow—the heat radiating off his body is overwhelming. I didn't intend to get this close to him. "That is the entire reason I'm here. I was supposed to be with Dad."

Across the room, Mom and Rob are sitting together, leg pressed against leg, his arm around her waist, her hand on his knee, and chatting with Thea. They're all smiling.

"It's good that you're helping, though." Jimmy shrugs. "Even if it means changing your plans. I mean, your dad'll still be there when we get back."

But I can't stop staring at them. "I have my dress and

shoes. The only wedding magazine I've looked at was when Imogene showed me which dress to buy. I don't know why I need to be here."

Xander scoffs. "Because she's your mother."

I don't look at him. I'm not supposed to respond.

"She wants you here." Jimmy's voice is soft, kind.

I shake my head.

On the far couch, she's laughing with Thea. Smiling. Happy. When in the world has she ever been happy? And in her hand, she holds a small glass of water. Simple water. She doesn't look remotely uncomfortable about the array of alcoholic drinks in the room, including the glass of Champagne in Thea's hand, only a few feet away.

"I don't know why."

"She loves you."

Jimmy says it like it's obvious. Like there's no way I could've missed it. And when you consider Thea Powell, you can see why. But while Mrs. P is the epitome of warmth, calm, and affection, my own mother was anything but.

In my head, I say the words again.

She loves me?

I don't know why.

"Anything to drink?"

I blink to clear my vision and look up at the smiling face of Charlie Powell. He holds out a flute of Champagne to me, a second one in his other hand.

I shake my head. "I'll get some water in a little bit."

Charlie nods before offering the flute to his son, who takes it without hesitation, and moves on.

Several bubbles jostle free and slide up the side of the flute as Jimmy sets it on the end table at his elbow, and I tear away to survey the room again.

On my other side, Xander closes his DS. The device clicks as it powers off. "You don't want Champagne?" His voice is quiet but firm, guarded.

I shake my head. "I'm not drinking."

He shifts in the seat. When he uncrosses his legs, the nearest one brushes mine. "That's new."

My mother presses a kiss to her fiancé's lips. Her arms wrap around his neck, his hand tightens at her waist. I could use that water right now.

"I half-expected you to drink in front of her out of spite." Xander shifts again. His bitter words cut deep. "It wouldn't be much of a stretch considering how much you've been drinking this semester. This must be killing you."

My jaw tightens. I'm not an alcoholic.

"Thanks for your concern, but I'm fine."

But he doesn't let up. "By 'not drinking,' do you mean while you're here? Keeping up appearances for your mom? Or are you going to hang out with Dahlia Finnick without alcohol involved?"

I frown. "I haven't thought that far ahead."

He lays the DS on the armrest. "How would you manage to talk to anyone without the alcohol? You don't know how to talk about your feelings sober, but, hey, at least you'll remember the conversations in the morning."

"Xander." Quiet as it is, Jimmy's voice comes out as a warning.

There are plenty of things I said to him that night I wish I hadn't, but none of it was an outright confession. I'm not sure what I would confess anyway. It's certainly not odd for me to be attracted to him. We've had sex, and it wasn't entirely unremarkable.

But his wording makes me pause.

Did I say something while I was hurling up my guts in his bathroom? Something I don't remember? Or is he speaking generally?

Either way, the idea of baring my soul—of telling him everything—is absolutely terrifying.

I feel sick.

I rise from the couch. "I'm going to grab that water."

Neither of them says anything as I leave.

In the kitchen, I lean against the granite counter and down my glass of water before refilling it with filtered water from the fridge. I didn't bother with the overhead lights, so the pendant lights that dangle over the sink are the only light source.

Honestly, I don't know why I'm so concerned about this. What could I have told him? There's nothing to tell. Despite what Jimmy might think, I don't have feelings for Xander. I cannot allow myself to have feelings for Xander.

I take a sip and close my eyes. My stomach is full now, but I don't know what else to do.

Footsteps echo as someone approaches, and I turn away. Someone in heels that *click clack* across the ceramic floor.

"Oh, hi, Billie." My mother's footsteps stop. "Are you feeling alright?"

I take another drink.

"Do you want to talk about it?"

I try not to scoff, but it seeps out.

When I open my eyes, concern is etched in her furrowed brow. "You can talk to me about anything, Billie."

I set the glass on the counter. "Where in the world did you get that idea, Mom? The last time we talked you blackmailed me. How can you possibly think I'd want to talk to you about anything?"

She sighs. "We're worried about you. I'll do anything within my power to fix this."

I turn to her sharply. "I'm not your special project. You don't need to fix me now that I'm the only unruly part of your life left. And worrying doesn't give you the right to manipulate me."

"I'm your mom."

"Biology isn't enough for you to qualify as my mom. That's a role you have never filled before."

Her face contorts, but she isn't quick with a rebuttal. What could she say? Denial would be disingenuous and futile.

"How would you know anything going on in my life anyway?" I turn away again. "It's been months since I saw you. I did that on purpose. I'm here because Imogene asked me to come—not because of you."

Mom ponders this a moment. "Would you have attended therapy if your sister had asked you to?"

My brow furrows, but I focus on the stainless steel sink. "What does that have to do with anything?"

"If you wouldn't have done it for me or yourself, would you have done it for Imogene?"

"I am doing it for Imogene."

She shakes her head. "Would you have done it if she'd asked you to?"

"It doesn't matter anymore. What's done is done."

Her pretty dress shimmers in my periphery as she leans

against the counter a few feet away. "Yes, it is done."

The words come out with a sense of finality that's out of character for any version of this woman I've known.

"I know I wasn't there for you growing up. I'm sorry for that. I can be better if you give me a chance. I can understand what's going on if you let me."

How typical of my mother to make promises everyone knows she can't keep.

I try not to roll my eyes—I don't try very hard. "No, you can't. Even if you could, I don't want to talk to you about anything."

"You don't have to tell me." She's staring at the floor, her arms crossed over her chest. "I already know."

I freeze. "Know what?"

For a moment, she doesn't say anything, hesitating, but when she finds her voice again, she looks up. "Everything—or as much as I can. As much as your father was willing to admit."

"Know what?"

She glances around the room to make sure we're alone. "About the abortion, Billie."

"He told you? He swore he wouldn't say anything."

"The clinic used your insurance card. You're my dependent. I received a letter listing the services used a month after you got home for the summer. I know."

All I can do is shake my head. "You don't know anything."

"I called your father to ask him, but he barely confirmed it happened. I was shocked."

I grab the glass off the counter and take a long drink. This cannot be happening.

"Why didn't you talk to me about it? I understand."

My fingers clench around the glass. "Do you?"

"When your father and I—when we were first together, when I found out I was pregnant, we debated for a long time…"

"I know. You've told me."

Her face falls. "Then you know I understand how hard a decision that is. I know what you must've gone through."

My jaw clenches. "Is that what I know? Because that's not what I learned from hearing your drunken rendition at age fifteen."

For a moment, she's speechless.

"Besides, having an abortion doesn't mean I need therapy. Just because you needed therapy after you got pregnant with me doesn't mean I do. At least I won't have a child who spends her entire life wondering why her own mother doesn't want her."

She turns to me again with a sharp glare. "That's out of line—"

"And your solution is to threaten to take away my relationship with my sister because you think I've fucked up my life? When in the world did you become the reigning judge of mental health in the family? I will never forgive you for this."

She opens her mouth, but I slam my glass on the counter and stalk from the room.

In the hallway, unable to see anything through my blurry vision, I collide with something—someone—solid.

Twenty

Xander scrutinizes me. His hands grip my shoulders. He can always tell when something's off—though I imagine the tears glistening in my eyes is a dead giveaway. I cannot look away.

I press a hand to his chest. "Keys?"

He cocks his head to the side, but he reaches into the pocket of his jeans and pulls out his key ring.

I snatch it from his hand, grab him by the shirt, and drag him to the front door.

"Where are we going?" he asks as soon as we're in the car.

"Why do you care? I just need to go away for a little bit."

I shove the key into the ignition, press my foot on the clutch, and jiggle the stick—yes, it's in neutral—before starting the engine. It roars to life, but I pause.

"What?"

I bite my lip. "Is there any way I can convince you to go inside and grab a bottle?"

He raises an eyebrow. "I'm not going to answer that. You're upset. You don't need alcohol."

"It didn't bother you last time."

He lets out a hollow laugh. "And I learned my lesson,

Besides, I'm not sure you should even drive right now."

I scoff. "I'm not going to hurt your precious car. I doubt our friendship could survive that."

I'm still not convinced it will survive our most recent fight.

I direct the car down Pickwick, left onto Bennett, and drive till I hit Glenstone, the next large cross-street. I take a right onto the avenue and drive. No destination. No idea where to go. It's less than an hour till midnight on New Year's Eve.

Xander points out the window. "That's a big cemetery."

I don't bother looking. I have nothing to say.

And he doesn't try to force anything.

"Look." I adjust my hands on the wheel. "I just want to be able to breathe. Can we be quiet?" I locate the switch on the door, and the wind whips through my thick hair, down for once. I shove the corkscrew curls back over my shoulder.

"Then why did you bring me along?"

My grip tightens. "Taking the car without you would've been stealing."

He releases a mirthless laugh and presses close to his window. "I'm still trying to figure out why you care. You think I would've reported you?"

My hands grip the steering wheel so hard my knuckles are white. I wouldn't put it past him with how pissed he's been at me.

"You wanna breathe, to think?" He shifts in his seat to face me partway. "How about you cut the bullshit and be honest for once?"

I blink a few times. Finally, tears actually fall. "What do you want to talk about?"

Xander nods his head in the direction we came from. "Whatever the hell happened with your mom. Why you're crying."

I shake my head. "Not crying."

He scoffs. "Fine, have it your way. We can pretend those aren't tears. But that's not an answer."

The light ahead changes to yellow, then red, and I slow to a stop.

"She surprised me." I shift back down to first gear. "I don't know what to make of her anymore. She is nothing like the mother I grew up with, but she's exactly the same."

The other car, no longer waiting for the light, turns left to go the opposite direction of us, and the light changes back.

"This summer was the strangest experience. She's been angry, she's been crazy, depressed, jealous, paranoid—she's been manic, but this was the first time I've ever seen her happy. She's never been happy before."

The light's green again—has been for a minute—but there's no one around. I press on the gas and clutch and shift gears as we speed up.

"Not even with your dad?"

I laugh. "Never. That would require them to be in the same room."

The signal ahead changes to yellow, and I slam on the brakes to stop in time. Xander clucks his tongue disapprovingly.

I send him a sheepish smile. "I don't know where I'm going."

"Let's go back."

But that thought terrifies me. Seeing her right now terrifies me. The idea that I might have to talk about what happened last semester sends a chill through my body.

And Xander can read me like an open book. "We don't have to go inside, but you shouldn't be driving. You're too upset."

I don't want to admit it, but I turn right and head back to the houses.

It doesn't take long to reach the Powells' driveway again, and I park on the concrete with the car running. He reaches over to pull the parking brake, shift the car into neutral, and turn off the engine, but he leaves the keys in the ignition.

"What now?"

I can't look at him. My hands grip the steering wheel. "I don't understand her."

"I'm not sure we're supposed to understand our parents."

"My entire childhood was divided. My dad worked at the university, and if I was able to, I joined him. Otherwise, I stayed in my room, occasionally hung out with Jimmy. She never raised me."

Xander leans his seat back. All he does is listen, and I have to keep talking.

"She was diagnosed with bipolar when she was sixteen, and she met my dad a year later. She didn't tell him about it. By the time she was eighteen, she was pregnant. She could never keep a job, always jumping from place to place. I don't think he knew what was going on."

I rest my head against the steering wheel and clench my eyes shut. "But when Mo came around, my mom was excited. She actually wanted a kid. She stayed at home to take care of us, but that woman doesn't have a motherly bone in her body."

"What happened?"

I push away from the wheel and finally release my hands. My knuckles ache from staying in such a tense position for too long. "She was overwhelmed, off meds, and that's when everything got out of hand. I was four or five, Mo was two. I had no basis for a comparison. I thought it was normal, that this is what everyone's family is like. Until I met Charlie and Thea at least." I laugh. "But that was years later."

I stretch my fingers and pop my knuckles, but I'm tense everywhere. "I don't know how Dad missed it. It was so obvious. But I don't think the thought crossed his mind. After he started his job at the university here, they never had to spend time together. They never loved each other."

Xander reaches out but stops before his fingers touch my arm. "Even if that's true, your parents both care about you."

When I look at the Powells' house, still sparkling with Christmas lights, I let out a low bitter laugh. "She never wanted me."

"What do you mean?"

"If she'd had her way, they wouldn't have gotten married after they discovered the pregnancy—and I wouldn't exist. It was my dad who insisted on a wedding, on keeping me."

Xander shakes his head. "That was before you were born. She's had nineteen years to change her mind."

"That's a nice thought. Doesn't make it true." I pause, but I might as well say everything. "She told me I had to go to therapy or I couldn't come here to see Mo anymore."

"She's worried about you. She isn't the only one who worries."

I scoff. "Do you have any idea how condescending it

185

is for someone to say they're worried about you? Jimmy's spent half our friendship worrying about me, trying to help, pitying me. It's not helpful. Even with good intent, it isn't nice."

"He worries because he cares. You've been friends forever. You're an important part of his life."

I heave a sigh. "It'd be nice if he could just listen instead of trying to fix my problems."

But Jimmy always sends me that sad look and says he wants me to be happy—as if that will solve everything, as if the thought never occurred to me. He means well—he always means well—but he never understands.

"You don't pity me, do you, Xander?"

He snorts. "You're a fully capable person, Dixon. Doesn't matter how much you fuck up, how many mistakes you make, or how upset I am with you, I will never pity you."

There's no room for argument in his tone. That is so good to hear.

When he speaks again, his voice is barely above a whisper. "That doesn't mean I don't worry, though."

My eyes flit to him before returning to the Powells' house.

"The divorce was mutual, then?"

I nod.

"What was the final straw?"

I release something between a laugh and a sigh. "Bradford. He was an associate professor at the university here, and yeah, Bradford's a smaller school, but it was a higher position, more pay, private, smaller classes—exactly what he was looking for."

"But your mom didn't want to go?"

"I don't know why. She had no friends here and no job. All that's here is Jimmy and his parents. But when the time came, he made the decision, and they agreed on a divorce, on me and Mo staying here with Mom, and he left at the end of the school year. It was all incredibly civil."

Xander makes a small humming sound. "Then why do you always talk like he walked out on you guys?"

I send him a glance, frowning. "He was the one that raised me, and suddenly, he was gone. What else was I supposed to think?"

"What about Imogene?"

I shrug. "She's taken care of our mom since she learned how to walk and talk, and I spent all my time with Jimmy, pretending it never happened because I didn't know how to handle it. I didn't know how to handle Mom." I lean against the seat and shut my eyes. "I was selfish."

Rough fingers press to my forearm. "You're not the only person who's ever been selfish, Dixon."

"No, but I've definitely been my fair share of selfish. Especially when it came to you." I turn and open my eyes to find him watching me. "I thought you were stealing my best friend. Jimmy was the only person who cared, and I was scared you were going to take that away from me."

"I know." He sends me a rueful smile. "Obviously, that's not the case."

"I know."

"And he's not the only person who cares."

I almost laugh, but it comes out as a strangled sigh. "Logically, I know that's true, but no matter how hard I try, there's a voice inside my head that tells me everyone's lying. That I'll always be alone. That no one will understand."

His fingers slide down my arm to entwine with mine. "My dad started his business before I was born."

I frown, surprised by the change in topic—but more because of his sudden, unsolicited openness.

"He worked constantly, and my mother went through a series of potential businesses, far too many to remember. She's been running that boutique for four years now—I'm impressed she hasn't moved on to the next venture yet." He lets out a short laugh before continuing.

"We moved around a lot. Every time he started up a new location, we moved there until the project was done, and then off to the next one. The business grew really fast, and we were all over the country. I've lived in California three different times, in Alaska of course, New York, Chicago, Albuquerque, and the hotel in Miami was the most recent addition."

I squeeze his hand, and his fingers tighten around mine.

"By the time we reached Florida, I didn't have expectations. I stopped trying to make friends, stopped putting in an effort because we'd just move again in six to nine months. But then, he decided to stay. I went to a private high school there, but I didn't socialize with anyone beyond the soccer team. The closest thing I had to a best friend was Em."

"Wasn't she the one that stabbed you with a pencil?"

He laughs, almost reminiscently. "She was exactly what my parents wanted for me. Her dad's in the fashion business, and he'd started her in junior modeling. But I hated all of it. I resented my parents for everything. When I turned sixteen, my dad wanted me to join the company in the lowest possible position so I could build from the ground up like he did. He didn't consider that I wasn't interested.

That wasn't an option."

Even as I can hear the frustration in his voice, he remains calm, his hand relaxed in mine.

"So I bought this Camaro off the dad of one of my team-mates—the only guy I hung out with outside of practice. I got a minimum wage job at a local auto parts store so I could get discounts. I read, researched every day on the bus to and from work, and I learned from the guys there, figured out how to fix this thing." He laughs. "The learning curve sucked. Prior to this, I'd had a chauffeur. I knew literally nothing about cars, but I fell in love with it."

I rub my thumb across the back of his hand, and he squeezes me.

"My dad tried to force me to quit several times. He tried to take the car away. But I wouldn't let him. He thought I was being a rebellious teenager and I'd grow out of it." He scoffs. "Em thought the same thing, constantly joked about me getting my act together. She freaked out when I told her I was going to a tiny-ass town in Vermont after graduation."

"Is that when she stabbed you?"

"No, that was five minutes later when I asked her to go with me." He grins. "Temporary lapse in judgment. I thought things could be different if we went on our own, but she hated that idea. And when I left, I swore I'd never go back."

I frown at our connected hands. I can't imagine letting go. "I'm sorry."

Xander gives a one-shouldered shrug. "Don't be. I have no regrets." With his free hand, he reaches into his pocket to retrieve his phone. "We should go back inside. It's almost midnight."

I pull out my own phone to check. It's 11:58 p.m., and there's a text from Jimmy: *Are you okay? Where did you go? It's been an hour.*

"Okay." I grab his keys and open the door.

We pause in front of the hood, and he turns to me, his hand brushing mine. "Keys?"

Right.

I reach into my pocket and pull them out, my fist clenched around them.

He's watching me, and I want to say something. But I don't know where to begin or what to say. This is the first time we've had a heartfelt conversation in months. Somehow, he manages to make me feel at ease while baring my soul.

It's hard not to feel comfortable with him, even when I'm at a loss for words. Because, really, I don't want to speak. I'd rather just be with him—especially after a month of being apart. I want so much to be close to him.

The clock on my phone turns from 11:59 to twelve. "It's midnight." I slide the device into my pocket.

Xander quirks a smile. "Happy New Year, then."

I return the smile, step closer to set the keys in his waiting hand, and push up on my tiptoes to kiss him.

He drops the keys and pulls me into his arms, and my eyes flutter shut. I press a hand to his jawline, and he shoves his fingers into my wind-tousled curls, drawing me closer. The kiss is overwhelming, and all I can do is melt into his embrace as he holds me flush against his body. His lips are insatiable and hypnotizing. My knees are weak.

All too quickly, he releases me and leans his forehead against mine.

When I step back, my legs brush the hood.

On the ground, the keys sparkle in the glow of the street-lights, and I snatch them from the pavement before offering them again. "Here you go."

He grips them loosely. "Dixon…"

I offer a small smile. "I just wanted to say thank you—for listening, for sharing with me, for making me feel better. You always know what to say, even if I don't want to hear it."

He nods, dazed. "Right."

I thread my fingers through his empty hand and turn to the Powells' house. But next-door, my childhood home is dark and deserted. "I think I'd rather go to bed."

Xander clears his throat but doesn't say anything.

"Will you walk me to my door?"

We trace the path around the fence line and up to the kitchen side door. I didn't bother bringing the key with me, but the latch gives when I twist the knob. I crack the door to make sure it isn't my imagination.

"What are your plans?" Xander's thumb rubs circles on my hand. "Can you go to sleep yet? It's only midnight."

I purse my lips and release him. "I'll watch some TV or something first. I won't be up late."

He laughs. "You're sweet to try to placate me, but I don't believe that for a second."

I roll my eyes. "What, do you need to come up to make sure?"

The smile falls from his face. "And what, watch the show with you? What about after that?"

"It's not like anyone is home." I push the door open the rest of the way. "My mom and Rob are leaving for Eureka Springs any minute. The car's already packed. You could stay the night."

Xander places his hand over mine on the doorknob to stop me. "Dixon, are you asking me to bed with you?"

I release a low snicker. "We both know I'm not that subtle."

But he follows me inside the house.

Twenty-One

WE LEAVE THE LIGHTS OFF AS I WALK HIM THROUGH THE kitchen, into the hallway, up the stairs, and stop at the closed door of my bedroom. His fingers are tense around mine, but when I twist the knob and pull him inside, there is no resistance. The latch clicks into place behind us, loud and final.

And we're alone. Completely and utterly alone. In my bedroom.

I hesitate by the door, my fingers clenching tighter around his. Despite this, his grip relaxes.

Xander brushes against my side as he leans close to my ear. "Are you waiting for something?"

I clear my throat. "Turn around."

For a moment, he doesn't move or make a sound, but his breath rustles my loose hair. He's still close, still touching me, and despite myself, I lean into him.

Finally, he steps back and spins around.

I too turn away, breathing a quiet sigh of relief, and undo my jeans. If we're going to sleep, I have to be comfortable. It's not a good idea for him to watch me undress.

"I've seen you naked, you know." When I glance back,

he's facing the wall. "What's the big deal?"

I'm too busy kicking the jeans to the floor and pulling off my Marvel sweatshirt to respond. Underneath the sweatshirt, I have a white camisole and a padded bra, and I reach under the shirt to unclasp and yank off my bra.

"You said your mom put you in therapy? When did that happen?"

I pause, then nudge my clothes toward the foot of my bed. "She wanted me to go at the start of the semester—made appointments for me and everything—but I refused. When she called me Halloween night, she didn't give me a choice." The bed creaks as I sit.

By the door, he's still facing the wall, his hands tucked casually into his front pockets. In the moonlight cascading through the window, the contours of his clothes are easily discernible—the dress shirt across his broad shoulders, not tucked in at his waist, the tight jeans creased at the point where his ass meets his legs, his legs spread leisurely.

It takes a moment to register he's talking.

"...had me in counseling for years—it was their way of ignoring their job as parents while still feeling good about themselves. But it was mostly playing with toys and answering simple questions. I was maybe ten."

"Right."

"What's yours like?"

"My what?"

He starts to look over his shoulder but changes his mind. "Your therapy."

"Oh." I scoot close to the wall and pull the covers all the way over my chest. "It's tedious. You can turn around now."

At last, he withdraws his hands from his pockets and

spins on the balls of his feet. When I finally look up to his face, there's a smirk playing on his lips. "And what am I supposed to sleep in? Did you think of that?"

If possible, I press closer to the wall. I didn't. I didn't consider that we'd share the twin bed I grew up in. There's no way we won't touch. I am wet and aching at the thought.

I open my mouth to speak, but his eyes lock with mine, and his hands unbutton the shirt from the collar down. All I can do is watch, mouth agape, as he undoes each button at a tantalizingly slow pace. Dear God, his abs...

He drops his shirt to the floor, and his hands move to his belt. I try to look away—I'm outright staring—but I can't. He unclasps the buckle, then undoes the button, the zipper, and then, he's shoving the jeans down his legs and kicking off his Vans.

He's down to a pair of bright blue boxers and socks. The face of the distinctive blue hedgehog almost ruins the view. The socks come off after that.

I definitely didn't think this through.

"Is this okay?" He takes a tentative step toward the bed.

Mute, I can only nod, and when he pulls the satin sheets away to lay down beside me, I swallow audibly.

"Do you talk about me when you're there?"

"What?" My voice is breathless.

Under the covers, his leg touches mine, his arm presses against my shoulder. "In your therapy." He twists onto his side to face me. "Do you talk about me in your therapy?"

"He's never heard of you."

Without warning, Xander presses a finger to my nose. His friendly smile twists into a smirk. "That's a shame. I'm a pretty hot topic." Even after his hand withdraws, he's inches from my face. "In fact, I'm a pretty hot everything."

I snort and shove his shoulder. "You're so conceited."

He smirks again. "Am I?"

"Yes."

"Is it conceit if it's based on fact?" His hand caresses my bare arm. "It'd be a safe bet to say you think I'm hot. That's not conceited."

I turn to the ceiling as heat rises to my cheeks. "That sounds pretty conceited. I've given you no indication I find you attractive."

Xander laughs and moves closer. His bare chest presses against my arm. His lips brush my ear. "Dixon, you've been attracted to me since the day we met. You haven't been able to stop thinking about me since we had sex." His whisper sends shivers down my spine and a jolt of pleasure through my heat. "Don't forget, I know what your arousal smells like."

I open my mouth, but I'm at a loss for words.

Without warning, he retreats, putting as much space between us as possible in the small bed. "Weren't we going to watch TV?"

I clear my throat. "Right. Uh, what do you want to watch?" I sit up to find my laptop, nestled on the desk at the foot of my bed, and I crawl out from under the sheets to reach it.

"Dixon."

I glance back, my fingers grazing the case. "Yeah?"

He's staring at my ass. "You're not wearing pants." His hand outlines the curve of my ankle.

I sit up, leaving the laptop behind, my back to him. "Neither are you."

Then, Xander rises into a sitting position and traces up my leg, stopping mere inches from my ass. His hand wraps around my waist and pulls me into his lap. My back rests flush against his chest, and he leans his forehead against my shoulder, coils of hair in his face. Everything below his waist is beneath the covers, but his erection is eager and hard through the sheets.

My tense body relaxes in his arms, and I lean into him. I lay my hand over his on my stomach and thread our fingers together.

"Why didn't you drink tonight?" The vibrations send shivers through my body. "You surprised me."

I try to breathe steadily, but he places a kiss against my skin and I have to resist moaning. "Maybe this semester didn't turn out how I wanted it to." I press closer. I need to feel him. "Maybe my grades could've been better. Maybe I don't know what I'm doing. Maybe I missed you."

His other hand slides upward, and he pauses before his fingers engulf my breast, squeezing lightly.

This time, I do moan.

"Maybe—" his voice is thick and slow in my ear "—I didn't handle the situation well. I shouldn't have been so hard on you." He pinches the erect nipple through my shirt.

I gasp, and my fingers clench around his.

He nips at my neck, kisses the sensitive skin, and his fingers slide down again. He passes our clasped hands, slips between my legs, and cups my heat over my underwear. I roll my hips against his hand.

"To be fair," he says between placing kisses up my neck, "I don't make the best decisions when it comes to you. You drive me insane." The husky desire in his voice says this isn't

197

a problem right now. His fingerpad rubs a line up and down my underwear.

"Trust me—" I twist my neck to kiss the closest part of him I can reach, his temple "—the feeling's mutual."

I'm impatient, and he doesn't disappoint. He tugs the hem of my underwear aside and circles my clit. I whimper, desperate for more, and he plunges inside, but he can't reach very far in this position.

I try to kiss him again, and he turns to meet me. Our lips meld together in an excruciatingly slow kiss, and all I want to feel is his mouth on mine. His thumb sweeps across my clit. I moan into his mouth and reach up to clutch his face. His hand now free, he envelops my breast again. Between his lips and his hands, I cannot contain myself.

But then, he breaks the kiss. His hands retreat, and he slowly leans back on the bed, pulling me down on top of him. I toss my glasses away and twist to kiss him again.

He tears the camisole over my head, his lips barely leaving mine before we're attached again. I straddle him, press my heat against his throbbing erection, but the sheets still separate us. There are too many layers between us.

He grips my waist as I rock against him. His kisses are insatiable, and I meet him tit for tat. When he nips and sucks at my lower lip, I slip my tongue into his mouth, eager to taste him. His hands nudge my underwear out of the way, following the curve of my ass, caressing me with unparalleled tenderness.

But I retreat from his embrace.

I trail kisses down his chest, pausing to yank the satin sheets away. The boxers are next. I need to see—to touch—everything.

His body tenses as my fingers trace down, then come to a stop at the trimmed hair at his groin. I graze his base, and he takes a deep breath at the touch.

"Dixon…" Xander entangles his hand in my hair, but he's blurry without my glasses.

His hand tightens in my corkscrew curls as I grasp his cock and press my lips to its head. I trail a line of kisses down one side, then drag my tongue up the other. My hand pumps up and down slowly, testing the waters.

"Oh, fuck."

His hips lift to reach me better, and I take him into my mouth.

"Wait, Dixon." He tugs on my hair, and I lift my head enough to find his blurry face, his head still in my mouth. "I just—you know, there's typically a condom for this."

I release him. "You want me to stop?"

"No, no." He swallows. "I need you to know you don't have anything to worry about, okay?"

"Oh." I relax again and place another kiss atop his erection. "Well, ditto."

He starts to respond, but I take him in again, and a quiet groan escapes his lips. He takes a few deep breaths to speak again. "More pressure."

I tighten my lips around his erection and squeeze in tune with my mouth—

"Shit."

I pull back at the sudden change in his voice. "What?"

"Condom." Xander exhales loudly, and his tense abdomen relaxes. His voice is shaking, but the desire is all but gone. "I don't have a condom, and I don't imagine you do either."

Dammit.

I push up on my elbows. "Why would I have a condom in my mother's house?"

He sighs and shakes his head. "And why would I have one? We weren't even talking three hours ago."

The wall is cool when I lean against it, his legs still circling me. "Don't most men carry one in their wallets or something?"

Xander scoffs. "If you're an idiot. Everyone knows that renders it useless."

My body goes cold. I pull up my legs.

If I had known that, everything would've been different. If I had known, I could've insisted on a different condom. I could've used this knowledge to put an end to it, to leave. I wouldn't have gotten pregnant.

Xander sits up and presses a hand to my shoulder. "You alright?"

I nod silently.

"Come here." When he reaches for me, I let him pull me into his arms. He has to stretch to draw the sheets over us. "There are plenty of things we can do that don't involve penetration." He presses a kiss to my forehead. "Or we don't have to do anything at all." He's naked and erect, but his touch is gentle.

"I'm tired," I mumble into his chest.

He tucks my head under his chin, and our legs tangle together beneath the sheets. "Then go to sleep." One hand caresses my thick curls. The other keeps me tight in his arms.

I curl around him. Here, in his embrace, I'm safe. "Are you really going to stay the night?"

"Of course. Do you have any idea how long I've wanted to spent the night with you while you're naked?" His hand slides down and snaps the elastic hem of my underwear, halfway down my ass. "Well, almost naked."

I nuzzle my face into the crook of his neck. "You're ridiculous."

"Maybe, but you don't have to worry about a thing. I'm not going anywhere."

Twenty-Two

THE ROOM IS EMPTY.

I'm still wearing only my underwear, and my pillow smells like Xander. Last I was awake, he was in this bed, holding me.

Where did he go?

His clothes are gone from the floor, but mine are folded neatly on the foot of the bed, and my glasses sit on the nightstand—the only visible evidence he was here. The rest of the room is as vacant as I left it at the end of the summer; nothing here is mine anymore.

I tear off the sheets and scramble out of the bed to get dressed. Maybe he's downstairs. I poke my head through the curtains to check the driveway. The faded red car is parked on the pavement, where we left it. He's around here somewhere.

I yank on my jeans, then grab a new shirt from my bag.

Downstairs, the living room is empty. The bathrooms are all empty. The dining area is empty. But Imogene sits at the breakfast nook in the kitchen, eating a bowl of cereal.

She looks up at me when I burst into the room and beams. "Did you have a fun night?" Her voice is far more cheerful than any of the other times we've talked since my arrival.

I glance around, still hoping, but there's nowhere else he could hide. "Um, it was eventful." I move to the side door to catch a glimpse of the Powells' house.

He must've gone back.

"Quick question." She doesn't pause for a response. "Are you and Xander sleeping together? I thought you weren't talking."

Heat rises to my cheeks, and I stumble over my words as I turn around. "Of course not. He didn't—we didn't—I don't know what you're talking about."

Her snort is loud and abrasive. "Don't play coy, Billie. I caught him sneaking out of your room with his shirt half-buttoned twenty minutes ago."

I turn away. "We didn't…"

Why did he leave? Why didn't he wake me up first? Why didn't he say goodbye?

"I mean, he spent the night, but we didn't have, you know, sex."

She clucks her tongue. "That sucks."

I collapse onto the stool next to her, my chest wrenching with unspoken emotion. Because she's right, it does suck. But the suckiest part is that he's gone. He said he wouldn't go anywhere, but he's gone. "What am I supposed to do now?"

Imogene raises an eyebrow. "Why does that matter? I mean, if all he did was spend the night, how is this a big deal?"

I open my mouth but don't want to say it out loud. If I say it, it's admission that he's not the only one with feelings. It's a confession that I slept better last night than any night since I stopped drinking. If I say it, those kisses, those touches, that insatiable attraction—it all actually happened.

But maybe it was just another insane dream.

"My recommendation is, spend the next few days with him in your bedroom. It's not like Mom is here, and I can, I don't know, hang out with Jimmy or something. But you guys have a lot of shit to sort out." She pauses. "I've got a big pack of condoms you can have."

I blanch at the words. "That's not—that's not appropriate, Mo."

She laughs, then drains the milk from her bowl. "It wasn't supposed to be appropriate. The point would be for you to be inappropriate together. Maybe you'll finally defuse the tension between you—sexual and otherwise."

"That's not going to happen."

"You should reconsider." She rinses the bowl and spoon in the sink before loading them in the dishwasher. "What do you have to lose?"

More than I feel comfortable risking. Even when we argue or ignore each other, Xander remains one of my closest friends. He is the one person who simultaneously believes in my abilities and holds me accountable for my actions.

I rest my elbows on the counter and lay my head in my hands.

"Whatever you do," Imogene says, closing the dishwasher, "you better decide fast. Charlie and Thea asked us to join them for brunch since Mom and Rob are on their little vacation." She pauses, quiet. "You want help with your hair?"

I raise a hand to my hair. The auburn curls are twisted and knotted from our activity last night. "That would be nice."

Imogene smiles.

◆

Charlie Powell lets us into the house when we arrive. "You're a little early. The boys are up in Jimmy's room. They've been holed away in there all morning. We'll eat in twenty."

He gives us each a quick hug before sending us on our way, but Imogene runs into me when I freeze at the top landing of the stairs.

"What's the holdup?" She steps around me but pauses when she sees my face. "Don't be so paranoid, Billie. It'll be fine." She links her arm with mine and leads the way to Jimmy's bedroom, a bounce in her step.

The door is shut, and she raps her knuckles against the wood before twisting the knob. It doesn't turn.

It takes a moment for him to come unlock it, and Jimmy's pink face appears. "Hi." His smile is hesitant, but he pulls the door open the rest of the way.

Imogene barges in without hesitation, and I follow closely behind her, still being led by the arm. Jimmy hovers by the door behind us. On the edge of Jimmy's made bed, Xander sits up when we enter.

For a moment, we only stare, but then, his face breaks into a smile, and I can't do anything but smile back.

Imogene's lips move in my periphery, but he's still smiling and I can't look away. Finally, she nudges me in the arm. "Hey, we're going downstairs for drinks."

I nod and glance around.

Jimmy's out the door, having barely said a word, and Imogene follows him.

But Xander hesitates. "Hey, can we talk?"

I pause, suddenly uncertain, and turn back to him. My silence is my acquiescence, and he approaches from the bed and closes the door for privacy.

"We should talk about what happened last night." His voice is soft, quiet—it's unnerving. "I meant to stay and talk this morning, but Jimmy called. I needed to come back because he was having a crisis." He rolls his eyes. "But that's another story. I'm sure he'll tell you about it later. Anyway, we need to talk."

Nervous, I step back. "I don't know what to say."

He frowns, and for a moment, he doesn't say a thing. "We still need to talk about it. This is a big deal. We almost—"

I shake my head. "But we didn't. Maybe it would be better if we didn't."

His jaw tightens, his lips purse. "I understand if you need more time, but we cannot avoid this conversation."

"I'm not avoiding it."

"Yes, you are." He steps closer, less than a foot away. "You're shutting me out, and it's only going to make things worse."

"We need to be realistic."

He scoffs, looking away. "It's pretty realistic to discuss last night. We would've had sex if we had a condom. Don't you dare deny that."

"But we didn't," I say again, adamant. "If we had, this would be a different conversation."

Xander crosses his arms over his chest and glares. "Maybe

we should pretend we did. Maybe then you'd have this conversation." He shakes his head. "Why can't you admit you have feelings for me? Why do you have to make this more difficult than it needs to be?"

I take a deep breath, but I don't know where to begin.

Maybe the intense attraction that's been building for the past year. Maybe the way his smile or holding his hand can relax me. Maybe how distraught I was this morning when I realized he was gone.

"We should be on the same page." His voice is steady now, no evidence of agitation or distress. "But I'm not sure you've thought about it, have you? You haven't considered where our relationship is going. You haven't thought about why you're so attracted to me."

I stare down at my feet. The problem is, I think about how attractive he is too much—to the point where it's distracting. He drives me insane, and apparently, a little alcohol is all it takes for my desires to spew out.

But that's not what he's asking.

"There's nothing to think about." My voice is small. "I'm not attracted to you."

He laughs—and I would too in his position. The denial is so weak it isn't worth rebutting. But he offers an unimpressed smile. "Is that so?"

I nod, emphatic despite the obvious lie.

Xander's face breaks into a smile, and he steps closer. One hand clutches my waist, and with the other, he guides me to look him in the eyes. "Then I haven't thought about kissing you all morning."

Before I can consider speaking, his lips are on mine.

The kiss is slow but irresistible, and he walks me backward till I'm trapped against the wall. I hesitate, until he presses his body against mine. I am lost.

My arms wrap around him, and I open my mouth. Then, his hands are on me, running up and down my sides, squeezing and teasing. He grips my ass and lifts me into the air, my back still pressed against the cold wall, and I hook my legs around his waist.

We stumble to the bed. He collapses on the edge of the mattress, his arms tight around me. My legs spread across his lap, and his cock nudges me through the jeans. I break the kiss to gasp at the pressure, leaning my head back, and his hand squeezes my breast over the shirt. He trails kisses along my jaw and neck, and I roll my hips. His erection responds fervently.

"You know," he mumbles between kisses, "I do have a condom now."

"Thank God." I pull him into another kiss, then slide my hands down to untuck his dress shirt. My fingers spread across the hot skin underneath, touching his back, around the sides, along his abs. "We need it." I want him naked.

The tiny buttons are difficult when I'm in a hurry, but I tear the shirt off, and he releases me long enough to drop it to the bed. His hands return to me in an instant, tugging at the hem of my shirt, but I push him away.

His eyes widen when I pin him to the mattress, and his grip on my waist tightens as I drag my tongue down his bare chest. His breath quivers, then a quiet moan. I nip the skin along his ribs, relishing the sound, but I want more. I buck against him, eliciting another hoarse moan.

I fumble with his belt buckle, desperately trying to release the erection beneath, and he pushes my shirt out of the way to unclasp my bra.

The door squeaks.

"Oh, shit."

I leap off him and look toward the door, now open to reveal Jimmy, wide-eyed and staring.

Xander slams his head against the mattress. "You've got to be fucking kidding me."

I scoot back until I hit the dresser. "It's not what it looks like." I'm not sure my cheeks could be any redder.

For a moment, they both stare at me.

Then, Xander pulls his shirt back on. "What exactly does this look like?" He does up a couple buttons.

I don't know what to say.

Jimmy clears his throat. "Okay, should I pretend you weren't about to have sex on my bed? Is that what we're doing now?"

I adjust my shirt, and Xander pulls out a cigarette. "I'll see you down there." When he heads out the door, he's already lighting the cig.

I run a hand through my hair and lean against the dresser. That could've gone better.

"You should've locked the door." Jimmy leans against the door frame. "Or better yet, go next door and have sex in an empty house instead of one with my parents in it."

I shake my head. "Or we could not do it at all."

Jimmy cocks an eyebrow. "Why not?"

"We're friends." My throat aches, and I cough in an attempt to relax. I can't get emotional about this. "It's better if we stay friends."

"You can be friends and in a relationship. I'm pretty sure those are the better, healthier relationships."

"Who said anything about a relationship?"

Jimmy snorts. "I'd have thought that was a given. You're not still pretending you don't have feelings for him, are you? At least he's past denial. You have no idea how many months of nagging it took for him to admit how he feels about you." He laughs. "I spent all last year trying to get him to say something, especially with everything that happened with Za—you know. I hoped his jealousy would spur him to make a move."

I frown but decide not to broach the subject. "I'm not..." But the words escape me. I try again. "I'm not convinced it would be a good idea."

He sighs. "Please don't waste this opportunity, Billie. I know you're figuring a lot out, but don't miss something big because you're scared."

The dresser is hard against my head, but the pain is almost a comfort. "I'm not ready for this conversation."

"So when will you be ready?" He heaves a sigh. "You were about to have sex on my bed, but you're not ready to talk about it?"

I close my eyes. Logically, I know, it doesn't add up. "I need to control myself better."

"What happened last night?"

"He spent the night."

Jimmy chuckles. "I figured that out when he didn't come back."

"I kissed him. And we kind of...messed around, I guess."

"You guess?"

"But it got weird, and I panicked and said I was tired, and we sort of went to sleep, and we were cuddling and basically naked, but it was really awkward." I groan. "And then, he was gone when I woke up. He just left. He didn't say anything."

"That may have been my fault." He runs a hand through his messy brown hair and sends me a sheepish smile. "My timing sucks."

I try to smile, but it's obviously not convincing.

"Why can't you let it be and see where it leads? You don't have to keep everything organized in a pretty little box all the time. You don't have to make everything perfect."

I push away from the dresser, frowning.

How long would it take to figure that out? And what does that entail? Am I supposed to sleep with him until I sort out my feelings? That would be unfair to him. He's not looking for just sex.

"I don't know."

He starts toward the open door. "I was sent up here to tell you it's time to eat. Let's go downstairs. We're late."

I follow.

On the ground floor, I hesitate. Everyone else is in the kitchen for a laid-back brunch, but Xander's probably on the deck having his smoke.

Jimmy pauses a few feet ahead. "You okay?"

I cannot stop staring down the hallway toward the backyard. "I'll be in there in a minute."

"Sure."

Jimmy watches as I turn away.

As expected, Xander is leaning against the railing, staring at the Powells' expansive backyard, a half-smoked cigarette in one hand. He doesn't turn to look as I close the door, but his body stiffens.

211

"Hi."

He grunts as a greeting.

I lean against the railing next to him, facing the dark gray siding. "You're right."

He raises an eyebrow.

"I'm not sure what page I'm on. I'm still trying to sort everything out, and I'm not ready to talk yet. I don't know when I will be, but I can't have the conversation you want."

Xander takes another drag from the cigarette and surveys the yard again. "Yeah, I know."

I force a smile. "It was stupid to deny I'm attracted to you, but you deserve better than just attraction. Right now, that's all I can give you."

You deserve better than me.

He purses his lips around the cig, takes one last drag, then smashes it on the deck with his foot. "I don't understand how you can think so little of yourself."

I frown, uncertain how to respond, and look away when he turns to me.

"You know, it's kind of funny, but you have no idea how jealous I get when I see your drawings of other people." He quirks a smile. "I like to think that's something special you reserve for me. Stupid, I know. But then, I look more closely. You pour so much emotion, so much effort into them, and none of them more so than the portraits you do of me. I love being one of the few people who gets to see them—who gets to see your secret world. It's nice to know how implicitly you trust me."

I smile, but it's a reminder that I've barely drawn anything outside of class since befriending Dahlia. I certainly haven't shared anything with him in the last month.

"The point is, Dixon, you're not great with words or emotions. Your strengths lie elsewhere. So I understand you need more time, and that's fine, but I need you to know this."

I tilt my head. "What?"

"You're enough." He lays his hand over mine on the railing. "If you need to talk like last night, I'll listen. If you need someone to sit with in silence, I'm there. If you need a distraction, I can subject you to hours upon hours of *Pokémon*." He pauses when I laugh. "And no matter what you're thinking, no matter what anyone else says, no matter how much we're fighting or how long it's been since we've talked, you are enough."

Before I can stop myself, I twist toward him and pull his mouth to mine. The kiss is brief, but he holds me in his arms after our lips have parted and tucks my head under his chin. His shirt, still partially unbuttoned despite the cold, soaks up my tears.

"I will always care. Never doubt that."

For a moment, I cling to him, inhaling the cigarette smoke. "Can you help me with something?"

"What?"

I take in a deep breath. "Byrdie, my therapist, gave me a list of little experiments to try, and I was wondering if, um, I could go running with you."

There's a rumbling in his chest that feels remarkably like laughter, but the sound never leaves his mouth.

"After we get back," I add. "I want to see if it's something that might help."

Xander runs his hand up and down my back. "You can do anything you set your mind to, Dixon."

213

I burrow closer.

"It's definitely something we can try." He's still trying not to laugh. "Let's get back in there. Mrs. P's probably holding food for us, you know." When he pulls away, he takes my hand and leads me inside the house.

Twenty-Three

"DAMMIT!" JIMMY SLAMS HIS CONTROLLER ON THE COUCH beside him, jaw clenched, and turns to Imogene with a glare. "Stop doing that."

"What, winning?" Her laughter echoes through the Powells' family room. "It's not my fault I'm the only heavy class. You shouldn't pick someone completely useless."

The term "family room" is probably used too loosely, considering it's a small living space attached to the main living room. When we were little, this was Jimmy's play room, and that hasn't changed. But the toys transitioned from Slinkies and echo microphones to *Ocarina of Time* and, in this case, *Mario Kart*.

"Yoshi isn't useless."

"Then why have I won the last three races?"

Jimmy pushes himself into the corner of the couch, arms crossed. "Stop gloating about a video game. You're using your overpowered character to crush me on purpose."

Imogene laughs again. "If you didn't have a useless character, Bowser wouldn't defeat you so easily." She scoots closer and jabs him in the ribs. "Admit it—I'm better at this game than you."

215

On the floor beside me, Xander nudges me with his elbow and flashes a smile. "How long do you think they'll argue about *Mario Kart*? Because this is going to get annoying."

I chuckle. "'Going to'? It's already annoying."

He laughs too, then turns to the television and switches back to the disc menu. "I'm gonna grab a drink." He nods toward the kitchen and sets his controller on the coffee table. "You wanna join?"

When he stands, he offers me his hand, and I take it without hesitation. Jimmy and Imogene are still bickering about the game.

In the kitchen, Xander examines the fridge's contents with pursed lips, and I lean against the counter nearby, my elbows on the granite behind me. It's brighter during the daytime— the Powells have an enormous south-facing window above the sink—and the countertop sparkles in the sunlight.

"I didn't realize *Mario Kart* was such an antagonistic game."

Xander scratches the back of his head. "They're having fun. Weren't you?"

"I'm not as into the game as either of them." I tilt my head as he bends down for a better view of something. My view is an improvement too. "But I suppose that's why I'm in here, right?"

He casts a laugh over his shoulder. "Oh, you didn't come in here for my company?"

I smile. Of course I did. No matter how hard I try to deny myself this pleasure, I yearn for his company more than anything else. I want to be close to him.

Finally, he pulls out a pitcher of red liquid. "Have you heard from your mom yet?"

I frown at the subject change. "No, but she'd call Mo. They're supposed to get back tonight."

Xander approaches but pauses immediately in front of me. "Who were you texting earlier?" There's a tinge of... concern, maybe irritation, in his voice. He's staring, anxious for a response.

"I was trying to reach Dahlia, but she hasn't responded yet."

We haven't talked since I arrived in Missouri, and that's strange. We've been joined at the hip for the last two months, but she hasn't responded to a single text.

Xander's furrowed brow deepens. "She'll get back to you when she can." His words are tense. Is he worried? Or jealous?

"Yeah, she must be busy."

Then, he steps closer. "In the meantime, you're supposed to have fun with us. Am I not fun?"

"Oh, trust me, you're plenty of fun." I lay my hand on his shoulder, laughing. "Far too much fun."

Xander grins, and there's a distinct look on his face that says he wants to pull me into his arms and kiss me. Instead, he stretches over my shoulder and pulls a glass from the cabinet behind me. "That's good to hear."

I tighten my hand on his shoulder to draw his attention. "I'm glad I came back for New Year's, and I'm glad I spent that night with you."

There's that look again as he says, "I'm glad you're here too."

This time, he abandons the glass on the counter, placing

his hands on either side of me. I hold him by the shoulders, as if trying to keep him at bay, but it's an invitation more than anything else.

Our last kiss was two days ago, and Imogene has insisted we spend all our waking minutes here at the Powells' while Mom and Rob are away. There have been too many moments, too many almost-kisses, too many of those charming smiles—and way too many times I've wanted to throw that conversation out the window and escort him to my bedroom. He would've said yes every time.

He steps closer, pushing me against the counter, and I wrap my arms around his neck, drawing his face in, eager for his lips on mine, desperate for his hands to touch me.

Footsteps stomp into the room, and he pulls away before I can kiss him.

"Did Jimmy come in here? He ran off in the middle of our discussion."

Hovering in the doorway, Imogene is unfazed by what she walked in on. She mostly looks annoyed that we don't answer her right away.

I clear my throat. "Uh, no, he didn't come in here."

She purses her lips and turns around. "Fine."

Xander looks at me again, and I smile before slipping out of his grasp. "I should make sure he's okay, right?"

"Yeah." He grabs his empty glass from the counter and pours out the red drink with an unsteady hand.

Imogene comes back into the kitchen with a huff. "Are you two done making out yet?"

I frown. When we left them in the family room, she couldn't stop laughing—mostly at Jimmy's misfortune. What put her in such a foul mood so quickly?

"Did you bother looking upstairs?" Xander asks.

Mo shrugs. "I hadn't gotten to that yet. He's only been gone a minute, but he disappeared while we were talking, and it was weird."

I heave a sigh and head for the stairs. "I'll check. He probably went to his bedroom to grab something."

Jimmy's bedroom door is half open, and inside, he's curled up on the floor by his bed, plucking a few chords on his first guitar. He stops to read over the scribbled words in the notebook on the floor beside him, then repeats the chords, mumbling under his breath. In the shadow of his queen bed, his hunched form fidgets with each anxious strum.

He doesn't notice when I nudge the door open farther, and I lean against the frame. "What're you doing?"

He looks up, eyes wide, and pulls his notebook closer. "Nothing."

I cock my head to the side. The floor is uncomfortable when I join him, resting back against the bed frame, and reach for the notebook. He hesitates but allows me to take it. "What's this?"

His messy scrawl spreads across the page, tight and difficult to read. Short lines with a few longer ones interspersed. Only a few words stand out, but the message is clear. He doesn't have to say the name Cynthia for me to know it's about her.

"I've been writing a few songs," Jimmy says in a quiet voice.

I hand the lyrics back, and he holds the notebook to his chest. "You haven't written anything in five years."

"I know." He runs a hand through his hair. "I'm out of

219

practice, and it's awful, but practice is the only way to get better, right?"

I flit through the lyrics again in my head. "It's not awful, I promise. I just…I wish you could get over her."

For a few beats, Jimmy doesn't say anything. "I do too, but every time I think I'm past it, there she is, reminding me how big of an idiot I am."

"You're not an idiot." I nudge his arm. "I'm sorry I said those things at the party. It was totally uncalled for, and I was a jerk. I know you care about Cynthia, but I want you to find someone who cares about you as much as you do about them."

His grip tightens on the guitar neck, but then, he laughs. "Well, suffice it to say, we were both jerks that night. Alcohol does neither of us any favors."

"Yeah, but it shouldn't have taken me this long. At least you apologized the day after, in spite of an awful hangover."

Jimmy turns to me with a small smile, his freckled cheeks scrunching against his black frames. "Well, when we live together in May, I won't have to walk half a mile to apologize for being a drunken idiot."

I smile. "Are we seriously going to rent a house?"

He moves his guitar to the stand and sits up. "Depends on how intensely you and Xander continue flirting. If you keep this up, I won't be able to put up with living under the same roof as you two."

Heat rises to my cheeks.

"Trust me, Billie, I want you to be with someone who makes you happy too. I just wish you'd take a chance instead of worrying so much."

"Knock, knock." We turn to see Imogene rapping

her knuckles on the open door. "There you are. You disappeared."

"Uh, yeah." Jimmy closes his notebook and slides it into his nightstand drawer, a tinge of pink on his cheeks and ears. "Sorry."

He rises to his feet, and I follow.

"I talked to Mom." Mo leans against the door. "We can expect them home in a couple hours."

"Alright," I say.

She falls into step beside Jimmy when he exits the room, and I follow a few paces behind. "So," Imogene says, her voice upbeat as she punches him in the arm, "you'll have to deal with me kicking your ass for a little while longer."

Jimmy grimaces and rubs his arm, but when she beams, he smiles too.

Twenty-Four

The bell above the door chimes as we enter, and Mom and Imogene examine the small displays. They stop and smell the flowers, and I meander around the small shop.

Imogene dragged me out of bed this morning. Not that I'd been able to sleep. I woke at 5:30 and tossed and turned for an hour. I can't sleep anymore.

Rob fried empanadas and sprinkled them with sugar for breakfast, but it made my stomach queasy. I settled for the fruit he cut up to go with it. Afterward, Rob left for work, and my mother, Imogene, and I piled into her car.

The first stop was a shoe store for a pair of white kitten heels, where I sat on an open chair and waited while flipping through my phone. My mom asked my opinion once. After a shrug, she didn't ask again.

The second stop was so she could drop off the updated menu with the caterer, a local restaurant on the south side of town. Mo and I sat in the car while she ran in.

Our final stop before her dress fitting is this small flower shop a few blocks from the restaurant.

"Welcome, welcome!" Out from the back walks a tall thin woman with high cheekbones and black hair that falls down to the small of her back. Her face contorts into a small, unconvincing smile. "Is there anything I can help you find today?"

My mother steps forward, and they begin discussing options for the wedding before the shopkeeper leads them to a side room.

I lean on the edge of one of the shorter displays and unlock my phone. There are a couple texts from Dahlia. She finally got back to me this morning.

How's your trip? she asks. *You bored without me yet?*

I smile. *We're picking out our bouquets. It's incredibly interesting.*

I imagine her light-hearted giggle and the grin on her small lips, and her text comes in a second later. *Definitely bored without me. We want to do a big shindig when you get back. Don't make any plans for the first Friday after classes start.*

Footsteps echo on the concrete floor as the shopkeeper, my mother, and Imogene emerge from the adjoining room, talking animatedly. "Let me put in the order," the shopkeeper says. "One bridal bouquet, two bridesmaids, and one boutonnière?"

My mother nods, and I push my phone back into my pocket.

Imogene approaches with a frown. "Did you have fun in here by yourself?" She heaves a sigh. "I know you don't want to be here, but you could at least pretend for Mom's sake. This is important to her."

"Yeah, I noticed." I shrug. "I'm tired, that's all."

Her jaw is tense with irritation, but her voice is calm when she speaks. "You should've gone to bed sooner."

That's a lot easier said than done.

"I don't want to talk about this, Mo."

Mom and the shopkeeper are still talking, and Imogene steps closer, frustrated but keeping her voice low. "You never want to talk about anything. This is exactly why you need therapy."

I can't look at her.

I wasn't sure if she knew about the therapy. I've barely told anyone—Dad, of course, and Xander on New Year's Eve—and I didn't expect Mom to shout it from the rooftops either.

"I'll be outside."

She doesn't follow me.

◆

Springfield's bridal store is smaller than Burlington's, but the interior is the same. Mom chose her dress back in August, but she needs to go through several fittings before the big day.

The sales assistant, an older woman who introduced herself as Alicia, lets her into a dressing room and hangs the dress in its white bag on the hook inside. I sit on one of the viewing chairs while she changes, and Imogene reluctantly takes the seat next to mine.

Alicia waits outside the door while Mom slips into the gown. "Are you ready for me to zip you up?"

For a moment, silence. Then, Mom unlocks the door, and Alicia steps inside to help. After a minute of muffled voices, Alicia holds the door open for her.

I look at my phone again.

Beside me, Imogene stands, bubbling with emotion. "You look beautiful, Mom."

"Thank you, dear."

Finally, I look up.

The cream cloth wraps around her in a simple Bohemian style. Braided fabric forms the shoulder straps, and her dark blond hair falls behind her shoulders in soft waves. A bright smile spreads across her features as she admires herself in the mirror.

Alicia grabs a small veil and places it nimbly atop my mother's head to finish the look.

"What do you think, Billie?" Her eyes meet mine through the mirror.

I nod. "It'll be perfect for the wedding."

When I turn to the mirror directly to my left, I frown at my own reflection. The girl that stares back at me is small with stringy hair and bags under her eyes. She doesn't belong here.

The sales assistant motions over their seamstress, who leans close to my mother's waist to tighten the dress and measure how much fabric needs taken in.

Mom glances at me through the mirror again. "Have you found a date for the wedding, Billie? Your sister asked her boyfriend Colin to come."

I seek out Imogene, who grimaces.

Mom keeps talking: "I want to see you put yourself out there."

"Mom, I'm not looking for a boyfriend."

"I'm just asking you to take a chance on someone."

I frown at my hands. I've taken chances, and I have no interest in doing so again, even if Xander's smile is very convincing.

"Have you even considered asking Xander?" Mom's quiet voice carries through the empty store. "I'm sure he'd be happy to go. I almost invited him when we saw him on Christmas Eve."

I purse my lips and look toward the entrance. A young woman, determined and carrying a clipboard, enters the store, two friends behind her. They stop at the reception desk.

"Well, I'm glad you didn't. You don't need to secure a date for me. I probably won't bring anyone."

"Really, Billie."

I turn back and meet her disapproving eyes. She's turned around to face me now, and the seamstress is measuring the length of the skirt. "I don't know what you expect, Mom. I'm not dating. That should be enough for you."

Before she can respond, the seamstress stands to discuss their options before going off to calculate the cost. I pull out my phone again.

No new texts from Dahlia, even though I sent the last three. She's usually far more prompt than this.

"Now that she's found her 'one true love,' she can't stop forcing it down everyone else's throat." I look up as Imogene takes the chair beside me, her lips pulled taut in a line. "Colin and I broke up a month and a half ago, and she can't remember Ethan's name. It's not like it's difficult to pronounce."

I snort. "It's a common name."

Although, I imagine the difficulty comes from the fact that Imogene can't keep a boyfriend longer than two weeks.

"I asked Ethan—" she slumps against the wall "—but he

said no, so I don't have a date."

"Yeah, but how long are you going to date this guy?"

Imogene laughs. "Till I get bored."

I shake my head. "If you know it's going to fail, why bother?"

She sends me a tight, sad smile and links her arm with mine. "Because I'd rather try and fail than never try."

This isn't quite the turn I was expecting.

I thread our fingers together, but my eyes are on Mom, who's too busy having a quiet but heated discussion with the seamstress to pay any attention to us. "I'm glad I came back, Mo, but I'm ready to go home."

She squeezes my hand. "I know."

Twenty-Five

"How was your break, Billie?"

This time, it's watercolors. I've never worked with them, but I appreciate the focus and intent required. The way the paintbrush glides across the cardstock. The sheen of the water before it soaks in. But this sixteen-pigment tray was made for ten-year-olds.

The plastic yellow brush bangs against the side of the water cup—an old sour cream container—as I rinse it. "It was a bust."

Byrdie simply waits for me to explain.

"More shopping for the wedding. I don't know why I had to be there. I'm not good at girly things." I twirl the paintbrush in the deep purple and slide it across the cardstock—it doesn't have enough tooth for watercolor, but it's adequate for this purpose.

"Why do you think that is?"

I snort. "That would require me to have a guide. If you haven't guessed by now, my mom was far too busy getting drunk to teach me how to apply makeup—and it's not like she'd have any tips for my skin tone."

Byrdie nods. "How many of your friends are women?"

228

When I pause, the water and pigment pools on the paper where my brush is still touching. "What are we considering 'friends'?"

"However you define it. Everyone sees things a little differently."

I lift the brush off the paper, but a couple drops fall next to the small pool. "I don't have very many friends in the first place. Aside from, you know, relatives, there's Dahlia and…maybe Prudence. Both of those are new friendships, though."

Not that I've been a particularly good friend to Prudence.

"And before them?"

I shake my head. "No one."

"What about men?"

Jimmy. Xander. Brent. Am I close enough with Darius to count him? Probably not.

"Three or four. And I've been friends with Jimmy forever."

"Prior to this year, you've only had male friends?"

"Girls are harder to talk to, more complicated. You know where you stand with a guy." But as the words pass my lips, there's an awful taste in my mouth.

That may be true with Jimmy, but no one else has fit the criteria. I spend every day trying to figure out where I stand with Xander, and we've known each other for a year and a half. Brent shifts easily between acting cool and collected and being ridiculously over the top, and I'm never sure which version I'm talking to. Darius, silent most days—unless he's trying to wear a toga—is entirely closed off. How could I know?

And then, there's Zane.

He spent months wearing me down, and I was stupid enough to let him. Despite my efforts to remain unaffected by his advances, I put myself in the worst position. A small part of me may have realized what he was doing, but for the most part, I was oblivious. I definitely didn't know where I stood with him—especially when he tweaked parts of his story to counter my hesitation.

"Men are less emotional," I try again, but that doesn't sound right.

Between Jimmy's constant worrying and Xander's constant frustration with me, they're way more emotional than Dahlia.

Byrdie is silent for a moment. "Why do you think you have a hard time connecting with women?"

"I never had a woman to connect to before this year," I say after a pause. "My mom was never available and never cared, and Imogene was always busy—taking care of Mom, cheerleading, student government, her perfect popular friends."

"Were there other girls in your class?"

I shake my head and rinse the paintbrush again. "I've never been good at making friends, let alone keeping them. I think I stopped having female friends in middle school." That was also when popularity and who your parents were mattered more.

This time, I dip my brush into cerulean and sweep the brush along the paper's edge.

Byrdie lets me work, watching without comment or movement.

But when the brush is dry, I set it in the water for a minute and clasp my hands together. "I quit drinking."

"Hmm?"

"The handout you gave me. You said alcohol decreases your serotonin levels over time. I quit drinking."

He nods. "I didn't realize you drank, Billie."

"And Xander, he runs every morning. He said I could run with him. We're starting Monday."

"That sounds like a good idea. I'm glad to hear you're willing to try."

I shake my head. "It's a test," I remind him.

"Of course."

Not a full commitment.

◆

My apartment is empty when I get back. Nothing has been touched. Lacey and Camila haven't returned from their break, but Dahlia never left campus. I've been back for two days. She hasn't been around the apartment at all in that time.

I drop my keys and wallet in my bedroom before making a bowl of ramen.

As I lean against the counter while it cooks, the front door opens.

Dahlia's face breaks into a grin when she spots me. "You're here!" She drops her bag on the counter and pulls me into a hug. "I missed you."

In my arms, she is thin and frail and smells like vodka, but I missed her too.

At last, she pulls back to grab the bag she abandoned on the counter behind her. "I brought some wine to celebrate. I'm keeping you to myself. Brent and Dar will have to wait."

She brandishes a dark bottle aloft.

I give a one-shouldered shrug. "Alright, fine."

She twists off the cap. "Can you grab a couple cups?"

I grab one, then hesitate before pulling the second from the cupboard. "It's barely after four," I say, setting them down on the counter.

She laughs as she pours a generous helping into each, then places the bottle on the counter. "Do you suddenly care that it's four in the afternoon?" The burgundy liquid stains her lips when she takes a drink.

The microwave beeps.

The bowl is steaming when I pull it out, and I stir it to help it cool. "Maybe after I'm done eating." The pint-sized cup she poured for me is full to the top.

"Have it your way." She nods me into the living room, and I follow her with my ramen.

I join her on the couch. "Where have you been? I got back on Tuesday."

Dahlia offers a small aloof smile. "Yeah, sorry. I've been distracted the last few days. Stuff with Dar."

What sort of "stuff" with Darius would prevent her from being at our apartment? Is it the same reason she rarely texted me over break?

"How's planning for your mom's wedding going?" She doesn't bother hiding the derisive smile.

I twist my fork in the noodles and try to remain unaffected. "Tedious, as expected. She won't stop nagging me to find a date—as if a boyfriend will materialize because she wills it."

Dahlia laughs. "And let me guess, if you don't bring a date, you're going to be alone forever and no man will ever want you." She scoffs. "And if you try to bring a girlfriend home instead…well, why even come home anymore?"

I frown but carry on. If she wanted to talk about her own mother, she would. She wouldn't generalize like that.

"Since the divorce, my mother has always worked her world around whichever man she was sleeping with." I shrug. "Why would she expect anything different from me?"

But that's not true with Rob. He's part of her world more than she's part of his. None of the other men were in the house for more than a couple hours, if at all. They didn't spend the night. They didn't meet the kids. And they definitely weren't boyfriends.

"Dating is overrated." Dahlia leans back and laughs, but it's not happy. "It's impressive she got a man to commit at her age. It's hard enough to get a twenty-year-old to commit publicly. I can't imagine getting a guy to admit he's sleeping with me, let alone dating, when I'm old and ugly." She pauses, wincing, then takes another drink. "Not that your mom is…you know."

"Yeah."

She laughs. "I'm sorry, I'm reading way too much into this. Obviously, I have a pretty skewed view of mothers."

I shrug it off. "It's fine. I do too."

I finish my ramen and return the bowl to the kitchen, but she wants me to bring the bottle back with me.

For a moment, I stare at the cup she poured for me, still sitting on the counter. The wine inside is a deep red-violet, too thick to be translucent. There's no way to get around the topic now. No way to avoid the discussion.

I grab the cup and bottle and return to the living room, where Dahlia's draining her drink. She motions me over, and I take my seat again, leaving my own cup on the coffee table in front of us. She shoves her cup toward me, and I pour her more, then dump in the whole bottle because she purses her lips when I only fill it halfway.

"Have some." She's already lifting her cup to her lips.

I take a small sip. It's dry, bitter, heavy—more so because I haven't had anything to drink since the last time I saw Dahlia two weeks ago.

"Okay!" She turns to me, her voice overwrought with excitement. Her upper lip is red from the wine. "Classes start Monday, and we're getting together next Friday for a little party. Nothing big, just us, but you need to be prepared to get sloshed." She giggles.

I return the full glass to the coffee table, and she keeps talking, unaware.

Twenty-Six

I meet Xander at his apartment Monday morning at six a.m., as promised.

He answers the door with a tight smile. "Took you long enough, Dixon." He's wearing a stretchy, gray v-neck and tight, black pants with a red stripe down each side.

For a moment, I can only stare at him.

When he woke me up that time, I was too hungover to notice what he was wearing, but now I can't stop. God, this is going to be hard. You can see pretty much everything.

"Are you coming in?"

I scurry inside the apartment. "Sorry."

"I'm having a snack." He heads for the small kitchen. "You should eat something before we go out there."

I'm too busy watching him walk to speak. This was a terrible idea.

His snack is half eaten on a plate in the kitchen, and he looks up at me between bites. "Is that what you're wearing?" He casts a skeptical glance over my form.

I look down at my t-shirt, jeans, and Converse. "I brought something. Can I change here?"

Xander nods toward the hallway. "Go ahead. You'll want

to shower when we're done. You're welcome to do that here."

It wouldn't be the first time I've showered in their apartment.

I lock his bedroom door behind me before changing. All I own in the way of exercise clothing is basically pajama pants, and I switch to a sports bra and a t-shirt I don't care about. I look ridiculous.

In the living room, he's tying his sneakers.

"Sorry."

He looks up with a cocked eyebrow.

"I guess I don't really know what I'm doing."

He laughs. "There's nothing to be sorry about. You ready, Dixon?"

"Yeah, I guess."

He leads the way out the door, and I follow silently.

◆

Xander is confident and determined in his movements, but I trail behind him. He slows to let me catch up.

After what seems like an eternity, I slump on a bench along St. Clare's only park and drop my head in my hands. "Oh, God, I hurt everywhere. My feet hurt. I think I pulled a muscle—or twelve. And why are my legs numb and itchy?"

Xander plops down next to me. He doesn't bother to hold back his laughter. "When your blood vessels expand, it stimulates your nerves, and your brain interprets it as itchiness." He shrugs. "It goes away when you exercise on a regular basis. You're out of shape, Dixon."

"Yeah, well, I never realized how drastically out of shape I am until this moment." I wipe another layer of sweat from my forehead. "This is gross."

But he's barely broken a sweat.

"I ruined your workout, didn't I?" I glance around the park, but I've only seen it from the interior of his car before.

Up close, it is a long strip of land, located a few blocks from downtown, with a long trail running through it and lots of trees. A small gazebo sits on the edge of a pond at one end—I can only see it because winter means the trees are bare—and a few benches line the brick trail.

We aren't in the park, though. A ten-foot-high, wrought-iron barrier separates the greenspace from the rest of town, with a large open gate at each end.

"How far have we gone? We've been doing this forever."

Xander shakes his head. "We've done a little over a mile in twenty minutes."

"That's horrible."

He nods, but he's smiling. "I usually get back right about now."

"How far do you go?"

"Three miles minimum every morning."

I snort. "Oh, fuck that. That's not happening."

He bursts into laughter and tugs on my sleeve as he stands. "Come on, Dixon, let's get some food in you."

Despite a severe lack of appetite, I follow him. "I'm really not hungry."

He doesn't bother looking at me. "I don't care how hungry you are. You're eating something." He pauses to let me catch up, and we walk side by side. "Part of the reason you took so long is because you don't eat. You don't have enough glycogen stored to have the energy to run. You should've had a snack when I offered."

"I wasn't hungry."

"Yeah, well, if you want to exercise, you need to eat. You used up all your energy in twenty minutes. How do you intend to get through the rest of the day like that? You need to eat." He shoots a quick glare my way. "You can't run with me if you don't eat."

I frown at the sidewalk. "Fine."

"Good." A victorious smirk spreads across his face. "A high-carb snack before the run, and a half-protein, half-carb breakfast afterward. That's the deal."

I let out a low growl but nod my assent.

"A couple other things." Xander tugs on my arm, and I look at him again. "Your feet will hurt a lot less if you have shoes with arch support, and tight, light-weight clothes mean less chafing, less baggage, more general comfort."

"You're making me go shopping so I can exercise?" I heave a sigh. "Are you sure you don't want me to wear tight clothes so you can check me out?"

He laughs. "Like you weren't checking me out earlier?" When I don't respond, he says, "An added benefit."

I come to a stop, rubbing the sweat from my brow. "Oh, who am I kidding? This isn't going to work. I'm terrible at it."

Xander stops a few feet ahead. "Yeah, you're pretty awful." It takes no time for him to cross the distance between us, and when he lays his hands on my shoulders, I look up to find him smiling. "But it's cute to watch you try so hard."

I roll my eyes. "Don't be so condescending."

He leans down. "Think of it this way, you can only get better. I bet we can cut five minutes off that time by having you eat something."

I snort. "You have too much faith in me."

"Well, somebody's got to. You don't have any faith in yourself." He pushes a stray hair behind my ear, and I lean into his touch, shutting my eyes. His hand stays close. "Is this part of your therapy?"

"Kind of."

"Part your idea?" His voice is deep, husky, closer than before.

"The list Byrdie gave me has a bunch of things he thought might help. This was one of the higher options on the list. Endorphins are natural antidepressants, apparently, and there's the added benefit of increased levels of vitamin D since we're outside."

"You know…" He pulls his hand away, and I open my eyes. "Running isn't the only thing to release endorphins." He's smirking.

I laugh. "Are you seriously trying to sell us having sex like that? You want me to go to bed with you to boost my mood?"

The smirk doesn't leave his face. "I'm willing to help out with whatever you need."

"How generous of you."

"I know." He grins and steps away, heading down the sidewalk again. "Also," he calls over his shoulder.

I rush to catch up.

"Studies have shown that seminal fluid is rich in oxytocin, serotonin, and endorphins—all things that boost your mood."

"You really want me to give you a blowjob, don't you?"

"You can't argue with facts."

I laugh and shove my elbow in his direction, but he's too

fast. He sidesteps and catches me when I stagger, my hands trapped against his chest. We stumble to a halt.

"Facts?" I couldn't move from his grasp if I wanted to. "Do you memorize these 'facts' to get women in your bed?" I don't want to.

Xander laughs, and his grip tightens around me. "Most women are more interested in what goes on in my bed than using our little rendezvous to improve their mental health. Most of them aren't interested in facts." He smiles. "You're different."

If I weren't already pink from exertion, I'm red now. "I do like facts."

"A little too much." His lips look soft and warm. They're mesmerizing. "But I wouldn't want you any other way."

My fingers play with the neckline of his shirt, and my body presses closer to him. I want nothing more than to kiss him right now.

But he smiles and releases me. "Come on, Dixon, we should get back."

Right, back to the apartment.

I swallow down my feelings to calm the aching in my chest and trail behind him.

◆

"Is Jimmy here?"

"It's not even seven yet. He doesn't get up for another hour—or longer." Xander pushes open the door and steps inside. "His class is at 9:30 today, but he's got that test later, so he could be cramming."

Before I'm even inside the apartment, he tears off his

shirt and drops it on the couch. I stumble to a stop as he flips on the kitchen light. His lean muscles glisten with sweat under the soft glow of the incandescents.

But I force myself to move, shutting the door and joining him in the kitchen. While he rummages through the fridge, I use the nearest counter for support. "What do you do now?"

Xander pulls out a loaf of whole wheat bread. "Breakfast, a shower, and homework before classes. I usually set up in my room." He throws a couple slices in the toaster and shoves the loaf back in the fridge. "This is a lot nicer than last year—not having to worry about waking him up. I spent the first two months tiptoeing around till I realized he could sleep through a train wreck."

I laugh. "How'd you figure that out?"

When the toast pops, he grabs it from the toaster and smears on a layer of peanut butter. "That's a long story." He laughs. "Suffice to say, there was blood and cussing on my part, and snoring on his." He slides a slice to me and shoves the other between his teeth as he screws the lid on the peanut butter jar.

I take a small bite. "Something tells me this is a meager breakfast."

He chuckles through his toast and pushes the jar against the wall. "Wait for it," he says after taking a bite and snatching the slice from his mouth. There's peanut butter and crumbs on his lips when he smiles at me.

I clutch the counter. My legs still feel like jelly.

He takes another bite and sets his toast on the counter before moving to the blender. "Smoothie?"

I eat my toast and watch as he pulls together an assortment of ingredients: a bag of frozen berries, a banana, plain Greek yogurt, some ice. The whirring blender, though mind-numbingly loud this early in the morning, isn't enough to wake Jimmy all the way in his bedroom. The twelve-ounce glass he passes me a moment later is full.

I eye the glass suspiciously. "Not sure I can drink this much."

Xander laughs as he pours the rest in his own glass, then he takes a sip and moves toward the sink. While he rinses and takes apart the blender for a run in the dishwasher, I finish my toast. He bends over to organize things in the dishwasher, and I release a little sigh—I clear my throat and take another drink to cover up my sound.

"You say something?" He glances back and smiles.

I swallow down more smoothie and wipe my mouth with the back of my hand. "You constantly surprise me."

He closes the dishwasher, but he's not done cleaning up. "Why?" He piles the smoothie ingredients inside the fridge and freezer.

"Because," I say, pausing to add a short laugh, "you got drunk every weekend last semester. And now... I never realized how much you care about your body—I mean, of course you do, just look at it, but um, that's not what I mean."

When he closes the fridge, there's a little smirk playing on his lips. "Well, what do you mean?"

I turn away to hide my hot face. "You care about how healthy you are. I didn't expect that."

He shrugs. "Why wouldn't I? I'm twenty years old—this thing's supposed to last."

I cock my head to the side. "How do you excuse the

drinking and the smoking?"

A heavy frown spreads across his face. "I never smoked much in high school because of soccer, but it increased a lot when I came here. Over the summer, when I started working out again, I realized I had to cut back if I wanted to run more than a block." He grabs his drink from the counter but pauses. "And of all the people employed at Draft Horse, I gotta tell you, I drink the least."

I watch as he gulps down half his smoothie. It is a strange thing. Freshman year, he smoked multiple cigarettes a day and downed alcohol the way he's downing that smoothie now. This year is the complete opposite.

"It's nice to see how much you care."

He licks the remnants off his lips as he sets down the glass. A tiny smirk plays at the edge of his mouth, and I'm continually impressed by how easily he shifts from quiet introspection to cracking jokes. "It's nice to hear you admit how much you look."

Heat rises to my cheeks again, and I finish my smoothie despite how full my stomach is.

Xander laughs while rinsing out his own glass, and when he's done, he brushes past me to go down the hall. When did he finish eating? His food's gone. I was too busy checking him out to notice.

"You wanna shower first or should I go?" he calls over his shoulder.

I'm not sure I need more incentive to think about him naked.

"Either way's fine," I say in a small voice.

He pushes his bedroom door open, but by the time I start down the hallway, he's walking out in only his boxers,

243

I stumble to a stop.

He pauses at the bathroom doorway, opposite Jimmy's closed door. "I'll be quick."

I sit on the edge of the couch to wait.

I told him I needed more time, dammit. That means I can't stare at him for an hour straight, no matter how half-naked or sweaty he is.

The bathroom door opens a few minutes later, and he exits with a loose towel wrapped around his waist. His hair, damp, is pushed out of his face, and he hasn't finished drying off. The towel barely covers the top of his ass.

Oh, fuck.

I lock the bathroom door as soon as I'm inside. The water's hot when I turn it on, and I tear off my clothes and jump in.

While he may have only needed a rinse-off, I'll need a lifetime supply of water to wash away everything that's dirty.

God, does he have to be such a smug bastard about it? I don't ogle him on purpose.

The hot water streams down my body, and I glide my hand over my cold flesh. My afro, still up in the high ponytail, presses against the cold tiles as I lean back, and I slip a finger between my folds. My fingers seek out my clit, using my own lube to rub the bundle of nerves. I am wet from thinking about him.

Only a couple weeks have passed since New Year's Eve, and everything is still vivid. His soft lips against mine, his reverent hands as they explored my body, his taste, his smell, his desire for me.

I can mimic his hands, moving one to massage my breast,

but I can't mimic his mouth on mine. More than anything, I want to kiss him, to hold him.

I need to buy a vibrator.

When I turn off the water, it takes a moment to gather myself together and find the towel he pulled out for me, sitting on the counter. But I was in such a hurry I forgot to grab my clothes.

Shit.

Inside his bedroom, Xander's hunched over one of his textbooks, mechanical pencil between his fingers, wearing nothing more than a pair of boxers. His towel is spread across his bed, as he was unable to hang it while I was using the shower. He doesn't look up when I walk into the room, despite the fact that I'm only wearing a towel. I kneel next to my bag and rifle through the contents.

"That took a while."

I stop and barely manage to stutter out a response: "Um, yeah, I just, you know, have a lot of…hair."

He snorts and writes something in his notebook.

He fucking knows, doesn't he?

I hug my clothes to my chest and head for the bathroom again.

"You know," he says when I reach the door. I pause, my hand on the frame, but he doesn't look up from his textbook. "You can get dressed in here. I promise I won't look. Too much."

I shake my head. "I'll be back."

He laughs as I rush to the bathroom.

Fully clothed, I sit atop the toilet lid, the towel hanging from my neck. I have to shake off any remaining thoughts about the half-naked man in the next room over and how he must have figured out why my shower took so long.

But the only thought that crosses my mind is: After knowing him for a year and a half, I finally learned when he does his homework.

Twenty-Seven

PRUDENCE TAKES THE SEAT BESIDE ME AND FLASHES A SMILE. "Okay, so super short notice." She places her hands on her knees. "Please tell me you don't have plans for lunch."

I glance around the painting classroom as the students pack up their things and file out of the room. Felix teaches Painting I in addition to my drawing class last semester, and the new studio is only a couple doors down from previous semester's. Most of the studios in the Kelley Center are exact replicas too, so the only real difference is, we have huge metal easels and rolling carts for our supplies instead of the wooden drawing horses and cubby wall.

Felix grabs the remaining syllabuses and his phone off the window sill and heads for the door. The first lesson is always the shortest.

"Not exactly."

Prudence forces a smile and shoulders her backpack. She is one of the few people from Drawing who's taking Painting as well. "That's fine. I'll see you next class, then." She passes me, heading for the door.

Dammit. She thinks I'm blowing her off again.

"Wait." I rush to catch up. "I'm sorry. I'm not avoiding

247

you. I have some errands I need to run, and I left my bike at my apartment this morning. I don't have time to eat lunch."

Prudence stops just inside the door, an almost-smile on her lips. "What errands?"

I pull my backpack over both shoulders and hold the straps. "I have to go shopping for exercise clothes and athletic sneakers." My Converse, after all, have no arch support.

Prue snickers. "Since when do you exercise?"

I send her a sheepish smile. "This morning."

She cocks an eyebrow.

"I'm not sure I'd call it exercise. It was more a thrashing and flailing attempt than anything else." I clear my throat as her face breaks into a grin. "Did you know Xander runs every morning?"

"Even during the winter?"

Everyone else is gone now, and Prudence follows me down the hallway, matching her pace to mine.

I snort. "He doesn't even complain about how cold it is. So now I have to go buy some before we run again tomorrow morning."

Prudence stops halfway down the hall, and I pause. "Wait, you're exercising with Xander?" Her eyebrows shoot up to her brown bangs. "Weren't you two fighting?"

I flush. "We made up. Well, something like that."

"There you are!"

I spin round.

Dahlia, a grin on her heart-shaped face, leans against the wall by the elevator. "Are you coming or not? It's lunch time."

Since returning to Bradford, my time alone with Dahlia has been limited, aside from that first time with the ramen and the wine. Lunch after Drawing used to be the norm, but we don't have the same class anymore—hers is an art history class on the first floor. She doesn't know about the therapy, let alone running with Xander.

"Uh, I can't today. I have errands."

Prudence turns her full attention to me. "Do you want some help? I could drive you. It'd save time."

I pause, considering, and when she offers a small smile, I say, "Sure."

Her smile widens. "I'm parked in the lot below. I had to drop off a package, so I drove over here this morning."

Dahlia steps away from the wall, joining us in the middle of the hallway. "I'm coming with you guys."

Prue hesitates, then smiles. "Sure."

My enthusiasm is tainted by the tenacious look on Dahlia's face.

◆

"What about these?"

Prudence flips through one of the nearby racks, searching through exercise pants, and I frown as I look around the area. Most of the athletic wear for women are yoga-style clothes. Would those work for this purpose?

A few feet away, Dahlia half-heartedly moves hangers along a rack, skimming over the options.

The pair Prue shows me is a dark gray with long legs and a thick band around the waist. "You think those will fit me? They're tiny."

Prue laughs. "You're tiny. Besides, they're supposed to be tight. It helps with friction and stuff."

I pull the hanger from her hands and look at them. "That's what Xander said."

Dahlia examines them over my shoulder. "When did you start working out? And why in the world are you working out with him?"

Prudence grabs a couple other options, and we head for the dressing rooms.

"I'm trying to be a little healthier, I guess."

Prudence shoves the other hangers in my hands and pushes me toward the nearest dressing room.

"But with Xander?" Dahlia asks.

When the door closes behind me, I peel off my clothes to try the pants and shirts Prudence picked out. The material stretches and contorts as I slide it over my skin.

Outside, Prudence laughs. "It's a lot of effort to give yourself blue ladyballs, but I'm glad you're trying something new."

I snort at her phrasing, but even in this confined space, the heat rises to my cheeks at the memory of this morning. "I'm not doing it so I can ogle him."

Most people see Xander's aloof attitude and cool demeanor, the way he suavely holds himself in their company, the ease with which he bounces from person to person and conversation to conversation, and of course, his fit body…but they miss everything else. They don't see the kindness, the intense loyalty, or his efforts to rein me in and calm me down when I'm overreacting. They don't realize his ridiculous jokes and snarky smirks are a front, an excuse to remain enigmatic, but also an opportunity to defuse tense situations.

They're attracted to the persona he displays for the world,

but that's not remotely the most attractive thing about him.

Outside the dressing room, Prudence says, "Right, that's an extra benefit." She pauses. "Speaking of benefits, I've been dying to ask. When did you two have sex?"

I pause halfway through pulling on a shirt, then tug it down the rest of the way and step out of the room to show them.

"It looks good," she says as I spin around, and beside her, leaning against the wall nonchalantly, Dahlia nods.

"I'm gonna try on another pair. I should have more than one, right?"

I return to the dressing room and change into a different pair, and outside, Prudence continues her interrogation.

"I know it's none of my business, so you don't have to say anything you don't want to. I just—I'm confused, you know? Like, did you know Connor and Blayne encouraged everyone in our hall to make bets on when you'd sleep together?"

I frown. Connor and Blayne lived in the room next to Jimmy and Xander in our freshmen dorm building, and the four of them shared a bathroom. They were incredibly quiet. I can't imagine them starting a betting pool.

"No." My voice is so quiet I'm not sure they can hear me. "I didn't know." I check myself in the mirror as I pull on a new pair of athletic pants. "Did Val?"

Prue laughs but stifles the sound; her voice is quiet and sad when she speaks. "She was never as oblivious as you."

At least she doesn't know it happened.

"It was January," I say as I open the door again. "It's Monday, right? So in three days it'll have been a year."

This time, Prudence does laugh. "You remember the

251

exact time and date it happened?"

I shrug. "Jimmy had a night class on Thursdays that semester, so it was the first Thursday of the semester. It's not that difficult to remember."

To be fair, I remember everything about that night.

Leaning against the wall, Dahlia looks uninterested, but she still asks, "Why?"

I turn to her, skeptical. "Why what?"

"Why'd you sleep with him?"

I grip the door and consider it. There were a number of reasons, most involving my own insecurities and short-comings, things I didn't want to deal with, and somehow, doing that would make it better. Obviously, I was wrong in that assessment.

But maybe, just maybe, there was already something there. Or more likely, I'm retroactively projecting his appeal.

"I wanted to have sex, and he was willing."

"Yeah, I'd say," Prue adds. She has to hold back a laugh. "How do these look?"

They examine the new pants.

"They look a little long," Dahlia says.

I frown at the loose material around my ankles. "I'm five-six."

"It's the cut," Prudence adds. "Maybe stick with the skinny ones. They'll be better for the friction anyway."

I try on the last pair of pants and show them off, but the general consensus is to get a couple pairs of the first option. When I'm done, we return to the racks to grab a couple extra pairs before heading to the register.

"Out of curiosity," I say as we get in line, "who won the bet? Or, I guess, who would've won if everyone had found out last year? If you remember."

Prudence considers for a moment. "If I recall correctly, David guessed January 31, so probably him."

I snort. "Our RA was in on it? You've got to be joking."

She turns to me with a laugh, and behind us, Dahlia grabs a drink from the aisle fridge.

Twenty-Eight

THE RUN IS DECIDEDLY EASIER WITH ACTUAL RUNNING sneakers, but I still have to pause fifteen minutes in to catch my breath.

He stops not far from me, jogging in place, and watches as I lean over, my hands clutching my knees.

"Sorry, gimme a minute..."

"Take your time. This is only day four." He comes back to me and slows to a stop. "Let's keep going. We don't want to lose momentum. We can walk." He holds my hand and leads the way.

I tighten my grip on his warm hand. My thin fingers are still frozen.

"Have you decided yet?" he asks.

"Decided what?"

"If you like running."

I let out a short laugh but quickly regret releasing most of my air. My chest is constricted, tight, desperately seeking oxygen. "I feel like that's a trick question. It's awful and I hate it and it's hard to get out of bed for this, but I can't help enjoying this."

Although, to be fair, I can't decide whether "this" is the

running or holding his hand.

Xander nods.

I don't often wander off campus. The coffee shop and Walmart are the only places I go, but little St. Clare remains eerily silent on these morning runs. Perhaps because it's January and still cold, or perhaps because the town is always quiet at 6:30 in the morning.

After a moment, Xander says, "What about when it gets hot?"

I glance at him, brow furrowed. "Huh?"

He shrugs. "If you're going to keep doing this, did you get clothes for warmer weather? Or will this little experiment end in a month or two?"

I look down at my pants and long-sleeve shirt. "I didn't think that far ahead."

"I was just curious," he says in a sly voice.

I roll my eyes. "You just want me to wear those stupid little short-shorts, don't you?"

He grins. "To be fair, half your pajamas are those 'stupid little short-shorts.'"

"I don't wear those in public, do I?"

"No, but I get to fantasize about your ass no matter where we are."

My face is instantly on fire. "That's incredibly inappropriate."

A cloud of fog billows out when he laughs. "Then here's something else to think about: Come May, if we do rent a house together, the amount of time I spend fantasizing about your ass will dramatically increase."

I squeeze his hand as a warning, but he rubs his thumb along my knuckles affectionately. "That's if we get a house to rent. I have to save up money since I can't get an off-campus job before my study abroad, and Jimmy will need to find a job off campus too."

Xander shrugs, but there's an uneasy edge to his voice. "Well, even if you two go back to Missouri, I'm not leaving St. Clare for the summer. I'll get my own apartment or live in my car if I have to. I'm not going back there."

I tighten my hand around his. "You won't have to."

He doesn't say anything, but his grip is firmer and there's a small smile on his face.

"Let's go." I tug my hand away and break into a run so he has to catch up.

◆

The apartment is bright when we get back, and Jimmy is eating a bowl of cereal and working on his laptop at the kitchen table. A big stack of papers and a couple magazines spread across the surface, but the space immediately surrounding him is empty.

I sit beside him and peek over his shoulder to see what he's looking at. It's the housing section for St. Clare on Craigslist. "The semester isn't over for four months. What're you looking on there for?"

He sends me a small smile before returning to the browser. "We need to keep a lookout for a quality place, though."

Xander heads for the kitchen. "You sleep alright?"

With a shrug, Jimmy says, "I was up late writing. Doesn't matter how hard I try, I cannot get...this out of my head."

Xander, a scowl on his face, puts together a quick breakfast for us.

On the screen, Jimmy flips from listing to listing, searching for three-bedroom houses in a reasonable price range. This small town doesn't have many options. The ten tabs of rentals quickly diminish to three, and he shows me a two-story cottage, pointing out the location. Only a couple blocks from downtown. The white porch looks like a new addition.

When he accidentally clicks to a different window—a word processor—he quickly switches back to the internet.

"Are those your lyrics?"

He switches back and closes it before I can see anything other than a line about blond hair and bright eyes.

"Have you talked to her since the party?"

For a moment, he won't look at me. "The party?"

I frown. Not a night I want to bring up in more detail. I assumed the question was self-explanatory.

"Oh, right." He shakes his head. "No, but we have a class together this semester. Gen ed shit, but still."

Between Jimmy's Music major and Cynthia's focus on biology and medicine, gen ed is the only way they'll have a class together.

Oddly, though, he doesn't sound thrilled.

When Xander brings me a plate, I push away the papers on the table, but they barely budge. "What is all this shit?" I set the plate on the nearest page so I don't have to hold it.

"Ask the asshat." Jimmy simply shrugs.

Xander joins us, sans food, and piles together the pages. "Research."

I cock an eyebrow, and he lays the freshly organized pile to the side and retrieves his own plate. "Research for what?"

I grab the couple papers he neglected from beneath my plate.

The top page is a faint sketch of a dragon, but he snatches it from my hand before I can look too closely.

He shrugs. "I can't decide what to get."

"For what?"

I pause mid-bite when he releases a loud bark of laughter. "I'm twenty years old, and I don't have a tattoo yet. Obviously, this needs rectified."

"Obviously." I glance at the stack again. They're too far away to decipher anything. "How much research does that require? Why don't you get 'Rory and Jess Forever' on your chest and be done with it?"

Xander gives me a light push on my arm. "I'm pretty sure you're supposed to put more thought into something so permanent."

"I've never thought about it."

He finishes his food quickly and glances down the hall before returning his attention to me. "You going to take a rinse-off?"

"Yeah."

He eyes my half-eaten food. "Apparently, I have to wait for you. I can't trust you to eat all that without my constant prodding."

I huff but force myself to finish, and victorious, he takes our plates to the kitchen before heading to the bathroom for his shower.

I slump my head on the table and listen as the water starts in the bathroom. It takes deliberate effort not to picture him stripping in there. I spend too much time thinking about him naked.

My hand reaches across the table to grab the topmost papers on his stack, and I examine the sketches.

"How much time are you going to need?" Jimmy asks in a quiet voice.

I sit up again to look at him. His bowl of cereal is empty, and he studies the screen. Did he say that? Or am I imagining things?

"What?"

"You said you needed more time, right?"

My face falls. For once, they have been talking about me. "Yeah."

"So how much do you need?" Finally, he looks down the hallway after Xander, then turns to me. "How long are you going to make him wait?"

I study the sketch again. "It's not that simple."

"This is killing him, but it's you and you're special, so he's going to keep doing it long past the point where it becomes unhealthy. You're supposed to care about him. Don't you?"

I open my mouth, uncertain. I want to tell him he's being ridiculous and melodramatic. To release a biting remark about his own "unhealthy" romantic ambitions.

But I'm silenced by the shower shutting off.

When Xander opens the door a minute later, Jimmy continues in an amiable voice: "What're you doing tomorrow night? I don't work, and Xander's shift is earlier than normal."

Uneasy, I answer in a shaky voice. "I can't. I'm hanging out with Dahlia."

He may have moved on, but there's still a sickness in the pit of my stomach.

Twenty-Nine

My phone vibrates again. I glance over as Xander's name flashes across the screen before it fades to black.

If I were anywhere else, I'd open it and reply within seconds. We've been texting constantly—he jokingly insists we need unbroken communication to make sure I'm eating enough for our morning runs—and I admit, there's a bolt of excitement every time I see his name and silly picture light up my phone.

But I don't want to draw attention to it—to him—while I'm here.

"Wait a minute." Darius leans forward in his typical armchair. "Are you actually studying? That's lame, Billie. You can study later."

I strike a smile but pull my French book closer. If I get behind this semester, I could be disqualified from the Honors Program or study abroad. "Two birds with one stone." Or worst of all, I could lose my scholarship. If I lose that, study abroad and Honors don't even matter.

In the kitchen, Brent's voice is nonchalant. "I don't care how many birds you murder, but you do need to talk to us, not just pretend you're here."

The frown spreads across my face, but I try to hide it with my hair. I'm not pretending to be here—I'm physically here.

Dahlia, who has been helping Brent with the drinks, plops down on the couch beside me. "Seriously, Billie, I need you to pay attention to me." She holds a bubbling, bright green cocktail.

"This is important," I say, imploring her to understand. "I can't afford to let my grades slip this semester."

Beside me, Dahlia takes a sip and swishes the liquid around in her mouth, considering. "It's barely the start of the semester, Billie. I like that you care so much about school, but you can slack off a little bit instead of being completely anal." She takes a long drink, and Brent comes into the living room with a couple cups.

He hands Darius his, then sets one down beside my textbook. The liquid sloshes in the cup. "Vodka and Mountain Dew. Your studying will go a lot faster once you've got a little alcohol in your system."

Through the translucent red cup, the drink looks a dirty brown. After the liquid settles, the only surface disturbance is the rising carbonation bubbles.

My phone vibrates again, and I slide it toward me before Dahlia gets too curious.

Xander again.

Jim claims he's found the perfect house. He does realize this is almost four months out, right?

Then, the second message: *Now the idiot's sent the land-lady an email.*

Hey, I type back, *if she posted an ad, she's literally asking people to contact her about the house.*

261

I almost power off the screen but pause. His response is prompt—he's off work tonight for once.

The ad did say she's looking for tenants starting in May. The current tenants are seniors. So that's doable.

Location?

His next text is the address, and I pull it up in my navigation app. The house is on Sandalwood, a small street that runs primarily through downtown St. Clare. This means it's only four blocks away from Draft Horse—Xander wouldn't have to drive to work—but it's a decent distance from Bradford. Easy enough on my bike, but it's probably time for Jimmy to invest in some form of transportation.

While I'm zooming in, another text arrives: *We can look at the ad when you get back. You're coming over after your study session, right?*

I hadn't considered it, but I smile as I read the text a second, then a third time. As far as I'm concerned, time spent with Xander is time well spent.

"Who're you texting?"

I look up in the middle of the message to find Dahlia staring with a suspicious scowl. "Stuff about housing next year." I finish the text and lay the phone on the table.

When the device vibrates again, Dahlia seizes it before I move. She's seen me unlock it enough she doesn't have to think about the passcode. "'Can't wait.'" She follows the words with an irritated cluck of her tongue.

She scans through the long series of texts, and I wait uncertainly. Our conversations aren't anything to hide. And she's aware we're talking again, though she doesn't know how often. But my stomach twists uneasily.

Those messages, no matter how benign or mundane, are

private. They're a window into a relationship I'm incapable of maintaining, despite my yearning to be near him.

"You know," she says, drawing my attention, "I was starting to think going to bed with him would help you move on, but obviously, that didn't work."

I flush at the words.

Dahlia looks down, and I follow her gaze to my cup, sitting where Brent left it. "Have a drink, Billie."

When I turn back, her hands are on the keyboard, already writing a second line of a text.

"Wait, what are you doing?" I reach for the phone, but she scoots away, unperturbed by my weak attempt to confiscate it. "Give it back, Dahlia."

"Take a drink." She finishes the message, turns off the screen, and grips the phone in both her hands.

Her stare is challenging while mine is hesitant, waiting for Xander's response to light up the device. But when no response arrives, I break eye contact.

"I'm not drinking tonight."

"Are you sick or something?" When I turn, Brent is relaxing against the counter, his face wrinkled in confusion. "Headache?"

I shake my head. "No, I'm just not drinking right now."

Dahlia makes a small indifferent sound. "Since when? That's new, right?"

"Yeah, I guess."

Brent interrupts before she can speak again. "Like you're not going to drink ever again? Why would you do that?"

I bite my lip. "I haven't thought that far ahead yet. For now, I'm not drinking."

I didn't expect them to understand—they're drunk, after

all—but it'd be nice if they tried.

Brent pushes away from the counter and joins us on the couch, his oversized drink in his hand. "Then what are you going to do?"

My eyes wander back to the French book. "Homework?"

Then, there it is.

The opening notes of the blink-182 song play, and I turn my full attention to Dahlia, who holds the phone up with exaggerated surprise. "It's for you."

I snatch the phone from her and answer it as I rush to the bathroom, but Xander blows right past salutations.

"Are you drinking?"

"What? No, of course not." I twist the lock into place behind me and take a seat on the toilet lid in the dark.

He starts to speak a couple times before he manages to say, "So you thought sending that was a good idea?" His voice is quiet now, but guarded.

"I didn't." I take a deep breath. "I mean, I didn't send that. Dahlia took my phone. They're all drinking. I don't know what she texted you."

"Don't worry about it." Xander clears his throat. "If they're drinking, why are you over there? That can't be a good idea."

So I'm learning.

"What did the text say?"

"Really, Dixon." He scoffs. "It's not a big deal. You can look at it yourself."

"Right."

"I should go. I'll see you when you get here, right? You're still coming over?"

"Of course."

"Great. I'll see you then."

He hangs up before I can get another word out. The screen fades to black in my hands, and I sit in the dark.

But I want to hear him say it.

What could she text that would make him believe I've been drinking and trying to hide that fact? I don't want to consider the multitude of embarrassing propositions she could have sent him.

Finally, I light up the phone and unlock it to read the message.

I can't stop thinking about you. I want you.

It's not untrue, though not necessarily at this instance. But certainly not something Dahlia should be texting him, even if she's pretending to be me.

What the hell was that text supposed to achieve? She's made it abundantly clear she doesn't want me to date him, that I should spend my time drinking with her instead.

I pocket the phone and unlock the door.

◆

On the opposite side of the square table, Cynthia has her chemistry book splayed open, along with a wire-bound notebook, where she jots down her notes.

In contrast, Prudence faces me with an eager smile and scoots her chair in. "Okay, but Felix is a better painting teacher than drawing teacher."

I dip my final fry in my mayo cup. "I might agree with that if we stop doing still lifes. I'm tired of painting boxes and topiaries. How am I supposed to be motivated if we never paint anything interesting?" I pop the fry in my mouth and pile all my trash into the food basket.

It's rare that I eat at the Eyrie anymore since I can keep snacks on-hand in my apartment—plus, after working here for a year, Xander has no interest in eating here—but Cynthia has been set up at this table for the last five hours. Her morning lab class was canceled, and she has a test in Inorganic Chemistry at one.

"We have to study the basics before we can do the interesting stuff." Prue pauses to take a drink. "You're taking Fundamentals now, right? Now that's basic."

I'm stuck in Fundamentals of Creative Design with the freshmen. I could've had it with Prudence if I took it last year.

"It's torture, but like you say, learning the basics."

Growing up, the only person who encouraged my drawing was Imogene. I never got up the nerve to take an art class in high school. I taught myself, and now, I have to relearn everything. At least this time I have a guide.

"I need more to drink." Prue nods around the corner toward the drink station. "I can grab you some if you like."

"I'll come with."

Prudence leads the way to the Coke machines at the front of the Eyrie. While she pops the lid on her to-go cup and fills it with lemonade, I lean against the counter beside her, waiting my turn.

A few feet away, Dahlia peruses the pre-made meal options in the cooler.

I smile. "Hey. Are we getting together to study on Thursday?"

Dahlia's smile doesn't reach her eyes. "Maybe, I'm not sure." Her voice is subdued, restrained, and she grabs a box of sushi.

Prue steps away from the fountain machine. "You going to get something, Billie?"

I cast a glance at the Coke machine, but my mind is still struggling to wrap around Dahlia. "Yeah, sorry." I move closer and fill my cup with Sprite.

"Let's go back."

Behind us, Dahlia pays for her sushi and walks out of the Eyrie's front door, and once she's out of earshot, Prue glances after her. "When did that get super awkward?"

"I'm not sure."

Dahlia's dismissive attitude isn't anything new. But this is the first time she's been so dismissive of me. I don't think she's been sleeping much lately. Her bedroom light is always on when I get up to pee at three in the morning and struggle to fall back to sleep.

"I don't think she's in a very good place."

It's hard to be mad at her. No matter how dismissive she is, I can't fault her for having a difficult time when she's been there for me during all my difficult times since we became friends.

I turn toward our table again but stumble to a halt when someone brushes my arm. Prudence stops behind me. "Sorry, I wasn't looking," I say, twisting to see the other person.

With pursed lips and narrow eyes, Regan Foster stares back. "No, I don't imagine you were."

My gaze falls to my hands. I open my mouth to speak, but nothing comes out. There's nothing I could say to her, now or ever, that would excuse my behavior. Even if I could make it up to her somehow, I doubt she'd be interested.

But I force myself to look at her again. "I'm sorry, Regan."

She scoffs. "Sorry for what?"

"I never meant to be so…"

Regan turns to me sharply. "Mean?"

I grimace. Not the word I wanted to use. Certainly accurate.

"And you had no reason to be. He's always liked you. He still does. Although, I don't know why he'd be interested in such a bitch." She doesn't give me a chance to respond before stalking toward the exit, her layered skirt swishing with each furious step. I didn't realize she was here.

I clench my eyes shut.

"Wow." Prudence lays her hand on my arm. "You okay?"

What's there to be upset about? Regan may have been harsh, but she was honest. She didn't say anything more or less than I deserve.

My eyes flutter open, and I force a smile into place. "It's fine."

When we sit down with Cynthia, who doesn't look up from her notes, Prudence is still watching me, her lips tight in a frown. I can't look at her.

Thirty

THE HOUSE ON SANDALWOOD IS A TWO-STORY BRICK BUILD-
ing with tall windows and a front porch, painted white. A
balcony, supported by thick pillars, is immediately above
and connected to one of the bedrooms upstairs.

Xander parks his Camaro in the driveway and surveys
the building with a skeptical scowl.

The landlady said she'd meet us here at four while the
tenants are out, so we're not bothering them during the tour.
She meets us on the front step, and Jimmy steps forward to
introduce us. They shake hands, and after a few quick hellos,
she invites us inside.

"Excuse the mess." She holds the door for us, and we trail
inside. "The tenants cleaned up a little, but I told them not
to worry too much."

The foyer is small with hardwood floors and a wire shoe
rack in the corner. Wide arched doorways lead into two
large living spaces, one on each side of the entryway. The
space on the right is set up with an Xbox, old box TV, a ratty
couch, and a couple wooden stools as end tables.

I'm pretty sure that's supposed to be a living room, not a
mess. This house is definitely rented by college guys.

"This is the dining room." She gestures to the room on the left, but they don't have a table. The only thing inside is a small bookshelf in one corner with a few miscellaneous items—no actual books.

The landlady leads us through a few doorways, past a set of stairs, to the kitchen. Electric stove. Small fridge. Limited counter space. A small table in one corner with two chairs. There's one small bathroom between the kitchen and living room.

Then, she leads us up the narrow staircase to the bedrooms.

"It's three bedrooms, and there's a full bathroom with a tub and shower combo. This room—" she points to the one on the left "—has access to the balcony out front. It's the largest room, and the other two are the same size."

One of the other bedrooms is right next to the master. The entrances are immediately across from each other. Right across from the stairs, there's the bathroom, and the last bedroom is in the opposite corner. Another smaller door is down there too—she says it's storage.

Jimmy pauses beside me. "I want the room as far away from you two as possible."

He's joking, but I avert my eyes and pause beside the two bedrooms on the left side of the stairs. Everyone else heads downstairs, but I'm stuck examining my surroundings.

Is living with them a good idea?

It's not like I can afford to live on campus anymore, especially if my grades fall again. I dropped my photography class like Felix asked, but if I don't perform well in all my classes this semester…

I could always move in with my dad. He'd love that, and

I crash there regularly. I already have a key. He wouldn't ask me to pay rent.

But I did the math. I could lose my Presidential Scholarship. Without that, I can't afford college. Period. Housing wouldn't matter anymore.

"You look serious."

I glance over my shoulder. Xander's right beside me, a small smile on his lips, and when I spot him, he steps forward to look into the larger bedroom. Jimmy and the landlady are downstairs, and his eager questions filter up through the stairwell.

"You should take the big one," I say, quiet. "Balcony access for smoking and all."

He shrugs. "It's whatever." He peruses the room, sparsely decorated—the bed doesn't even have a frame. "I'm fine in any room. My need to smoke isn't that overwhelming."

I release a long sigh and lean against the wall between the two bedrooms, and Xander joins me.

"What do you think of the house? It's a good price."

"Yeah." I peek an eye, but he's staring off into space. "In this town, we'd be lucky to find anything else available and at a decent price."

He scoots closer and lays his hand on my waist. "Then what's the problem, Dixon? You chickening out?"

I shake my head. "No, I—"

What can I say? Three people makes the house more affordable, and I don't want to bail on them.

But what happens when we have one of our fights and don't talk to each other for a month? What happens when he brings home a girl? What happens when I have to listen to him having sex with someone else?

271

Xander squeezes my hip and steps close enough his unzipped leather jacket brushes my stomach. "You okay?" His other hand caresses my cheek.

And there's that look again. The look that says he wants to kiss me, and yes, the look that makes me want to melt into his embrace. The look that says he can see me at my core.

Before I can do anything stupid, I wrap my arms around him under the jacket and bury my face in his chest.

"Oh, come on, Dixon." His thumb traces my jaw. "We're going to rent a house. This should be exciting. And I can't think of anyone I'd rather live with."

Yeah, that's exactly the problem, though.

"I'm fine." I burrow deeper. "I am excited, but it's also a little overwhelming, you know?"

"Then let's do something to help you relax tonight."

My grip tightens. I can think of far too many relaxing things I'd like to do with him tonight.

I swallow to quell the thoughts in favor of something more realistic.

"Let's play *Mario Kart*. Just you and me this time." His chest vibrates as he chuckles. "No Jim or Mo fighting over who's better at the game—even though, let's be honest, it's definitely your sister."

I release a long laugh. "That would be fun."

"Jim has to practice for his ear training class, so he won't be there to butt in."

"That sounds perfect."

"Good." He presses a kiss to the top of my head and starts to pull away. "We should get back down there."

After a short nod, I release him, and we head for the

stairs.

His phone rings.

He stops after a step to answer. "Yeah, what's up?"

I pause, my hand on the railing, and watch.

"At six?" He frowns but nods all the same. "Yeah, I can do that. Not a problem."

When he hangs up a moment later, he turns to me with an uneasy smile. "Kylie asked me to cover for Tiff tonight. I'll be done early, though, since she's a server, but we'll have to put video games on hold."

"Right."

"Sorry." He takes a step toward me, but I start down the stairs. There is no way to ignore the immense disappointment.

◆

Xander drops me off at my dad's house before he and Jimmy head for their apartment. He has to get ready quickly.

Dad pores over a stack of worksheets, a bright green felt-tipped pen in his hand. He glances up over the dining room table as I take the seat across from him. "I didn't expect to see you." He quickly returns to grading.

I hunch over the table and rub my neck. "I know. My plans got messed up because Xander had to take a shift last minute."

"That's a shame," Dad says.

"Can I stay the night here?" It takes me a minute to undo the bun on top of my head. When I remove the hair tie and bobby pins, the corkscrew curls cascade down my shoulders. I run a hand through the frizzy locks to straighten my part. "I don't want to go all the way back to my apartment tonight."

"Of course." He flashes me a quick smile. "You can sleep here any time. That's why I gave you a key."

"Right." I lay my arms on the table and rest my head on top.

"You tired?"

I shake my head.

"What's wrong, Mina?"

I lift my head to look at him. "I don't know. I don't like it when my schedule gets messed up. I want everything to be organized."

Dad lays down his pen. "I imagine you were looking forward to spending the evening with Xander."

I give a one-shouldered shrug. Of course I was, but it's not like there's a shortage of evenings spent with him. "Maybe."

"You two are much closer than you used to be."

"There was a lot of room for improvement." I let out a short laugh. "We didn't get along at all when you met him, Dad."

But he brushes away my comments with a shake of his head. "You care about each other quite a bit."

"He's one of my best friends."

Dad forces a small smile and picks up his pen again. "The way you care about each other isn't platonic, Mina." He peruses the next worksheet.

My eyes gravitate toward the stairs. "Do I still have that eighteen-by-twenty-four drawing pad upstairs?"

"I haven't done anything with it." I turn back, he says, "About Xander—"

274

"There's nothing to say about Xander."

But Dad continues, despite my protests. "I may be old, but I'm not stupid. Things have been different this year, since your…procedure. The way you look at each other, the flirtations, the touches. You lack subtlety."

"Dad, there's nothing going on between us."

He assesses the top worksheet, then flips the page. "I'm well aware. My question is, why?"

"There are a number of reasons. He's one of my best friends. I don't want to ruin that friendship. We're not that compatible. We fight all the time. Plus, you know, he has a reputation around campus."

Dad raises an eyebrow. "Are you worried he wouldn't be interested after you have sex?"

I toy with the strands of auburn hair splayed over my shoulders. "Technically, we had sex a year ago."

For a moment, my dad is silent, and I can't meet his eyes. But then, he says, "Isn't that a moot point? He cares about you more now than he did then, Mina, and it has nothing to do with sex."

I frown. Not the reaction I expected, especially with his intense hostility toward a potential relationship with Zane and how that ended.

"Dad, I'm not ready for a relationship." My words are barely loud enough for him to hear. "I'm not in a good place right now, and I don't want to risk a friendship with one of the most amazing people to have it ruined when we break up. You know romance has never been a priority for me. There's so much I want to do with my life."

"Good," he says, and I'm struck by the resolve in his words. "Do those things. Have high priorities, take chances, learn as much as you can. But also realize you can do those things while being in a relationship, Mina. A healthy relationship is a supportive one. You should be encouraging each other, not holding one another back."

I shake my head. "Dad, I don't want to make another mistake."

He reaches a hand across the table to find mine. "Mina, you can't assume that every relationship is a mistake. He's not Zane Nelson."

I stiffen at the name and pull away. "I never said he was."

Dad opens his mouth, but I head for the stairs.

"I'm going to grab my drawing pad. I need to practice."

Thirty-One

I SIT DOWN AT THE BACK TABLE INSTEAD OF THE ARMCHAIR without prompting, and Byrdie joins me.

"How has your week been, Billie?" He pulls out a few magazines, a glue stick, a pair of scissors, and a couple legal-sized sheets of paper and lays them on the table between us.

I heave a sigh. "It's been long, but mostly good. What are we doing today?"

"I thought it might be fun to make a self-portrait."

I tilt my head. "With magazine cutouts?"

Byrdie smiles. "A collage self-portrait. Take whatever stands out to you—images you like, words that speak to you, pictures of people you aspire to be, anything—and we'll make a collage using them. It doesn't have to be artistic or beautiful. I'm going to do one too, and trust me, I have no skill in this field."

I laugh and accept the paper he passes to me. "This sounds too simple."

"Actually, most people find it difficult to pick out the images. You're quite creative, so you might have more luck." He grabs one of the magazines and flips through the pages. "Did anything interesting happen this week?"

I grab one of the remaining magazines and flip through the pages of advertisements, celebrities, and an article about Taylor Swift's latest breakup. "We found a house—me and Xander and Jimmy. We signed the lease. Move in at the end of May."

"That's a little early, isn't it?" Byrdie tears out a couple pages from the magazine and lays them atop his blank paper. "It's only February."

"Yeah, but I'm relieved to get it out of the way. At least one part of my life is sorted out." I let out a short laugh. "One minuscule part of it."

Byrdie tears out another page to add to his stack. "How is our experiment going, Billie?"

I trade my current magazine for a *National Geographic* and find a few photographs of a craggy coastline. "I don't know how to assess that."

"Well, how do you feel?"

I find an image of a falcon and sigh. "Better, but that probably has more to do with not being hungover all the time instead of my actual mental state."

He nods. "There are a lot of factors that could affect it. What else has changed that could alter the results?"

I've been spending more time with Xander and Jimmy again. That doesn't necessarily put me in a better mood. Especially when Jimmy looks at me with his stupid sad eyes and I want to punch something.

"I don't know. I'm exercising every morning with Xander now, running around town in the freezing cold. I'm terrible at it, but he's always so encouraging. And he makes sure I eat well—enough protein, no sweets."

"How are your sleeping habits?"

I close my magazine. "I don't know how to fall asleep. I have to wait until I'm so exhausted I literally cannot stay awake. And I don't sleep for long anymore. Otherwise, I wouldn't be able to go running at six in the morning." And it's gotten worse since I stopped drinking—that's what helped me fall asleep in the first place.

Byrdie makes a quiet humming sound. "How many hours, do you think?"

I shrug. "Two or three."

"Have you tried something simple like drinking chamomile tea?"

I chuckle. "My dad's a tea enthusiast. I've tried every kind of tea, trust me."

He cracks a smile. "Well, what I would recommend would be setting up a bedtime routine. You stay up until you're exhausted when you should be trying to relax your body and mind. Take a bath, read a book, drink a cup of tea, use lotion. Spend your evening with someone who you feel completely comfortable around. Or if you'd rather not be around anyone, make sure you're alone so you can fully relax."

He grabs the scissors and cuts out sections of the pages he's torn from his magazine. "Whatever routine you decide on, do the same things in the same order every night. Start it so the routine will finish at the time you normally manage to fall asleep, and move it forward by small increments each night, even by ten minutes."

When he's done cutting out his images, he places the scissors between us, and I grab them to cut out my falcon and a few big words from headlines.

"I suppose that could help."

But all I can think about is Xander and how easy it was to relax in bed with him. Replicating that would be a bad idea.

"Do you drink coffee?"

"In the morning."

"That could be contributing, but I also imagine making it through the day without the coffee is difficult. As long as you're not drinking it excessively, I don't recommend changing it."

I nod.

Byrdie glues down some of his images. "What do your friends think of the situation? You're a college student, Billie, and quite frankly, drinking is expected and encouraged. How do your friends view the change?"

I shrug.

Xander has been especially affectionate and kind. He's thrilled by the change, but things have been less smooth with everyone else, even Jimmy. Brent won't stop making curt jokes about my abstinence, and Dahlia has distanced herself. I don't know if that has to do with my lack of alcohol consumption, or if she has something else going on.

My stack of cutouts is tall enough the top images slide off, and I pull my paper over to organize them. "It's been a mix of everything." The backgrounds, the cliffs and forests from the *National Geographic*, go down first, then a few images of a falcon, a girl with asymmetrical hair, a couple sleeping, a green Luna moth, and the snippets I tore from article titles.

The odd thing is, last time I saw them, Dahlia and Brent asked me to study with them tonight. Of course, a study session with the two of them is an excuse to smoke hookah and drink while they "do their homework."

"Some people are more understanding than others." I rearrange the images, trying to find the perfect composition.

Nevertheless, I agreed.

◆

It's rare that I make the walk to Brent and Darius's apartment alone, but Dahlia's not in our apartment when I get back from therapy. And she doesn't arrive in the hours prior to the decided study time with the others.

When I text her, there's no response, but Brent sends me a short direction half an hour before we were supposed to head over: *Come over whenever. Lia's hung up at the moment.*

Without Dahlia, the trip is shorter, lonelier, but also oddly nice.

University Park is cold and sterile in the winter. All the small trees between the buildings are still bare; it's easier to see Zane's old apartment as I pass near it, but I avert my eyes. He isn't there anymore.

Brent opens the door with his typical goofy smile and invites me inside. "Lia won't be here for half an hour," he says as he returns to the living room. "Or more."

The hookah is set up, ready for the charcoal to be lit. A large frozen drink in a fancy glass sits on the coffee table, half gone.

I sit down on the chair usually occupied by Darius and open my backpack. "Where's Darius?"

Brent smiles. "Didn't Lia tell you? He's got a hot date tonight."

"Oh." I glance down the hallway toward Darius's shut

bedroom door. "I didn't realize that was tonight."

He returns to the kitchen. "You want something to drink?"

"Don't worry about it." I pull out my French textbook and flashcards. "I need to concentrate."

When he takes his seat on the couch, he holds the charcoal with the tongs and lights it. He sucks on the hose till smoke pools out as he exhales. He offers it to me then. "It's peach."

I shake my head, flipping through the cards.

"Your loss."

I pause to watch as he takes another long draw on the hose, then sets it down to drink from his glass. The pale brown iced drink moves slowly as he gulps it down.

"What're you drinking?" I have an intense need to fill the silence. Usually, there's music playing and people laughing.

He sets the empty glass on the coffee table firmly. "It's a mudslide." He's already smiling more.

I return my attention to my French II homework. "Cool."

"You want one? Can't be too hard to make it virgin, right?" His voice is mildly perturbed, but I ignore that.

"If you want."

He heads to the kitchen, pours himself another glassful from the blender, and sorts through the fridge.

I flip through my flashcards. Everything in our current curriculum is about sports and health, and I test myself while Brent runs the blender.

My phone, sitting on the coffee table next to my textbook, lights up. I can't hear the vibrations over the whir of the blender, but the light draws my attention.

Dahlia's response is a full four hours after I texted her: *Sorry, heading your way now. I won't be there till after 9.*

I check the time and frown. It's barely 8:30.

"Hey…"

But between his drink, now almost gone again, and the blender, which is for some reason still running, Brent can't hear me.

"*Brent!*"

He turns to me swiftly, but it takes him a moment to turn off the blender. The room is eerily silent once the machine stops. For a while, he stands there, appraising me, then he turns back to the blender, pours the drink into a new cup, and brings it to the living room.

He sets it down in front of me. It was blending so long, most of the ice has melted. He actually made me a virgin mudslide.

"What's up?" He sits on the couch and picks up the hookah hose again.

"Thanks." I pick up the glass, but I hesitate. "What's Dahlia doing today? She said she's on her way over but it'll take thirty minutes. Where's she coming from?"

Actually, I haven't seen her in a few days.

Brent's brow develops a deep furrow. "She's been in Montpelier. For a couple days."

"Oh."

The look on his face tells me not to ask.

I return to the glass in my hand and take a drink. The liquid, no longer frozen, looks and tastes like chocolate milk. Incredibly sweet, strong coffee flavor, but there's a hint of something else beneath.

"What's in this?"

Brent looks at me. It takes him a minute to speak. "Huh?"

I set the glass down. "What's in my drink?"

"Oh. Kahlua and Bailey's. I left out the vodka for you."

I frown at the glass. "You do realize Kahlua and Bailey's have alcohol in them, don't you?"

He shrugs. "They're just liqueurs."

"They're not 'just' liqueurs. They're alcoholic. You said it would be virgin."

"I don't have the stuff to make it virgin." He leans against the armrest nearest me. "I don't see what the problem is. What does it matter if there's alcohol in it or not? It's relaxing, and trust me, you need to relax."

I scoff and push the drink toward him, out of my way. "'Why does it matter?'" I slam my book shut and gather up my vocab cards, piling them in an unruly stack on top of the book before wrapping the rubber band around them again. "Why do you think it fucking matters, Brent? If you don't have the ingredients, you fucking tell me that. You don't pour an alcoholic drink and give it to someone who doesn't drink."

"You're ridiculous."

I shove the book and flashcards into my backpack. "I don't care if I'm being ridiculous. You're being an asshole." I zip the bag shut. "You don't get to choose whether I drink. That's my decision, and only my decision. You don't get to judge me because it makes you feel good about yourself. And you don't get to give me a drink because you think it's fine. That's not your choice."

Brent stands up with me. "Lia's mentally unstable too, but she's gonna drink when she gets here. I don't see the problem."

"The problem is you didn't ask me. You made it alcoholic without my permission and handed it over without telling me." I grab the drink and brandish it toward him. "This is a breach of trust. You lied to me."

"Sin of omission isn't lying." He shakes his head, but he stumbles and grips my arm to prevent himself from falling.

I shove the drink into his hands and sling my backpack over my shoulder. "You knew this wasn't okay. It might as well be."

As I turn, he stumbles again. A faint crash echoes from the apartment as the heavy door slams behind me.

My feet head to the first place I can think of.

Thirty-Two

Footsteps pound on the stairs.

It's dark now.

I pull my legs closer to my chest. I don't know how long I've been waiting.

My head is fuzzy. I can't focus, but the footsteps draw closer, closer, closer.

"Dixon?"

They stop.

Xander.

"What's wrong? What are you doing here?"

My body is shaking. I can't look at him. He'll see the tears.

He leans close, his head near mine. "Dixon, look at me." When I don't say anything, don't even move, he pulls me into a standing position, an arm wrapped around me, keeping me from falling. My hand clutches my backpack strap. "I'm not going to bother asking if you're okay. You're obviously not."

I lean into him, pressing my forehead to his collarbone. He smells like cigarettes and beer and leather. He always smells like cigarettes.

He unlocks the door with the keys from his pocket and walks me inside the apartment. The door shuts quietly behind us.

"Jim's working late tonight at the Eyrie." He pushes a few strands of auburn curls from my face, but I can't look at him. "You want some water?"

I give a barely discernible nod, and he pulls away. My fingers release the strap, and the backpack falls to the linoleum.

"Hold on a sec. Let me change out of these dirty clothes, and I'll grab you some water."

He leaves me by the door.

I don't want to be alone.

I follow him.

His bedroom door is wide open, and he's undressing next to his dresser. He doesn't notice me—even as he strips off his boxers and tosses them in the hamper.

"Xander."

He jumps and spins toward me, supporting himself with the dresser. "Fuck. You startled me, Dixon." He's still naked and, in perfect Xander fashion, unbothered by the fact that his soft dick is on display.

I lean against the door frame. "Can I sleep here?"

"Uh, yeah." He grabs new underwear from the top drawer. "Have a seat." He gestures to his bed before pulling the boxers on.

I sit on the edge of the mattress and shed my hoody on the floor. "Do you have something I could change into?" The only thing under my Marvel sweatshirt is my sports bra. I'm not sleeping in either of those.

Xander opens the next drawer down and tosses me the

bright red shirt on top. Apparently, I get to be Charmander.

"I'll get that water now." He doesn't wait for a response before heading out the door.

I pull off my sweatshirt and bra and don the Charmander tee before crawling under the covers of his twin bed.

I'm still uncomfortable.

I push off the blankets and tear off my jeans and socks as well. They fall to the floor with the rest of my clothes, and I wrap the covers around myself. I was in the cold far too long.

He returns, a glass of water in his hand, and sits on the edge of the bed. "Do you want to talk about it?" He offers me the cup.

I sit up and take a long drink. "No, I really don't." The glass fogs up with my hot breath. "I'm glad you're here."

"How long were you waiting? You should've called me."

I shake my head. "I don't know. It could've been hours or minutes. What time is it?"

"Ten-thirty." Xander scoots closer and wraps an arm around me. "Tell me what happened."

My head droops onto his shoulder. "Nothing happened. I'm completely overreacting. I shouldn't be this upset about it. I shouldn't even be surprised."

His grip tightens. "Don't be so hard on yourself, Dixon. It's okay to be upset, even if it's illogical. You don't need to emulate Spock all the time."

A small bit of laughter bubbles from my mouth, but the tears fall too. "It's the same thing over and over. Once again, I'm being manipulated and lied to, and for what? He doesn't even want to fuck me, but he's exactly the same."

"Who is?" His voice is unnervingly quiet; he's trying to

keep his emotions at bay.

I open my mouth, but it takes a second for the words to come. "Brent. We were…studying."

"Please tell me that's not a euphemism for anything."

I shake my head. "It's not. He was doing what they always do when we 'study'—drinking, smoking, anything but actual studying. I don't know why I keep going back there, expecting it to be different, expecting them to be different. Expecting me to be different."

He returns the glass to the nightstand and tugs me closer. His arms wrap around me. His lips press to the top of my head. And I cling to him, lean my face against his hot skin. I'm shaking again. I didn't realize I was that cold.

"Don't doubt yourself," he whispers in my ear. "You're doing so much better. You don't realize how much better you're doing."

"Then why don't I feel any better? Why do I put myself through this day after day? Why can't I get a good night's sleep? And hell, why can't I have a good day either? One that's not tainted by my brain doubting and hating and wishing I were anywhere but here, no matter where 'here' is."

His hand massages my back, and I push closer. "There will always be bad days. And bad ideas and bad situations and bad people. But it's not every day."

"Yes, it is."

"It doesn't have to be."

"But I don't know how to make it stop. I don't know how to make my brain stop." I sniffle. "It would be nice if, for once, I could not worry about everything. If I could finish the day without feeling drained and overwhelmed,

Or conversely, if I could relax for more than a few minutes without the help of alcohol."

Xander holds me closer but doesn't speak.

"He knows I'm not drinking, but he poured it anyway." I take a moment to steady my breathing—to stop my voice from quivering. "No matter what bullshit reason he comes up with, it was because he genuinely doesn't care when I say no. He doesn't care enough to put in the time or effort to understand why I stopped drinking. Because he doesn't care about me. He never did."

The tears fall again, and I toss my glasses toward the nightstand. They clatter to the floor. "This is fucking *déjà vu*. No matter how much he said he cared, that he wanted to date me, he never did. How could I have been so stupid? He wanted me in bed and that's all. I was a challenge, a prize he won the second I gave in, a trophy to stroke his ego. I'm so fucking stupid."

"You're talking about Zane Nelson."

It's not a question. There's a finality in his quiet words, even as he runs his fingers down my spine.

"Yes."

"I wish you'd talk to me about that. About any of it." He places a kiss on my forehead and leans his temple against my head. "I know you told Jimmy something, but not much. He was so worried. You have to realize what happens when you don't explain these things, right? We assume the worst."

I swallow. "What's that?"

"You know, the 'R' word."

I shake my head. "It wasn't rape."

"Then what happened?" He heaves a sigh. "All I know is, you avoided us for weeks afterward—and God, it wasn't because Jim found out we had sex. You panicked every time you saw Nelson, avoided him, wouldn't even mention his name. You still don't. What else am I supposed to think?"

I take a shaky breath. "He—we had sex after that stupid fight in the cafeteria. He took me back to his apartment and he—it was awful." My arms clamp around his shoulder blades to keep from shaking.

"Awful how? Did you want to have sex with him?"

My grip tightens. "I don't know."

"Yes, you do."

"No, I don't."

He scoffs. "Of course you know. No one knows better than you."

I bury my face in his chest, and my words muffle against his skin.

"Dixon, I can't understand you."

I pull back just enough to speak. "No, but he didn't know that. I didn't know at the time."

"Did he ask you?"

"Kind of."

"And what did you say?"

"I didn't say anything. He didn't give me a chance. He just kept kissing me, undressing me."

Xander's jaw tightens. "You were angry and upset, and he didn't wait for you to confirm you wanted sex? You spent the next month freaking out whenever you saw him. That's not consent."

"It wasn't rape." I pull away so I can see him. "It wasn't."

"It sounds remarkably like rape to me."

I shake my head. "Don't say that."

But his hand clenches in a fist atop his knee.

291

"Don't you realize…?" I struggle to find the words. "When you say that, you completely devalue my ability to make a decision. I wasn't drunk or high or incapacitated in any way. He didn't purposefully hurt or threaten me. I was emotionally bereft, and God, it was a stupid fucking decision—but it was still my decision."

He purses his lips. "And in your internal monologue, does Zane Nelson receive any of the blame?"

Of course he does, I want to say, but the words refuse to pass my lips.

"I was stupid," I say instead. "I put myself in that position. I knew what he wanted by then—some part of me did. Some part of me had to."

Just like I shouldn't be surprised about Brent. Why in the world would he care about me? What did I expect to happen when I quit drinking? Our entire friendship was based around alcohol.

Xander's hand wraps around my shoulder firmly. "Not everything is your fault."

I close my eyes. "I don't want to talk about Zane anymore."

"Then what do you want to talk about? Brent and the alcohol?"

"No. Just no. I don't want to talk at all."

He sighs and pulls away again. "What do you want?"

My eyes flutter open. I look around, locate the blurry glass of water on the nightstand, and reach for it. "For once," I say after a sip, "I want someone to care about me. Actually care, not pretend for their own benefit. I want someone to see me and want me. Why am I never enough?" I return the glass to the table.

Xander releases a small sigh, and his hand finds my jaw and turns me to him. "How many times do I have to tell you, Dixon? You are enough. You will always be enough."

It's nice to hear, but I don't believe him.

I exhale slowly and close my eyes. "Xander, will you care for me?"

His fingers run along my jaw. "I do." His breath grazes my face.

"No." My eyes blink open, and I pull away to uncover my bare legs and space for him to join me under the sheets. "No, I mean, will you care for me?"

When I look up again, his eyebrows are arching under his black hair. "Wait, now? Now is when you want to have sex?"

I don't have to say anything. He can see the answer in my eyes.

His voice is uncertain, but he searches my half-naked body. "Having sex with me won't make you feel better."

"Please tell me you have a condom." I press his hand to my Charmander-covered breast.

"Dixon, this is a bad idea." But his fingers squeeze. "You're upset; we shouldn't have sex when you're upset."

"Do you have a condom?"

At my sharp tone, his eyes find mine. "Yeah."

I press a short kiss to his mouth. "Then show me how much you care."

The twin bed is small, but he slides his legs under the covers without protest. Lying down, our heads on his pillow, bodies entangled, we don't take up much space.

His arms wrap around me, and he presses another kiss to my forehead, but I push closer. I want to feel every inch of his hot skin.

For a moment, Xander holds me, his arms stiff, but his breathing is shallow as I trail my lips across his scruffy neck—he didn't shave this morning. My hands run along his tight muscles, and his chest sears my cold fingers.

In the last year, I have fantasized about him far too often. More often than is healthy. Especially after New Year's Eve. But no matter how real those fantasies have felt, they are nothing compared to the moment his skin touches mine.

I shift positions to kiss him on the lips again.

After a moment of hesitation, he pulls me flush against him, and his tongue darts out to meet mine. All signs of hesitation dissipate, and I melt into the kiss.

I shift to slip my hand between us and grasp his hardening dick, already straining against his boxers. His breath hitches at the contact. He stiffens in my hand.

"Are we really...?" His words come as a whisper, but the sound is jarring in the silent room, and he presses another kiss to my lips.

But I don't want any distance between us. I need his skin against mine—and he agrees. He breaks from my mouth to tear my shirt up and out of the way and flings it to the floor. His lips are on mine again in an instant.

It doesn't last long.

Gradually, he pulls away and cups a hand to my cheek, his touch soft and reverent. He eases me onto my back, and his hands skim down my ribs to my waist. "You're beautiful, did you know that?" A finger tugs at the underwear band, and my swallow in response is audible.

I want him, there's no doubt about that. I'm wet and aching and my skin is on fire under his touch, but we've spent so long toying with this idea that it's hard to believe this is really happening. That we're actually going through with it this time. I am eager—no, desperate—for this, but he asks for my permission with his eyes again, and my chest tightens.

Xander retracts his hand. "You can change your mind, you know. We don't have to."

My eyes clench shut. "I want to."

"Then why are you hesitating?"

I pull him into another kiss, entangling one hand in his hair, and he responds fervently. One hand grasps my breast, squeezes and rolls the nipple between his fingers, and I nip his bottom lip, begging him not to hold back. I don't want to think right now. I don't want to change my mind.

Beneath the covers, my hands find his boxers, and I propel them down his legs with a little help from my foot. The moan that slips from his lips as he rocks against me is small but throaty.

I need him to make that sound again.

Using his own momentum, I twist him against the wall and onto his back, and his breath is ragged when we break the kiss. That still doesn't stop him: "Dixon, we don't have to do this. You don't have anything to prove. To me or anyone else."

But I press a short kiss to his lips and slip down between his legs to take in the full view of his throbbing erection. I touch a finger to him, then a second and a third and my thumb, and I rub a short line down the side. "I want to." I lay a small kiss to the head. "I want you."

"I want you too." His voice is short and clipped, and a hand clamps down on my shoulder when I take him into my mouth. He releases a subtle gasp, his abdomen tense and firm, at the sudden attention. "Dixon…"

I roll my eyes. He's breaking my concentration.

But when he says my name again, frantic, unguarded, my chest constricts. I can't complain. Not when he says it like that.

His grip on my shoulder is strong, but it doesn't bother me in the least. A soft moan escapes his lips when I take him deeper, and he gasps again. Every sound is powerful—deafening, even—and I am entranced by each tiny noise, by each minuscule movement. Under normal circumstances, these things would be insignificant, but here and now, his desperation is my self-indulgence.

From this far away, his face is too blurry to decipher, but then, I don't have to.

He tugs on my shoulder, and I allow him to pull me into his tight arms.

I lean my forehead against his, but his eyes are shut, his brow sweaty, and I laugh to remove the anxious bubble in my stomach. "No need to get worked up. I can't be that good at it yet."

His lips twist into a smile, and his chest shakes with laughter. "We can practice as much as you want."

I snort. "What a sacrifice."

His erection presses against my thigh, hard and wet, and he sends me a little wink before pulling me into an intoxicating kiss.

Like always, Xander's ability to leave me breathless catches me off-guard. His kisses are furious and overwhelming, but I push closer. More than anything, I need to feel his skin against me right now.

I reach down to stroke him and break the kiss. "Where's that condom?"

He glances toward the nightstand, and I stretch across him and fumble with the drawer. His lips trail kisses from my breast to my hip—almost too much of a distraction to locate the condom. But there's a small box at the front of the drawer, torn open but full. I release a soft sigh at his delicate touches and clutch one condom to my chest.

His lips move farther south, and he snags the hem of my underwear between his teeth and tugs them over my ass.

Somehow, he's still more aware than I am. I barely notice when his fingers slip the condom from my hand.

For a minute, he fumbles with something between pressing quick kisses near my core. Then, he yanks the underwear out of the way and buries his face in my heat. My body was already begging for him, but I didn't anticipate the sudden and unwavering attention.

I grip the headboard, gasping, trying to hold back a moan, but he circles my clit.

All hope is lost.

When he retreats, I whimper, desperate to get him back, and twist to find him. I don't know when he put the condom on, but he's ready for me, and I'm tired of waiting.

I straddle him, and he guides me by the waist to my destination. My breath quakes when he enters me, and I pause, hands resting on his stomach as I adjust.

"You alright?"

I bite my lip but nod. I slowly rock against him, trying to find a rhythm, but I am tottering. His gentle hands steady me, guide me, but it isn't enough. My rhythm is spastic.

After a minute, he thrusts with me, pushing deeper. I

gasp at the pressure.

Slowly, he increases his speed, and I lose my rhythm, letting him take over. Despite my initial flustered attempts to remain quiet, I moan in time with the thrusts. Who cares about the squeaky campus bed or maintaining my dignity? No one else is here anyway. And I'm not sure I'd care if anyone were. I give in to the feeling completely.

The pressure builds in my abdomen, and I shut my eyes. More than anything, I don't want to think or remember. Just feel him touching me, thrusting inside me. My breath is unsteady, but he keeps me stable and secure. That feeling— that one wonderful feeling—is what holds me afloat. One hand trails up to grasp my breast again, and when he pummels into me, clenching in time with the thrust, I cannot contain myself. I do not want this moment, this feeling, to stop.

But then, he slows down, almost stopping.

I look down at him to speak, to protest. But I can't breathe, let alone talk, and before I can catch my breath, he rolls us over, his arm wrapped tight enough he doesn't pull out. His mouth presses to mine in a hungry kiss. My left arm is caught against the cold wall, but I don't care because he pulls out almost entirely and thrusts back inside slowly, carefully, tenderly.

Needy, I latch my ankles together around his waist, holding myself higher, and his next thrust delves deeper. My aching swells as he languorously increases his speed. His kisses are heady; his lips leave me begging. Every second is a struggle to hold on, and I don't know why I want to.

I curl around him, and he whispers my name between frenzied kisses, and I am lost.

I am so lost.

There's a long while where I'm not sure of anything but the feel of his lips on mine—soft, careful, sincere—and I revel in his touch. The kiss is gentle, sensual, and I don't want it to end. I prolong it as long as he allows.

When he pulls away, he pushes a clump of tangled curls from my face. I have no idea when he finished, but all his movements slowly cease. "God, you have no idea what you do to me." His lips, brushing mine when he speaks, send shivers down my spine.

One final kiss, and he slips from my embrace to dispose of the condom in the small trash can by his nightstand.

He takes a moment, sitting on the edge of the bed, to catch his breath, and I clutch his hand. He runs his fingers through his hair, but he can't rein in the sweaty mess, and when he casts an exhausted smile over his shoulder, I'm compelled to kiss him again.

Afterward, I rest my face on his shoulder, clinging to his arm, my fingers laced with his. "You said I could stay the night?"

Xander's arm slips from my grasp, but he pulls me into his warm embrace. "You can stay as long as you want."

I place another kiss on his neck, smiling. I can't imagine wanting to leave.

Thirty-Three

THE ROOM IS EMPTY. HE'S GONE. AGAIN.

I crawl to the edge of the bed. Where are my glasses? My phone? What time is it?

The phone sits on the nightstand, and I light it up. It's 11:21 a.m. I don't know the last time I've slept in that long.

But he's gone.

Did he have work?

I lie down again and stare at the blurry ceiling. There's an odd full feeling in my abdomen—the number one reminder I had sex last night. For the first time in nearly a year, I had sex. And sex has gotten infinitely better.

But now is not the time to reminisce.

With a deep breath, I push aside the sheets and search for my glasses. They could be anywhere, but like the phone, they're sitting on the nightstand. He must've picked them up.

The moment I pull them on, the doorknob twists. I scurry to cover myself with the sheets again.

Xander slips inside the room and closes the door behind him. A smile spreads across his lips when he sees me. "You're up." He's wearing gym shorts, but otherwise, he hasn't even combed his hair. "You haven't been awake for long, have you?"

"I thought you left."

He chuckles. "This is my apartment and my bedroom. Where do you think I'd go?"

"Work?"

"I don't work until seven. I'm training some newbies tonight." He joins me on the bed, close enough our arms brush. "I had to piss, and then, I got distracted by Jim. I was wondering how long you'd stay in bed."

"Oh, I'm sorry. I should leave." I lean down to find my clothes, but he catches my arm, still holding the sheets over my chest.

"You don't have to go."

I glance up.

"Dixon, you are exactly what I want to wake up to. I want you to be here."

I pull up and entwine my fingers with his. "I want to be here."

He nods, but his face twists in thought. "What happens now?"

I look at his alarm clock, a bright red in the dark room. "Now, I have to get dressed and go see my dad. We're supposed to eat lunch at noon."

He frowns. That's not what he meant.

But I don't know how to answer his question.

He releases my hand, but I grip tighter and tug till he looks at me. "Do you want to come with me?"

His skeptical eyebrow, his little smirk, his snarky "Really?" when I don't expand—but underneath all that, there's a twitch at his lips that makes me pause.

301

I nod, squeeze again, and release him so I can find my clothes. As I stand, his hand glides down my side and pauses to squeeze my butt. I turn to him, laughing, and bat his hand away. "I have to get dressed."

He raises an eyebrow. "Do you have to?"

"Well, I don't think it's a good idea to have lunch with my dad in this state of undress, do you?"

"Or we could go back to bed."

I smile and step between his legs. His hands are on me instantly, and he yanks me against his chest. But after a quick kiss, I pull away again. "Ask me later." I stoop to grab my underwear and pull them on. "In the meantime, we need to get dressed to have lunch with my dad. You are coming, right?"

He's looking everywhere but my face. "You want me to come?"

I roll my eyes. "Not everything I say has to do with sex, Xander. Get ready."

He smirks as he rises from the bed. "I guess I should put on actual clothes then." When he nudges the gym shorts to the floor, the only thing beneath them is his hardening dick.

I nod, but it's half-hearted. I'm staring. "Actual clothes would be good in front of my dad."

He pulls me into a quick kiss. "Are you sure you want to wait till later?"

I press a hand to his chest. "I don't want to be late."

"How much would he mind?"

"I don't know. I've never been late before."

"There's a first time for everything." He kisses me again, and he doesn't even strain as he lifts me into the air and lays me on his mattress. His hands eagerly tear off the underwear

I just put on, and his mouth moves downward, trailing kisses along my abdomen.

I stifle a gasp when he reaches my heat. His tongue darts out to circle my clit, and I grab hold of the pillow, clinging to whatever's in reach. "Wait, you said Jimmy's here. He's still here?" He kisses me again, and I bite my tongue to stifle a moan when his tongue grazes my clit. "We need to be quiet."

He moves a hand from my thigh to push a finger inside my entrance, then a second, and he pulls back far enough to say, "I don't care. I don't want you quiet."

"Right, you want me embarrassed."

"No." Despite my protests, his fingers delve deeper and arch forward, eliciting a long moan I try to smother with the pillow. "I want to hear you come."

For a moment, I can't do anything but pant. The words send a deep aching through my body, and I can no longer protest. Even as he pulls away to grab a condom, I can only watch as he prepares himself, dying for him to touch me again.

He's more than happy to oblige, and I can't deny him his pleasure either.

◆

Xander's fingers squeeze mine beneath the table, and Dad sets a fresh pot of tea on the table. Lunch is long over, and I don't have any room for more tea, but Dad pours out a few cups and takes his seat again.

"How are the wedding plans going?" Dad asks. "The wedding is three weeks away now, isn't it?"

I sigh. "Yeah, I guess. I haven't thought about it. They've taken care of everything." The Earl Grey scalds my tongue when I take a sip. "I'll only be there for five days, and half of that's after the wedding."

Dad nods, and beside me, Xander quietly drinks his tea. Beneath the table, his thumb rubs back and forth across the back of my hand. I relish the discreet contact.

"I imagine it'll be a large affair? Your mother was always disappointed by our small ceremony."

"I don't know."

I almost feel guilty. I've been focusing on getting ahead in classes, following Byrdie's suggestions, and Xander. I've definitely been focusing on Xander.

Dad nods again before turning his attention to Xander, who hasn't spoken much during our visit. "It's good to see you, Xander. You're always welcome to visit with Mina. I don't see you often enough."

Xander smiles as a show of appreciation. "That's very kind of you to share your time with her, but I imagine you'd prefer to have her to yourself."

Dad shrugs. "Of course, but you'd prefer to have her to yourself as well, wouldn't you?"

A blush rises to my cheeks, but Xander releases a shallow laugh. "I wouldn't want to be too selfish." He sends me a conspiratorial smile as I grab my tea in an attempt to hide my face. "I should apologize for us being late. I wanted to come at the last minute."

I nearly inhale the hot liquid in my cup. It takes a few coughs to clear my windpipe.

Xander sends me a sidelong glance. "You alright?"

"Of course," I say after a minute.

There are a couple dishes sitting on the table from lunch, and Dad rises from his seat and escorts them to the kitchen. "I'll be right back."

I elbow him in the side as soon as Dad's out of sight. "Do not fucking say that."

Xander smirks. "Why not? It's true."

I scoot my chair closer, glaring. "Just because it's true doesn't mean you should say it out loud to my dad."

He shrugs. "You may be right, but I don't care." He pulls me into a kiss, and I latch on to him, happy to have his lips on mine for the first time in over an hour. One long, torturous hour.

When I push closer, practically climbing on his lap, he smiles against my lips. One hand slides down to grab my ass over my jeans. I want more than anything for all barriers between us to disappear. I need to feel him again.

I moan into his mouth as he squeezes.

A cough sounds behind me.

I break the kiss and scoot my chair closer to the table as my dad comes into the room. My shaky hand grabs my teacup, but beside me, Xander stifles his laughter.

Dad stands next to the table and accepts Xander's empty cup. "Perhaps, you'd like to take advantage of some alone time right now. I should get back to grading tests."

I down the rest of my tea and push the cup across the table toward him. "Right, I wouldn't want to be a distraction." The words tumble out of my mouth.

Xander rises from the table, and I follow suit.

Dad bids us goodbye at the door, pulling each of us into a hug. As he parts with Xander, he says, "I hope to see you again often."

Xander shoots a small smile my way. "I'd like that very much, sir."

In the safety of the red Camaro, I hunch over and press my face into my hands. Xander takes the driver's seat and starts the engine. The stereo bursts to life, blaring Journey, but he turns it off.

"Oh my God, I can't believe that happened."

"Which part?"

I glare at him through the cracks between my fingers. "The part where my dad sent us away so we can have sex and then invites you back like it's no big deal. God, why do both my parents adore you?"

Xander grins. "Because I'm adorable. Besides, is it a big deal if your dad knows we've slept together?"

"Well, no. It's just embarrassing." I push my hands through my hair and turn to glare at him. "Not that you have any idea what it's like to get embarrassed."

He shrugs and shifts into gear. "Your dad's a smart man—he figured it out the second you showed up wearing my shirt. And I tend to take the advice of smart men. Alone time sounds nice."

I scoff. "At some point, you have to get ready for work, you know." Charmander probably did make it obvious—it is Xander's favorite shirt, after all.

"I don't go to work for four hours."

Outside, we pass houses as he drives back to campus. It's the same short trip I walked on a weekly basis the second half of freshman year.

"So what, you'll take me back to bed for that long?"

There's something in my chest that feels tense, unnerved,

but I can't place it. It's not that I'd mind going back to bed with Xander. He is ridiculously attractive, comforting, and more generous than I imagined. Being with him is worth the months of waiting.

But I don't know what last night meant. I don't know if it was a good idea.

"Do you want to go to bed?"

And this morning? That shouldn't have happened, no matter how tender or soothing or pleasurable a lover he is. Not unless I know what I'm getting into.

"I don't know."

As we pull into the Plaza Apartments parking lot, I glance at him, expecting irritation or disappointment at my minor evasion. But Xander simply shrugs. "You wanna play *Super Mario*? Or should you be studying?"

Thirty-Four

WHEN FELIX RETURNS TO THE PAINTING STUDIO TO announce it's clean-up time, the first thing I do is stick my paintbrush between my teeth and check my phone. When I smile, the brush nearly falls from my mouth. I have two texts from Xander.

You need to stop being so sexy, the first message reads. It was quickly followed by: *That, or I should drop my 8 a.m. class so I can climb back in bed with you without tempting fate. Almost late again today.*

I flush at the reminder, but I can't help grinning.

To be fair, this morning was my fault. We shared a rinse-off shower after our run, and shower sex proved too difficult. Afterward, when he elected to do his homework instead of me, I took matters into my own hands. He changed his mind pretty quickly after I showed him I could have fun without his help.

"Billie, you haven't started cleaning up."

I press my phone to my chest, pull the paintbrush from my mouth, and look up. "Sorry, Prue, I got distracted."

Prudence flashes me a smile. "You're lucky we don't have class right after this or you'd be late. Now, come on. You can sext Xander during lunch."

I fidget with my phone for a moment, then finally slip it into my pocket and grab the roll of plastic wrap to seal my palette.

She snatches my water cup and dirty brushes and heads toward the sinks. "I'll help," she throws over her shoulder.

I cover the palette to keep the paints wet till the next time I can come in, then take one last look at the painting. We've moved on to color instead of grayscale at least, but this painting is yet another still life.

"That's a nice topiary, Billie."

I glance over and smile at Felix when he pauses by my work station. "Thanks, I guess." I turn to the canvas with a furrowed brow. "I don't know what I'm doing."

He chuckles. "If you did, you wouldn't need to take my class. There's always more to learn." He steps forward to assess my work. "As always, your line work is great. That's your strongest quality. Your brush strokes are a little mechanical, though. Remember to use your whole arm, not just your wrist."

"Right."

Felix faces me with a big smile. "Billie, your progress is fantastic. I'm glad to see your focus has improved this semester."

"Thanks."

"You're doing great." He squeezes my shoulder before moving on.

Even after he's gone, I stare at the painting. Felix has said on multiple occasions that you shouldn't be able to see the effort that an artist puts into their work. Even Van Gogh's paintings, full of seemingly haphazard brush strokes, appear effortless.

The hours I've labored over this canvas are obvious from a glance. I have a lot of work to do.

My pocket vibrates.

You work tomorrow morning, right? Xander asks. *I switched shifts and have the day off for once. What do you want to spend the rest of your weekend doing?*

I smirk as I text back my response: *I'm sure we can think of something.*

"You ready to go yet?"

I grab my backpack from the floor as I turn off my phone. "Yeah, let's go."

Prudence and I walk in step as we leave the studio, and in my hand, the phone buzzes again.

I see you have something in mind.

◆

Stacks of thick-toothed paper and a pile of bright red scraps of leather cover the back table. A ball of twine, an awl, a long metal ruler, a set of binding needles, craft scissors, and a bone folder are lined along the edge.

"This is a little more complex than what we've done so far," Byrdie says as I sit down beside him. "Do you keep a journal, Billie?"

I shake my head no.

"I suspected." He grabs two pages of the loose paper, hands one to me, and folds his in half. "We're going to make journals using something called Coptic stitch, so the first thing we need to do is make a template."

He spreads the paper out again and grabs a mechanical

pencil to mark six dots along the interior fold, and I follow suit.

"The Coptic stitch is a type of bookbinding process that was used by early Christians in Egypt. The best thing about it is, it's easy to learn and doesn't require glue." He pushes the awl through the dots as he speaks. "Because of the way it's sewn together, the pages lay flat. It could make a great art journal."

I take the awl when he's finished and do the same. "Couldn't I buy a new sketchbook?"

"You could, but this way, you can design it any way you like. You can mix and match colors, or use parchment. It's customizable."

He gathers together a group of papers and folds them together to form a signature. "I'm going to use regular paper for this, since it's our demo. The smaller your signatures are, the flatter the book will lay, so a lot of small ones would be best for our purpose."

I fold my paper into ten signatures of four sheets each, then follow his lead as he applies his template to the signatures. When he's done, he hands me the awl again. The work is simple and tedious, but he waits for me.

"This is our last meeting before spring break, isn't it?" He asks it as if he's double-checking his calendar.

"Yeah."

"When are you leaving for your mother's wedding?"

I push the awl through the papers until the tapered metal is fully revealed on the other side, then move on to the next dot. "We're flying out next Saturday. Early morning."

Byrdie raises an eyebrow. "'We'?"

"Well, Jimmy's my next-door neighbor, and the wed-

311

ding's in his backyard, so it'd be a little weird if he weren't there too."

"Ah."

"And…" I hesitate. "And I asked Xander to go with me."

Byrdie doesn't say anything, but I can feel his eyes on me as I put the holes in my final signature.

After a moment, he clears his throat. "The next step is a little harder. Assuming you want a cover, we need to cut these leather scraps into the right shape and punch the holes through them as well."

We pick out our leather and outline the template on the interior for cut lines. This time, he lets me go first. With the large craft scissors, I shear through the thick red leather.

I pass the scissors to him. "What am I supposed to use the journal for?"

"Whatever you want. You can paint, draw, cut and paste anything you like. You could make a collage or add favorite quotes. You can write out your feelings if you're inclined." He finishes cutting out his cover and pushes the scissors to the side. "The options are endless. The point is for you to shape what you do around what you need most."

He grabs two of the bookbinding needles and threads one with linen thread. He demonstrates the stitch with his own book, and I follow his lead.

"What happens after the wedding?" he asks.

I shrug as I work. "I'm not sure. The wedding's on Wednesday, and we're not getting back till Friday evening. I don't know what's supposed to happen while I'm there. I'd think Mom and Rob would want to go on a honeymoon or something, but it hasn't been mentioned."

"What are you thinking in the final weeks before the

big event?"

I haven't been thinking about it much. My thoughts have been occupied by studying for midterms, whether Dahlia knows about my argument with the drunken Brent, and everything Xander.

I haven't seen Dahlia yet, and we live together. Not that I've been there much. I've spent every night for the last two and a half weeks in bed with Xander.

"I'm ready for it to be over. I don't like the stress, and I'm not thrilled to see my mom again."

The last time I saw her, after all, didn't go well.

"I don't think I've ever seen you in a skirt. Will you be uncomfortable as a bridesmaid?"

I let out a short laugh. "I'm uncomfortable thinking about it, but I don't have an option. My mom doesn't think I should get a choice in life-changing decisions."

"Why do you say that?"

Right. He either still doesn't know about what's essentially blackmail or he's playing dumb to get me to talk. I haven't been able to determine which.

"You know I didn't want to come here, to see you." I choose my words carefully. "But my mom insisted, no matter what I said."

"You're an adult, Billie. You never had to attend these meetings."

I sigh. "Yeah, an adult who didn't want ties with her sister forcibly cut as retribution for not attending."

Byrdie's motions slow to a stop. "For what it's worth, I've enjoyed getting to know you, Billie."

I have to push the needle with all my might to get it through the hole in the signature and nearly stab myself on the other side, still considering how to respond.

But he doesn't give me the chance.

"You might find it helpful," he says, moving on, "to write down the most important things in your life. List the things and people you're most grateful for, so that on the bad days, you can look inside this book and remember."

He turns to me with a small smile, and I return it.

"Often, we forget the most important things when we're in our darkest places."

Thirty-Five

When I get back to the apartment, I don't bother knocking.

Jimmy sits at the table with his laptop and a textbook, studying for his music theory class. He smiles at me before returning to his work. "Xander's not back for twenty minutes."

I purse my lips and drop my backpack on the floor as I take the seat beside him. "I don't only come here for Xander."

He snorts, and his eyes glisten with laughter. "You do hear what you're saying, right?"

Heat rises to my face. "He's not the only reason I'm here."

"No, but he's the number one reason." Jimmy looks back at his laptop and starts typing, then pauses. "Please don't pretend that your primary interest in being here isn't to curl up in his bed and have loud sex."

I slide down in the chair. "You're my best friend. I'm here to see you too."

"Yeah, my best friend whose orgasms I have the privilege of listening to while trying to fall asleep at night." His tone says it's anything but a privilege.

I open my mouth to insist that only happened once—maybe twice—but he'd counter it with some other argument. Besides, despite his irritation, he's not angry. For the first time in months, his smile is genuine.

"You know how happy I am for you guys," he says, "but in a couple months, things are going to be very different. You two can hardly keep your hands off each other when you don't live in the same house. I'm trying not to imagine how bad this will be after we move in together."

I frown.

I'd forgotten about that. About the house. About the three of us living together for a year.

"I don't know."

Jimmy shrugs it off. "Seriously, though, I don't think I've ever seen Xander this happy."

My stomach twists, and I look away. Surely his happiness isn't dependent on me? I can't support my own happiness—how am I supposed to keep him happy as well? How could I manage that?

I keep my voice low. "I'm glad he's happy."

He starts to speak again, but the door opens.

Xander steps inside, shutting the door loudly behind him, and his face lights up when he sees me. "I was hoping you'd be here."

When he smiles, I rise to greet him. "I finished my therapy and came straight over. I missed you."

A frown flickers across his features, but it passes quickly, and I follow as he heads down the hallway.

He flips on his bedroom light, and I lay on the bed as he puts away his textbooks. "I work at five," he says grudgingly, "so I'm sorry I don't have much time." He glances over and smiles. "But I'm glad I get to see you, even if it's for a little while."

"How long will you be gone tonight?"

How late will I have to stay up waiting for him?

Xander sits on the edge of the mattress, contemplating his response, but I've waited too long to kiss him.

I yank him down onto the bed with me and press my lips to his. He kisses me with equal fervor, wrapping an arm around my waist. The other dives into my mass of curls and refuses to let me pull away. Not that I want to.

But the moment I pull off his t-shirt, music bursts to life from the kitchen.

Fuck. We left the door open.

With a groan, I slide from Xander's arms to shut the door, but he holds my wrist before I can get off the bed. "What?"

"I won't be back for a while." He tugs me back into his arms and kisses my temple. "Maybe it'd be better if you went back to your apartment for the night."

My fingers trace his shoulder blade. "It's not a bother to stay here. I can hang out with Jimmy. We haven't talked a lot lately, and you know, we can study together. I still have a midterm tomorrow—"

"Or you could stop worrying about the possibility of running into Dahlia if you go back." His voice is quiet and solemn, and I don't know how to respond. "I know you're scared, but you can't keep avoiding her. You never did anything wrong."

I frown. "How would she know that? If Brent told her anything…he was so drunk, I doubt he remembers it accurately."

He combs my hair with his fingers. "Maybe he told her you did something awful, maybe he didn't tell her a thing. You may never know. But you won't know if you never get up the nerve to go back to your apartment." He presses a kiss to my mouth, but it's too short. "You have to pack for the trip somehow."

I push closer to him, and he slides an arm around my shoulders. "I know. I just—it's so much easier to stay away."

He flashes a smirk. "Well, as much as I enjoy you staying here, I have a serious problem with you hiding." He gives me a moment to respond, but when I don't speak, he adds, "You have to face your fears eventually."

"I know." I heave a sigh and lay my head on his chest. "I know that."

◆

Camila is pulling out her keys when I reach the apartment door. When she sees me, she jumps, then laughs, her keys dangling and jingling in her hand. "Oh, hey, Billie. How've you been?"

I shrug. "Busy studying for midterms."

She retreats away from the door instead of locking it. "Why do you think I'm leaving? The library's calling my name. Have you seen Dahlia lately?"

I frown. "No, why?"

Cam raises her eyebrows. "I think she's been sick or something. She doesn't look too good. She's been staying at the apartment and sleeping a lot the past week." She passes me along the hallway and smiles.

When I push open the apartment door, it's eerily quiet.

My bedroom is dark, and when I flip the light switch, one of the bulbs flickers and goes out. It's dim in the half-light.

This is the first time I'll have been here for more than a quick stop. I've grabbed textbooks, but every night since Brent gave me that stupid mudslide has been spent in Xander's bed. I haven't seen Dahlia in over two weeks.

I sit on the edge of my mattress and look around.

I don't know what to do with myself now that I'm here. This is not the safe haven it was meant to be, even with my own bedroom, my own personal space.

Beyond the open door, there's shuffling. A door closing. Footsteps coming closer, then veering off toward the kitchen. The fridge door opens and, a second later, closes.

That has to be Dahlia.

I take a deep breath and head out to the kitchen.

Dahlia is standing next to the microwave with a large box of Chinese leftovers in her hands. She glances at me when I grab a glass from the cupboard a couple feet away, but the second her eyes meet mine, I'm stunned by her gaunt face. She is particularly skinny, and her breathing is labored.

I fill my glass with water from a pitcher in the fridge, and when I turn around, Dahlia is assessing me.

"You're back," she says indifferently. She turns back to the microwave. "I was under the impression you didn't live here anymore."

I frown. Says the person who disappeared for three days without a word.

"Where have you been?"

I take a sip of my water. "Spending more time with Xander and Jimmy lately. Nothing spectacular."

"Really?" She pauses to give me a chance to say something, but I wait. "You know, when I got to Brent's apartment, I was surprised you weren't there. Why'd you leave?"

"I—"

But what am I supposed to say? Surely he told her something.

"I needed some time to myself."

She scoffs. "Time to yourself? That you then spend with Xander? I thought we agreed he's an asshole."

I take another drink. "I never agreed to that. I would never agree to that."

Dahlia's face twists into a sneer.

"He may be the asshole who ruined your night when he kicked everyone out of his party, but he is one of the truest friends I could ask for."

She's unimpressed. "What, are you fucking him now or something?" She follows it with a small laugh, but her laughter dies the second she sees my face. "You're kidding."

"We're not 'fucking.'" I cling to my glass, but Dahlia cackles.

"Are you dating, then? Is he your boyfriend?"

Behind her, the microwave beeps, and she turns around and opens it. Steam pours from the box's cracks.

"No, he's not—I mean, maybe." I stifle the sigh as I exhale. "I don't know."

She snorts as she opens the paper box and stirs the contents with her chopsticks. A cloud of steam rises, and she leans away. "You two must make quite the couple."

I frown. "Why do you say that?"

She moves past me, setting her Chinese food on the nearest counter, and I step away from the fridge so she can poke her head inside. Despite her tired face and slow response time, she's stronger than she looks—she must think so too because she grabs a bottle of Chardonnay with a twist-off lid and tears it open before she has the fridge door shut.

When she sets the bottle on the counter next to her Chinese food, she levels me with an intense stare. "I can't imagine dating someone who wants to control my every move, but hey, if that's how you get your kicks, have fun. At least the sex'll be good with how much experience he's had around campus." She gives me the minutest of moments to respond before adding, "That doesn't bother you, does it?"

I sip my water to quell the nausea bubbling in my stomach. "He doesn't want to control me. He's helping."

Dahlia turns on me then, a wild look in her bloodshot eyes, and her pink lips form a thin line. "Oh, I didn't realize telling someone what to do was helpful—and if he's such an essential part of your so-called recovery, what happens when he isn't around anymore?"

For a moment, I am frozen, trying to rebut, but the words escape me.

"Most college relationships fail," she says with a short shrug. "Common knowledge. Do you think it's a good idea to rely on him so much? I'd hate to see you distressed when things don't work out. The odds are not in your favor."

She doesn't wait for me to speak. Instead, she takes a swig of her Chardonnay, grabs her food, and heads toward the safety of her bedroom.

I stand by the counter, clutching my glass to my chest.

Thirty-Six

Xander presses his fingers over mine as the airplane wheels out to the runway. A few feet away from us, the flight attendant explains safety procedures, and on Xander's other side, Jimmy glances through the corresponding pamphlet.

This is the first time I've been on the same flight as Jimmy and Xander on one of our trips to Missouri.

I twist my hand so our fingers lace together and look out the tiny window to take in the gray Vermont sky. As the plane turns, several runways come into view.

Xander leans against my arm. "You're not scared of flying, are you?"

I shake my head, but I can't look away from the window.

He tugs on my hand, and after a moment's hesitation, I turn his way. "Hey." He flashes me a smile. "Stop worrying about the wedding. I'm here to help with whatever you need. That's why you asked me here, right?"

I heave a sigh. "I wish I could curl up in a ball until this is over."

He squeezes again, and I reciprocate. "I hear distractions can be a huge help." He's smiling when I look at him.

"Like what?"

He shrugs. "I can think of a million things, Dixon. Use your imagination."

I stifle a laugh. "But this is you. I'm sure you have your preferred methods of distraction, right?"

"What are you insinuating? I'm insulted."

"No." I poke his chest with my free hand. "You're ridiculous."

He grins, and I lay my head on his arm. "Well," he says in a quieter voice, "would you prefer to talk instead of avoiding it? What are you so worried about?"

I nuzzle his shoulder. "What I'm always worried about—everything."

"Specifics would be nice."

I try to shrug, but it's difficult in this position. "Seeing my mom again. Meeting my new 'family.' Having to stand during a ceremony while wearing heels when I've never worn heels before."

And you.

But how could I say that out loud? How can I voice my concerns without hurting his feelings? Without displaying my irrational fears for the world to see and judge?

"Is it bad that I'm excited to see you wearing a dress?"

I roll my eyes, and the plane turns onto our runway. "Of course you are. You're not helping."

He snickers. "Fine, fine."

"I'm going to fall over during the ceremony. I don't know how to balance in three-inch heels."

"You should walk around in them for a while to get used to them." He laughs again and presses a kiss to the top of my head. "They make your ass look good, and trust me, your ass is already perfect."

"You know, you're going to have to keep your hands to yourself on this trip."

"Will I?" I can hear the frown in his voice, then a melodramatic sigh. "I suppose I can manage."

His hand tightens around mine as the plane lifts into the air, and there's a moment where his skin against mine is the only thing I want to feel.

"Will I have to steal kisses while no one's looking?" he asks, more seriously. "Or are we talking no touching whatsoever?"

Even as my stomach clenches from the pull of gravity, I laugh. "I mean, if we're being discreet, it wouldn't hurt. I do rather like kissing you."

Xander pulls me closer. "That's good to hear."

◆

When the flight lands in the tiny Springfield-Branson National Airport, Charlie and Thea Powell are waiting for us by the luggage carousel. They swarm around us with hugs and kisses as soon as we're in range.

"No Mom?" I ask as Thea pulls away from a second hug.

She shakes her head. "Your mom's got a full house tonight, you know. Rob's relatives got into town yesterday, and half the family's staying at your house."

I grimace. "Oh, that's awesome."

"I'm sorry, dear." A frown forms on her face. "I thought your sister would've told you."

"We've been having trouble communicating. It's not a problem."

"Hey." Jimmy comes closer and nudges me in the side.

"You can stay the night at my house. You were going to anyway, right?"

Charlie places a hand on his shoulder. "We always have a room ready for you."

It's a subtle insinuation—from Jimmy, not his dad—but I bite my lip. "Maybe."

Xander's beside me, close enough our arms brush, and as we make the short trek to their navy-blue Impala, I link my hand with his. He doesn't look at me, but a small smile forms on his lips.

"Knowing my mom," I say, quiet so only he can hear me, "she's given away my bedroom to some guests."

He chuckles.

Once the luggage is stowed and we're all buckled in, Charlie glances in his rear-view mirror. "You kids want to stop and grab dinner before heading over? We did promise to make an appearance after picking you up."

"I'd hate for Imogene to feel left out." Xander's voice is unnervingly quiet. He's talking to me and Jimmy, not the whole car. "It must suck being there without anyone her own age to mess around with."

I shrug. "I'm pretty sure Rob's brothers have kids our age. Besides, she should've come to the airport to meet us if she wanted to get away."

On Xander's other side, Jimmy lurches forward as the car starts to move. "Dinner sounds delicious, Dad. We're starved."

Xander nudges my side. "Right, Dixon?"

I rub my ribs and send him a quick glare. "I'd be a lot hungrier if I weren't being elbowed in the stomach, asshat."

He grins. "I specifically aimed above your stomach."

I snort. "Thanks for your consideration."

"I know." He leans close. "I'm very generous."

I open my mouth to argue, but he waggles his eyebrows, and I can't deny that. Instead, I purse my lips and turn away.

"Oh, come on." Xander pokes my side, but I push his hand away. He draws nearer to whisper in my ear. "Don't you want to play with me?"

His lips on my earlobe send a shiver down my spine, and I lean into him. The seatbelts holding us apart are a mild irritant, but he wraps his arm around my abdomen and presses a kiss to my exposed neck. Cuddling is discreet, right? I lay my hand over his and thread our fingers together.

On my other side, Jimmy pulls a face and checks his phone. He has a couple messages, and he busies himself with responding to them.

Up front, Charlie Powell directs the car toward town. "Let's stop and get some Indian food."

◆

When we reach the house, there are several cars in the driveway and on the street. My mom's car is parked under the carport with two cars blocking it in, mere inches between them so they fit.

Charlie stops in their own driveway but leaves the car running. "Do you want to take your bags upstairs first?" He twists in his seat to look at us.

It's almost like he knows I'm not looking forward to this.

But I shake my head. "I should go inside."

Beside me, Xander squeezes my hand. "Do you want me to go with you? They can put everything away, right?"

I turn to him and nod, then glance at Charlie.

"Not a problem," he says. "We'll be over in a few minutes."

The walk from the Powells' driveway to my mother's house is a maze, and I hold Xander's hand, leading the way through the cars to reach the front door. I hesitate at the door, then pull away from him to open it.

For once, the interior of my mother's house is loud and bright. The space is crammed with a couple fold-out tables covered in snacks and bottles of soda and juice, and the living room is packed with people. A few of the nearer guests turn at the sound of the door.

"*Billie!*"

Oddly enough, out of everyone here, it's Rob who steps forward with a grin. He wraps an arm around me in a quick hug before looking at Xander. "And your boyfriend, right? Alexander?"

"It's just Xander."

A look crosses Rob's face that says he's not sure whether I answered one or both of his questions.

He moves on.

"You can meet my family, Billie." He motions around the room as he talks, pointing out his many brothers and their families. "My oldest brother Jorge and his wife Daniella. His daughter Sofia is here, but Mathias is in Spain. And then, there's Gio and Carmen and their kids Gabriel and little Dante. Marco and Liz, and Eduardo and Beliana, and last of all, my little brother Fernando—he is not married."

I try to place the names with the smiling faces around the room, but none stick, and then, Imogene emerges from the hallway.

Rob claps me on the shoulder before rejoining my mother on the couch. She offers me a small smile from afar. I breathe a sigh of relief when she doesn't rise to greet us.

Xander steps closer. "You want a water or something?"

When he's gone, Imogene takes the place beside me. "I was starting to think your flight was delayed." She glances behind us toward Xander, frowning. "You never said you were bringing Xander."

I shrug it off. "Who else would I have asked?"

"Are you together now?"

I glance back, but Xander's busy getting our drinks. "I don't know."

Imogene sighs. "Well, at least you have a date. Mine bailed when I told him his band sucked giant donkey balls."

I cover my mouth, trying to hide my snort.

But Imogene is unfazed. "Go ahead and laugh. It's pretty funny in retrospect, but I can never get back the hours I spent listening to them play to be 'supportive.' I was looking for a reason to get out of that relationship anyway."

Xander reaches his arm around me to hand me a water. "There are plenty of musicians who aren't shit. I'm sure you can find someone better."

She laughs. "Thanks, I guess." Then, she looks back toward the living room, shrugging. "I've already got someone in mind."

I roll my eyes. Of course she does.

And Imogene moves on easily. "Where are the Powells? Didn't you get here somehow?"

"They're putting away the luggage," Xander says.

I turn to my sister anxiously. "I thought it might be better to sleep over there. You know, to give my room to

328

somebody who might need it?"

Imogene assesses me silently. "Are you sure?"

"If you think Mom wouldn't be too upset." I hold my arms close to my chest. "I mean, I'll spend a couple nights there anyway."

She turns away. "You're right. I have no interest in listening to my sister's orgasms."

"What?" I turn on her with wide eyes, but she doesn't notice. "How do you—?"

But the door opens a few feet away and in stumbles the answer to my unfinished question.

Jimmy doesn't pause before joining us. "Hey, Imogene." He beams at her, then assesses the rest of the room, his goofy smile still in place. "You having a good break?"

Charlie and Thea come in afterward and get drinks from the fold-out table before going to greet my mom and Rob.

"My break is next week," Imogene says noncommittally.

"Oh, I'm sorry."

She turns to him with a laugh. "Why're you sorry? I get to skip classes to wear a pretty dress and dance. This is going to be fun."

Jimmy shifts his weight from foot to foot, unsure how to respond, and I nod Xander toward the stairs.

When we slip inside my childhood bedroom, it doesn't look like anyone has moved in yet. I don't bother turning the light on, and we sit in the dark on the edge of my old twin mattress. He doesn't let go of my hand.

"This is going to be a long trip."

"We're here for five days—four and a half really. The wedding's the day after tomorrow."

I nod. "Yeah, and the plan for tomorrow sucks. We're

getting mani-pedis. Mo's braiding my hair, which takes forever. And my mom wants to do a run-through of the ceremony. I'd prefer not to have to do that more than once."

Honestly, I'd rather hang out all day with him than spend half an hour with my mother. We could goof off. There's a vast list of things we could do that are far more fun and engaging than getting a manicure.

Xander laughs. "Well, what can I do to help?"

I frown at our conjoined hands. "'Help'?"

"Yeah. What would be stress-relieving or reassuring or whatever you need right now?"

My fingers tighten around his. He's far too good for me.

"I'm here for you, after all."

Before he can add anything else, I pull him into a short kiss. "Just keep being you." I press my mouth to his again.

Thirty-Seven

"At last!"

Mo yanks me inside the makeshift dressing room. I barely catch myself on the door frame before tripping over the threshold. She latches the door behind us and rejoins our mother in the far corner. The cream dress is half buttoned up the back. Mom's hair hangs with long beautiful curls down past her shoulder blades. The hairdresser pinned a fresh lily in her dark blond locks.

"Get dressed." Mo nods toward the closet, where my dress bag dangles from a hanger. "What took you so long? We have twenty minutes till the photos. Thank God your hair's already done."

I force a smile and cross the room. The zipper echoes through the quiet room as I unveil the frilly pink dress. I've been dreading this moment for too long, but it's finally here. I slip it on and pull the zipper up my side, careful not to pinch my skin. The heels—the very ones I've hidden in the back of my closet since I bought them three months ago—sit on the floor.

When Imogene finishes buttoning Mom's dress, she returns to me. "Are you ready? You still need your makeup.

Come sit down."

She leads me to the vanity, where the cosmetologist is waiting. A palette of pinks, browns, and golds sits open on the counter. A small brush leans against the compact. Imogene heaves a sigh and relaxes against the wall nearby.

The cosmetologist applies a thin layer of foundation, and I shut my eyes. All I can do is wait for it to end.

"Where have you been?" Mo asks. "You were supposed to be in here an hour ago."

I have to force myself not to pull a face. I'm not sure I'm even supposed to talk. "I was helping Thea."

Not that Thea wanted my help. She gave me a few odd jobs in the beginning to appease me, but after that, it was constant reminders that I needed to be here, helping my mom.

But unless she's suddenly acquired an ability to walk noiselessly, my mother hasn't moved since my arrival. Maybe she's nervous. Although, this is her second wedding. Either way, I don't know what she needs me for.

"Yeah, postponing this. We're supposed to take pictures before the ceremony, and we can't do that if you're not ready. You're going to hold everything up."

"I'm here now, Mo."

"I'm surprised you didn't spend the entire morning holed away with Xander. What's he doing right now?"

My jaw tightens.

Trust me, I wanted nothing more than to spend the whole day with Xander, but he insisted we had to get up instead of make out and cuddle on my mother's wedding day. I'm not convinced that was the right decision.

"I don't know. Maybe he's helping direct guests or

something."

More likely, he and Jimmy are playing a video game while I'm stuck in here.

"Hey." The cosmetologist smiles—a gentle smile to match his quiet voice. "I need you to relax."

◆

After an extensive photo session, I slink away to wait out the final half hour in peace. Unfortunately, the Powells' residence is teeming with family, caterers, and guests. While they always have a beautifully-landscaped garden space by the deck, it's early spring, and only a few flowers are blooming. The tulips, grape hyacinth, and daffodils are separated from the lawn by a narrow brick trail and small solar walkway lights. The landscape is enhanced by strings of lights, streamers, and marbles in mason jars a la Pinterest.

The only place I can find that's remotely secluded is the family pool shed, shoved in the far corner at the back of their property, but Xander sidles over, a bottle of water in his hand.

"I thought I saw you sneak over here." He leans against the wall beside me and offers me the bottle. "Nervous?"

I accept a drink. "Something like that."

"You know, you're pretty good at faking a smile for the camera, but I can tell how uncomfortable you are in that thing." That doesn't stop his eyes from wandering. "Still, this outfit will take center stage in a few fantasies of mine."

I snort. "Me in a dress? Considering how many times we've had sex in the last few weeks, that's a tame fantasy." I set the water bottle on the shed window sill behind us.

He swings an arm around my shoulders. "I wouldn't say the dress is the only feature, but it's a start."

From our secluded spot, the Powells' empty pool, covered for winter still, and picturesque lawn and gardens look massive. Everything for the wedding was set up by ten this morning, and many of the guests have arrived. They're standing, chatting, waiting.

"How long do we have till the ceremony?"

I lean against him, my hand clutching his dress shirt. "Maybe thirty minutes. Why?"

His chest rumbles with laughter. "Dixon, you're wearing a push-up bra, strapless dress, heels, makeup, your hair's styled—I can't decide whether I like it or if it's weird, but you definitely look hot."

I laugh. "You're biased."

His fingers trail along my shoulder, across the expanse of my neck, stopping at my chin, and he drags my face up. "Incredibly biased." His other arm tugs me closer, and he presses a soft kiss to my lips.

But I press a hand to his chest. "You'll mess up my makeup."

There's a hint of pink on his lips—I wipe it with the back of my hand, holding back a laugh.

"Besides," I say, casting a glance toward the party, "we shouldn't do that here."

Xander doesn't say anything but retreats immediately. He leans against the pool shed again, a grimace on his face. His body is tense. He won't look at me.

"Hey."

When he doesn't turn, I take his hand and lead him around the corner and inside the shed. He follows silently but without resistance.

With the door shut, the building is dark and dusty. A few cobwebs fill the corners, but it's not otherwise dirty. Shelves line one side, and on the opposite wall, a counter with drawers beneath sits immediately below the grimy window. It's barely spring, and the Powells won't fill the pool till May; the shed is unused this time of year.

I lean against the counter, gripping his hand, and he watches as I pull my phone from the side of my bodice. "I need to be in the dressing room in twenty minutes." I set an alarm for the allotted time and lay the phone on the counter, out of the way.

"And until then?" He glances around the interior before turning to me. "We're going to hide in the pool house so you can avoid people?"

"Maybe you could distract me."

Xander cocks an eyebrow. "How would I manage that?" But he steps closer, pressing his hands against my skin, across the dress, over my breasts. "If I can't kiss you, what can I do?"

I press my forehead to the front of his violet shirt. "I don't know. I really wanted to touch you."

He presses his mouth to my neck, and I repress a quiet moan at the heat of his lips. "Well, your makeup has to be preserved, and your dress can't get dirty." His whisper against my skin sends a jolt of desire coursing through my body. "That doesn't leave me many options."

I grip his shoulders, leaning back, and his lips trail down to the cleavage revealed by the sweetheart neckline.

"What're the odds you have a condom?"

He laughs against my breast and pulls back. "Pretty good.

I thought I might drag you away during the reception—you know, when it doesn't matter if you get dirty. Not now."

My hands move down to undo his belt. "You could get a little dirty, though, right? You don't have to look pretty for the ceremony."

Xander opens his mouth but doesn't speak. Instead, he allows me to slide the dress pants down to his ankles, and he gasps when I pull his partial erection through the fly. I hold him in my hand, squeezing, rubbing till he stretches, hardens, lengthens in my grip.

He clutches my bodice, and his eyes are needy and insatiable. "We don't have time for this."

I want to push him against this stupid counter and take him into my mouth. I want to kiss him, revel in his taste and his touch, and I want to swallow him when he comes.

Unfortunately, we don't have time for all the things I want—he's right about that.

"We have a little bit of time." I spin him around and nudge him up onto the counter. I press a kiss to his erection, and surprised, he grips my bare shoulder. "Where is it?"

"Huh?"

"The condom."

He pulls it from his breast pocket. It crinkles in the wrapping. "This?"

Grinning, I pull him into a quick kiss, breaking it to tear open the wrapper. The latex is slippery with lube, and I test it to make sure it'll roll on without issue. "We're going to have to figure out some logistics." I place the condom at his tip and slide it down.

His laughter is breathless. "Yeah, how do you think this is going to work? How many layers does this dress have?"

He tugs at the pink skirt.

I push him against the wall, making room on the counter and his lap, and he helps me climb on top. His hands hold me by the waist as I adjust myself, but they slip under the dress to find the wetness between my legs, massaging my inner thighs as they travel. He kisses me again.

The cotton underwear is in the way, but he moves it aside. Despite his words, there's no hesitation in his movements. Without doubt or delay, his rough pads graze my clit, and I shiver in his arms.

He pulls back from the kiss. "You need to get back."

I quirk a smile. "I set a timer. We're fine."

For a moment, he can only stare at me. Then, his finger plunges between my folds, and I roll my head back and release a long moan at the contact. Spending this day apart has been torture, and I am eager to be close to him again.

"Xander…"

He pulls me into another kiss, and I rake my fingers down his side. The layers upon layers of tulle prevent me from reaching him, but his hands are already down there. I whimper when he pulls away, but he guides me by the hips, repositioning me above him, and holds my underwear to the side.

I ease down.

Once the tip nudges inside, he doesn't want to wait. He yanks me down around him, and I tear away from his mouth to release a loud cry. Lips press to my exposed breasts, trailing across every inch he can reach. Every minute touch sends an aching desire to my core, and I want this to go slowly as much as he does.

I rise again till he's almost out, then force my way down.

His hands tighten on my hips, guiding me, helping me keep a rhythm. My knees dig into the hard, wood surface—this shed hasn't been updated in a long while, so I'm probably getting splinters. But all I care about is having him inside me.

He places his lips just below my ear. "There are a lot of people out there." He steadies my movements, and I writhe, trying to hold on without losing my momentum. "You should be quieter." But his words are followed by him yanking me down again.

I cling to him, stifling my moan with the collar of his shirt. My forehead clenches together as I try to regain my rhythm.

Wet kisses sweep across my neck, then his hot tongue. His teeth nip, so light it tickles, and I spasm in his arms, wrenching him deeper.

The counter vibrates, but it's not the timer—it's a text message. I don't bother looking closely.

He retreats from my neck, but the space between us dissipates the second our eyes connect. He crashes his mouth to mine in a heady kiss, bites my lip—a little rougher than at my neck—and squeezes my ass. I spasm and squirm, and his mouth muffles my moan. I can't hold on anymore.

I lean my forehead against his, heaving, my body limp as he slows his motions. I swallow to wet my dry throat before trying to speak. "Xander," I whisper, and he looks up.

But suddenly, I don't remember what I was going to say. I try again. "Xander."

My voice is louder this time, and he cocks an eyebrow. "Yeah?"

What can I say?

I don't know how to articulate my feelings. There aren't words to describe the overwhelming pleasure he provokes, let alone how glad I am these intimate moments are spent with him. I don't know where to begin.

I pull him closer. "Kiss me."

He doesn't hesitate before obliging.

The kiss is soft, sensual, and he drags a hand from under the skirt to cup my face. His other hand keeps the condom in place as I break the kiss and dismount.

I stumble to the floor, my hands gripping the counter to keep from falling. He pulls off the condom, knots it at the open end, then pauses. I don't have time to figure out where we're supposed to put a used condom.

I snatch my phone from the counter as the alarm sounds and read the text: *Get your ass back in here.* Imogene, of course.

I flatten my dress, swipe a section of braids over my shoulder, and tuck the phone inside my bodice before turning to him. "Do I look remotely presentable?"

Xander smiles. The condom's gone, and he zips up his dress pants and dusts off the black slacks. "You're absolutely gorgeous."

That's not an answer to my question.

I scoff but place a quick kiss on his lips before rushing back to the house.

Thirty-Eight

HALFWAY TO THE TABLE, IMOGENE SNAKES HER HAND around mine and yanks me back. "I can't believe you."

Fifteen feet away, our circular table is filled with a few of our new cousins-in-law and Xander and Jimmy, but Imogene is too frustrated to finish the short walk from the house to our chairs—even though we're supposed to be seated by the time Mom and Rob make their entrance.

I turn to her. "It's fine."

She keeps her voice low—we're on the edge of the guest tables. "Mom's stressed out enough. You cannot disappear for half an hour so you can get laid. Next time, you can walk down the aisle with your makeup all over your face. I won't help you fix everything."

I pry her hand off my arm, glowering. "We were late by maybe five minutes. That's negligible. And I don't think Mom has any intention of getting married again."

Her jaw clenches. "You could at least have the decency to deny it. To say you weren't off fucking Xander in the bushes somewhere."

Before I can respond, the speakers blast to life, and Charlie Powell announces: "Ladies and gentlemen, let's give a big round of applause for Roberto and Susan Herrera!"

Imogene and I pause to clap as Mom and Rob walk down from the house to their personal table.

When they take their seats, I turn to her again. "And if I did deny it, you'd stand there pissed off and say, 'You could at least have the decency to be honest.'"

Her face darkens, and she turns on her heel and marches to our table. I follow.

She takes her seat between Jimmy and someone whose name I've already forgotten, and I collapse on the chair beside Xander. But I'm not ready to let this go.

"There's nothing I could do to make you stop being mad at me, is there?" I struggle to keep my voice low. "Will you stop being pissed off once tonight is over? Or do you feel so displaced by Mom's new husband that you'll take it out on me for no reason?"

My hand clenches into a fist atop the table, but Xander lays his fingers over mine.

"Hey, your mom's here now," he stage-whispers to both of us. "The two of you need to chill."

I shake him off, and across the table, Imogene doesn't pay him any mind either.

"You bailing on Mom right before the ceremony because you want to get laid rather than learn how to deal with your own emotions is a damn good reason to be mad at you."

I purse my lips. "Even if that were true, how does this make it any better?"

Rob takes the microphone and begins his welcome speech, but we tune him out.

"It doesn't, but you've been complete shit during all the preparations. You haven't done anything to help—even when you were here. You haven't been supportive."

"What the hell should I have done from halfway across the country?"

"You could at least pretend to care, but you're too pissed about the fucking therapy." She scoffs.

My hand grips the table edge. "You'd be pissed about the therapy too if she made an appointment without saying anything and guilted you to go. She just wants to feel better about herself so she can start her new family without complications."

"No." Imogene slams her hand down on the table, and a few nearby guests glance our way before turning back to Rob. "No, she's doing it because I asked her to."

"What?"

"I'm worried about you, Billie." Her voice is no longer harsh, but the words still cut. "I thought when things got better with Dad, they'd get better with you, but they haven't. You never would've listened to me, never would've done anything to help yourself."

I scoot my chair back and stand up.

Guests are starting to gather as my mother and Rob stand to take their first dance, but I push past them.

Not a single drink here is alcoholic—for the best considering how much I want a drink now—but the table offers a wide array of sodas, bottled water, and sparkling juice. An attendant offers me a drink, and I grab a bottle of water.

"You've been here a while."

Everyone has eaten, and there's dancing and frolicking and laughter, and I hate it all. But that doesn't stop Xander from leaning against the pool shed beside me like earlier.

When I look over at the dance floor, Imogene is dancing with Charlie Powell and smiling despite our argument earlier. She can paint on a pretty face and carry on with the night like nothing happened.

"You going to come back to the wedding? I know you're not close, but she is your mom."

I heave a sigh. "I know. I know I should." I tug on my braids, trying to slide them back into place. "I'm getting up the nerve, I guess."

"Do you need help?"

I frown. "I don't know what I need."

He offers me his hand. "You wanna dance?"

I hesitate, but he smiles, and I can't say no.

He leads me toward the crowd, but his pace is slow. He's giving me time to adjust. At the edge of the circular tables, he pauses and nods toward the dance floor.

The song has changed, and when I follow his eyes, Imogene's partner has changed too. Jimmy's hands are wrapped around her waist, hers around his neck, but there's a good foot between them. Her movements are slow, fluid, and confident, but he shuffles his feet—he always insists he's a terrible dancer.

I grimace. "Ew."

Xander laughs. "You're only saying that because you're mad at her. They're dancing the arm's-length-away middle school slow-dance." He entwines his fingers with mine and tugs me to the dance floor.

The deejay's playing Christina Perri's "A Thousand Years"—my mother's choice—and I rest my head against his chest. His arms hold me tight.

"I know you don't want to hear it," he says in a quiet

voice, "but she's your sister. I'm not saying it was the right thing to do, and she shouldn't have had your mom as the driving force, but she did it because she loves you."

I sigh. "I know."

"You know she's right, don't you?"

I inhale his scent and wait for him to continue. His kind voice makes everything slightly better.

"You need to talk to someone. I know you're trying, you're working on opening up—I know that firsthand—but you're still doing it half-assed." His hand rubs up and down my back, and he pauses to press a kiss to my temple. "And about your mom…"

"What?" I pull back, but he's looking elsewhere.

I follow his gaze to the center of the dance floor, where my mother is clinging to her new husband, a serene smile on her face.

"Why can't you let her be happy?"

I lean against him again. My arms tighten around his torso, and he rests his chin on my head. Heat and the scent of his citrus cologne emanate off his body.

"Xander," I mumble into his shoulder.

"Yeah?"

His cologne is overpowering. Or maybe that's the music. Or my own insecurities.

"Nothing. Never mind."

But he stops dancing and pulls back. When I refuse to look at him, he drags my face toward his by the chin. I blink away the tears forming.

"Hey, talk to me." He caresses my cheek, but I shake my head, and he leans forward.

I want to give in as he presses a gentle kiss to my lips—

344

that desire is unshakable—but I pull away. "Not right here. Not right now."

His grip slackens, and he looks away, but then, he resumes dancing. I follow suit, holding him tight. The music transitions to Train, and I lean against him again. His body is tense under my touch.

Then, he stops. "Dixon, what the hell are we doing?"

I look up.

"We've been having sex for three weeks, but I don't know what the hell is going on. Are we friends with benefits? Or do you—"

I turn away. "Can we not have this conversation right now?"

"How long do you intend to postpone it? Do you think there's going to be a convenient time to discuss this? Or are you hoping I'll magically forget?" He runs a hand through his black hair. "I can't be your booty call."

"You're not."

"Then what the fuck am I? What are we doing?"

I pull him closer again, hug him tighter, bury my face in his chest. "Please don't do this. This is the worst timing. Did you forget about the fight I just had with Mo? We're at my mother's wedding."

His hand pats my back stiffly, but his voice is firm. "Yes, and I came as your date. Does that mean anything?"

I cling to him. "Of course it does. Of course you do."

"But you don't want to be with me, do you?"

I hold tighter, trying to steady my breathing with his heartbeat. "Look, I'm not okay. I know I'm not. Can't you tell what a mess I am? Don't you see it? I don't want to drag you into this, and I can't rely on you just to have you walk

345

away. Did you know most college relationships fail?"

He scoffs. "Most relationships fail. What does that have to do with us?"

I lift my head. "Please trust me when I tell you it's a bad idea. You don't want me, Xander. I'm not in any place for what you need—I'm broken, I'm—"

His lips meet mine in a searing kiss, and I latch on to him, trying not to fall. His mouth is fierce, determined, and I melt into his arms.

When he pulls away, he leans his forehead against mine. I'm panting.

Xander doesn't wait. "You don't get to choose what I want." He places another small kiss on my lips. "I don't care about any of that—it's bullshit. I want to be with you, the good and the bad."

I pull away. "But I care, and I get to choose what I want. I can't do this right now."

"What do you mean 'right now'?" He grits his jaw, not ready to give up. "What are you waiting for? You cannot miraculously get fixed. You're not broken."

"You don't understand."

His eyes narrow. "No, you don't understand. There's nothing wrong with you. But until you figure that out for yourself, I can't change your mind." He lets me go; I'm instantly cold. "Doing it alone and doing it on your own aren't the same thing. It's okay to ask for help."

"I know that." I hug myself, but I cannot make up for the heat I lost when he retreated. "I know that, I do. But I can't give you what you want."

His exhalation is shaky. He takes another step away. "That's your final answer?"

"Yes."

"Fine." He glances back, pulling out a pack of cigarettes. "Just know that I'm not going to pine after you. I'm not going to wait for you." He sticks a cig in his mouth, lights it, and takes a long drag before looking at me one last time. "I'm going for a walk."

Without another word, he's gone.

Thirty-Nine

THE POWELLS' KITCHEN IS COLD AND STERILE. THERE'S A bit of clutter from the catering, but otherwise, the space is clean and organized and silent and perfect.

I fill a glass with ice water and hover by the sink. Eyes shut. Leaning against the dark gray granite countertops. Listening to the silence. Drinking the cold liquid.

I'm scared to go back out there. Scared for someone to see me with smeared makeup and tear-stained cheeks. Scared he's back. Scared he hates me. Scared he won't come back at all.

From the hallway, the back door squeaks as it opens and closes, shutting off the party noise almost as soon as it began. And footsteps.

I gulp down more water and lean over the sink so my braids fall in my face.

"Billie?" Jimmy comes to stand beside me at the sink, but one glance at his face says everything. "I just talked to Xander. What the hell happened?"

I cannot look at him. "I don't know."

"What does that mean?"

"I don't know."

"I thought you guys were—"

"We never actually were."

Jimmy scoffs. "Please don't tell me you're back to pretending you don't have feelings for him."

"I'm not pretending." I take another drink and set the glass on the counter. "I'm being honest. I don't want to hurt him, and if anything happened between us, that's all it would be."

"But something has happened—that was a hell of a lot more than sex, whether you want to admit it or not—and you are hurting him." He heaves a sigh and leans against the counter. "This isn't a Blue October song where it's beautiful and romantic to sacrifice the relationship to make the other person happy because, oh, God forbid you make him happy. He's a real person who has real feelings for you, and you know you reciprocate. Tell him how you feel and be done with it."

I close my eyes. "It's not that simple. I'd fuck it up. That's what I'm good at."

He releases a groan. "No, what you're good at is being ridiculously emo."

I don't say anything, and he takes a moment to calm down before trying again.

"I don't understand what's going through your head. You're happy with him, and he's happy with you. Why do you have to stop that? Why are you—?"

But I turn on him with a glare. Tears prick my eyes again. "Why do you have to stick your nose in everyone else's business? I cannot handle you doing this right now."

He retreats, taken aback. "What?"

"You can't possibly have nothing better to do with your

life than stand on the sidelines of mine and judge me. You don't get to write off my point of view because you don't understand what I'm going through. I don't have the perfect life or the perfect family, but that doesn't mean you get to stare at me with those stupid sad eyes and pity me. It doesn't mean you get to tell a room full of people who I've slept with because you've had too much to drink."

For a moment, he can only stare, mouth agape.

I blink away the tears, but he's already seen them. "Seriously, Jimmy, don't do this. I cannot handle you berating me about this of all things."

"I said I'm sorry," he finally manages. It takes him a moment to regain his momentum. "You have to understand that you're not the only person who matters. Xander is my best friend too, and you might not have meant to, but he's hurting already, and you did that."

I turn away, but he doesn't stop.

The words blur together, an endless cycle of frustration that echoes through the cold room like a striking crescendo. Cymbals blaring. Sirens screaming. The heavy reverberations of a gong.

And then, it stops.

I blink, but the granite and stone and gray-painted wood of the kitchen all blend into a mist. I blink and blink again. Slow inhalations.

When I look back, a hand holds Jimmy's shoulder. His face is white, and he backs out of the way as she steps forward. Her blond hair frames her face with a braid, the lily tucked in the golden locks. She watches me curiously before turning to him. "That's enough, Jimmy. Go back to the party."

He doesn't say anything, doesn't nod, doesn't even move for a moment. He can't look at me, but then, his eyes shift upward for a brief moment before he turns on his heel and leaves.

The room is silent again.

She turns to me. "Billie..."

I look away. "You should be out there. This is your dream wedding. You shouldn't spend the reception in a kitchen."

She sighs. "I know we don't always get along. I know I've never been a good mother. But you're still my daughter."

I step closer to the counter and lean against the granite. The cold numbs my skin, and I lay my hands on the rock, desperate for the chill to permeate my exterior, to numb me through and through. "I don't think I can go back out there."

"What happened?" She presses a hand against the counter next to mine.

I shake my head again. "I don't know. Somehow, I always fuck everything up, even when I'm not trying. I don't know what happened. Everything happened. It always spirals out of control."

"Then you're not trying hard enough."

I freeze, then try again. "I push everyone away. It's—"

"A defense mechanism," she supplies. "The more distance you have, the better. That doesn't solve anything. It doesn't protect them."

I release a short laugh and look down at our hands, so close yet so far away. Her new wedding ring glints under the tiny pendant lights. "No, but at least I can take solace in the fact that no matter how much I make them hate me, they'll never hate me as much as I hate myself."

"Nobody here hates you." Her voice is quiet and reserved. Aside from when she's with Rob, this is the norm after starting her medication.

"They should."

For a minute, she doesn't say anything. "Tell me about Xander."

"I don't know what to say." The tears start again before I can prevent them.

"You have to know how deeply he cares for you."

I let out a short laugh. It doesn't matter how much he cares. I'll never be okay enough.

"Not anymore. We probably can't be even friends after that. I don't think I can manage that much damage control."

"Your sister said you're dating."

I grimace. "Not exactly. We've mostly been...having sex." Before she can say anything, I have to ask. "Mo said she asked you to put me in therapy. I'm confused."

Mom leans against the counter, considering. "Your sister has been worried about you since she turned thirteen. I wasn't in a place to listen to her until last summer."

"Does she know?"

She raises an eyebrow.

"About the abortion. Does she know?"

A forced smile, and she shakes her head. "No. She tried to talk to me as soon as you got back for summer break. I didn't take her seriously until I saw the insurance paperwork."

I breathe a sigh of relief, but my chest aches. "Everything was supposed to get better when things with Dad started to mend—and for a little while, it did. I don't know if it was elation or relief—complete and utter relief—but as soon as that faded, I'm the same as I've always been. I don't know how to stop. I don't know how to move on. I don't know how to stop worrying about everything. How to stop working as if somehow constantly doing something will keep me busy enough that I forget. But I never forget and I never stop." I close my eyes. "I don't know how to stop... being me."

She presses her fingers over my hand, and I lay my head atop my arm. "Some days are easier, sometimes even normal—but you're not taking the steps to get there."

But I don't know what steps I'm supposed to take. I'm drowning. No matter how hard I try to grab for something, it's always just out of reach. I am suffocating.

"I don't see how it could change."

And if I can't change, what's the point?

"He wants more?"

I nod. "A relationship."

"How much does he know?"

"About what?"

"About your feelings? About the abortion? Was it his?"

"No, I was...so stupid." I catch her gaze again. "Mo never told you I had a boyfriend?"

Mom frowns. "We didn't talk about you often."

I take in a deep breath and look down at our conjoined hands. "I tutored him, but... It was fake. Everything he said and did was a lie, even when he told the truth. I knew he was manipulating me, but I let him. He manipulated me into a relationship that wasn't a real relationship and into sex that wasn't really sex." I heave a sigh. "And apparently, it was too difficult to tell me the condom was defective."

"How much does anyone know about this?"

"Dad is the only person who knows about the abortion. I couldn't have paid for it without him. I used all the money I'd gotten from tutoring, but it wasn't enough since the insurance didn't cover any of it." I sigh. "But he doesn't know much about what happened with Zane. No one does."

She releases a small sigh. "I was surprised when I spoke to your father. He spent so long convincing me to keep you that it never crossed my mind he would support someone else's decision." She squeezes my hand. "Your father loved you from the moment he knew of your existence. He worshiped you." Her voice breaks. "And I wasn't sure I was capable of love."

Even as the tears prick my eyes, I laugh.

Her hand clenches around mine. "Sometimes, I'm still not sure."

My throat hurts, and I can't speak. Mostly because she's already said everything. Sometimes—often—I'm not sure I'm capable of love either.

For a moment, she stares at the counter, her jaw tightening, loosening, then tightening again. "I know we haven't always gotten along. I've never been good at showing you I care."

I take in a shaky breath and wipe away the tears. "Why couldn't you get better until after I left? What is so wrong with me that you couldn't do it while I was here? Was it that much of a relief for me to be gone?"

Her grip slackens, and then, she releases me altogether. "You remind me too much of your father. You have his eyes, his brain, his manner of walking. But I do care about you, Billie, and I don't want you to make the same mistakes I did. You can ask for help."

"I've been too stubborn."

Mom shakes her head, the movement almost erratic. "I don't think I would be here today without therapy."

My breath comes in sniffles. "Do I have a choice?"

She offers me a small smile. "Of course you have a choice."

"You won't force me to go anymore?"

She shakes her head. "Billie, you have to want to do it for it work."

I nod, slowly, steadily.

"What are you going to do about Xander?"

I gulp down air, circumventing my nose. "He wanted an answer now, and I gave it to him. The damage is done."

"Even if that means you can never be with him?"

"Maybe it's for the best."

"Are you sure you're not self-sabotaging?"

I snort. "No."

She hunches over the counter and slides my half-empty glass against the wall. "Having someone special can make the hard days easier."

I inhale deeply.

"Are you ready to go back out there?" She offers me her hand, and when I take it, she leads the way to the backyard.

Forty

"YOU BAKED A CAKE."

Dad takes it out of the oven with a pair of green and white striped potholders. "Well, last year, you were here for your birthday, but we didn't do anything special. I want today to be special."

Last year, my birthday was one day in a long string of days I spent avoiding people. That's not to say I didn't have a good reason—it was two weeks after I gave in to Zane's intentions, and I wasn't ready to see anyone yet. Not the most noble impetus for spending the day with my dad.

This year's birthday dinner has been in the works for over a month, though, and for once, I'm not the one doing the avoiding.

Despite this, I smile. "Dad, it's just a birthday."

"But it's your birthday." He sends me a careful smile as he closes the oven. "Where are Jimmy and Xander?"

Pressed between my thin fingers, my glass is empty now. This is a conversation topic I've glossed over since my mother's wedding. Although things ended on an oddly good note with Mom, the rest of the break didn't fare so well. I spent the two days after the wedding on my mother's couch, watching Jane Austen movies with Mo and Beliana, Rob's youngest sister-in-law. I much prefer Jonny Lee Miller as Sick Boy or Dade to Edmund or Mr. Knightley, but Mo chose the movies. I didn't care what we watched.

I join him near the oven to get more water. "They're not coming."

He lays a cloth over the top of the cake pan and turns to me with a creased brow. "Why not? It's your birthday, Mina, and they're your closest friends. They should be here."

With fresh water from the fridge, the glass is cold again. I hold it to my chest. "Because I screwed everything up."

"Surely the blame can't be laid entirely at your feet."

But it is my fault. I pushed them away. Not because I didn't care but because I was scared.

I am so tired of being scared.

Dad rests a hand on my shoulder, drawing my attention. "I don't want you to spend your birthday alone again."

"I'm not alone, and I wasn't last year." I force a smile. "I'm here with you."

He smiles back, but like mine, it doesn't reach his eyes. "What about the girl you spent all of winter break with? Her name was a flower..." He pulls me closer and wraps an arm around me.

I lean against his chest. "She wasn't a very good friend, it turns out."

"Then who are your friends?"

"I don't know."

On the counter, my phone buzzes.

Who in the world would be texting me?

When I return to my seat and unlock it, the text is simple: *What time am I picking you up?* Prudence.

I forgot. She insisted on taking me out tonight. Though in a town where there's nothing to do except go to one of the four bars, none of which let in people under twenty-one, I'm not sure what we'll do. Besides, she knows I stopped drinking.

Any time, I send back. *I'm at my dad's for dinner.* I attach the address and look back to Dad.

"Well, Prudence is going to pick me up to do something. Are you happy now?"

His face breaks into a smile. "Prudence? She's in your painting class, right?"

"Yeah."

My phone vibrates again. *We'll be there soon. I'm bringing my closet.*

I frown. Her whole closet?

Dad slips onto the stool beside me and clasps his hands together. "I spoke to your sister this morning."

I set the phone down. "She mentioned she'd call you soon."

"Your mom's back from her honeymoon. They got in yesterday morning."

"Yeah." Despite sitting on the couch together and watching hours upon hours of Jane Austen films, we've barely spoken. We simply pushed our argument under the rug and moved on. "Mo stayed with Charlie and Thea while they were gone so she wasn't alone."

"I'm sure they enjoyed having her company. They're probably still getting used to not having Jimmy in the house. I understand the feeling." He casts me a conspiratorial smile.

I nudge him in the side. "I'm here now."

"Which makes me very lucky." He playfully pinches my

arm. "She mentioned she wants to visit over the summer."

I open my mouth, but I don't know what to say.

Mo hasn't mentioned anything like that to me. Plus, I'll be gone for two months during summer break.

"Oh," I finally say. "She'd stay here?"

He nods, then moves on. "What are you and Prudence going to do tonight?"

I glance at my phone again. "She didn't say."

My phone lights up and vibrates, but it's not Prudence's smiling face that stares at me. The text is from Jimmy.

When he sees the sender's name, Dad goes to check on the food still in the oven.

What are you doing tonight? I thought we might do something for your birthday if you're not busy.

With a heavy sigh, I text back, *I have plans.*

His response is quick, and it says nothing more than: *Okay.* He doesn't have to be physically present for me to feel his disappointment.

To be fair, while Xander has been avoiding me because of our "breakup," Jimmy has avoided me mostly out of frustration and guilt. The past few days, he's reached out in an attempt to make amends. I've been blowing him off.

"You hungry, Mina? Food's ready."

When Prudence and Cynthia arrive after dinner, Prue is carrying a thirteen-gallon trash bag full of clothing.

Grudgingly, I lead them to my bedroom.

"This is a cute house." Prue drops the bag on the floor and surveys the quiet room. "Are you living here now?"

It's not technically mine, but I've made this guest room more of a home than my apartment with Dahlia ever was—

more so because I've spent every night here since spring break. The dresser and closet are filled with my clothes, the nightstand is full of my sketchbooks—on top and inside—and my art supplies are shoved in multiple bins inside the closet. Like always, Dad's kindness is unmatched. He wouldn't let me hang up my posters, though.

I shrug. "I haven't wanted to see Dahlia."

She sends me a rueful smile.

Behind her, Cynthia doesn't hide her grimace as she perches on the edge of the bed. Someone got roped into this against their will.

"You're taking me out?" I glance between them, but my eyes stop on Prudence, who sends me a toothy grin.

"It's your birthday, so you have to get dressed up." She pulls out a few dresses, skirts, and frilly tops from the black trash bag and drops them in a pile beside Cynthia. "You need to look hot."

I roll my eyes. "Are we going clubbing? Are we old enough to do that?"

She laughs into the bag. "We are. But no, I'm not going to subject you to that. We're going bowling." She sends me a quick wink. "Nothing too traumatizing, I promise."

"Then why in the world do I need to look 'hot'?" I move to the mirror above the dresser. I barely look presentable. My ponytail is a mess. When I yank the tie out, the afro falls around my shoulders and down my back. "A fancy dress isn't going to make me look beautiful. Especially when my hair looks like this."

Prudence walks up beside me, her lips in a tight frown. "What are you talking about? Your hair's gorgeous."

"No." I cast her a small smile. "It's annoying and in the

way and takes way more effort than I care to put into it."

"We could cut it."

It's a suggestion—one that causes a gleam in her brown eyes—but her voice is soft and soothing.

"Huh?"

"Having it shorter would make it more manageable for someone who wants low maintenance hair." She tentatively fingers a strand, examining it. "I mean, when was the last time you cut it?"

"Ninth grade."

Prue frowns and, when I don't protest, she steps closer for a better look. "Please tell me you've trimmed it since then." My split ends are a good indication of the answer.

I laugh. "A few times."

"Do you have scissors?"

"Of course." I pull my craft scissors from my art bin in the corner—they're the only kind of scissors I own. "Are you really going to do this?"

She takes them when I offer, then pauses. "If you want me to, sure. I grew up cutting all my sisters' hair, and I cut Cynthia's a few times, right, Cyn?" She glances toward the bed, where Cynthia looks pale next to the enormous pile of Prudence's flashiest outfits.

"Oh, yeah." Cynthia tries to smile assuringly.

Prudence's smile is much more convincing. "And Ruby let me cut hers a couple times. She used relaxers instead of keeping it natural, but she told me a few things."

It takes a moment to remember who Ruby is—Prue's girlfriend last year—and I flash her a sad smile. "Okay, sure."

Her eyes light up.

"Why not?"

She directs me to sit on the vanity chair and runs through my hair with a pick comb. "Your curls will be tighter with it short. You might still be able to put it in a bun or ponytail."

I frown. "How short are you going to cut it?"

"You'll be able to braid it."

When she finishes untangling the coils, Prue drops the comb on the dresser, then grabs the scissors and measures out sections of my hair. "Have you talked to him at all?"

I take a deep breath and shut my eyes. "No. I haven't seen him."

Xander and I haven't had any classes together this year and won't again. We've both taken the majority of our gen ed classes, and there's no overlap between Fine Arts and Business Management. It's easy for him to avoid me.

"How's that possible?" The scissors snip as she makes the first cut.

"Are you and Jimmy still fighting?"

My eyes flash open to locate Cynthia, who uttered the question, through the mirror. "Um, not exactly. We've needed time apart." I sigh. "I've needed time apart."

At some point, we have to stop being co-dependent. It might as well be now.

Prudence makes a few more cuts.

Behind us, Cynthia shifts on the bed. "But you're still friends?" She pushes a few blond strands behind her ear.

"Yeah, of course."

Prudence pauses to catch Cynthia's attention. "Hey, Cyn, why don't you show Billie some of the clothing options?"

Cynthia scoots farther onto the mattress and lifts dresses and shirts one by one. After demonstrating, she tosses each on a new pile at the opposite end of the bed. There are short sundresses, sleek and slinky tops, strapless rompers, floral short-shorts.

"I'm not sure you brought enough clothes," I tell Prudence over my shoulder.

She laughs. "Yeah, I know. I wasn't sure what you'd like."

"Usually, jeans and a t-shirt."

She snickers as Cynthia holds up a navy-blue halter-top. "Well, tonight isn't a 'usual' night. You need to look nice."

But I frown as Cynthia lifts another shirt for me to inspect.

"If you'd rather wear your jeans, that's fine," Prue says, "but you should pick out a pretty shirt."

Cynthia shows me another article of clothing from the bottom. A green romper with long pants. Prudence is one of the few adults that can pull off a romper.

"Oh, hold on, Cynthia." She turns back to me. "We need to take off your glasses." She waits for a second, then removes the spectacles. Everything but her face is blurry.

"Wait," Cynthia says in a quiet voice.

"What?" Prudence throws the question over her shoulder as she grabs the scissors again.

Cynthia clears her throat. "This isn't yours, is it, Prue?"

"What? No." She squints toward the bed, confused. "That's Xander's."

I scramble to grab my glasses and twist to see Cynthia holding up the bright red t-shirt. A smiling Charmander stares back at us. I must've left it on the bed.

When Prudence sees my face, she laughs and returns to my hair. "Billie, why do you have his shirt?"

Cynthia folds it in half and tosses it onto the nightstand, and I lay my glasses back on the dresser. Prue grips the scissors tighter and grabs a strand of hair.

"He lent it to me a while ago."

"And you kept it."

For a moment, the only sound in the room is the scissors snipping locks of my auburn hair, but then, Cynthia's small voice echoes through the room: "Are you going to give it back to him?"

I clench my eyes shut.

There's a number of reasons I haven't, but mostly, I don't want to give away the one thing of his that I have. I'm not ready to let him go.

"Eventually."

Forty-One

Bradford's cafeteria is busy when I arrive at six—it's prime dinnertime—but I swipe my ID for my to-go box and drink and head straight for the drink station.

There's a short line, and I wait until the ice machine is available before filling my foam cup with ice water. The lids are located to the side of the fountain machine, and I slip the flimsy plastic on and insert a straw.

"Billie?"

I pause, not wanting to look.

But I have to.

When I turn, Jimmy assesses the auburn halo around my face. "Your hair…"

I sip my water and step away from the drink station. "Prudence cut it."

He nods, then he tries to smile. "I've been wanting to talk to you."

I flip open my to-go box and start walking. "I have to get dinner."

"Right." He rushes to match his pace with mine. "Can I walk with you?"

"Do whatever you want."

I stop at the first section, and the attendant spoons gnocchi into the large section of my box, then a slice of chicken Parmesan. Jimmy waits beside me, quiet but anxiously tapping his foot.

"I fucked up," he says the moment I pull away from buffet.

I stop, eyes wide.

Jimmy's never said "fuck" before in his life.

"Seriously, I fucked up. I was selfish and stupid. I never should have put pressure on you when I knew what a difficult decision that had to be. I was totally out of line." He takes a deep breath and runs a hand through his hair, unable to look at me for a moment. "I'm sorry."

When I sigh, the tension in my muscles fades. "I'm sorry too. I wasn't in the best mindset. I shouldn't have said those things."

"No, you were right." He closes the distance between us. "I haven't been the best friend. You know, things changed a lot after your parents divorced—you changed a lot. We've been friends for a long time, and I still struggle to see you like this. So no, I don't understand, and maybe sometimes I pity you—I don't mean to—but I'm always here for you."

I force a rueful smile. "When I'm upset, I'm not looking for you to solve all my problems or even to make me feel better. Most of the time, all I want is for you to be there and listen."

I scan the length of the cafeteria, searching for her usual table. Dahlia, Brent, Darius, and everyone else—they're talking and laughing, not remotely affected by my absence.

When I look back, Jimmy's face droops, his brow furrowed, his eyes shimmering, and I smile. "We're not always going to get along, you know?"

"I know that." He sighs and sends me a teary smile. "But we normally do, so I don't know what to do when we don't. I'm sorry I missed your birthday."

"It's alright. Prudence and Cynthia took me bowling, believe it or not."

He raises an eyebrow. "Really?"

"Yeah." He follows as I move to the next line. "It was strange, but Prue insisted on dressing me up and taking me out on the town."

Jimmy stifles a broken laugh. "What town?"

"That's what I said."

A smile spreads across his quivering face, but he doesn't say anything.

"You're not going to ask me about Cynthia?" I raise an eyebrow. "You spent the last year and a half mooning after her, and suddenly you're silent on the matter."

He shrugs and looks away, his ears tinging pink. "I'm not sure I have a shot there."

I stop at the salad station and fill the vacant parts of my box with veggies and a fruit cup. "What gave that away? The months she ignored you? The time she blatantly rejected you? Or did something else happen?"

"I don't know. I guess it hit me that no matter how hard I try, she isn't going to see me like that. Or you know, at all." He sighs. "Besides, maybe she's not the only girl out there."

A laugh escapes my lips. "You think? Half the world is covered with women, Jimmy. You're certainly not limited to Cynthia Allen."

"I guess."

I close my box, ready to go. "You're not convinced yet."

"I wanted to marry her."

I turn on him and lean against the counter in front of the salad bar, lips pursed. "You said you wanted to marry Mandy Hawkins in high school. That didn't go anywhere either." I laugh. "Somehow, you crush on the most apathetic girls. Maybe you should set your sights on someone who realizes you exist."

"The thought has crossed my mind."

"Good."

Neither of us says anything, and I glance toward the exit now that my box is full. He understands and walks over with me.

We stop near the two enormous glass doors leading out of the cafeteria, and he places a hand on my arm. "Come over later."

Despite myself, my eyes drift to our usual table. The only thing there is Jimmy's half-eaten plate and his jacket slung on the back of his chair. If Xander was here, he's gone now.

"That sounds like a bad idea."

Jimmy shakes his head. "Xander won't be there. He's... well, he has a date tonight."

I take a drink, trying to judge my own reaction. "Good for him," I finally say. "I'm glad he's happy."

But Jimmy's anxious face shifts to irritation. "If I'm not allowed to placate you, you're not allowed to lie so blatantly to me."

"It's not a lie that I want him to be happy."

"Sure, but please don't lie and say you're glad he's happy with someone else. Besides, we both know he isn't happy, whether he's going on a date or not."

I inch toward the door. "That doesn't matter, though. I

made my decision, and it was the right decision—and now, everyone has to live with it."

"Fine." He slips his hands into his jeans, but his fingers still clench and unclench inside his pockets. "I know it's a little selfish, but I wish you considered what sort of position you put me in. You guys are my best friends, and now you can't be in the same room together."

I roll my eyes. "I'm sorry, but thinking about you wasn't high on my priority list."

"I know."

"I'm not asking you to choose."

"And I wouldn't. This is just awkward. We're going to live together in six weeks, you know. All three of us. How will that work?"

I stare at the white foam box and cup in my hands. "I don't know. I've been trying to figure that out, but I don't know."

"We signed the lease. All our names are on it. It's good for a year, and none of us can afford to break it." He sighs. "It's pretty tight quarters, if you remember. You'll share the same living room, kitchen, bathroom, everything."

"I know that."

"I'm not trying to pressure you or anything, I promise. I want to figure out how this is going to work."

"Well, so do I. And I'm sure the thought has crossed his mind too."

Jimmy hesitates, brow creased. "Is it going to be like this all the time? Am I going to have to divide my time between you two? Will every interaction be strained?"

"I don't know how to change that. I don't know what I could do to make this easier."

The look on his face says it all, and part of me agrees: I could go to him. I could tell him how much I care, how much I miss him, how much I want to be with him. It wouldn't be a lie. It's been nearly a month since spring break, and I am more lost than ever.

But I'm not convinced that's the right idea. I cannot throw away my resolve, and it wouldn't be fair to expect him to dive back in when I still have doubts.

Besides, he's already dating, moving on. He's not waiting for me, just like he said. I led him on for too long. Maybe now he'll be able to have a real relationship, to find someone who loves him.

If nothing else, he'll get laid tonight.

I feel sick.

I take another sip of water and look at the exit again. "Time. Time will make it easier."

"Then take the first step, Billie."

I turn to him, frowning. "What's that?"

"Come to the apartment. Hang out with me. He won't be there, so you can start to, you know, adjust to being in his space again."

I shake my head and cast a rueful smile in his direction. "I'm not sure how much good that'll do."

I've memorized his face, his voice, his smell, his unhealthy habits, his disgruntled expression when I mock *Gilmore Girls*, how his eyes light up when he spots me, how tight he holds me at night.

Held.

I sigh.

Held. Past tense.

"But I'm willing to try."

When I look at Jimmy, he's smiling. "Good. When can you come over?"

◆

Jimmy sends me an encouraging smile as we reach the top of the stairs. "You don't have to stay long."

I follow him inside the familiar apartment and settle uncomfortably on the couch, a place once so relaxing and soothing. While he grabs drinks, I pull out my phone.

A moment later, he joins me on the couch with a couple glasses of water, still trying to smile. I drop my phone on the coffee table and accept a drink.

The door at the end of the hall opens, and Xander walks out in a t-shirt and jeans. He makes it all the way to the living room before he spots me. Then, he freezes.

I look away.

Jimmy's mouth gapes. "Oh, I thought you were..."

"I was." Xander starts walking again and pours himself a drink in the kitchen. "Now I'm not."

He returns to his bedroom without another word.

Jimmy turns to me, unnervingly quiet. "I'm sorry. He wasn't supposed to be here. That's the only reason I suggested this. I thought—"

"I know. It's okay. It was going to happen eventually. We'll definitely run into each other once we move into the Sandalwood house."

He releases a shaky breath. "I know, but I thought maybe we could smooth the journey."

"It's fine. I'm fine."

Eventually, I'll be fine.

"Right." He nods, an encouraging smile in place. "Let's move on, I guess."

"Let's."

"How's your painting class going?"

I focus on his words and the cup in my hands. "I have a lot to learn. The more classes I take, the more I realize I have no idea what I'm doing. Prudence is really good, though."

"I didn't know she painted."

"Yeah, she does." I force a smile, but behind him, at the end of the dark hallway, light and "Rock N Roll" by The Runaways sneaks through the door cracks. He doesn't want to hear my voice.

"Hey." He lays his hand on my knee and squeezes. "You don't have to stay. I understand."

I shake my head. "No, I just—I need to say something."

His eyebrows shoot up under his messy brown hair, but I rise from the couch and walk around. I have to do this while I have the courage.

But when I reach his door, I can't move.

We've fought a million times. Silly arguments. We're both too stubborn. But this is vastly different. This cannot be joked, explained, or apologized away.

I rap my knuckles against the wood.

He won't answer. He must know it's me, and he has no reason to talk to me. There's nothing I could say that could make this situation better.

I knock again.

Then, the music stops. Footsteps approach. The knob jiggles, and the door opens slowly. But only a crack.

His face is expressionless, and he's fully dressed. There's a first time for everything.

"Hey. Can we talk?"

"What is there to talk about, Dixon?"

I clear my throat, but all I can do is stare at my hands. "We're going to live together in six weeks. I'd like for things to not be this awkward. Maybe we could be friends again."

And I miss you.

There's nothing else to say, really. It's my own fault, my decision, but I miss him more than I thought possible. More than I've missed anyone.

"Do you think we could be friends?"

He assesses me, his blue eyes contemplative, and when he speaks, he looks away. "We can try." The words are forced, reserved, cold.

I nod. "Good. I'll, um, let you get back to whatever you're doing, then."

He shuts the door.

In the living room, I grab my phone off the table. Jimmy looks at me, curiosity etched into his brow, but I don't know what to say. I turn away. "I'm sorry, I need to go."

The door shuts before he has time to respond.

I bolt down the stairs, taking two, even three, at a time, stumbling.

At the bottom step, I collapse. That was harder than it should have been. Harder than I thought it could be. I can't imagine how difficult living with him will be.

I can't breathe. My eyes blur. It takes a second to realize what's blocking my vision. I heave, gasp, try to prevent the tears from pooling over the edge. I can't.

A hand touches my shoulder. Jimmy.

He tries to smile, but I launch into his arms, and all he can do for a moment is hold me. "It'll be okay." He squeezes tight, trying to steady my breathing.

I know he's right.

But it doesn't stop the wrenching, clenching, constricting in my chest, and it doesn't stop the tears that stream down my face.

Forty-Two

"Thank you for bringing this, Billie."

For the first time in months, Byrdie and I sit in the armchairs instead of at the back table with the art supplies.

"A journal is incredibly personal." He nods to the book he asked me to bring. "I don't expect to see anything inside it. I just want to talk about it, see how it's working for you."

On my lap, the leather-bound tome is worn, its pages frayed and soft on the edges.

He motions to it. "How often do you use it?"

"I didn't at first. Between everything with the wedding, I didn't feel like I could take the time—it wasn't a priority."

"The wedding was a month ago. Are you using it more now?"

My fingers tighten around the soft leather cover. A single strand of twine wraps around the middle of the book, fastening it shut. "Yes. Almost daily. I've had a little more time on my hands, and it's been a nice companion the last couple weeks."

Byrdie nods, a tight smile spreading across his full cheeks. "Do you mind telling me what you use it for?"

We designed it as a journal, but I've never kept a journal

before. Instead, I've filled it with drawings. Unlike my regular sketchbooks, the drawings are accompanied by messy scribbles, short phrases, mixed media designs. I've tried—and failed—to work with watercolors a few times.

When we put the journals together, he suggested a number of abstract uses and how it could help. My attempts have not been very successful. I try to outline and illustrate my day—random sketches of events or emotions and a few choice words or quotes that fit the tone of my day—but it feels forced.

"Drawings, you know, to center myself."

Byrdie nods, unfazed by my unwillingness to explain further. "Do you think it helps center you?"

I close my eyes for a second. "I don't know. Sometimes, it's like, dredging up the day's emotions makes everything worse. Maybe I'm doing it wrong."

He hums, considering. "There's no wrong way to keep a journal, Billie, but you might experiment with some other methods while you're adjusting. I have a few suggestions if you like."

"Sure."

He grabs a pad of sticky notes from his desk and scribbles something down. "You might look up Lucia Capacchione. She stipulated that drawing with your non-dominant hand could help you better access your creativity, spirituality, emotions." He tears the top note off and offers it to me.

I stare at the name, holding the paper in my hand, as he continues.

"You've shown me some of your drawings, Billie—you're not lacking any artistic skills, but I think you still struggle with accessing your imagination. Your art classes this year are helping you explore more, but drawing with your left hand might give you an extra boost, get you out of your own head."

I nod.

"Another option," he says, "is using it as a dream journal. You'd need enough time in the morning to record everything, though. Or you could do what's called a mandala journal—you draw a circle on each page and use that as a template."

I flip open the book in my lap and glance through the pages. I've filled a third of it with ink drawings, Linkin Park and Blue October quotes, and my awful attempts at watercolor painting.

"How is everything else, Billie?"

I look at Byrdie again, and I close the journal. "Classes are going well. I got all A's on my midterms, and we're starting our final all-color painting in my Painting I class. Felix says I've improved a lot." A smile spreads across my face. "My study abroad is officially confirmed. I got my passport in the mail earlier this week. From the third of June to the end of July, I will be in Paris."

He returns the smile. "That has to be exciting."

"Vermont is the only place I've been outside of the Midwest. This is my first time leaving the country. I'm thrilled."

"What about your friends? Are you still exercising? Eating healthy? No alcohol?"

Not the direction I'd like the conversation to go.

"For the most part, things are going well."

The initial weeks after my mom's wedding were difficult. I'm not sure how well I would have managed without

Dad. Or Prue, for that matter. When she learned what happened—from a week-long attempt to pry all the details out of me—she started asking me to join her at the gym every evening.

Byrdie nods. "Do you think it's helped?"

Depends on what he means by "help." While eating better—or rather, eating at all—and not drinking means I stay mentally focused, they don't otherwise provide much assistance. Exercising acts as a distraction more than anything else.

"A little."

"But not enough." He offers me a grim smile. "I've been hesitant to make a diagnosis based on how your symptoms have presented, even with your family history, but the next step is typically—"

"Medication?"

"Yes." He jots down a short comment in the notebook on his lap. "I'm not a psychiatrist, though, so I would need to consult with a colleague before we could prescribe anything. I would, of course, need your permission to share your case with her."

"What would that mean?" My fingers clench around the journal. "It took months for my mom's medication to work right, and I'm about to go halfway across the world for seven weeks. I don't want to be less emotionally available than I already am."

"Unfortunately," Byrdie says, laying his pen on the notebook, "lack of motivation and energy is a common side effect in the beginning. That usually fades, but your study abroad trip will complicate the process. You have to understand, though. There are many potential side effects. It will take time for any medication to make a difference. It isn't a magic pill, and it will not make years of untreated depression go away. It can help, but you have to do the heavy lifting."

I frown. "I have to do the heavy lifting anyway, though, right?"

"You already are, Billie."

He smiles, and I try to smile back, but nothing I've done so far has made a difference. How in the world is that "heavy lifting"?

"It would be safer to wait until you're back from study abroad to try medications. You would have to be diligent about taking your pills. Depending on the medication, missing even one dose can cause withdrawal."

That would be a big commitment. Would it be worth it?

"It's perfectly alright if you want to think about it." He scoots upright. "We can discuss it again at our next meeting. How does that sound?"

"That sounds like a good idea."

"Do you mind if I discuss your case with my colleague? She could come to our next meeting—her name is Dr. Belinda de Luca. We can discuss the options together, all three of us."

I nod, but there's still an uneasy feeling in my stomach. "So…this is our next step?"

Byrdie inclines his head. "Yes, if you're ready."

The leather in my hands is smooth and deep red, and my grip tightens around the small book. "I don't know if I'm ready." My quiet voice quivers. "But I owe it to myself to try."

Acknowledgments

This book was an emotional roller-coaster to write, and that wouldn't have been possible without the endless support and affection of my family and friends, especially that of my husband. He is the love of my life, my best friend, and my strongest support, and I am continually amazed by his love and kindness. Thank you especially to my friends Samantha, Marissa, and Shane for allowing me to rely on you and for helping shape this story. Thank you to Michelle for your marvelous editing skills and for your generosity and encouragement. Thank you to Sarah for her skills with design and composition. Thank you to Rayona for her thoughtfulness and expertise. And thank you, readers, for giving this book a chance. I am grateful for your time and effort.

D. L. Pitchford

A Note on the Author

D. L. Pitchford is a wife and mother of two,
living in Springfield, Missouri. She graduated
from Drury University with a Bachelor's in
English, Writing, and Fine Arts in 2013.

Learn more at:
www.DLPitchford.com

A Note on Reviews

If you enjoyed this book, please consider leaving a review on Amazon or Goodreads. Reviews are like food for new and aspiring authors. This is not an instance where you shouldn't feed the wildlife. Please feed the starving artists with your reviews.